When the wagon was l.
In the silent and empty ... e
broken hoe and broug... ...l
peacefully in the shade...

Once mounted, he startled the good little burro with his heels and they departed from Ciudad Real at a brisk canter. He didn't see the trail or the countryside. The auto de fé was a foretaste of the cruel way he would die when he was caught. Something in him screamed that he must seek out a sympathetic priest. Perhaps it was not too late to beg for the chrism and lead a life of careful Catholic rectitude.

But he had made a promise to his father's memory, to God, to his people.

To himself.

For the first time, his hatred of the Inquisition was stronger than his fear. He couldn't erase the images, and he spoke to God not as a supplicant but in demanding fury.

What can be the Divine Plan that causes so many of us to be Hanged Men?

And, *For what purpose have you made me the last Jew in Spain?*

THE
LAST JEW

NOAH GORDON

WARNER BOOKS

A *Warner* Book

First published in the United States in 2000 by
Thomas Dunne Books, an imprint of St. Martin's Press
First published in Great Britain in 2000 by
Little, Brown and Company
This edition published by Warner Books in 2001

A CIP catalogue record for this book
is available from the British Library.

ISBN 0 7515 3062 X

Typeset by MRules
Printed and bound in Great Britain by
Clays Ltd, St Ives plc

Warner Books
A Division of
Little, Brown and Company (UK)
Brettenham House
Lancaster Place
London WC2E 7EN

With love
For Caleb and Emma
and Grandma

Acknowledgements

Many people made it possible for me to write this book. If there are errors in my interpretation of information given to me by those cited below, they are mine alone.

For answering questions in the field of medicine I thank Myra Rufo, Ph.D., senior lecturer in the Department of Anatomy and Cellular Biology at the Tufts Medical School; Jared A. Gollob, M.D., associate director of the Biological Therapy Program at Beth Israel Hospital and assistant professor at the Harvard Medical School; Vincent Patalano, M.D., ophthalmologist at the Massachusetts Eye and Ear Infirmary and assistant professor at the Harvard Medical School; and the staff of the Centers for Disease Control, in Atlanta, Georgia. Louis Caplan, M.D., director of the Stroke Unit at Beth Israel Deaconess Medical Center and professor of neurology at the Harvard Medical School, answered several questions and was kind enough to read the manuscript of the American publication.

In Spain, historian Carlos Benarroch walked the old

Jewish Quarter of Barcelona with me and gave me glimpses into the lives of the Spanish Jews of the Middle Ages. I am grateful for the courtesy shown me in Girona by Jordi Maestre and Josep Tarrés. Two families in Girona opened their homes to me so that I might get an impression of how some Jews had lived in Spain hundreds of years ago. Joseph Vicens I Cubarsi and Maria Collel Laporta Casademont showed me a wondrous stone structure, complete with a wall oven, which was found beneath their interesting house when the earthen floor of their cellar was excavated. And the Colls Labayen family took me through the gracious residence which in the thirteenth century was the home of Rabbi Moses ben Nahman, the great Nahmanides. In Toledo courtesy was shown to me by Rufino Miranda and by the staff of the Museo Sefardi at the Sinagoga del Tránsit.

At the Museu Marítim in Barcelona, Enrique Garcia and Pep Savall, speaking to my son Michael Gordon who was representing his father, discussed travel by sail and suggested Spanish ports of call that might have been made by a sixteenth-century packet. Lluis Sintes Rita and Pere Llorens Vila showed me some of the waters along the coast of Menorca, taking me out on the *Sol Naixent III*, Lluis's boat. They brought me to a secluded island facility that once had been a hospital for patients with infectious diseases and now is a holiday resort for the doctors of Spain's national health service. I thank the director, Carlos Guitierrez del Pino, and the staff guide, Policarpo Sintes, for their hospitality and for showing me the museum of early medical artifacts.

I thank the American Jewish Congress and Avi Camchi, its erudite chief guide, for enabling me to participate in a tour of Jewish historical sites in Spain, while permitting me to go off on my own for several days at a time and then rejoin the tour; and I thank a wonderful group of people from Canada and the United States for repeatedly letting a working writer through their ranks so he could get his tape recorder close to every lecturer.

In America, for answering my questions I thank Rabbi M. Mitchell Cerels, Ph.D., former director of Sephardic Studies at the Yeshiva University; Howard M. Sachar, Ph.D., professor of history at George Washington University; and Thomas F. Glick, Ph.D., director of the institute of medieval history at Boston University.

Father James Field, director of the office for worship of the archdiocese of Boston, and Father Richard Lennon, Rector of St. John's Seminary in Brighton, Massachusetts, on several occasions answered an American Jew's questions about the Catholic Church, and I'm grateful for the kindness of the Latin department at the College of the Holy Cross, in Worcester, Massachusetts.

Rabbi Donald Pollock and Charles Ritz each helped me to find dates of Jewish holidays in the Middle Ages. Charlie Ritz, my lifelong friend, also allowed me to borrow freely from his personal library of Judaica. Gilda Angel, wife of Rabbi Marc Angel of the Spanish and Portuguese Synagogue in New York City, talked with me about the Passover celebration of Sephardic Jews.

The University of Massachusetts at Amherst gave me faculty privileges at the W.E.B. Du Bois Library, as it has for a number of years. I am particularly grateful to Gordon Fretwell, the assistant director of that library; to Betty Brace, head of user support services; and to Edla Holm, former head of the interlibrary loan office. For courtesies I also thank the Mugar Memorial Library and the Library of Science and Engineering at my alma mater, Boston University; the Countway Medical Library and the Widener Library of Harvard University; the library of the Hebrew College; the Brookline Public Library; and the Boston Public Library.

I found that historians offer different estimates of the population of Spanish Jewry at the end of the fifteenth century and sometimes depict the events of that period from differing viewpoints. When this occurred I felt free to choose what seemed to me the most logical and likely of the versions.

A word of warning. I based my descriptions of herbal remedies on material found in the writings of Avicenna, Galen, and other early physicians. But there was little science used in the compounding of medications by early physicians and apothecaries, and their nostrums are relics of a vast ignorance. It would be irresponsible for any person to try the remedies described in this book, as they may be dangerous or life threatening.

There has been an active market for the theft and sale of religious relics, some of them spurious, since the beginning of Christianity, and it continues today. Relics of St. Anne, revered by Christians as the mother of the Virgin Mary, are to be found in many churches and in different parts of the globe. I based the fictional story of my relic of St. Ann, up to and including the period of Charlemagne, on events that may be found in Catholic histories of the saints.

The events that occur to the relic after the era of Charlemagne are fictional, as are the Priory of the

Assumption in Toledo and the valley and village of Psadogrande. All monarchs mentioned and bishops with the exception of Enrique Sagasta and Guillermo Ramero are historic.

I am grateful for the warm support and friendship of my German publisher, Dr. Karl H. Blessing of Karl Blessing Verlag; my American agent, Eugene H. Winick of McIntosh & Otis, Inc.; and my international agent, Sara Fisher of the A.M. Heath literary agency in London.

My publishing house in Spain, Ediciones B, was exceedingly helpful in a number of ways and I thank its publisher, Blanca Rosa Roca, and Enrique de Hériz, editor-in-chief.

I sent the manuscript to Germany and Spain in segments, so translations could begin in each of those countries while I was still writing. Historian and journalist José Maria Perceval vetted my pages, offered advice and sought to ensure that the names of my characters would match the language and culture of the Spanish regions in which the action of the story took place. The difficult task, for which I thank him, made revisions an ongoing necessity, and I owe special thanks to the patience and skill of editors Judith Schwaab of Karl Blessing Verlag, in Munich, and Cristina Hernandez Johansson of Ediciones B, in Barcelona. For much of the writing of my novel I enjoyed the luxury of having Herman Gollob as my editor of first sight, until he left for England to research a a book on his relationship with Shakespeare. He is a great editor who loves the product of writers, and this novel is much better than it would have been without him. My American publisher, Thomas Dunne of St. Martin's Press, offered valuable suggestions that made this a better book, and I am grateful for help and courtesies shown me by Peter Wolverton, associate publisher, and Carolyn Dunkley, editorial assistant.

My daughter Jamie Beth Gordon was ever watchful for "a book Dad might find useful," and I always feel cherished and stengthened when I find one of the little notes she leaves for me. My daughter Lise Gordon, my own unfailing source of good books to read for interest and pleasure and always my toughest yet tenderest editor, read some of my early script and edited all of my finished copy. My son-in-law, Roger Weiss, answered innumerable cries for help whenever my computer swallowed whole sections of prose and wouldn't spit it out; he always saved the day. My daughter-in-law, Maria Palma Castillón, translated, interpreted, read the proofs of the Spanish edition, and whenever we were in the same country plied us with great Catalan food. My son Michael Seay Gordon was constantly there with intelligence, clippings, phone calls, advice, and support. He interviewed people on my behalf and was the best of companions on several of my trips in Spain.

Lorraine Gordon, still the quintessential writer's wife, gives me so much I would not try to put it into words. She has allowed me to fall in love with her repeatedly, which I have been doing now for these very many years.

Brookline, Massachusetts
February 9, 2000

Part One

THE FIRST SON

Toledo, Castille
August 23, 1489

1

The Silversmith's Son

The bad time began for Bernardo Espina on a day when the air hung heavy as iron and the arrogant sunshine was a curse. That morning his crowded dispensary had been almost emptied when a pregnant woman's water burst, and he banished from the room the two patients who remained. The woman was not even a patient but a daughter who had brought her old father to see the physician about a cough that wouldn't go away. The babe was her fifth and emerged into the world without delay. Espina caught the slick, rose-colored boy child in his hands, and when he patted the tiny nates the thin yowling of the lusty little *peón* brought cheers and laughter from those who waited outside.

The delivery lifted Espina's spirits, a false promise of a fortunate day. He wasn't committed for the afternoon, and he was thinking he would pack a basket with sweetmeats and a bottle of *tinto* and go with his family to the river, where the children could splash while he and Estrella sat in the shade of a tree and sipped and nibbled and talked quietly.

He was finishing with his last patient when a man wearing the brown robe of a novice bobbed into the courtyard on a donkey that had been ridden too hard in a day of such heat.

Full of contained excitement and importance, the man stammered that the señor physician's presence was requested at the Priory of the Assumption by Padre Sebastián Alvarez.

'The prior wishes you to come promptly.'

The physician could tell the man knew he was a converso. The demeanor contained the deference due his profession, yet there was insolence in the tone, almost but not quite how the man would have addressed any Jew.

Espina nodded. He made certain the donkey would be given small amounts of water, and the man, food and drink. He himself took a cautionary piss, bathed his face and hands, swallowed a piece of bread. The novice was still eating when Espina rode out to answer the summons.

It had been eleven years since his conversion. Since that time he had been fervent in his chosen faith, a man who observed every saint's day, attended Mass with his wife daily, and was ever eager to serve his Church. Now he traveled without delay to answer the priest's demand, but at a pace that would protect his animal under the copper sun.

He arrived at the Hieronymite priory in time to hear the molten sound of bells calling the faithful to the Angelus of the Incarnation, and to see four sweaty lay brothers bearing the basket of hard bread and the cauldron of *sopa boba*, the thin friar's broth that would add little flesh this day to the bones of the hungry paupers gathered at the priory gate.

He found Padre Sebastián pacing the cloister, deep in conversation with Fray Julio Pérez, the sacristan of the chapel. The gravity in their faces reached out to Espina.

Stunned was the word that flickered into the physician's mind as the prior sent the sacristan away and greeted Bernardo Espina somberly in Christ's name.

'The body of a dead youth has been found among our olive trees. The youth was slain,' the priest said. He was a middle-aged priest with a chronically anxious look, as if he worried that God wasn't satisfied with his work. He had always been decent in his relationship to conversos.

Espina nodded slowly, but his mind already was heeding a warning signal. It was a violent world. With unfortunate frequency someone was found dead, but after life has fled there is no reason to call a physician.

'Come.'

The padre prior led the way into a friar's cell where the body was laid out. Already the heat had brought flies and the sweetish stench of human mortality. He tried breathing shallowly against the odor, but it did no good. Under the blanket that offered a final modesty the husky young corpus wore only a shirt. With a pang Bernardo Espina recognized the face and crossed himself, not knowing whether the reflex was for the slain Jewish boy or for himself or due to the presence of this cleric.

'We would learn about this death.' The priest looked at him. 'Everything. As much as it is possible to know,' Padre Sebastián said, and Bernardo nodded, still mystified.

5

Some things both of them were privy to from the start. 'He is Meir, son of Helkias Toledano,' Bernardo said, and the priest nodded. The murdered boy's father was one of the leading silversmiths in all of Castille.

'This boy had scarce fifteen years, if my memory is correct,' Espina said. 'At any rate, his life barely went beyond boyhood. This is the way he was found?'

'Yes. By Fray Angelo, picking olives in the early coolness after Matins.'

'May I examine him, Padre Prior?' Espina asked, and the prior waved his hand impatiently.

The boy's face was unmarked and innocent. There were livid bruises on his arms and chest, a mottling on the thigh muscles, three superficial stabs on his back, and a cut in his left side, over the third rib. The anus was torn and there was semen between his buttocks. And bright beads of blood across a slit throat.

Bernardo knew his family, devout and stubborn Jews who loathed those, such as he, who had volunteered to abandon the religion of their fathers.

After the examination, Padre Sebastián bade the physician to follow him into the sacellum, where they dropped to their knees on the hard flagstones before the altar and recited the Paternoster. From a cabinet behind the altar Padre Sebastián lifted out a small sandalwood box. Opening it, he removed a square of scarlet silk, heavily perfumed. When he unfolded the silk, Bernardo Espina saw a dry and bleached fragment, less than half a span in length.

'Do you know what this is?'

The priest seemed to surrender the object with reluctance. Espina drew close to the dancing light of the

6

votive candles and studied it. 'A piece of a human bone, Padre Prior.'

'Yes, my son.'

Bernardo was on a narrow and tenuous bridge, teetering over the treacherous abyss of knowledge gained in long secret hours at the dissection table. Dissection was forbidden by the Church as sin, but Espina had still been a Jew when he apprenticed to Samuel Provo, a Jewish physician of renown who was a secret dissecter. Now he looked directly into the prior's eyes. 'A fragment of a femur, the largest bone of the body. This, from close to the knee.'

He studied the raddled bone, taking note of its mass, the angulation, the landmarks and the fossae. 'It is from the right leg of a woman.'

'You can tell all this simply by looking?'

'Yes.'

The candlelight turned the prior's eyes yellow. 'It is the most sacred of links to the Savior.'

A relic.

Bernardo Espina regarded the bone with interest. He had never expected to stand so close to a sacred relic. 'Is it the bone of a martyr?'

'It is the bone of Santa Ana,' the prior said quietly.

It took a moment for Espina to comprehend. The mother of La Virgen María? Surely not, he thought, and was horrified to realize he had stupidly spoken aloud.

'Oh, it is, my son. Certified so by those who deal with such things in Rome and sent to us by His Eminence Rodrigo Cardinal Lancol.'

Espina's hand holding the object trembled in a way strange to one who had been a good surgeon for years. He returned the bone to the priest carefully, then he sank

7

to his knees again. Blessing himself quickly, he joined Padre Prior Sebastián in renewed prayer.

Afterward, outside again in the hot light, Espina noted that armed men who didn't appear to be friars were on the grounds of the priory.

'You didn't see the boy last night while yet he was alive, Padre Prior?'

'I didn't see him,' Padre Sebastián said, and told him, finally, why he had been summoned.

'This priory commissioned the silversmith Helkias to fashion a reliquary of chased silver and gold. It was to be a remarkable reliquary in the shape of a ciborium, to house our sacred relic during the years it will take us to finance and build a suitable shrine in Santa Ana's honor.

'The artisan's drawings were magnificent, showing every promise that the finished work would be worthy of its task.

'The boy was to have delivered the reliquary last night. When his body was found, near it there was an empty leather bag.

'Possibly those who killed the boy are Jews or perhaps they are Christians. You are a physician with entry in many places and many lives, a Christian yet also a Jew. I wish you to discover their identity.'

Bernardo Espina struggled with resentment at the insensitive ignorance of this cleric, to think that a converso was welcome everywhere. 'I am perhaps the last person you should entrust with such a charge, Reverend Padre.'

'Nevertheless.' The priest gazed at him stubbornly, and with the implacable bitterness of one who has given up earthly comfort to wager everything on the world to come. 'You are to find these thieving murderers, my son. You must point out our devils that we may gird ourselves against them. You must do God's work.'

2

The Gift from God

Padre Sebastián knew Fray Julio Pérez was a man of unimpeachable faith, someone who doubtless would be elected to lead the Priory of the Assumption should he himself have to leave it through death or opportunity. Yet the sacristan of the chapel was flawed by an innocence that was too trusting. Padre Sebastián found it disquieting that of the six men-at-arms Fray Julio had hired to walk the perimeter of the priory, only three of the hard-eyed guards were known personally by either Fray Julio or himself.

The priest was achingly aware that the priory's future, to say nothing of his own, rested in the small wooden box hidden in the chapel. The presence of the relic filled him with gratitude and renewed wonder, yet it increased his anxiety, for having it in his charge was both high honor and terrible responsibility.

As a boy of scarce twelve years in Valencia, Sebastián Alvarez had seen something in the polished surface of a black ceramic ewer. The vision – because this is what he knew it to be – came to him in the mid of the frightening night, when he awoke in the sleeping chamber he shared with his brothers, Augustin and Juan Antonio. Staring at the black ceramic in the moonlit room, he saw our own Lord Jesus on the rood. Both the Lord's figure and the cross were amorphous and without detail. After seeing the vision he drifted back into a warm and pleasant sleep; when he awoke in the morning, the vision was gone, but the memory of it remained clear and perfect in his mind.

He never revealed to anyone that he had been chosen by God to receive a vision. His older brothers would have jeered and told him he had seen the hunter's moon reflected in the ewer. His father, a baron who felt that his lineage and lands gave him license to be a sodden brute, would have beaten him for being a fool, and his mother was a chastened figure who lived in fear of her husband and seldom talked to her children.

But ever after the night of the vision Sebastián's role in life was clear to him, and he had demonstrated a piety that made it easy for his family to shunt him into the service of the Church.

After ordination he had been content to serve humbly in several undistinguished roles. It was in the sixth year following ordination that he was helped by the growing prominence of his brother Juan Antonio. Their brother Augustin had inherited the title and the land in Valencia, but Juan Antonio had made an excellent marriage in Toledo, and his wife's family, the powerful Borgias, had arranged for Sebastián to be assigned to the Toledo See.

Sebastián was named chaplain to a new Hieronymite priory and assistant to its prior, Padre Jerónimo Degas. The Priory of the Assumption was exceedingly poor. It had no land of its own save for the tiny piece on which

11

the priory stood, but it rented an olive grove, and as an act of charity Juan Antonio allowed the friars to plant grapes in the corners and on the thin edges of his land. The priory attracted little money in donations from Juan Antonio or anyone else, and it called no wealthy novices into lives of holy service.

Still, after Padre Jerónimo Degas died, Sebastián Alvarez had succumbed to the sin of pride when the friars had elected him prior, although he suspected the honor came because he was Juan Antonio's brother.

The first five years of directing the priory had diminished him, sapping his spirit. Yet, despite the grinding pettiness, the priest dared to dream. The giant Cistercian order had been started by a handful of zealous men, fewer and poorer than his own friars. Whenever a community had sixty white-robed Cistercian monks, twelve of them were sent out to start a new monastery, and thus they had spread throughout Europe for Jesus. Padre Sebastián told himself that his modest priory could do the same if only God would show the route.

In the year of the Lord 1488 Padre Sebastián was excited – and the religious community of Castille was invigorated – by a visitor from Rome. Rodrigo Cardinal Lancol had Spanish roots, having been born Rodrigo Borgia near Seville. As a youth he had been adopted by his uncle, Pope Calixtus III, and he had grown to be a man to fear, a man of tremendous churchly power.

The Alvarez family had long ago proven itself friends and allies of the Borgias, and the close ties between the families had been strengthened by the marriage of Elienor Borgia to Juan Antonio. Already, because of the Borgia connection, Juan Antonio had become a popular figure at court functions and was said to be ⟨...⟩ the queen.

Elienor was first cousin to Cardinal Lancol.

'A relic,' Sebastián had said to Elienor.

He hated to plead to his sister-in-law, whom he could not abide for her vanity, insincerity, and spitefulness when irked. 'A relic of a martyr, perhaps of a minor saint. If His Eminence could help the priory obtain such a relic, it would be the making of us. I am certain he will come to our aid if you but ask it of him.'

'Oh, I could not,' Elienor protested.

Nevertheless, Sebastián became more abject and more insistent as the time of Lancol's visit approached, and she softened. Finally, to rid herself of a nuisance and for the sake of her husband only, she promised Juan Antonio's brother she would do whatever was humanly possible to benefit his cause. It was known that the cardinal would be entertained in Cuenca, at the estate of her father's brother, Garci Borgia Junez.

'I shall talk to Uncle and ask that he do it,' she promised Sebastián.

Before Cardinal Lancol departed from Spain, in the cathedral of Toledo he officiated at a Mass attended by every friar, priest, and prelate in the region. After the service Lancol stood surrounded by well-wishers, the cardinal's miter on his head, his great shepherd's crook of a crosier in his hand, and about his neck the pallium given him by the pope. Sebastián saw him from afar, as if experiencing another vision. He made no attempt to approach Lancol. Elienor had reported that Garci Borgia Junez had indeed made the request. Uncle had pointed out that knights and soldiers from every country in

13

Europe had passed through Spain after each of the great Crusades. Before they returned home they had stripped the country of its holy relics, digging up the bones of martyr and saint, and pillaging relics almost at will from any church or cathedral along their route. Uncle had told Lancol ever so gently that if he could but send a relic to the Spanish priest who was their relative by marriage, it would earn the cardinal the adulation of all of Castille.

Sebastián knew that now the matter would be decided by God and by his appointed servants in Rome.

The days passed slowly for him. At first he dared to imagine receiving a relic that would have the power to answer Christian prayer and the tender mercy to heal the afflicted. Such a relic would draw worshipers and donations from afar. The small priory would become a great and thriving monastery, and the prior would become . . .

As the days turned to weeks and months, he forced himself to put the dream aside. He had almost given up all hope when he was summoned to the offices of the Toledo See. The pouch from Rome, which was sent to Toledo twice a year, had just arrived. Among other things it contained a sealed message for Padre Sebastián Alvarez of the Priory of the Assumption.

It was very unusual for a humble priest to receive a sealed packet from the Holy See. Auxiliary Bishop Guillermo Ramero, who handed it to Sebastián, felt the itch of curiosity and waited expectantly for the prior to open the packet and disclose its contents, as any obedient priest should have done. He was furious when Padre Alvarez merely accepted the packet and hurried away.

14

It was not until Sebastián was alone within the priory that he broke the wax seal with trembling fingers.

The packet contained a document entitled *Translatio Sanctae Annae*, and as Padre Sebastián sank into a chair and started to read numbly, he began to understand that it was a history of the remains of the Blessed Virgin's mother.

The Virgin's mother, Chana the Jewess, wife of Joachim, had died in Nazareth and was interred there in a sepulcher. She was venerated by Christians from their earliest history. Soon after her death two of her cousins, both named Mary, and a more distant relative named Maximin, set out from the Holy Land to spread the Gospel of Jesus in foreign places. Their ministry was solemnized by a gift of a wooden coffer containing a number of the relics of the Blessed Mary's mother. The three crossed the Mediterranean and landed at Marseilles, both women settling in a neighboring fishing village to seek converts. Because the coastal region was subject to frequent invasion, Maximin was entrusted to bring the holy bones to a safe place, and he continued on to the town of Apt, where he enshrined them.

The bones rested in Apt for hundreds of years. Then, in the eighth century, they were visited by the man his soldiers called Carolus Magnus – Charles the Great, King of the Franks, who was stunned to read the inscription on the shrine: 'Here Lie the Remains of Saint Anne, Mother of the Glorious Virgin Mary.'

The warrior king lifted the bones out of their moldered winding sheet, feeling the very presence of God, amazed to hold in his hands a physical link to the Christus.

He presented several of the relics to his closest friends and took a few for himself, sending his own to Aix-la-Chapelle. He ordered an inventory of the bones and forwarded a copy to the pope, leaving the remainder of the relics in the stewardship of the Bishop of Apt and his successors. In A.D. 800, when decades of his military genius had conquered Western Europe and Carolus Magnus was crowned Charlemagne, emperor of the Romans, the embroidered figure of Saint Anne was conspicuous on his coronation robes.

The rest of the saint's relics had been removed from the sepulcher in Nazareth. Some had been enshrined at churches in several countries. The remaining three bones had been given into the care of the Holy Father and for more than a century had been stored in the Roman catacombs. In the year 830 a relic thief named Duesdona, a deacon of the Roman Church, conducted a wholesale theft of the catacombs in order to supply two German monasteries, at Fulda and at Mulheim. He sold the remains of Saints Sebastian, Fabian, Alexander, Emmerentina, Felicity, Felicissimus, and Urban, among others, but in his plundering somehow he overlooked the few bones of Santa Ana. When Church authorities realized the depredation that had occurred, they moved Santa Ana's bones into a storeroom, where for centuries they gathered dust in security.

Padre Sebastián was now notified that one of these three precious relics would be sent to him.

He spent twenty-four hours giving thanks on his knees in the chapel, from Matins to Matins without food or drink. When he attempted to rise he had no feeling in his legs and he was carried to his cell by anxious friars. But eventually God sent him strength, and he brought

16

the *Translatio* to Juan Antonio and Garci Borgia. Suitably awed, they agreed to underwrite the cost of a reliquary in which the fragment of Santa Ana might be kept until a suitable shrine could be achieved. They mulled over the names of prominent craftsmen to whom such a task might be given, and it was Juan Antonio who suggested that to fashion the reliquary Sebastián commission Helkias Toledano, a Jew silversmith who had captured attention because of his creative designs and graceful execution.

The silversmith and Sebastián had conferred regarding the composition of the reliquary and had negotiated a price, and they had achieved a rapport. Indeed, it occurred to the priest how pleasing it would be if he could win this Jew's soul for Christ as a result of this work which the Lord had made necessary.

The design sketches Helkias had rendered revealed that he was an artist as well as a craftsman. The inner cup, the square base and the cover were to be made of both smooth and massy silver. Helkias proposed to fashion the figures of two women out of spun silver filigree. Only their backs would be seen, graceful and clearly female, the mother on the left, the daughter not quite a woman grown, but identified by an aura about her head. All over the ciborium Helkias would place a profusion of the plants with which Chana would have been familiar: grapes and olives, pomegranates and dates, figs and wheat, barley and spelt. On the opposite side of the grail – figment of things to come, as far from the women as future time – in massy silver Helkias would fashion the cross that would become a symbol of a new religion well after Chana's life. The infant would be set at the foot of the cross in gold.

Padre Sebastián had feared that the two donors would delay approval of the design, demanding that their own conceptions be heeded, but to his delight both Juan Antonio and Garci Borgia appeared highly impressed by the drawings Helkias submitted.

Within only a few weeks it became apparent to him that the priory's impending good fortune was not a secret. Someone – Juan Antonio, Garci Borgia, or the Jew – had boasted of the relic. Or perhaps someone in Rome had spoken unwisely; sometimes the Church was a village.

People in Toledo's religious community who had never noticed him now stared, but he noted that their glances contained hostility. Auxiliary Bishop Guillermo Ramero came to the priory and inspected its chapel, its kitchen, and the friars' cells.

'The Eucharist is the body of Christ,' he told Sebastián. 'What relic is more powerful than that?'

'None, Your Excellency,' Sebastián said meekly.

'If a relic of the Sacred Family is given to Toledo, it should be owned by the see and not by one of its subject institutions,' the bishop said.

This time Sebastián didn't reply but he met Ramero's glance squarely, all meekness gone, and the bishop snorted and led his retinue away.

Before Padre Sebastián could bring himself to share the momentous news with Fray Julio, the sacristan of the chapel learned of it from a cousin who was a priest in the diocesan Office of Worship. Soon it became obvious to Sebastián that everyone knew, including his own friars and novices.

Fray Julio's cousin said that the various orders were responding to the intelligence with preparations for drastic action. The Franciscans and the Benedictines each had forwarded strong messages of protest to Rome. The Cistercians, built upon worship of the Virgin, were furious that a relic of Her mother was to go to a priory of the Hieronymites, and had arranged for an advocate to plead their case in Rome.

Even within the Hieronymite order, it was hinted that so important a relic should not go to so humble a priory.

It was clear to Padre Sebastián and Fray Julio that if something should occur to halt delivery of the relic, the priory would be placed in an extremely precarious position, and the prior and the sacristan spent many hours kneeling together in prayer.

Yet finally, on a warm summer's day, a large, bearded man dressed in the poor clothing of a *peón* came to the Priory of the Assumption. He arrived at the serving of the *sopa boba*, which he accepted as eagerly as any of the other hungry indigents. When he had swallowed the last drop of the thin broth, he asked for Padre Sebastián by name, and when they were alone he identified himself as Padre Tullio Brea of the Holy See of Rome and extended the blessings of His Eminence Rodrigo Cardinal Lancol. From his ragged bag he took a small wooden box. When it was opened, Padre Sebastián found a highly scented wrapping of silk the color of blood, and within that was the piece of bone that had traveled so very far.

The Italian priest stayed with them only through the most exultant and grateful Vespers ever celebrated in the Priory of the Assumption. Evensong was scarcely over when, as unobtrusively as he had arrived, Padre Tullio took his departure into the night.

In the time that followed, Padre Sebastián thought wistfully of how carefree it must be to serve God by wandering the world in disguise. He admired the cleverness of sending so precious a prize with a solitary and humble messenger, and he sent word to the Jew Helkias, suggesting that when the reliquary was finished, it should be delivered by a single bearer, after darkness had fallen.

Helkias had concurred, sending forth his son as once God had done, and with the same result. The boy Meir was a Jew and thus could never enter Paradise, but Padre Sebastián prayed for his soul. The slaying and the theft revealed to him how beleaguered were the protectors of the relic, and he prayed, too, for the success of the physician he had sent out on God's errand.

3

A Christian Jew

The padre prior was the most dangerous of human beings, a wise man who also was a fool, Bernardo told himself moodily as he rode away. Bernardo Espina knew he was the least likely of men to learn anything from either Jews or Christians, because he was despised by the members of both religions.

Bernardo knew the history of the Espina family. It was legend that their first ancestor to settle on the Iberian Peninsula had been a priest in the Temple of Solomon. The Espinas and others had survived under the Visigothic kings and alternate Moorish and Christian conquerors. Always they had scrupulously followed the laws of the monarchy and the nation, as their rabbis directed.

Jews had risen to the highest stations of Spanish society. They had served the kings as viziers and they had thrived as physicians and diplomats, moneylenders and financiers, tax gatherers and merchants, farmers and artisans. At the same time, in almost every generation they had been slaughtered by mobs passively or actively encouraged by the Church.

'Jews are dangerous and influential, moving good Christians toward doubt,' the priest who had converted Bernardo had told him severely.

For centuries the Dominicans and the Franciscans had incited the lower classes – whom they called *pueblo menudo*, the 'little people' – at times whipping them into an implacable Jew-hatred. Since the mass killings in the year 1391 – fifty thousand Jews slaughtered! – in the only mass conversion in Jewish history hundreds of thousands had accepted Christ, some to save their lives, others to advance their careers in a Jew-hating society.

Some, like Espina, truly had taken Jesus into their hearts, but many nominal Catholics had continued in privacy to worship their God of the Old Testament, so many that in 1478 Pope Sixto IV had approved the establishment of a Holy Inquisition to ferret out and destroy backsliding Christians.

Espina had heard some Jews call conversos *los Marranos*, the Swine, insisting they were eternally damned and wouldn't rise again at the Final Judgment. With more charity, others called the apostates *Anusim*, the Forced Ones, insisting that the Lord forgave those who were coerced, understanding their need to survive.

Espina wasn't among the coerced. He had first become intrigued with Jesus as a Jewish boy, glimpsing through the open doors of the cathedral the figure on the cross that his father and others sometimes referred to as 'the hanged man.' As a young apprentice physician seeking to alleviate human suffering he responded to the suffering of Christ, his initial interest gradually ripening into burning faith and conviction, and finally into a desire for personal Christian purity, a state of grace.

22

Once committed, he fell in love with a godhead. He thought it a much stronger love than that of a person simply born into Christianity. The Jesus-passion of Saul of Tarsus couldn't have been more powerful than his own, unshakable and certain, more consuming than any yearning of man for woman.

He had sought and received conversion into Catholicism in his twenty-second year, one year after he had become a full-fledged physician. His family had gone into mourning, saying the Kaddish for him as though he had died. His father, Jacob Espina, who had been so full of pride and love, had passed him in the plaza without acknowledging his greeting, without a sign of recognition. At that time Jacob Espina already was in his last year of life. He had been buried for a week before Bernardo learned he was gone. Espina had offered a novena for his soul but could not resist the urge to say Kaddish for him as well, weeping alone in his bedchamber as he recited the memorial blessing without the comforting presence of the minyan.

Wealthy or successful converts were accepted by the nobility and the middle class, and many married Old Christians. Bernardo Espina himself married Estrella de Aranda, daughter of a noble family. In the first flush of family acceptance and new religious rapture he had hoped against all reason that his patients would accept him as a coreligionist, a 'completed Jew' who had accepted their Messiah, but he wasn't surprised when they continued to scorn him as a Hebrew.

The magistrates of Toledo, when Espina's father was a young man, had passed a statute: 'We declare that the so-called conversos, offspring of perverse Jewish ancestors, must be held by law to be infamous and ignominious, unfit and unworthy to hold any public office or benefice within the city of Toledo or land within its jurisdiction, or to be commissioners for oaths or notaries, or to have any authority over true Christians of the Holy Catholic Church.'

Bernardo rode past other religious communities, some scarcely larger than the Priory of the Assumption, several the size of small villages. Under the Catholic monarchy, service in the Church had become popular. *Segundones*, the younger sons of noble families, excluded from inheritance by the law of majorat, turned to the religious life, where their family connections assured swift advancement. The younger daughters of the same families, because of the excessive dowries demanded to marry off firstborn females, often were sent to become nuns. Churchly vocations also attracted the poorest peasants, to whom holy orders with a prebend or a benefice offered the only chance to escape the grinding poverty of serfdom.

The growing number of religious communities had led to fierce and ugly competition for financial support. The relic of Santa Ana could be the making of the Priory of the Assumption, but the prior had told Bernardo there was scheming and planning among the powerful Benedictines, the wily Franciscans, and the energetic Geronomites – who knew how many others, all eager to wrest away ownership of the relic of the Sacred Family. Espina was uneasy lest he be caught between powerful factions and crushed as easily as Meir Toledano had been slain.

Bernardo began by attempting to recreate the youth's movements before he was killed.

The home of Helkias the silversmith was one of a group of houses built between two synagogues. The chief synagogue long since had been taken over by Holy Mother Church, and the Jews now held religious services in the Samuel ha-Levi Synagogue whose magnificence reflected a time when things had been easier for them.

The Jewish community was small enough for everyone to know who had left the faith, who pretended to have done so, and who remained a Jew. They did no business with New Christians if it could be helped. Still, four years before, a desperate Helkias had consulted the physician Espina.

His wife, Esther, a woman of good works who had been born into the Saloman family of great rabbis, had begun to waste away, and the silversmith had thought only of sustaining the mother of his three sons. Bernardo had worked hard over her, trying everything he knew, and praying to Christ for her life even as Helkias had prayed to Jehovah. But he had been unable to save Helkias's wife, may the Lord be merciful to her eternal soul.

Now he hurried past Helkias's house of misfortune without stopping, knowing that soon two friars from the Priory of the Assumption would lead a burro bearing the dead first son home to his father.

Earlier generations of Jews had raised the synagogues centuries before, obeying the ancient precept that a house of worship should be built at the highest possible point in the community. They had chosen sites at the top of lofty, sheer cliffs overlooking the Tagus River.

Bernardo's mare shied nervously, too close to the lip of the cliff.

25

Mother of God! he thought, pulling at the reins; then, as the horse settled, perforce Espina smiled at the irony.

'Grandmother of the Savior!' he said aloud in wonderment.

He pictured Meir ben Helkias here, waiting impatiently for the shield of darkness. He believed the youth had not been afraid of the cliffs. Bernardo remembered many a dusk when he had stood on these cliffs with his own father, Jacob Espina, searching the lowering sky for the glimmer of the first three stars that would signify the Sabbath was at an end.

He struck the thought away as he was wont to do with any disturbing memory of his Jewish past.

He saw the wisdom of Helkias having used a lone fifteen-year-old to deliver the reliquary. An armed guard would have announced to the world of banditry that here was treasure. A boy bearing an innocuous bundle through the night would have had a better chance.

But it had not been a good enough chance, as Espina had seen.

He dismounted and led the horse onto the cliff trail. Just over the edge was a stone hut built long ago by Roman soldiers; from it, they had thrown condemned prisoners to their deaths. Far below, the river wound in innocent beauty between the cliffs and an opposing granite hill. Boys growing up in Toledo shunned this place at night, claiming it was possible to hear the wailing of the dead.

He walked his horse down the cliff trail until the sheer drop became a manageable slope, then he turned off and followed a path down and down, to the water's edge. The Alcántara Bridge wasn't for him, nor would it have been for Meir ben Helkias. A short distance downstream

26

Bernardo came to the shallows where the boy would have crossed, and he remounted the mare. On the opposite bank he found the path that went toward the Priory of the Assumption. A short distance away there was rich and fertile agricultural land but here the soil was poor and sere, good only for limited grazing. Presently he heard the sounds of sheep and came upon a large flock cropping the short grass, tended by an old man he knew, Diego Diaz. The shepherd had a sprawling family almost as large as his flock, and Espina had treated a number of his relatives.

'A good afternoon, Señor Bernardo.'

'A good afternoon, Señor Diego,' Espina said, and dismounted. He allowed the horse to crop grass with the sheep, and he spent a few minutes passing the time of day with the shepherd. Then, 'Diego, do you know a boy named Meir, son of Helkias the Jew?'

'Yes, señor. Nephew of Aron Toledano the cheese maker, that boy?'

'Yes. When did you see him, the last time?'

'Yesterday eve, early. He was abroad delivering cheeses for his uncle, and for but one *sueldo* he sold me a goat cheese that was my meal this morning. Such cheese, I wish he had given me two.'

He glanced at Espina. 'Why do you seek him? Has he done something bad, that one?'

'No. Not at all.'

'I thought not, he is not a bad young shit, that young Jew.'

'Were others abroad hereabouts last night?' Espina asked, and the shepherd told him that not long after the boy's departure a pair of horsemen had passed, almost riding him down but unhailed and unhailing.

27

'Two, you say?' He knew he could depend on the old man to be accurate. The shepherd would have watched them closely, happy to see armed night riders go away without stopping to take a lamb or two.

'The moon was high. I saw a man-at-arms, a knight surely, for he wore fine mail. And a priest or a monk, I did not note the color of his robe.' He hesitated. 'The priest had a saint's face.'

'Which saint did he resemble?'

'No saint in particular,' the shepherd said, annoyed. 'I mean to express that he had a beautiful face touched by God. Features that were holy,' he said, and crossed himself.

Diego grunted, and ran to direct his dog toward four sheep moving away from the flock.

Curious, Bernardo thought. A face touched by God? He collected his horse and mounted. 'Be with Christ, Señor Diaz.'

The man shot him a sardonic glance. 'Christ be with you, Señor Espina,' he said.

A short distance beyond the hard-browsing sheep the earth became richer and fatter. Bernardo rode through vineyards and several fields. In the field adjacent to the priory's olive grove he stopped and dismounted, tying the horse's reins to a bush.

The grass was flattened and crushed by hooves. The number of horses seen by the shepherd, two, seemed to fit the amount of disorder.

Somebody had learned of the silversmith's commission. They knew Helkias had been nearing the end of his work, and they would have watched his house for signs of just such a delivery.

Here was the confrontation.

Meir's cries would not have been heard. The olive grove that was rented by the priory was in uninhabited open country, a stout walk from the religious community.

Blood. Here the boy received the cut in his side from one of their lances.

Along this grass-flattened swathe, down which Bernardo slowly walked, the horsemen had run Meir ben Helkias before their mounts like a quarried fox, inflicting the wounds on his back.

Here they had taken his leather bag and its contents. Nearby, covered with ants, were two pale cheeses of the type described by Diego – the young bearer's excuse for being abroad. One of the cheeses was intact, one had been broken and ground, as by a great hoof.

From here they brought the youth off the trail, into the added cover of the olive trees. And one or both of them took him.

Finally, his throat was slit.

Bernardo felt light-headed and faint.

He was not so distant from Jewish boyhood that he had forgotten the fear, the apprehension of armed strangers, the knowledge of terror because so much evil had gone before. Nor so distant from Jewish manhood that he did not feel these things still.

For a long moment, in his mind he became the boy. Hearing them. Smelling them. Sensing the giant, ominous shapes of the night, the huge horses moving at him, coming at him in the blackness.

The cruel thrusting of sharp blades. The rape.

Physician again, Bernardo wavered under the sinking sun and turned blindly toward the mare, escaping. He didn't believe he would hear the soul of Meir ben Helkias screaming, but he had little desire to be in this place when the next darkness came.

4

The Questioning

Espina realized quickly that he could glean only a small and finite amount of information about the murder of the Jewish boy and the theft of the ciborium. Almost everything he knew had come from his examination of the body, his discussion with the old shepherd, and his inspection of the site of the crimes. The most evident fact that faced him, after a week of fruitlessly going about the town asking questions, was that he had been neglecting his patients, and he threw himself into the safe and comforting daily work of his practice.

Nine days after he had been summoned to the Priory of the Assumption, he decided to go to Padre Sebastián that afternoon. He would tell the priest what little he had been able to learn, and that would be the end of his involvement in this matter.

His last patient of the day was an old man who was having difficulty breathing, although for a change the air was cool and fresh, a freak day of comfort in the midst of the season of heat. The thin body before the physician was depleted and worn, and there was more troubling it than the state of the weather. The skin of the chest was like thin leather; within, it was filled and clogged. When Espina put his ear to the chest he could hear a ragged rattling. He was reasonably certain the old man was dying but would take his time about it; and he was searching his pharmacopoeia for an infusion that would make the last days merciful when two slovenly armed men walked into his dispensary as if they were its new owners.

They identified themselves as soldiers of the *alguacil*, the bailiff of Toledo.

One of the men was short and barrel-chested and wore an officious air. 'Bernardo Espina, you will come with us now.'

'What is it you wish of me, señor?'

'The Office of the Inquisition requires your presence.'

'The Inquisition?' Espina sought to remain calm. 'Very well. Please to wait outside. I shall be finished with this señor in a very short time.'

'No, you will come at once,' the taller man said quietly, but with more authority.

Espina knew that Joan Pablo, his man of all work, was chatting with the old man's son in the shade of the dispensary shed. He went to the door and called to him. 'Go to the house and tell the señora I wish refreshment brought for these visitors. Bread with oil and honey, and cool wine.'

The bailiff's men looked at one another. The shorter soldier nodded. His companion's face remained without expression, but he made no objection.

Espina placed the old man's infusion into a small earthen jar and drove home the plug. He was finishing his instructions to the patient's son when Estrella hurried to him, followed by a servant woman bearing the bread and the wine.

His wife's features seemed to freeze when he told her. 'What can the Inquisition want with you, my dear Bernardo?'

'No doubt they have need of a physician,' he said, and the thought calmed both of them. While the men ate and drank, Joan Pablo saddled Espina's horse.

His children were at a neighbor's home, at which a monk weekly catechised a group of the young. He was comforted they weren't there to watch as he rode away flanked by the horses of the two men.

Clerics in black robes moved through the corridor where Espina sat on a wooden bench and waited. Others waited also. From time to time a white-faced man or woman was brought in under guard and was seated, or someone was escorted from the corridor and swallowed up by the building. None of the people who left the benches returned to them.

Espina was kept waiting until torches were lit against the encroaching dusk.

There was a guard seated behind a small table. Bernardo went to him and asked who it was he was waiting to see, but the man gave him a flat stare and motioned him back to the bench.

After a time, though, another guard came and asked the one behind the table about some of the people who were waiting. Espina saw them looking at him.

'That one is for Fray Bonestruca,' Bernardo heard the man behind the table say.

Toledo was becoming populous, but Espina was born

there and had lived there all his life, and – as Prior Sebastián had pointed out – as a physician he had a good working knowledge of both the lay population and the members of the clerical communities.

But he had no memory of a friar named Bonestruca.

At long last a guard came for him and took him from the corridor. They climbed a stone stairway and traversed several ill-lighted corridors similar to the one in which he had waited, and finally he was brought into a small cell where a friar sat beneath a torch.

The friar was someone new to the Toledo See, because if Espina had but once seen him in the streets, he would have remembered him without difficulty.

He was a tall man with a very Spanish head that demanded attention; Espina fought the impulse to stare. His quick glance noted a mass of thick black hair, long and badly cut. A wide forehead, black brows, very large brown eyes. A straight, narrow nose, a wide mouth with thin lips, and a somewhat square chin with a slight cleft.

Each of the features, if found with different features in another face, would have merited no interest. But seen here in this one man they combined in an extraordinary way.

The countenance of the friar was nothing like the face of Jesus as Espina had observed the Savior's visage in statues and paintings. This was a face of more feminine quality emerging from features of masculine beauty, yet Espina's initial reaction was a kind of awe.

A saint's face, the old shepherd Diego Diaz had called it. Diaz had been talking about this friar, Espina knew without a doubt.

Bonestruca was beyond handsomeness; his face at

first glance sent the viewer signals of reassurance and piety, the message that such complete and total comeliness must signify the essential goodness of God.

Yet when Espina looked into this friar's eyes, they carried him directly to a cold and frightening place.

'You have been about the town, asking questions concerning a reliquary but recently stolen from the Jew Helkias. What is your interest in this matter?'

'I . . . That is, Prior Padre Sebastián Alvarez . . .' Espina wished to look anywhere but into the knowing eyes of this strange friar, but there was nowhere else to look. 'He asked me to enquire into the loss of the reliquary and the . . . death of the boy who had carried it.'

'And what have you learned?'

'The boy was a Jew, son of the silversmith.'

'Yes, I have heard that.'

The friar's voice was gentler than his gaze . . . encouraging, almost friendly, Espina thought with hope.

'What else?'

'Nothing else, Reverend Friar.'

Friar Bonestruca's chest was hidden beneath the folds of his black habit, but his fingers were long and spatulate, with tufts of fine black hair between the second joints of his fingers and the knuckles. 'How long have you been a physician?'

'These eleven years.'

'Did you apprentice in this place?'

'Yes, here in Toledo.'

'With whom did you apprentice?'

Espina's mouth was dry. 'With Maestro Samuel Provo.'

'Ah, Samuel Provo. Even I have heard of him,' the friar said benignly. 'A great physician, no?'

'Yes, a man of renown.'

'He was a Jew.'

'Yes.'

'How many children did he circumcize, if you would suppose?'

Espina blinked at him. 'He did not circumcize.'

'How many babes do *you* circumcize in a twelve-month?'

'Neither do I circumcize.'

'Come, come,' the friar said patiently. 'How many of these operations have you done? Not only to Jews but also to Moors, perhaps?'

'Never . . . A few times over the years I have operated . . . When the foreskin is not properly and regularly cleaned, you understand, it becomes inflamed. Often there is pus, and to rectify . . . they . . . Both the Moors and the Jews have holy men who do the other, along with religious rites.'

'When you made those operations, did you say no prayers?'

'No.'

'Not even a Paternoster?'

'I pray each day that I will bring no harm but only good to my patients, Reverend Friar.'

'You are married, señor?'

'Yes.'

'Name of your wife.'

'Señora Estrella de Aranda.'

'Children?'

'Three. Two daughters and a son.'

'Your wife and children are Catholics?'

'Yes.'

'You are a Jew. Is this not so?'

'No! I have been a Christian these eleven years. Devoted to Christ!'

The man's face was so beautiful. That made the gray eyes fixing upon his own even more chilling. They had become cynical eyes that seemed aware of every human failing in Espina's history, and all his sins.

The gaze worked its way deep within his soul. Then, shockingly, the friar clapped his hands, summoning the guard who waited outside the door.

Bonestruca made a small movement of his hand: Take him.

As Bernardo turned to go, he saw that the sandaled feet beneath the table were well fashioned, with long and slender toes.

The guard led him down the corridors, down the steep flights of stairs.

Sweet Christ, you know I have tried. You know . . .

Espina was aware that in the lower bowels of the building were cells and the places in which prisoners were questioned. He knew for a fact that they had a rack called a *potro*, a triangular frame to which a prisoner was bound. Each time a windlass was turned, more bodily joints were dislocated. And something called a *toca*, for water torture. The prisoner's head was kept low in a hollowed-out trough. Linen was thrust into his throat. Water was poured through the cloth, blocking the throat and nostrils until suffocation brought on confession or death.

Jesus, I ask . . . I implore . . .

Perhaps he was heard. When they reached the exit, the guard motioned him on, and Espina proceeded alone, out to where the horse had been tied.

He rode away at a walk, fighting to compose himself so when he arrived home he could reassure Estrella without weeping.

Part Two

THE SECOND SON

Toledo, Castille
March 30, 1492

5

Yonah ben Helkias

'I will take Eleazar down to the river, perhaps to catch our supper. Eh, Abba?'

'The polishing is finished?'

'Much of it is finished.'

'Work is not finished until it is finished. You must polish it all,' Helkias said in the bleak tone that always wounded Yonah. Sometimes he wanted to stare into his father's distant eyes and tell him: Meir is dead but Eleazar and I are still here. We are alive.

Yonah hated to polish the silver. There were half a dozen large pieces still to do, and he dipped his rag into the stinking mess, a thick mixture of powdered bird dung and urine, and rubbed and rubbed.

He had learned the taste of bitterness early, with the death of his mother, and it had been very hard for him when Meir was killed, because by that time he had been older, past thirteen years, and had better understood the finality of loss.

Only a few months after Meir's death, Yonah had been called to the Torah to recite the law and become a formal member of the minyan. Adversity had matured him beyond his age. His father, who had always seemed so tall and strong, was diminished, and Yonah didn't know how to fill the space emptied by Helkias's grief.

They knew nothing of the identity of his brother's murderers. Some weeks after Meir had been killed, word had reached Helkias Toledano that the physician Espina was about the town, asking questions regarding the event that had taken his son's life. Helkias had brought Yonah with him to call upon Espina and speak with him, but when they had reached his house they saw it was abandoned, and Joan Pablo, the Espinas' former servant, was taking away for his own use all that remained of the furnishings, a table and some chairs. Joan Pablo had told them the physician and his family had gone away.

'Where have they gone?'

The man had shaken his head. 'I know not.'

Helkias had gone to the Priory of the Assumption to talk with Padre Sebastián Alvarez, but on his arrival he had thought for a confused moment that he had made a wrong turn in the road. Within the gate was a row of wagons and tumbrels. Nearby, three women were treading purple grapes in a large vat. Through the open door of what had been the chapel Helkias could see baskets of olives, and more grapes.

When he had asked the women where the priory had been moved, one of them told him the Priory of the Assumption had been closed and the Hieronymite order had rented the property to their farmer.

'And what of Padre Sebastián? Where is the prior?' he had asked. The woman had smiled at him and shook her head and shrugged, without stopping her treading.

*

Yonah had tried very hard to assume the duties of the eldest son, but it was obvious to him that he would never be able to take his brother's place. Not as an apprentice worker of silver, not as a son, not as a brother, not in any way. The dullness in his father's eyes compounded his own sorrow. Although three Passovers had come and gone since Meir died, the house and workshop of Helkias still were places of mourning.

Some of the pieces before him, wine flagons, were especially dark with tarnish, but there was no reason for him to hurry, because his father seemed suddenly to remember their conversation of half an hour ago. 'You will not go to the river. Find Eleazar and make certain both of you stay close to the house.

'This isn't a time for Jewish boys to take chances,' Helkias said.

It had been necessary for Yonah to assume Meir's responsibility for Eleazar, who was tender and apple-cheeked, seven years old. He told the younger boy stories about their older brother so Eleazar would never forget, and sometimes he picked out tunes on the small Moorish guitar that had been Meir's, and they sang songs. He had promised to teach Eleazar to play the guitar, as Meir had taught him. That's what Eleazar wanted to do when Yonah found him playing at war with stones and twigs in the shade of the house, but Yonah shook his head.

'Are you going to the river?' Eleazar said. 'Am I to go with you?'

'There is work to be done,' Yonah said, unconsciously mimicking his father's tone, and brought the smaller boy back into the atelier with him. The two of them were sitting in a corner polishing silver when David Mendoza and Rabbi José Ortega came into the workshop.

'What news?' Helkias asked, and Señor Mendoza shook his head. He was a strong, middle-aged man with a number of missing teeth and a bad complexion, a house builder.

'Not good, Helkias. It is no longer safe to walk in the town.'

Three months before, the Inquisition had executed five Jews and six conversos. They had been charged with conjuring a magic spell eleven years before, in which allegedly they had used a stolen communion wafer and the heart of a crucified Christian boy in an attempt to turn all good Christians raving mad. Although the boy was never identified – no Christian child had been reported missing – details of the alleged charge had been confessed by several of the accused after severe torture, and all had been burned at the stake, including the effegies of three of the condemned who died before the auto de fé.

'Some already are praying to the "martyred" child. Their hatred poisons the very atmosphere,' Mendoza said heavily.

'We must appeal to Their Majesties for their continued protection,' Rabbi Ortega said. The rabbi was small and skinny, with a froth of white hair. It made people smile to see him stagger about the synagogue bringing the large and heavy Torah scroll to be touched or kissed by the congregation. He was respected by most, but now Mendoza disagreed with him.

'The king is a man as well as a king, capable of friendship and sympathy, but of late Queen Isabella is turned against us. She was raised in isolation, molded by clerics who fashioned her mind. Tomás de Torquemada, the inquisitor general, may he expire, was Isabella's confessor during her girlhood, and he greatly influences her.' Mendoza shook his head. 'I fear the days ahead.'

'We must have faith, David, my friend,' Rabbi Ortega said. 'We must go to the synagogue and pray together. The Lord will hear our cries.'

The two boys had stopped polishing the silver cups. Eleazar was disturbed by the tension in the faces of the adults, and the obvious fright in their voices. 'What does it mean?' he whispered to Yonah.

'Later. I shall explain all to you later,' Yonah whispered back, though he wasn't certain he really understood what was happening.

The next morning, an armed military officer appeared in Toledo's municipal square. He was accompanied by three trumpeters, two local magistrates and two bailiff's men who also bore arms, and he read a proclamation that informed the Jews that despite their long history in Spain, they were ordered to leave the country within three months. The queen already had expelled Jews from Andalusia in 1483. Now they were ordered to leave every part of the Spanish kingdom – Castilla, León, Aragón, Galicia, Valencia, the principality of Cataluña, the feudal estate of Vizcaya, and the islands of Cerdeña, Sicilia, Mallorca, and Menorca.

The order was nailed to a wall. Rabbi Ortega copied it in a hand that trembled so badly he had trouble making out some of the words when he read them to a hurried meeting of the Council of Thirty.

'"All Jews and Jewesses, of whatever age they may be, that live, reside, and dwell in our said kingdoms and dominions . . . shall not presume to return to, or reside therein or in any part of them, either as residents, travellers, or in any manner whatever, under pain of death . . . And we command and forbid any person or persons in our said kingdom [to] presume publicly or secretly to receive, shelter, protect, or defend any Jew or Jewess . . . under pain of losing their property, vassals, castles, and other possessions."'

All Christians were solemnly warned against experiencing false compassion. They were forbidden 'to converse and communicate . . . with Jews, or receive them into your homes, or befriend them, or give them nourishment of any sort for their sustenance.'

The proclamation was issued 'by order of the king and queen, our sovereigns, and of the reverend prior of Santa Cruz, inquisitor general in all the kingdoms and dominions of Their Majesties.'

The Council of Thirty that governed the Jews of Toledo was made up of ten representatives from each of the three Estates – prominent urban leaders, merchants, and artisans. Helkias served because he was a *maestro* silversmith, and the meeting was held in his home.

The councillors were staggered.

'How can we be so coldly evicted from a land which means so much to us, and of which we are so much a part?' Rabbi Ortega said haltingly.

'The edict is yet one more royal scheme to gain fresh tax money and bribes from us,' Judah ben Solomon Avista said. 'Spanish kings have always described us as their profitable milch cow.'

There was a grumble of assent. 'Between the years 1482 and 1491,' said Joseph Lazara, an elderly flour merchant of Tembleque, 'we contributed no less than fifty-eight million *maravedíes* to the war effort, and another twenty million in "forced loans." Time after time, the Jewish community has gone steeply into debt in order to pay an exorbitant "tax" or to make the throne a "gift" in return for our survival. Surely this is but another such time.'

'The king must be approached and asked for his intervention,' Helkias said.

They discussed who should make the appeal, and there was a consensus that if should be Don Abraham Seneor.

'He is the Jewish courtier His Majesty most loves and admires,' Rabbi Ortega said, and many heads nodded in agreement.

6
Changes

Abraham Seneor had lived for eighty years, and though his mind was fresh and sharp, his body was very tired. His history of hard and dangerous service to the monarch had begun when he had arranged secret nuptials that on October 19, 1469, had joined in marriage two cousins, Isabella of Castille, eighteen years old, and Ferdinand of Aragon, seventeen.

That ceremony had been clandestine because it had defied King Henry IV of Castille. Henry had wanted his half-sister Isabella to become the wife of King Alfonso of Portugal. The Infanta had refused, asking Henry to name her as heir to the thrones of Castille and León, and promising him she would marry only with his approval.

Henry IV of Castille had no sons (he was mocked by subjects who called him Henry the Impotent) but he had a daughter, Juana, believed to have been the illegitimate child of Henry's mistress, Beltrán de la Cueva. When he tried to name Juana his heir, a civil war erupted. The nobles withdrew their support of Henry as their king and recognized as their sovereign Isabella's twelve-year-old brother, also named Alfonso. Within two years the young Alfonso was found dead in his bed, reputedly poisoned.

Isabella had not been raised or educated as a future monarch, but soon after her brother's death she had asked Abraham Seneor to set into motion the secret negotiations with influential Aragonese courtiers that led to her marriage to Ferdinand, Prince of Aragon. On December 11, 1474, when Henry IV died suddenly in Madrid, Isabella was in Segovia. Upon hearing the news, she declared herself queen of Castille. Two days later, surrounded by a cheering throng, she drew her sword, held it above her with the hilt upward, and led a procession to the Segovia Cathedral. The parliamentary Cortes immediately swore its allegiance to her.

In 1479 King John II of Aragon died and Ferdinand succeeded his father. In the ten years that had followed their secret wedding the royal couple had waged continual war, fighting back invasions from Portugal and France and dealing with insurgents. When those military campaigns had been won, they concentrated on war against the Moors.

Through all the years of combat Abraham Seneor had labored for them faithfully, raising money for the expensive business of war, developing a system of taxation, and guiding them through the political and financial pitfalls of uniting Castille and Aragon.

The monarchs had rewarded him well, declaring him rabbi and supreme judge of the Jews of Castille and assessor of Jewish taxes throughout the kingdom. Since 1488 he had been treasurer of the Hermandad, a militia that Ferdinand had established to maintain order and security in Spain. His fellow Jews didn't love Seneor – he had been the King's choice to be their rabbi, not their own.

But Seneor was loyal to them. Even before Jews from many parts of the kingdom could beg Seneor to plead with Ferdinand, he had acted. His first meeting with the monarchs was based upon their mutual affection and friendship, but his pleas for a reversal of the expulsion edict met with a cool rejection that dismayed him.

Several weeks later he requested another meeting, this time bringing with him his son-in-law, Rabbi Meir Melamed, who had served as Ferdinand's secretary and was the kingdom's chief administrator of tax collections. Both men had been declared rabbis by the king and not by their fellow religionists, but they had served effectively as advocates for the Jews at court. With them was Isaac ben Judah Abravanel, who was in charge of tax collections in the central and southern parts of the country and who had loaned enormous sums of money to the royal treasury, including 1.5 million gold ducats to achieve victory in the war against Granada.

The three Jews again pressed their plea, this time offering to raise fresh funds for the treasury, with Abravanel making it clear that he and his brothers would relinquish certain heavy debts owed them by the Crown if the expulsion edict were revoked.

Ferdinand showed undisguised interest when discussing the sums offered. The three petitioners hoped for an immediate ruling, so Torquemada and other religionists who had worked for years to have the Jews expelled would have no opportunity to influence the decision. However, Ferdinand took their request under advisement, and a week later, when the three appeared before the monarchs again, the king told them their request was denied. He had decided that the expulsion edict would be carried out.

Isabella stood beside her husband, a stern, pudgy woman of average height, but very regal in her bearing. She had large, imperious blue-green eyes and a tiny pursed mouth. Her reddish blond hair, her best feature, was beginning to be flecked with gray. She made the moment even more bitter for them by quoting King Solomon, Proverbs 21:1.

'"The king's heart is in the hand of the Lord as the water courses. He turneth it whithersoever he will."

'Do you believe this thing is come upon you from us? The Lord has put this thing into the heart of the king,' she told the three Jews disdainfully, and the audience was over.

Throughout the kingdom, Jewish councils met in new desperation.

In Toledo, the Council of Thirty struggled to achieve some sort of plan.

'I cherish this land. If I must leave this beloved place where my ancestors rest,' David Mendoza said finally, 'I wish to go where I will never be accused of murdering an infant in order to make matzos from his tender body, or stabbing the Eucharist, or insulting the Virgin, or mocking the Mass!'

'We must go where innocent folk are not ignited like tinder,' Rabbi Ortega said, and there was a murmur of agreement.

'Where might such a place be?' Yonah's father asked.

There was a long silence. They stared at one another.

Yet all had to go somewhere, and people began trying to make plans.

Aron Toledano, a stocky, slow-speaking man, came to

his brother's house and he and Helkias talked for hours, proposing destinations and rejecting them while Yonah listened, trying to understand.

There were really only three possible destinations, when all was said. To the north, the kingdom of Navarre. To the west, Portugal. To the east, the seacoast, offering ships to transport them to more distant lands.

But within days they learned new facts that helped narrow the choices.

Aron came again, his farmer's face dark with worry. 'Navarre cannot be considered. Navarre will accept only former Jews who have converted to the worship of Jesus.'

Less than a week later they learned that Don Vidal ben Benveniste de la Cavalleria, who had minted Aragon's gold coins and Castille's currency, had ridden to Portugal and received permission for Spanish Jews to go there. King John II of Portugal saw an opportunity and decreed that his treasury would tax one ducat from every immigrating Jew, plus one-fourth of any merchandise carried into his kingdom. In return, the Jews would be allowed to stay six months.

Aron shook his head in disgust. 'I hold no trust in that one. In the end, I think we would receive less justice from him than we have received from the Spanish throne.'

Helkias agreed. And that left only the seacoast, whence they would take ship.

Helkias was deliberate and gentle, a tall man. Meir had been shorter and blockier, like Aron, and Eleazar already showed the signs of a similar build. Yonah was built larger, like his father, whom he regarded with awe as well as love.

'To where shall we sail then, Abba?'

'I don't know. We will go where there are many ships, probably to the port of Valencia. Then we will see what shipping is available, and where the vessels are bound. We must trust that the Almighty will guide our path and help us make a wise decision.'

He looked at Yonah. 'Are you fearful, my son?'

Yonah struggled to form a reply but was slow to answer.

'It is not a shame to be afraid. It is wise to recognize that travel is rife with danger. But we will be three large and strong men – Aron, and you, and I. The three of us will be able to see to the safety of Eleazar and your aunt, Juana.'

Yonah was gratified to be counted as a man by his father.

It was as if Helkias read his mind. 'I am aware you have taken a man's responsibility, these last years,' he said quietly. 'I want you to know others have observed your character, also. There have been several overtures made to me by fathers of daughters who are ready to stand under the bridal canopy.'

'Have you spoken of a marriage?' Yonah said.

'Not yet. Not now. But once we arrive at our new home there will be time to meet the Jews who are there and arrange a fine match. Which I suspect you will welcome.'

'I shall,' Yonah admitted, and his father laughed.

'Do you not think I was once young? I remember how it is.'

'Eleazar will be very jealous. He will want a wife also,' Yonah said, and now they both laughed together.

'Abba, I am not fearful to go anywhere, so long as you are with me.'

53

'Nor am I afraid with you, Yonah. For the Lord will be with us.'

The thought of marriage was a new element in Yonah's life. Amidst all the tumult, his mind was confused and his body had changed. At night he dreamed of females, and even in the midst of crisis he daydreamed of his longtime friend Lucía Martín. When they were curious children, on several occasions they had explored each other's nudity at length. Now it was possible to see that beneath her clothing she had taken on the first ripeness of womanhood, and there was a new awkwardness between them.

Everything was changing, and despite his fears and misgivings, Yonah felt a thrill at the prospect of traveling to distant places at last. He imagined life in a new place, the kind of life Jews hadn't experienced in Spain for the past hundred years.

In a book he had found mixed among the religious tracts in the study house, by an Arab author named Khordabbek, he had read about Jewish merchant-traders:

'They take ship in the land of the Franks, on the Western Sea, and steer for Farama. There they load their goods on the backs of camels and go by land to Kolzum, which is five days' journey over a distance of twenty-five farsakhs. They embark in the Red Sea and sail from Kolzum to Eltar and Jeddah. Then they go to Sind, India, and China.'

He would like to be a merchant-trader. If he were a Christian he would prefer to be a knight – of course, of the sort that did not kill Jews. Such lives would be full of wonder.

But in more realistic moments Yonah knew his father was right. It made no sense to sit and indulge in dreams. There was work to be done, because the very foundations of their world were giving way.

7

The Date of Departure

Yonah knew many people who were already leaving. On the road outside of Toledo first a few travelers were seen and then a trickle, and then there was a flood of Jews night and day, a multitude of strangers from afar, going west toward Portugal or east toward the ships. The noise of their passing was heard in the city. They rode on horses and burros, they sat on sacks of their belongings in wagons pulled by cows, they walked under the hot sun bearing heavy loads, some stumbling, some falling. Sometimes women and boys sang and beat drums and tambourines as they walked, to keep their spirits up.

Women gave birth by the side of the road, and people died. The Toledo Council of Thirty allowed travelers to bury their dead in the Jewish cemetery but often could offer no other help, not even a minyan to say the Kaddish. In other times travelers in distress would have been given aid and hospitality, but now the Jews of Toledo were themselves leaving or preparing to leave and were struggling with their own problems.

The Dominican and Franciscan orders, pleased to see the expulsion for which they had worked and preached, set about energetically to harvest as many Jewish souls as possible. Some in Toledo who had been friends of Yonah's family for a very long time entered the city's churches and declared themselves Christians – children, their parents and their grandparents, with whom the Toledanos had broken bread, with whom they had prayed in the synagogue, with whom they had cursed the need to wear the yellow badge of a shunned people. Almost one-third of the Jews became conversos because they feared the terrible dangers of travel, or out of love for a Christian, or because they had achieved position and comfort they couldn't bring themselves to renounce, or because they had had enough of being despised.

Jews in high positions were pressured and coerced into conversion. One evening Yonah's uncle Aron came to Helkias with shocking news.

'Rabbi Abraham Seneor, his son-in-law Rabbi Meir Melamed, and their families have become Catholics.'

Queen Isabella had not been able to bear the prospect of being without the two men who had accomplished so much for her, and it was rumored that she had threatened them with reprisals against the Jews if they refused to convert. It was known that the sovereigns had personally arranged and attended the public conversion ceremonies and had served as godparents at the baptism.

Rabbi Seneor had changed his name to Fernando Nuñez Coronel, and Rabbi Melamed had changed his name to Fernando Pérez Coronel.

A few days later Seneor was appointed governor of Segovia, a member of the royal council, and chief financial administrator to the crown prince. Melamed was appointed chief royal accountant and he too became a permanent member of the royal council.

Isaac Abravanel refused to convert. He and his brothers Joseph and Jacob renounced the large debts owed to them by the king and the queen, and in exchange they were allowed to leave the country, taking with them one thousand gold ducats and some valuable belongings made of gold and silver.

Helkias and Aron were less fortunate, like the vast majority of the Jews struggling with calamity. The Jewish multitude was told that no one was allowed to take gold, silver, money, or precious stones from the realm. They were advised by the throne to sell everything they owned and use the proceeds for 'common goods' which they could sell when they reached their new homelands. But almost immediately King Ferdinand declared that in Aragon some of the Jewish land, homes, and chattels should be seized because of revenues 'owed' the Crown.

Jews in Toledo rushed to sell their property before a similar move by the monarchs would make it impossible to do so, but the process was a charade. Their Christian neighbors, knowing that the property must be abandoned or the Jews would die, ground prices down mercilessly, offering a few *sueldos* for real estate that should have sold for many *maravedíes*, or even many *reales*. A donkey or a vineyard changed hands for a piece of common cloth.

Aron Toledano, offered almost nothing for his goat farm, turned to his older brother for advice. 'I don't know what to do,' he said helplessly.

Helkias had been a prosperous and sought-after

artisan all his life, but the bad times had come when he was in a financial trough. He had been paid only a deposit on the reliquary. When it had been stolen before delivery no more money was forthcoming, although to make the ciborium he had invested heavily in the purest silver and gold. A number of wealthy patrons now held back their payments for objects delivered, sensing that events might make it unnecessary for them to settle their debts.

'I don't know what to do, either,' he admitted. He was in desperate straits, but he was saved because of the efforts and tender heart of an old and devoted friend.

Benito Martín was an Old Christian, a goldsmith who lacked the creative genius that had earned Helkias his reputation as a worker of silver. Most of Martín's work was simple gilding and repair. Both of them were young men when Benito had discovered that in his own city of Toledo a Jew created things of wonder out of precious metals.

He sought out the Jewish artisan and spent as much time with him as he could without becoming a nuisance, learning new ways to design silver and gold and spurred to extend his vision of the work of his own hands.

In the process of relearning his craft, Benito Martín had discovered a man.

Helkias had welcomed him and invited a sharing of skills and human experiences. Benito's admiration gradually had ripened into a true and certain friendship, so deep that during better times Martín had brought his children to the synagogue to visit the Toledano family at Passover, and to the sukkah during the Feast of Tabernacles. His daughter Lucía had become Yonah's best friend, and his son Enrique was Eleazar's most frequent playmate.

Now Benito was ashamed of the injustice rampant in Toledo, and he came to walk with Helkias one evening, early enough so they were able to stroll along the cliff top and greet the coming of night.

'Your house is sited so wonderfully, and your workshop has been planned so sensibly it invites good results. I have long coveted them.'

Helkias was silent.

When Benito named his offer, the silversmith stopped walking.

'I know it is very low, but . . .'

It would have been a very low offer in ordinary times, but the times were not ordinary. Helkias knew it was all Benito could afford, and it was far more than the rapacious offers made by speculators.

He went to the other man and kissed his shaven Christian cheek and embraced him for a long time.

Yonah noticed that the dullness was gone from his father's eyes. Helkias sat with Aron and contemplated how they could save their family. The emergency was immediate, and Helkias was responding by rising to meet it with all his energy and attention.

'Ordinarily, the trip to Valencia would take ten days. Now, with the roads thick with people seeking early arrival, the same trip will take them twenty days, requiring twice as much food and doubling the dangers of travel. So we must leave Toledo as late as possible, when once again there will be fewer travelers.'

On their farm Aron kept two pack burros and a pair of fine horses that he and his wife, Juana, would ride.

Benito Martín had acted for Helkias, purchasing two additional horses and a pair of burros for far less than a Jew would have been charged, and Helkias was paying his neighbor Marcelo Troca exorbitantly to keep the four animals in his nearby field.

Helkias told his brother they must find a way to get more capital. 'When we reach the port, sea captains will not be charitable to us. It will take a great deal of money to pay for our passage. And when we reach a land of haven, we must have money to sustain us until we can again work for our daily bread.'

The only possible source of money was the unpaid debts of Helkias's clients, and Yonah sat with his father and made a careful list of those customers and the amounts each owed.

The largest debt was sixty-nine *reales* and sixteen *maravedíes* owed by Count Fernán Vasca of Tembleque. 'He is an arrogant noble, summoning me as though he were king, describing each thing he wished me to make, yet slow to pay me even a single *sueldo* of his debt. If I can collect this debt we shall have mo.[.] than enough.'

Yonah rode with his father on a bright July day to Tembleque, a village outside Toledo. He was unaccustomed to riding a horse, but their mounts were tractable, and he sat in the battered saddle as proudly as any knight. The countryside was beautiful, and though Helkias was weighed down with heavy thoughts, still he was able to burst into song as they rode. He sang a song of peace.

> *'Oh, the wolf shall dwell with the lamb,*
> *And the leopard shall lie with the kid,*
> *And the cow and the bear shall feed,*
> *While the lion eats straw like the ox . . .'*

Yonah loved to listen to the deep voice singing the sonorous lines. *This is how it will be when we ride to Valencia*, he thought with pleasure.

Presently as they rode Helkias told his son that when he had first been summoned to Tembleque by Count Vasca, he had confided in his friend, Rabbi Ortega. 'The rabbi said to me, "Let me tell you about this nobleman."'

Rabbi Ortega had a nephew, a young scholar named Asher ben Yair, learned in several languages as well as in Torah. 'It is hard for a scholar to earn a living,' Helkias said, 'and one day Asher heard that a nobleman in Tembleque was seeking to employ a clerk, and he rode out to Tembleque and offered his services.'

The count of Tembleque was proud of his martial skills, Yonah's father told him. He had fought against the Moors and had traveled far and wide to participate in jousting tourneys, many of which he had won. But he was always alert for novelty, and in the spring of 1486 he had heard of a different kind of contest, a literary tourney in which the contestants fought with poems instead of lances and swords.

The contest was the Jocs Florals – the Flower Games. They had begun in France late in the fourteenth century, when some young nobles of Toulouse decided to invite poets to recite their works, the winner to receive, as the first prize, a violet fashioned of gold.

The contest was held in France periodically, until Violante de Bar, queen of Cataluña and Aragon and wife of King Joan I, brought the poetry competition and some of its French judges to Barcelona in 1388. The Spanish court soon officially adopted the Jocs Florals and celebrated them each year with great pomp. By the time they came to Count Vasca's attention the annual poetry competitions were judged by the royal court. The silver violet was now given as the third prize. Second prize was a rose fashioned of gold. The first prize, with a typical Catalan touch, was a single real rose, on the theory that nothing made by humans could surpass a flower made by God.

Vasca thought it would be splendid to be summoned to the court to receive such an honor, and he made plans to enter the Jocs Florals. The fact that he was illiterate didn't deter him, for he had the wealth to employ someone with writing skills, and he hired Asher ben Yair and told him that he must write a poem. In a discussion about subject matter Vasca said the poem should be about a great and noble soldier, and after a very brief time the count and the clerk agreed that Count Fernán Vasca himself was the warrior most suitable for description in such a work.

When the poem was completed and read to the count it didn't offend his ear. It was sufficient that his bravery and warrior skills were treated with reverence and no little exaggeration, and Count Vasca sent a copy to Barcelona.

The Vasca poem failed to impress the judges of the court. By the time news reached the Count that three others had won the prizes, Asher ben Yair had said good-bye to his uncle, Rabbi Ortega, and had wisely departed for the island of Sicilia, where he believed he could become a teacher of young Jews.

Count Vasca had sent for Helkias Toledano, a Jew who was reputed to be a remarkable worker of precious metals. When Helkias had gone to Tembleque he had found Vasca still enraged that he had been snubbed by a group of effete versifiers. He told Helkias about the Jocs

Florals and its imaginative prizes, and then revealed that he had decided to sponsor a more manly contest, a true jousting tourney, with a first prize far more remarkable and magnificent than any given in Barcelona.

'I wish you to fashion a rose of gold, with a silver stem.'

Yonah's father had nodded thoughtfully.

'Listen to me with care: it must be fully as beautiful as a natural rose.'

Helkias had smiled. 'Well, but—'

The Count had held up a hand – Helkias believed he was unwilling to abide very long discussions with a Jew. Vasca had turned away. 'Just go and do this thing. It will be required after Easter next.' And Helkias had been dismissed.

Helkias was accustomed to the unreasonable demands of difficult patrons, though the particular situation was made more difficult by the fact that Count Vasca had a reputation for brutalizing those who displeased him. He started to work, sitting before rose bushes for many hours, making drawings. When he had a depiction that satisfied him, he began to beat gold and silver with a hammer. After four days he had something very much in the shape of a rose, but it was disappointing, and he broke it apart and melted the metal.

He tried again and again, each time gaining small victories but meeting defeat in the aggregate effect. Two months passed from the day of his meeting with Vasca, and still he wasn't close to fulfilling his commission.

But he kept trying, studying the rose as if it were the Talmud, drinking in its scent and beauty, picking roses apart petal by petal to note the construction of the whole, noting how stems turned and bent and grew toward the sun, observing the way buds were born and ripened and tenderly unfolded and opened. With each attempt to reproduce the simple and stunning beauty of the flower he began to sense the essence and spirit of the rose, and in the attempts and failures gradually he evolved from the craftsman he had been into the artist he would be.

Finally, he had created a flower of glowing gold. Its petals curled with a fresh softness that was perceived by the eye instead of being sensed through touching. It was a believable flower, as if a master horticulturist had achieved a natural rose of a perfect golden color. Below the flower was a single golden bud. The stem and twigs and thorns and leaves were of bright silver, spoiling the illusion, but Helkias had five months until the date of delivery demanded by Count Vasca, and he allowed time to do its work. The gold retained its color but the silver darkened with tarnish until it took on color characteristics that made the flower believable.

Count Vasca was visibly surprised and pleased when he saw what Helkias had wrought. 'I will not give this away as a prize. I have a better purpose for it,' he said.

Instead of paying Helkias he gave him a large order for more objects, and then still a third order. Ultimately he became Helkias's largest debtor, and when the Jews were ordered to leave Spain the Vasca debt had led to their present grave difficulty.

The castle was large and forbidding as Yonah and Helkias approached it. The bars of the great gate to the keep were down. Helkias and Yonah stared up at the sentry station atop the high stone wall.

'Halloo the guard!' Helkias called, and presently a helmeted head appeared.

65

'I am Helkias Toledano, silversmith. I wish to speak with His Excellency the Count Vasca.'

The head withdrew but in a brief time it reappeared.

'His Excellency the count is not here. You must go away.'

Yonah stifled a groan, but his father persevered. 'I come on a matter of important business. If the count is not here, I must speak with his steward.'

Once more the sentry went away. Yonah and his father sat on their horses and waited.

Finally, with a squeal and then a groaning, the barred gate was lifted, and they rode into the castle yard.

The steward was a slender man who was feeding strips of meat to a caged falcon. The meat had been a white cat. Yonah could see the tail, which was still whole.

The man scarcely looked at them. 'The count is hunting in the north,' he said in an irritated voice.

'I seek payment for articles which I made on order and delivered to him,' Helkias said, and the steward cast him a glance.

'I pay no one unless the count commands it.'

'When shall he return?'

'When he wishes.' Then the man relented, perhaps to rid himself of them. 'If I were you, I should come again in six days' time.'

As they directed the horses back to Toledo, Helkias was quiet, lost in troubled thought. Yonah tried to recapture some of the pleasantness of the earlier ride.

'"Oh, the wolf shall dwell with the lamb . . ."' he sang, but his father took no notice, and they rode the rest of the way mostly in silence.

*

Six days later Helkias made the trip again, by himself, and this time the functionary said the count wouldn't return until fourteen days hence, the twenty-sixth day of the month.

'It is too late,' Aron said in despair when Helkias told him.

'Yes, it is too late,' Helkias said.

But the following day there were tidings that the monarchs in their mercy had granted one extra day for the Jews to leave Spain, moving the final date from the first day of August to the second day.

'Do you think? . . .' Aron asked.

'Yes, we can do it! I shall be waiting at the castle when he arrives. We can leave as soon as I am paid,' Helkias said.

'But to make the trip to Valencia in seven days!'

'It is not that we have a choice, Aron,' Helkias said. 'Without money, we are doomed.'

When Aron sighed, Helkias placed his hand on his brother's arm. 'We shall do it. We shall push ourselves and the beasts, and we will find our way.'

But even as he spoke, he was considering the uneasy fact that August the second was the ninth day of the Jewish month of Ab, an infamous date and perhaps a bad omen, for the ninth of Ab was the date of the destruction of the Temple in Jerusalem, when large numbers of Jews were forced to begin wandering the world.

8

The Fisher

There was no longer need for Yonah and Eleazar to polish the silver objects. Recognizing that he couldn't sell them for a fair price, Helkias turned all his stock over to Benito Martín for a small amount of cash.

On the middle finger of Yonah's right hand he wore a wide band of silver, given to him by his father after he had been called to the Torah for the first time. Helkias had made an identical ring for his firstborn son, but when Meir's body had been brought to him, the ring had been missing.

'Remove the ring from your finger,' Helkias told Yonah now, and the youth did so with reluctance. His father threaded the ring onto a length of thin but strong cord and placed the loop around Yonah's neck, so the ring was hidden inside his shirt.

'If the time comes when we must sell your ring, I promise to make you another as soon as possible. But it may be that with the help of the Lord you will be able to wear this ring again in another place,' he said.

*

Helkias brought his two sons to the Jewish cemetery outside the limits of the city. It was a heartrending place, for other families who were leaving Spain stopped at the graves of their loved ones to say good-bye, and their cries and sobbing frightened Eleazar so the boy wept too, although he didn't remember his mother at all and scarcely recalled Meir.

Helkias had mourned his wife and firstborn son for years. Though his eyes were filled he made no sound, but held his two sons close and dried their tears and kissed them before he set them to neatening the graves and finding small stones to lay on them as a sign they had been visited.

'Terrible to leave their graves,' Helkias said later to Benito. Martín had brought a skin of wine and the two friends sat and talked as they had so many times in the past. 'But worse, somehow, to leave my son's grave without knowing who placed him there.'

'If it were possible to trace the reliquary, its location might tell a great deal,' Martín said.

Helkias's mouth twisted. 'It has not been possible. By now, the thieves who deal in such objects would already have sold it. Perhaps it is in a church a great distance from here,' he said, and took a long swallow of the wine.

'And yet . . . perhaps not,' Benito said. 'If I spoke to those pastoring the churches of the region, I might learn something.'

'I had thought of doing the same,' Helkias admitted, 'yet . . . I am a Jew. I have been too fearful of churches and priests to take that action.'

'Let me do it for you now,' Martín urged, and Helkias nodded gratefully. He went to his drawing board and fetched sketches of the ciborium that Martín might show the churchmen, and gave them to Benito.

Martín was troubled. 'Helkias, feeling against you is high in the city. It's muttered that you refuse to leave Toledo and yet also refuse to convert. This house on the cliff top is especially exposed. It is too late to seek security in numbers behind the walls of the Jewish Quarter, since the other Jews have departed. Perhaps you and your sons should come to my home, to the safety of a Christian house.'

Helkias knew that an adult and two boys moving into the Martín home, even for a short time, would cause turmoil. He thanked Benito but shook his head. 'Until the moment when we must leave we will savor the home in which my sons were born,' he said.

Still, when Benito departed, Helkias took his two sons to the path down the cliff. Off the trail, he showed them an opening into a narrow L-shaped tunnel leading to a small cave.

If ever the need should arise, he told Yonah and Eleazar, the cave would be a safe hiding place.

Yonah was very aware of doing things in Toledo for the last time.

He had missed the spring fishing. Spring was the best time, when it was still cool but the first warmth of the sun had hatched mayflies and other tiny winged creatures that hovered over the surface of the river.

Now it was hot, but he knew of a deep pool just beyond a natural dam of large rocks and branches, and he knew fish would be lazing almost motionless at the very bottom, waiting for a meal to drift their way.

He gathered the small hooks made for him by a father

who knew how to work with metals, and then he went behind the workshop and collected the short wooden pole wound with strong line.

He had taken scarcely three steps when Eleazar was running after him.

'Yonah, are you taking me with you?'

'No.'

'Yonah, I wish to go.'

If their father heard, perhaps he would order them to stay close to home. Yonah cast an anxious glance at the door of the workshop. 'Eleazar, don't spoil it for me. If you fuss, he'll hear and come out.'

Eleazar looked at him unhappily.

'When I come back I'll spend the afternoon teaching you to play the guitar.'

'The whole afternoon?'

'The whole.'

Another moment and he was free, ascending the trail toward the river.

At the bottom he attached a hook and then spent a few minutes at the river's edge, overturning rocks. Several crayfish scuttled away before he found one small enough to please him, then he pounced and secured the bait.

It was his favorite fishing place; through the years he had used it well. A large rock overlooked the pool, easy to reach because its flat top was almost the height of the trail, while an overhanging tree provided shade for both the fish that gathered in the pool and the fisher who sat on the rock.

The baited hook entered the water with a plop. Yonah waited expectantly, but when there was no sign of a strike he settled down on the rock with a sigh.

71

There was a slight breeze, the rock was cool, and the quiet sounds of the river were calming and pleasant. Somewhere far downstream two men called to one another, and nearby, a bird trilled.

He wan't aware of drowsiness, just a diminution of sounds and awareness, until he slept.

He was awakened with a start when someone slid the end of the pole from under his leg.

'You have a fish,' the man said.

Yonah was frightened. The man was as tall as Abba, a friar or monk in black robes and sandals. His voice was soft and kind, and Yonah thought he had a good face. 'He is a very large fish. You wish the pole?'

'No, you may catch him,' Yonah said reluctantly.

'Lorenzo,' someone called from the trail, and Yonah turned to see another black-robed man waiting there.

The fish was lunging for the brush dam at the top of the pool, but the tall man raised the tip of the pole. He was a good fisher, Yonah noted. He didn't pull it up so sharply that it endangered the line, but he led the fish back by taking in the line with his left hand, a little at a time, until the catch, a fine bream arching back and forth on the hook, was hauled to the top of the rock.

The man was smiling. 'Not so big, after all, eh? They all seem very large at first.' He held out the fish. 'You wish him?'

Of course Yonah did, but he sensed that the man wanted the fish too.

'No, señor,' he said.

'Lorenzo,' the other friar called. 'Please, there is no time. He will be looking for us.'

'All right!' the tall man said irritably, and slid a finger

under a gill the better to carry the fish. Gentle eyes as deep as the pool looked at Yonah.

'May Christ bring you luck,' he said.

9

Visitors

The next morning the sky turned a greenish black and there were shuddering claps of thunder and a good deal of lightning, then the storm quieted, but it rained for two days. Yonah's uncle Aron and aunt Juana came to Yonah's house and Juana said it was unusual for rain to fall so heavily in the month of Tammuz.

'But not unheard-of,' her husband said.

'No, of course not unheard-of,' Juana said, and nobody suggested it was a bad omen. The air was hot even though the moisture fell, and on the second day the rain lightened and then stopped.

Benito Martín had ridden through the rain on both days, carrying Helkias's sketches rolled and wrapped against the wet in a piece of leather. He had unrolled the drawings at seven churches and two monasteries. By now, every priest and monk in Toledo had heard of the loss of the priory's ciborium, but nobody offered any knowledge of what had happened to the reliquary after it had been stolen.

His last stop had been at the cathedral, where he had knelt and said a prayer.

When he finished praying he stood and saw that he was being watched by a tall friar with an extremely handsome face. Martín knew from common gossip that the people in the plazas referred to this friar as El Guapo, the Beautiful One, and that he was with the Inquisition, but Benito couldn't remember his name.

He continued the business of showing the sketches to priests, of whom there was no shortage in the cathedral. He had shown the drawings three times, with the familiar lack of success, when he looked up and met the tall friar's eyes again.

The man crooked a forefinger.

'Let me see.'

When Benito gave him the sketches he studied each of them at length. 'Why do you show them to priests?'

'They are designs of a reliquary that has been stolen. The silversmith who fashioned it seeks to learn if its whereabouts are known.'

'The Jew Toledano.'

'Yes.'

'Your name?'

'I am Benito Martín.'

'You are a converso?'

'No, Friar, I am an Old Christian.'

'Helkias Toledano is your friend?'

It should have been easy to say Yes, we are friends.

Benito was fond of the cathedral. It was his habit to visit it often, because the lovely vaulted place always made him feel his prayers could go straight up, into the ears of God, but this friar was spoiling the cathedral for him.

'I am a goldsmith. At times we have conferred about matters of our trades,' he said warily.

'Have you relatives who are conversos?'

'I do not.'

'Has the silversmith already left Toledo?'

'He is soon to be gone.'

'Has he spoken to you of Jewish prayer?'

'No. Not ever.'

'Do you know whether he has spoken of prayer with any Christian?'

'No.'

The friar handed back the sketches. 'You are aware that Their Majesties have specifically forbidden any Christian to give comfort to Jews?'

'I have not given comfort,' Benito said, but the friar may not have heard, for he had already turned away.

Bonestruca, Benito remembered, that was the name.

The rain had stopped by the time he rode to the Toledano house.

'So, my friend,' Helkias said.

'So, my friend. Is it truly to be tomorrow?'

'Yes, tomorrow,' Helkias said, 'whether or not the Count of Tembleque returns so I can collect my money. If we wait longer it will be too late.'

Helkias told Benito they would pack the burros early. He and his sons were carefully separating the few belongings they could carry with them. 'What we leave behind is yours, as you wish.'

'I thank you.'

'For nothing.'

Martín gave Helkias his disappointing report, and Helkias thanked him and shrugged: the results were not unexpected. Then, 'You know the friar they call the Beautiful One, a tall Dominican?' Martín asked.

Helkias looked at him in puzzlement. 'No.'

'He is an inquisitor. When he saw me showing the sketches he made me understand he disapproved of my errand. He asked questions about you, too many questions. I fear for you, Helkias. Have you had dealings with that friar – perhaps some difficulty or unpleasantness?'

Helkias shook his head. 'I have never talked with him. But save your concern, Benito. Tomorrow night I will be far from here.'

Benito was ashamed that a friar could cause him nervousness.

He asked if he might bring Eleazar to the Martín house for the rest of the afternoon, so the child could say farewell to his beloved playmate, little Enrique Martín.

'He might as well stay the night, with your permission?' Martín said.

Helkias nodded, aware that the boys would never see one another again.

Yonah and his father had worked well into the evening by candlelight, completing the arduous details of their departure.

Yonah enjoyed sharing tasks with his father. It was not unpleasant to be alone with him, with Eleazar gone for the night. They made piles of their belongings, one pile composed of things they would leave behind, a smaller pile that they would pack onto the burros at dawn – clothing, foodstuff, a prayer book, a set of his father's tools.

77

Before it grew late, Helkias put his arm around Yonah and ordered him to bed. 'Tomorrow we travel. You will need your strength.'

But Yonah had only just fallen asleep to the comforting sound of Helkias sweeping the floor when his father shook him, roughly and urgently. 'My son. You must leave the house through the rear window. Hurry.'

Yonah could hear it, the sounds of many men coming down the road. Some were singing a fierce hymn. Others were shouting. They were not far off.

'Where? . . .'

'Go to the cave in the cliff. Do not come out until I come there for you.'

His father's fingers dug into his shoulder. 'Listen to me. Go now. Go at once. Let no neighbor see you.' Yonah threw half a loaf of bread into a small sack and thrust it at him. 'Yonah. If I don't come . . . stay as long as you are able, then go to Benito Martín.'

'Come with me now, Abba,' the boy said fearfully, but Helkias shoved his son through the window and Yonah was alone in the night.

He circled cautiously behind the houses, but at some point he needed to cross the road to get to the cliff. When he was beyond the houses he moved to the road in the darkness and for the first time he saw the lights approaching, terrifyingly near. It was a large group of men, and the torchlight glinted sharply on weapons. He was trying not to sob but it didn't matter, because their noise was very loud now.

And suddenly Yonah was running.

10
The Lair

The narrowness and shape of the tunnel to the cave cut out most sound but now and again something came to his ears, a muffled roar, a howl like the wind in a far-off storm.

He wept quietly, lying on the floor of rock and earth as if fallen there from a great height, heedless of the pebbles and stones under his body.

After a long while he sank into sleep, deeply and gratefully, escaping from his small stone prison.

When he awakened he had no idea how long he had slept, or how much time had passed since he had entered the cave.

He was aware that what had dragged him from sleep was the sensation of something small moving over his leg. He stiffened, thinking of vipers, but finally he heard a familiar faint scurrying and he relaxed, unafraid of mice.

His eyes long since had become accustomed to the velvet blackness but couldn't pierce it. He had no idea whether it was day or night. When he was hungry, he gnawed at the bread his father had given him.

Next time he slept he dreamed of his father, in the dream studying the well-known face, the very blue eyes set deep above the strong nose, the wide, full-lipped mouth above the bush of beard, gray as the springy halo of hair. His father was speaking to him. But Yonah couldn't hear the words or didn't remember them when the dream was over and he awakened to find himself lying in his animal lair.

He remembered the last thing his father had said to him, his stern instruction that Yonah was to wait in the cave until Helkias came to tell him all was well, so he finished the rest of the bread and lay there in the dark. He was powerfully thirsty, and he recalled that Meir had taught him to take a small pebble when there was no water, and suck on it to start the saliva flowing in his mouth. He searched with his hands, finding a pebble just the right size, brushing it off with his fingers. When he placed it in his mouth the saliva came and he sucked like a babe at a teat. Soon he remembered to spit out the pebble when he started to sink back into the deep well of sleep.

Thus time passed amid dry hunger and consuming thirst and escape into slumber, and a terrible, growing weakness.

The moment came when Yonah knew that if he stayed longer in the cave he would die there, and he began slowly and painfully to crawl out of his hole.

When he turned the corner of the L-shaped tunnel the radiance struck him a blow and he stopped crawling until he could see in the terrible light.

Outside, he noted by the sun that it was afternoon. The day was silent save for loud birdsong. He climbed up the narrow trail carefully, realizing the Lord had protected him during his desperate descent in evening darkness.

As he walked homeward he met no one. When he came to the cluster of houses he saw with a burst of joy that all appeared untouched and as usual.

Until . . .

His own house was the only one ravished. The door was gone, ripped from its hinges. Furnishings were taken or ruined. Everything of value – Meir's Moorish guitar! – was gone. Above each window a fan of black on the stone showed where fire had consumed the sills.

Inside there was waste and desolation and the smell of the torch.

'Abba!'

'Abba!'

'Abba!'

But there was no answer and Yonah was frightened by the sound of his own shouting. He went outside and began to run toward Benito Martín's house.

The Martín family greeted him with a stunned joy.

Benito was pale. 'We thought you were dead, Yonah. We believed they threw you over the cliff. Into the Tagus.'

'Where is my father?'

Martín went to the boy, and as they swayed to and fro in a terrible embrace he told Yonah everything without saying a word.

When the words came, Martín related a horrifying story.

A friar had gathered a crowd in the Plaza Mayor of Toledo. 'It was a Dominican, a tall man, name of Bonestruca. He had revealed great curiosity about your father when I showed drawings of his reliquary at the cathedral.

'They say this friar has the face of a saint. But he is no saint,' Benito Martín said bitterly. 'He drew a crowd of angry men about him in the plaza when he preached against the Jews who had left. Jews had slipped away from Spain without being properly punished, he told them. He spoke of your father by name, accusing him of being a Jew who had designed a ciborium that would work terrible magic against Christians, referring to him as the antichrist who had spurned the opportunity to come to the Savior, who laughed at Him with impunity and now was about to escape unscathed.

'He whipped them into madness and then stayed behind while they went to your house as a mob and slew your father.'

'Where is Abba's body?'

'We buried him behind the house. Each morning and each evening I pray for his immortal soul.'

Martín allowed the weeping boy to mourn. 'Why didn't he come with me when he sent me away?' Yonah whispered. 'Why didn't he flee as well?'

'I believe it was to protect you that he stayed,' Martín said slowly. 'If no one was in the house, they would have searched until your father was found. And then . . . you would have been found, too.'

Soon Benito's wife, Teresa, and his daughter, Lucía, brought bread and milk, but in Yonah's grief he ignored them.

Benito urged the food upon Yonah, who to his shame couldn't keep from wolfing it down once he had taken the first bite, while the man and the two females watched him anxiously. Eleazar was not there, nor was

82

Enrique Martín, and Yonah assumed the two small boys were playing somewhere nearby.

But then Enrique came into the house alone.

'Where is my brother?'

'The little boy is with his uncle, Aron the cheese maker, and his aunt, Juana,' Martín said. 'They think you are dead, as we did. They claimed Eleazar from us the morning after the trouble, and they left Toledo at once.'

Yonah stood in his agitation. 'I must go at once to Valencia, to join them,' he said, but Benito shook his head.

'They don't go to Valencia. Aron didn't have a great deal of money. I . . . paid him a sum I owed your father for the silver, but . . . he thought they would have better opportunity to secure passage if they went to one of the small fishing villages. They took the two horses from Marcelo Troca's field, so they could always rest two mounts while riding.' He hesitated. 'Your uncle is a good man, and strong. I believe they will be all right.'

'I must go!'

'Too late, Yonah. It is too late. To which fishing village would you go? And you have been three days in your cave, my boy. The last of the Jew ships will sail in four days. If you galloped day and night and your horse didn't die, you would never reach the coast in four days.'

'Where will Uncle Aron take Eleazar?'

Benito shook his head, disturbed. 'Aron didn't know where they would go. It depended on what ships were available, with what destinations. You must stay within this house, Yonah. Throughout Spain soldiers will be searching for Jews who may have scorned the order of expulsion. Any Jew who has demonstrated unwillingness to be saved in Christ will be put to death.'

'Then . . . what shall I do?'

Benito came to him and took his hands.

'Listen carefully, my boy. Your father's murder is linked to your brother's. It is not coincidence that your father was the only Jew slain here, or that his was the only house destroyed by the *menudos*, when not even a synagogue was harmed. You must remove yourself from danger. Out of love for my friend your father, and for yourself, I give you the protection of my name.'

'Your name?'

'Yes. You must convert. You will live with us, as one of our own. You will have the name that was my own father's, you will be Tomás Martín. Is it agreed?'

Yonah looked at him dazedly. In one swift turn of events he had been deprived of all relatives, forlorn of every loved one. He nodded his head.

'Then I am off to find a priest and bring him here,' Benito said, and in a few moments he departed on his errand.

11
A Decision

Yonah sat in the Martín house, stunned by the things Benito had told him. For a time Lucía sat next to him and took his hand, but he was too overcome by his emotions to respond to his friend, and soon she left him.

On top of everything, never again to see his beloved young brother Eleazar, who still lived!

There was ink and a quill and paper on Benito's drawing table. Yonah went to it. He picked up a quill and was about to take a sheet of paper, but Teresa Martín moved to him at once.

'Paper is dear,' she said sourly, regarding him without joy. Teresa Martín never had taken the pleasure from the Toledanos that her husband and children had done, and it was obvious that she was not gladdened by her husband's decision to add a Jew to their family.

On the table was a drawing of the silver cup Helkias had made, one of the sketches his father had given to Martín. Yonah took it and dipped the quill and began to write on the reverse side, which was blank. He wrote the first line in Hebrew and the rest of the message in Spanish, quickly and without pause.

To my darling brother Eleazar ben Helkias Toledano.

Learn that I, your brother, was not slain by those who took our father's life.

I write to you, beloved Eleazar, against the chance that some event unknown to me has kept you and our kinsmen from embarking from Spain. Or if by the ninth of Ab you will be on those deepest seas about which we were wont to speculate in happier childish days, perhaps the time will come when as a man you may return to our boyhood home and discover this letter in our secret place, to learn what befell here.

If you do return, for your safety understand that a powerful person, unknown to me, feels a special hatred for the family Toledano. I do not understand the reason. Our father, may he rest in the eternal peace of the righteous, believed the terrible death of our brother Meir ben Helkias was to make possible the theft of the relic cup commissioned by the Priory of the Assumption. Our father's good friend, whose name I do not write lest this letter be read by one who would do him harm, is convinced Abba's death is connected to Meir's, to the silver-and-gold cup he made, and somehow to a Dominican friar, Bonestruca by name. You must take great care.

I must take great care as well.

No Jews remain here, nought but Old Christians and New Christians.

Am I alone in Spain?

Everything for which our father labored is gone. There are those whose debts to us are unpaid. Even if you should find your way back here to read these words, it will be hard for you to collect them.

Samuel ben Sahula owes our father thirteen maravedíes for three large Seder plates, a kiddush cup, and a small silver basin for ritual washing.

Don Isaac Ibn Arbet owes six maravedíes for a Seder plate and two maravedíes for six small silver goblets.

I do not know where these men have gone. If it is the Lord's will, perhaps your paths someday may cross.

Count Fernán Vasca of Tembleque owes our family sixty-nine reales and sixteen maravedíes for three large bowls, four small silver mirrors and two large silver mirrors, a gold flower with a silver stem, eight short combs for female hair and a long comb, and a dozen goblets of which the cups were massy silver and the bases were electrum.

Abba's friend wishes to make me his Christian son, but I must remain our father's Jewish child though it be my ruin. Should I be hunted down, I shall not become a converso. If the worst may occur know I have been united with our Meir and our beloved parents and rest with them at the feet of the Almighty.

Know also that I would risk my place in that heavenly kingdom if I could but embrace my small brother. Ah, I would be your brother again! For all thoughtlessness, for any hurt I may have done you through careless word or act, my vanished and cherished brother, I beg your forgiveness and your love through eternity. Recall us, Eleazar, pray for our souls. Remember you are a son of Helkias, of the tribe of Levi, the direct descendants of Moses. Each day recite the

Shema, knowing that saying it with you is your grieving brother,
    Yonah ben Helkias Toledano

'My husband shall not buy your father's house now, of course. The house is ruined.' Teresa frowned at the paper. She was illiterate but she recognized Hebrew letters at the top of the page. 'You will bring disaster to *this* house.'

The thought chilled Yonah and awakened him to the fact that in a brief time Benito would return with the priest bearing holy water for his baptism.

Agitated, he took the paper and went outside.

The sun was sinking and the day cooling. Nobody stopped him, and he walked away from there.

His feet took him back to the ruins of the house that had been his home. Behind the house, he was able to see where the earth had been turned to make his father's grave. Strangely dry-eyed now, he said the mourner's Kaddish and marked well the location of the grave, promising himself that if he lived, one day he would move his father's remains to consecrated earth.

He remembered the dream he had in the cave and it seemed to him now that in the dream his father had been trying to tell him to remain who he was, Yonah ben Helkias Toledano, the Levi.

Inside the house, he did a search despite the gathering dusk.

All the silver mezuzahs, the amulets containing portions of the Scripture, had been torn from the doorposts. Everything of value was gone from the workshop, and the floors were torn up. The intruders had found what money Helkias had been able to gather for the voyage

88

out of Spain. But they hadn't found a cache of small coins behind a loose stone in the northern wall of the house – eighteen *sueldos* that Yonah and Eleazar had saved as their personal fortune. It wouldn't buy much, but it would buy something, and he fashioned a small bag from a dirty rag and placed the coins inside.

On the ground was a piece of parchment that had been torn from one of the mezuzahs and discarded, and he read the Scripture: 'And thou shalt love the Lord thy God with all thy heart, and with all thy soul, and with all thy might. And these words, which I command thee today, shall be on thy heart.'

He started to stow the parchment in the bag with the coins. But he was thinking with cold clarity now, and it came to him that discovery of this scrap in his possession would result in his death. He folded the fragment and placed it, with the letter to his brother, behind the stone where he and Eleazar had kept their coins. Then he walked from the house.

Presently he found himself passing the field of Marcelo Troca. Uncle Aron had taken the horses but the two burros his father had paid for were tethered and eating garbage. When he tried to approach the larger of the burros, it shied and kicked. But the other, a smaller and dubious-looking animal, peered at him placidly and was more tractable. When Yonah slipped the tether and mounted, the beast trotted off obedient to his kicking heels.

There was just enough daylight left to allow the burro to make his surefooted way down the steep cliff trail. When they forded the river the outcroppings of purple shale were like menacing black teeth in the last bit of light.

The burro's digestion was very bad, perhaps because of his garbage diet. Yonah had no destination in mind. His father had said that the Almighty would always guide their paths. This present path was unpromising, but once Yonah was away from the river he dropped the reins and let the burro and the Lord take him where they would. He felt neither like a bold merchant traveler nor a knight. Riding friendless into the unknown on a farting beast was not the kind of adventure of which he had dreamed.

For a moment he halted the burro and looked back at Toledo, high above. Oil lamps glowed warmly through several windows, and someone was carrying a torch while walking the familiar narrow street next to the cliff. But it was no one who loved him, and in a moment he nudged the burro with his knees and didn't look back again.

Part Three

THE *PEÓN*

Castille
August 30, 1492

12

A Man with a Hoe

The Ineffable One and the small burro moved Yonah southward all night under a round floating moon that kept them company and lit the ass's way. Yonah dared not stop. The priest who had come to the Martíns' house with Benito surely had reported at once that an unbaptized Jewish youth was at large, threatening Christianity. To save his life, he meant to go as far as possible from Toledo.

He had been in open country since leaving Toledo behind.

Now and again the shadowy outline of a finca, a farmhouse, appeared off the trail. Whenever a dog barked, Yonah kicked his heels to produce a trot, and he drifted past the few habitations like a burro-borne spirit.

In the first graying light he saw he had moved into a different type of land, less hilly than the terrain at home and host to larger farms.

The soil must be very good; he rode past a vineyard and an enormous olive grove, and a field of green onions. He had a great hollowness and he dismounted and gathered onions and ate hungrily. When he came to another vineyard he picked a bunch of grapes, not yet ripe but full of sour juice. His coins could have produced bread but he dared not try to buy it, lest questions be asked.

At an irrigation ditch containing a trickle of water he stopped to let the burro crop grass on the bank, and as the sun rose he sat and thought about his plight. Perhaps he should choose a destination after all. If he must wander, maybe he should direct himself toward Portugal, where some of the Jews of Toledo had gone.

Laborers carrying hoes and machetes had begun to appear. Now Yonah could see workers' quarters at the far end of the field, and clumps of men cutting and piling brush. Most of them barely glanced at the boy and the burro, and Yonah allowed the cropping animal to eat his fill. Amazed by the good nature of the beast, by his willingness to do as he was bidden, Yonah felt a rush of gratitude.

The burro should have a name, he decided, and gave it his consideration as he remounted and rode away.

The field was scarcely out of sight behind him when he heard the chilling thunder of galloping hooves. At once he directed the burro to the side of the trail in order to watch safely. There were eight horse soldiers, and to Yonah's consternation they drew up their mounts instead of passing him by.

They were a patrol, seven soldiers and their officer, fierce-looking men armed with pikes and short swords. One of the soldiers slid from his horse and began pissing loudly into the ditch.

The officer glanced at Yonah. 'How are you called, boy?'

94

He tried not to tremble. In his fright he clutched at the identity he had refused when it had been offered in Toledo. 'I am Tomás Martín, Excellency.'

'Where is your home?'

Doubtless the field workers had told these men they had seen a stranger. 'I am lately of Cuenca,' Yonah said.

'As you have ridden from Cuenca have you seen Jews?'

'No, Excellency. No Jews,' Yonah said, masking his terror.

The officer smiled. 'Nor have we, though we search. We are finally rid of them. They are either gone from here, or converted, or bound by fetters.'

'Let others have them,' the dismounted soldier, the pisser, said. 'Let the damn Portuguese enjoy them. Already the Portuguese have a plague of them, so many they kill them like vermin.' He cackled, shaking his member.

'What is your destination?' the officer asked idly.

'I am bound for Guadalupe,' Yonah said.

'Ah, you go a distance. What is to be found in Guadalupe?'

'I go there . . . seeking my father's brother, Enrique Martín.' It was not so hard to lie, he saw. Invention flowering, he added that he had left Cuenca because his father Benito had been killed last year while fighting as a soldier against the Moors.

The officer's face softened. 'A soldier's lot . . . You look strong enough. Do you wish to work so you may buy food between here and Guadalupe?'

'Food is good, Excellency.'

'They need strong young backs at the farm of Don Luís Carnero de Palma. It is the next farm down this road. Tell

José Galindo you are sent by Capitán Astruells,' the officer said.

'Many thanks, Capitán!'

The pisser scrambled back into the saddle and the patrol rode away, leaving Yonah relieved to be choking in their dust.

The farm of which the *capitán* had spoken was a very large one, and from the road Yonah could see it had many workers. It struck him that perhaps he shouldn't ride by, as had been his intention, since the soldiers in this place had already been satisfied with his story, while others he might encounter in other regions might prove – fatally – to be more difficult.

He turned the burro into the entrance path.

José Galindo asked him nothing once the name of Capitán Astruells was uttered, and soon Yonah was standing in a dry corner of a field of onions, hacking at stony weeds with a hoe.

Midmorning, an old man with thin, ropy arms took a small wagon about the field, pulling between the shafts like a horse, stopping by groups to dispense to each worker a wooden bowl of thin gruel and a fist of rough bread.

Yonah ate so fast he scarcely was aware of taste. The food eased his belly but presently he had to piss. Every now and again someone walked to the ditch bordering the field to piss or shit, but Yonah was aware of his circumcized penis, a Jewish badge. He retained the urine until, trembling with pain and fear, he walked to the ditch and grunted in relief. He tried to cover the head of the member as his body drained. But no one was looking at him, and he finished and returned to his hoe.

The sun was hot.

Where was everyone he knew?

What was happening to them?

He worked maniacally, trying not to think, slashing as if the hoe were David's sword and the weeds were the Philistines, or perhaps as if the weeds were the inquisitors' men he was certain were busy throughout Spain, engaged solely in searching for him.

When he had been there three days, exhausted and dirty and working mechanically, he realized the date was August second. The ninth day of Ab. The day of the destruction of the Temple in Jerusalem, the last day of the departure of the Jews from Spain. He spent the rest of the day in silent prayer as well as in work, begging God over and over again that Eleazar and Aron and Juana were safely on deep water, being carried farther and farther away from this place.

13
The Prisoner

Yonah had been raised a youth of the town. He was familiar with the farms of Toledo and on occasion he had milked his uncle Aron's dairy goats, fed and tended the herd, harvested hay, and helped to butcher or make cheese. He was strong, large for his age and almost fully grown. But he had never before lived through the harsh daily cycles of unremitting labor that define an agricultural life, and in his first weeks on the Carnero de Palma farm his limbs stiffened and protested fiercely. The younger men were worked like oxen, given jobs too hard for those with bodies used up by years of similar toil. Soon his muscles hardened and swelled, and as his face darkened in the sun his appearance became more like that of the other laborers.

He was suspicious of everyone, afraid of everything, aware that he was vulnerable, fearful that someone would steal his burro. During the day he tethered the burro where he could watch it as he worked. At night both he and the animal slept in a corner of the great barn, and he had an odd sense that the burro was guarding him like a watchdog.

The *peóns* seemed content with their hard days of labor. They included youths of Yonah's age, mature stalwarts, and old men using up their last strength. Yonah was a stranger. He spoke to no one and no one spoke to him, except to tell him where to work. In the fields, he became accustomed to strange sounds, the thuds of hoes biting the earth, the clicking of blades that struck stones, grunts of exertion. If he was called to another part of the field he went promptly; if he needed a tool he asked for it politely but without wasted words. He was aware that some of the others watched him with inquisitive animosity, and he knew sooner or later someone would pick a fight. He let them observe him sharpening a discarded hoe until it had a wicked edge. The handle was broken short and he kept it by his side at night, his battle ax.

The farm wasn't a comfortable haven. The brutal work paid only a few miserable *sueldos* and filled every moment of daylight. But there were bread and onions, and sometimes the gruel or a thin soup. At night he dreamed occasionally of Lucía Martín but more often of the meats he had eaten without thought in his father's house, roasted mutton and kid, a potted fowl every Sabbath eve. His body signaled for fat, screamed for fat.

As the weather turned cooler the farm slaughtered and butchered hogs, and the leavings and coarser cuts of meat were fed to the workers, who fell upon them with great relish. Yonah knew it was necessary for him to eat the pork; not to do so would be his doom. But to his great horror he found that the pink scraps were a delight and a pleasure. He said a silent blessing for meat over the pork, wondering what he was doing, knowing that God was watching.

It emphasized his isolation and increased his despair. He yearned to hear any human voice speaking Ladino or Hebrew. Each morning and evening, in his mind he recited the mourner's Kaddish, lingering over the prayer. Sometimes as he worked he desperately chanted soundless portions of Scripture, or the blessings and prayers that lately made up his life.

He had been at the farm seven weeks when the soldiers returned. He had heard others speaking of them and knew they were part of the Santa Hermandad, the Holy Brotherhood, an organization of local militias united by the Spanish throne to form a national police force.

He was cutting brush in the early afternoon when he looked up and saw Capitán Astruells.

'What! You are still here?' the *capitán* asked, and Yonah could but nod.

A short time later he saw Astruells engaged in earnest conversation with the farm steward, José Galindo, while both of them studied Yonah.

It chilled his blood. If the officer began making inquiries, Yonah knew what would follow.

He finished the day in a miasma of apprehension. When night fell he led the burro away into the darkness. He was owed a few coins for his labour but he forsook them, taking the broken hoe instead.

As soon as it was safe, he mounted the ass and rode away.

On a diet of grass the burro's digestion was greatly improved. The beast moved so steadily, so willingly, that affection for him welled in Yonah.

'You must have a name,' he said, patting the animal's neck.

After contemplation that covered a great deal of trotted ground, Yonah arrived at two names.

In his own mind and in the dark of night he would call the good and faithful beast Moise. It was the finest name he could think of, in honor of two men, his ancestor who led the Hebrew slaves forth from Egypt, and Moise ben Maimon, the great philosopher-physician.

'And in the presence of others, I will call you Pedro,' he confided to the burro.

They were fitting names for the companion of a *maestro* who also had several names.

Reverting to his earlier caution, for two nights he traveled in darkness and found secure daylight sleeping places for Moise and himself. The grapes in the roadside vineyards were ripe and each night he ate several bunches that were very good, except now it was he instead of the burro who developed wind. His guts growled for food.

On the third morning, a signpost at a crossroads pointed the way west to Guadalupe and south to Ciudad Real. Since he had announced to Capitán Astruells that Guadalupe was his destination, he dared not go there, and he turned the burro onto the southern fork.

It was market day and Ciudad Real was bustling. Enough people were there so that no one would question the presence of a stranger, Yonah thought, although several people who saw him grinned at the sight of such a lanky young man riding a burro, his feet so low they could almost have walked.

Passing a cheese maker's booth in the Plaza Mayor,

Yonah couldn't resist, and he spent a precious coin for a small cheese that he downed hungrily, though it wasn't as good as the cheeses Uncle Aron had made.

'I am seeking employment, señor,' he said hopefully.

But the cheese maker shook his head. 'So? I can employ no one.' But he called out meaningfully to a nearby man, 'Bailiff, here is a young soul seeking labor.'

The man who swaggered over was short, with a very large stomach. What little hair he had on his head was plastered greasily across his scalp.

'I am Isidoro Alvarez, the *alguacil* of this city.'

'I am Tomás Martín. I am seeking work, señor.'

'Oh, I have work . . . Yes, I do. What sort of work have you done?'

'I have been a *peón* on a farm near Toledo.'

'What did they raise on that farm?'

'Onions and grain. They kept a herd of milch goats, also.'

'My crop is different. I raise criminals and earn my bread by keeping them out of the sun and the rain,' the *alguacil* said, and the cheese maker guffawed.

'I need someone to clean the jail, empty my miscreants' slop buckets of their sweet-smelling shit, and throw them a little food to keep them alive while they are my responsibility. Can you do that, young *peón*?'

It was hardly an inviting prospect, but the *alguacil's* small brown eyes were dangerous as well as merry. Nearby, someone snickered. Yonah sensed they were waiting for an amusement to commence, and he knew he would not be allowed to refuse politely and ride away.

'Yes, señor. I can do that.'

'Well, then you must come with me to the jail so you will start doing it at once,' the *alguacil* said.

As he followed the man from the plaza the hair on the back of Yonah's neck prickled, for he had heard the smiling cheese maker tell a companion that Isidoro had found someone to tend the Jews.

The jail was a long and narrow stone building. On one end of the structure was the office of the *alguacil*, and on the other end was an interrogation room. There were tiny cells on both sides of the corridor connecting the two rooms. Most of the cells had an occupant lying curled up on the stone floor of that limited space, or sitting against the wall.

Isidoro Alvarez told Yonah that among his prisoners were three thieves, a murderer, a drunkard, two footpads, and eleven New Christians charged with being secret Jews.

A guard armed with sword and club sat sleepily on a chair in the corridor. The *alguacil* told Yonah, 'He is Paco,' and muttered to the guard, 'This one is Tomás.' Then he went into his office and closed the door against the powerful stink.

Yonah knew with resignation that any attempt at cleanliness in that place would have to begin with the slop buckets, filled to overflowing, so he asked Paco to unlock the first cell, in which a vacant-eyed female watched listlessly as he took her bucket.

When he tethered Moise behind the jail he had noticed a spade hung against the wall, and now he took it and found a sandy place where he dug a deep hole. He emptied the odorous contents into the hole and then twice filled the bucket with sand and emptied it. There was a tree nearby with very large heart-shaped leaves that he used to wipe out the sand, then he rinsed the

103

bucket in the trickle of water in a nearby ditch before returning it to the cell.

Thus he cleansed the buckets in five cells, his pity growing as he witnessed the poor condition of their occupants. When the door to the sixth cell was opened, he went inside and paused for a moment before picking up the bucket. The prisoner was a slender man. Like the other males, his hair and beard had been allowed to grow long and untended, but there was something in the face that Yonah seemed to know.

The guard grunted, irritated to be kept standing by the open door, and Yonah picked up the slop bucket and carried it outside.

It was only when he reentered the cell to return the bucket, trying to see the prisoner's face as it may have been with barbered hair and a neatly tended beard, that he received a blow of memory. It was a picture of his dying mother, and the man who had come every day for long weeks to bend over Esther Toledano and spoon medicines into her.

The prisoner was Bernardo Espina, the former physician of Toledo.

14
The Holiday

At night Yonah slept on the flagstone floor of the interrogation room. Once a day he fetched food cooked
nearby by the wife of the night guard, Gato, and fed the
prisoners. He ate what they ate, sometimes feeding it to
Moise to supplement the burro's slim fare of weedy
grass. He was waiting for a propitious time to flee. Paco
said there was to be a large auto de fé soon, with many
people in the city. That seemed to Yonah a good time to
leave.

Meanwhile he kept the jail clean and Isidoro, content
with his labor, left him alone. In his first days at the jail
the thieves were severely beaten by Paco and the night
guard, Gato, and then they were released. The drunkard
was released too, only to be returned three days later to
a different cell, sodden and shouting wildly.

Gradually, from the muttered curses or conversations
between Isidoro and his men, Yonah learned about the
charges facing some of the New Christians. A butcher
named Isaac de Marspera was accused of selling meat
prepared according to Jewish rite. Four of the others

were accused of habitually buying Marspera's meat. Juan Peropan was accused of owning pages of Jewish prayer, and his wife, Isabel, of willingly participating in Jewish liturgy. Neighbors of Ana Montalban had observed her using the seventh day of the week as a day of rest, laving her body each Friday before sundown, wearing clean clothes during the Jewish Sabbath.

Yonah began to be conscious of the eyes of the physician from Toledo, following him each time he worked near the man's cell.

Finally, one morning when he was working inside the cell the prisoner spoke to him in a low voice. 'Why do they call you Tomás?'

'What else should they call me?'

'You are a Toledano, but I don't remember which one.'

You know I am not Meir, Yonah wanted to say, but he was afraid. This physician could seek to trade him to the Inquisition in return for leniency, could he not?

'Ah, you are mistaken, señor,' he said, and he finished his sweeping and left the cell.

Several days went by without incident. The physician spent much of his time reading his breviary and had stopped staring at him. Yonah felt that if the man wished to betray him he would have done so.

Of all the prisoners, the butcher Isaac Marspera was the most defiant, at frequent intervals roaring out blessings and prayers in Hebrew, hurling his Jewishness in his captors' faces. The others accused of Judaizing were quieter, almost passive in their despair.

Yonah waited until he was once more within Espina's cell. 'I am Yonah Toledano, señor.'

106

Espina nodded. 'Your father, Helkias . . . Did he go away?'

Yonah shook his head. 'Killed,' he said, and then Paco came to let him out and lock the cell, and they stopped talking.

Paco was a lazy man who dozed when Isidoro wasn't near, his chair tilted against the wall. At such times he was very irritable when Yonah asked him to unlock the cells, and finally he handed Yonah the key and bade him work the locks himself.

Yonah had returned to the physician's cell eagerly, but to his disappointment Espina showed no further desire to talk, keeping his eyes fixed on the pages of his breviary.

When Yonah entered Isaac de Marspera's cell the butcher was standing and swaying, his tunic pulled over his head like a prayer shawl. He was chanting aloud, and Yonah drank in the sound of the Hebrew words and listened to their meaning:

> 'For the sin which we have committed before Thee by
>   association with impurity,
> And for the sin which we have committed before Thee
>   by confession of the lips,
> And for the sin which we have committed before Thee
>   in presumption or in error,
> And for the sin which we have committed before Thee
>   wittingly or unwittingly,
> For all these, O the Lord of forgiveness, forgive us,
>   pardon us, grant us atonement.'

Marspera was shriving himself, and with a small

107

shock Yonah knew it must be the tenth day of the Hebrew month of Tishri, Yom Kippur, the Day of Atonement. He wanted to join Marspera in the prayers, but the door to the *alguacil*'s office was open and he could hear Isidoro's loud voice and Paco's submissive one, so he swept around the praying man and locked the cell door when he left.

That day all the prisoners ate the gruel he brought to the cells save Marspera, who observed the strict fast of the high holiday. Yonah didn't eat, either, glad of a means to declare his Jewishness without risk. He served his portion of gruel and Marspera's to Moise.

At night, lying sleepless on the hard floor of the interrogation room, Yonah asked forgiveness for his sins and for any slights or injuries inflicted on those he loved and those he didn't. Reciting the Kaddish and then the Shema, he asked the Almighty to care for Eleazar and Aron and Juana, and he wondered if they still lived.

He realized that if he didn't take steps to avoid it, he would soon lose the Jewish calendar, and decided that to prevent this he would recite the Hebrew date to himself at every opportunity. He knew that five of the months – Tishri, Shebat, Nisan, Sivan, and Ab – had thirty days, while the remaining seven months – Heshvan, Kislev, Tebet, Adar, Iyar, Tammuz, and Elul – had twenty-nine.

At certain times, leap year, days were added. He didn't know how to deal with that. Abba had always known what day it was . . .

I am not Tomás Martín, he thought drowsily. *I am Yonah Toledano. My father was Helkias ben Reuven Toledano of blessed memory. We are of the tribe of Levi. This is the tenth day of the month of Tishri, in the year five thousand two hundred and fifty-three . . .*

15
Auto de fé

A new phase began for the prisoners on a morning when guards came and shackled Espina and took him in a wagon to the Office of the Inquisition for questioning.

It was night when they brought him back with both thumbs bloody and splayed, ruined by torture with the screw. Yonah brought him water, but he lay on the floor of his cell with his face to the wall.

In the morning Yonah went back to him.

'How is it you are here?' Yonah whispered. 'In Toledo we knew you for a willing Christian.'

'I am a willing Christian.'

'Then . . . why do they torture you?'

Espina was quiet. 'What do they know of Jesus?' he said finally.

The men kept coming with the wagon and took the prisoners away one by one. Juan Peropan returned from his interrogation with his left arm dangling, broken at the wheel. It was enough to unhinge his wife, Isabel. At her own interrogation she avoided torture by agreeing hysterically to everything her questioners suggested.

Yonah served wine to the *alguacil* and two of his friends to whom Isidoro was relating the details of Isabel's confession.

'She placed full blame on the husband. Juan Peropan never stopped being a Jew, she says, never, never! He forced her to buy Jew meat and fowl, forced her to listen to unholy prayers and participate in them, forced her to teach them to her children.'

One by one she had provided evidence against every prisoner accused of Judaizing, buttressing the charges against them.

Isidoro Alvarez said she even testified against the physician, a stranger to her, agreeing Espina had confided to her that he had fulfilled the covenant of Abraham by performing thirty-eight ritual circumcisions on Jewish babies.

The questioning of each of the accused took a number of days. Then one morning on the balcony of the Office of the Inquisition a red banner was displayed, indicating that soon capital punishment would be administered at an auto de fé.

Having abandoned all hope, Bernardo Espina suddenly became eager to speak of Toledo.

Instinctively, Yonah trusted him. Scrubbing the floor of the corridor one afternoon, he paused next to Espina's cell and they talked. Yonah related how his father had gone to the empty Espina home and then to the Priory of the Assumption, only to find that the priory was abandoned.

Espina nodded, showing no surprise to hear that the Priory of the Assumption had been discontinued. 'One morning Fray Julio Pérez, the sacristan, and two armed guards were found slain outside the chapel. And the relic of Santa Ana was missing.

'There are deep churchly currents here, young Toledano, cruel enough to swallow with ease the likes of you and me. Rodrigo Cardinal Lancol lately has become our new pontiff, Pope Alexander VI. His Holiness would not have suffered gladly a priory that allowed so sacred a relic to vanish. The friars doubtless have been scattered within the Hieronymite order.'

'And Prior Sebastián?'

'You may be certain he is a prior no longer, and that he has been sent to a place where he will serve out his priestly life in hard fashion,' Espina said.

He made a bitter face. 'Perhaps the thieves have united the relic with the ciborium fashioned by your father.'

'What kind of men would commit the sin of murder to steal sacred objects?' Yonah asked, and Espina smiled wearily.

'Unholy men who give the appearance of holiness. Throughout Christendom, the pious always have placed enormous faith and hope in relics. There is a vast and rich commerce for such objects, and deadly vying for them.'

Espina related how Padre Sebastián had charged him with discovering what had occurred in the murder of Meir. It was hard for Yonah to hear his observations about the scene of Meir's murder, and then Espina spoke of his own detention by Fray Bonestruca, the inquisitor.

'Bonestruca? I was told it was Bonestruca who enraged the mob and sent it to my father. I have seen this Bonestruca,' Yonah said.

111

'He has a strangely beautiful face, is it not so? But his soul must carry a heavy load.' Espina told Yonah that Diego Diaz had seen Bonestruca and a knight riding in the footsteps of Meir Toledano.

'Bonestruca was there when Meir was killed?' Yonah whispered.

'Almost certainly. And stole the ciborium your brother was seeking to deliver,' Espina said. 'He is a man who would easily destroy anyone who learns something that might bring trouble to him. I knew when I was released after his questioning that I must go away or he would collect me again, the second time for good. I was trying to think where I could move my family when Padre Sebastián sent for me. When the prior told me the relic had been taken as well as the ciborium, it was as if he had gone mad. He wept. He ordered me to recover the relic, as though that were in my power if only I wished to do it. He ranted about the enormity of the crime, and he begged me to redouble my efforts to find those who had moved so terribly against him.

'But only hours later, as I was crossing the Plaza Mayor, Bonestruca and I passed one another. The friar stared at me. That was all it took.'

Espina shook his head. 'I was convinced that if I stayed in Toledo even a moment more, I would be seized. I bade my wife to take our children to the protection of kinfolk, and I fled.'

'Where did you go?'

'North, into the high mountains. I found hidden places, traveled between small settlements where they were greatly pleased to see a physician.'

Yonah could believe they had been pleased. He remembered the tenderness with which this man had treated his mother and recalled that his father had said Espina had prenticed with Samuel Provo, the great Jewish physician.

Espina had lived a noble life, serving others. This physician who had abandoned the religion of his fathers nevertheless was a worthy man, a healer, and yet he was condemned. Yonah wondered if perhaps these conversos could be saved, but he saw no way. At night their guard was Gato, a mean-spirited man who slept all day and watched the cells with malevolent wakefulness. During the day, when opportunity might arise for Yonah to kill the napping Paco with his sharpened hoe, neither the prisoners nor Yonah himself would get very far in Ciudad Real. The city was an armed camp.

If God wished them to be saved, He would have to show Yonah some way.

'How long was it before they found you?'

'I had been abroad almost three years when they took me. The Inquisition casts a damnably wide net.'

Yonah was chilled, knowing it was the same net he must elude.

He saw that Paco was awake and the guard's hard gaze was on them, and he resumed his scrubbing.

'A good afternoon, Señor Espina.'

'A good afternoon . . . Tomás Martín.'

The Inquisition was careful to place executions in the hands of the civil authorities, and in the Plaza Mayor the *alguacil* directed laborers to raise seven wooden stakes, next to a *quemadero*, a circular brick oven being hurriedly assembled by masons.

Inside the jail some of the prisoners wept, some prayed. Espina appeared calm and resigned.

Yonah was washing the corridor floor when Espina spoke to him. 'I must ask something of you.'

'Anything I am able . . .'

'I have a son of eight years, name of Francisco Rivera de la Espina. Lives with his mother Estrella de Aranda and his two sisters. Will you deliver to this boy his father's breviary and blessings?'

'Señor.' Yonah was astonished and dismayed. 'I cannot return to Toledo. At any rate, your house is empty. Where is your family?'

'I know not, perhaps with her cousins, the Aranda family of Maqueda. Or perhaps with the Aranda family of Medellín. But take the breviary, I beg you. It may be that God will someday make it possible for you to deliver it.'

Yonah nodded. 'Yes, I will try,' he said, though the Christian book seemed to burn his fingers as he took it.

Espina thrust his hand through the grate of the cell.

Yonah grasped it. 'May the Almighty be merciful to you.'

'I shall be with Jesus. God watch over you and sustain you, Toledano. I would ask you to pray for my soul.'

A crowd gathered early in the Plaza Mayor, more thickly than for any contest with the bulls. The day was cloudless, a touch of autumn chill in the breeze. There was an air of suppressed excitement buoyed by the shouting of children, the rumble of conversation, the cries of food vendors, and the sprightly songs of a quartet: a flutist, two guitarists, and a lute player.

By midmorning, a priest appeared. He raised his hand for silence and then led the assembled in endless Paternosters. By now the square was dense with bodies,

114

Yonah among them. Spectators had filled all the balconies of the buildings overlooking the plaza and were crowded onto all the roofs. Soon there was a disturbance in the plaza as the watchers closest to the stakes were driven back by Isidoro Alvarez's men to make way for the arrival of the condemned.

The prisoners were brought from the jail in three farm carts, two-wheeled tumbrels pulled by burros. They were paraded through the streets to the jeers of spectators.

All eleven of the convicted Judaizers wore the pointed hats of the punished. Two men and a woman wore yellow sanbenitos marked with diagonal crosses. They had been sentenced to return to their home parishes to wear the sanbenito for long periods of penitance and reconciliation, Christian piety, and the disgust of their neighbors.

Six men and two women wore black sanbenitos decorated with demons and hellfire, signifying that they would die by immolation.

At the Plaza Mayor the condemned were pulled down from the tumbrels, their garments taken from them, and the crowd reacted to their nudity with a rustle and a surge like the sea tide, everyone wishing to scrutinize the nakedness that was an ingredient of their shame.

Through his numb gaze Yonah saw that Ana Montalban appeared older naked than when clad, with long, flat breasts and gray hair between her legs. Isabel Peropan looked younger, with the round, firm buttocks of a maiden. Her husband was prostrated with grief and fear. He could not walk but was supported and dragged. Each prisoner was taken to a stake, and their arms were pulled behind the posts and tied.

The hairy body of Isaac de Marspera was free of bruises; the butcher had escaped torture because his rebellious and constant use of Hebrew prayer had made his guilt obvious, but now for his defiance they had selected him for the *quemadero*. The opening left in the wall of the oven was small, and three men pushed and crammed his large body inside, while people cast gleeful insults and Isaac roared back the Shema. His lips didn't stop moving while masons worked quickly to brick up the entrance.

Espina was praying in Latin.

Many hands piled the bundles of brush and wood around them. The fagots rose to provide a semimodesty, covering their lower trunks, hiding bruises and abrasions, scars and the shameful stains of fright, and building around the *quemadero* until it was no longer possible to see the bricks of the oven.

The quartet began to play hymns.

Chaplains were standing next to the four prisoners who had requested reconciliation with Christ. Their stake had been fitted with garrotes, bands of steel fastened about their necks, to be tightened by screws set behind the posts. For their piety the blessing of churchly mercy was now showered upon them and they were strangled prior to the burning. Isabel Peropan went first; she had been condemned despite pleas of guiltlessness and her dooming denunciation of the others, but the Inquisition had granted her the mercy of the garrote.

It was applied next to Espina and to two brothers from Almagro as Isidoro went down the line with a lighted torch, touching off each pile of dry fagots, which ignited with a great crackling.

As the flames rose so did the sounds of the people

who responded according to their temperaments with shouts of awe and wonderment, exclamations of fear, or screams of merriment and glee. Men and women held up children that they might glimpse on earth the fiery hell from which the Lord God would save and protect them providing they obeyed father and priest and did not sin.

The fuel around the *quemadero* was burning with a great roar. Isaac the butcher was within, baking like a chicken in an oven except, Yonah told himself faintly, a fowl was not roasted alive.

The condemned writhed. Their mouths opened and closed but Yonah could not hear their cries for the noise of the crowd. Isabel Peropan's long hair went up in a burst, creating a yellow and blue halo about the purpled face. Yonah could not bear to look at Espina. Smoke billowed and blew, concealing all, giving reason for his weeping eyes. Someone was poking his shoulder, shouting in his ear.

It was Isidoro. The *alguacil* pointed to the dwindling wood, cursed him for a lazy lout, told him he must go help Paco and Gato load a wagon with fresh fagots.

When the wagon was laden he didn't return to the Plaza. In the silent and empty jail he collected his sack and the broken hoe and brought them to where Moise cropped peacefully in the shade.

Once mounted, he startled the good little burro with his heels and they departed from Ciudad Real at a brisk canter. He didn't see the trail or the countryside. The auto de fé was a foretaste of the cruel way he would die when he was caught. Something in him screamed that he must seek out a sympathetic priest. Perhaps it was not

117

too late to beg for the chrism and lead a life of careful Catholic rectitude.

But he had made a promise to his father's memory, to God, to his people.

To himself.

For the first time, his hatred of the Inquisition was stronger than his fear. He couldn't erase the images, and he spoke to God not as a supplicant but in demanding fury.

What can be the Divine Plan that causes so many of us to be Hanged Men?

And, *For what purpose have you made me the last Jew in Spain?*

16
The Farm Woman

Yonah led Moise across the Guadiana River, the young man and the burro swimming a short distance when they encountered a deep hole midstream, allowing the water to remove the smoke stink from his clothing if not from his soul.

Then he slowly rode southeast through a farm valley, the hills of the Sierra Morena always in sight on his left.

The tardy autumn was pleasantly mild. Along the way he stopped several times at farms, tarrying a few days at a time while he worked for food and shelter, pulling the late onions, picking olives, helping to tread the last wine grapes of the season.

As the year moved into winter, he traveled toward warmth. Far to the southwest, where Andalusia reached to touch southern Portugal, he passed through a series of tiny villages whose existence revolved about the presence of great farms.

In most of the farms the growing season was over, but he found hard employment in a vast farm owned by a nobleman named Don Manuel de Zúniga.

'We are making fields out of forest where there never have been fields. We have work if you wish it,' the steward told him. The steward's name was Lampara; Yonah found that behind his back the workers called him Lamperón, the grease spot.

It was the most demanding kind of labor, grubbing out and removing heavy stones, breaking boulders, felling and uprooting trees, cutting and burning brush, but inheritance had made Yonah large and constant labor on other farms already had hardened him. There was enough work on the Zúniga farm to make it possible for him to stay throughout the winter. A detachment of soldiers was assembled in a field nearby; at first he kept a wary eye out for them as he worked, but they never bothered him, occupying themselves with marching and drilling. The climate was soft, almost caressing, and food was plentiful. He stayed on.

The things he had seen and suffered kept him apart from the other *peóns*. Despite his youth there was something formidable in his face and eyes that kept others from trifling with him.

He flung his hard body into the labor, seeking to erase horror evoked by the brush fires. At night he dropped to earth near Moise and slept deeply, his hand on the sharpened hoe. The burro guarded him while he dreamed of women and acts of physical love, but next day if he remembered the dream he lacked the carnal knowledge to know if he had dreamed correctly.

He removed the silver ring he had worn hanging from his neck and placed it in the sack with his few other belongings, tying the bag to Moise and keeping the burro always tethered in his sight. After that he worked

120

without a shirt, enjoying the sweat that cooled his body in the tender air.

Don Manuel visited his farm and while he was there even the most indolent workers labored as industriously as Yonah. The owner was an aging man, small and pompous. He toured the fields and barns, noting little and understanding less. He stayed three nights, sleeping with two young girls of the village, and then went away.

When Zúniga was safely gone, everyone relaxed, and the men spoke disparagingly of him. They called him *el cornudo*, the cuckold, and gradually Yonah learned why.

The farm had directors and overseers, but the strong personality that dominated the *peóns* belonged to an ex-mistress of the don's, Margarita Vega. Before she was fully a woman, she had borne two children by him. But when Don Manuel returned from a year in France, to the vast amusement of the onlookers who worked for him he found that in his absence Margarita had had a third child by one of the farm laborers. Zúniga had given her a wedding and a house as parting gifts. Her new husband had run away from her in less than a year. Since then she had experienced many men, an activity that had resulted in three new children by different fathers. Now she had thirty-five years and was large-haunched and hard-eyed, a woman to be reckoned with.

The *peóns* said Don Manuel returned so seldom because he loved Margarita still and was betrayed anew each time she took a man.

One day Yonah heard the sound of Moise's braying and looked up to see that one of the other workers, a youth named Diego, had removed the sack from the burro's back and was about to open it.

Yonah dropped his hoe and flung himself on the

121

other, and they rolled in the dust, striking out. In a few moments they had found their feet and were landing looping punches on one another with work-hardened fists. Yonah would find out later that Diego was a feared brawler, and indeed, very early in the fight he received a smashing blow that he knew had broken his nose. Yonah was a few years younger than Diego but taller, and not much lighter. His arms had a longer reach, and he fought with the fury of all the repressed fear and hatred he had stored up for so long. Their fists impacted with the sound of mauls thudding into the earth. They were trying to kill each other with their hands.

The other workers came running, gathering to shout and jeer, and their noise brought in the overseer, cursing and striking at both combatants with his fists as he separated them.

Diego had a smashed mouth and his left eye was closed. He seemed content to pull away when the overseer commanded the onlookers and the fighters to return to their work.

Yonah waited until they were gone, then he carefully tied the cloth bag closed and fastened it securely to Moise's tether. His nose was bleeding, and he wiped the blood from his upper lip with the back of his hand. When he looked up he saw Margarita Vega with her babe in her arms, watching him.

His nose was puffed and purpled, and his bruised and swollen knuckles pained him for days. But the fight had brought him to the woman's attention.

It was impossible for Yonah not to notice her. It seemed to him that wherever he looked she had uncovered a large brown breast and was suckling her hungry

122

baby. The farm folk nudged one another and smiled, noting that Margarita often managed to turn up where the big, silent young man was working.

She was friendly to Yonah, at ease with him.

She directed him to perform small tasks about her house, calling him to come inside to have bread and wine. It was only a few days before he was naked with her, incredulously touching a female body, tasting the milk that had filled the infant who slept nearby.

Her heavy body was not uncomely, the legs muscular, the navel deep, the belly only slightly convex despite all the childbirth. Her thick-lipped pudenda was a small animal with a wild brown pelt. She readily gave instruction and made demands, and he learned how to have a dream correctly. The first coupling was over for him quickly. But he was young and strong and she made him ready again, and he put the same fury into his efforts that he had used against Diego, until the moment when he and the woman were spent and gasping.

In a while, half-asleep, he was aware of her fingering hands, as if he were an animal she contemplated buying.

'You are a converso.'

At once he was awake.

'Yes.'

'So. When were you converted to the true faith?'

'Ah . . . Several years ago.' He closed his eyes again, hoping she would desist.

'Where was it?'

'In Castille. In the town of Cuenca.'

She laughed. 'But I was born in Cuenca! I have been there within these eight years with Don Manuel. Two of my sisters and a brother are there, and my old *abuela* who has outlived both my mother and my father. At

123

which church were you converted, San Benito's or San Marcos'?'

'It was . . . San Benito's, I believe.'

She stared. 'You believe? You don't know the name of the church?'

'A manner of speaking. Yes, San Benito's, of course. A very nice church.'

'Beautiful church, no? And which priest?'

'The old one.'

'But both are old, yes?' She was frowning at him. 'Was it Padre Ramón or Padre Garcillaso?'

'Padre Ramón.'

Margarita nodded but got out of bed. 'Well, now you must not go back to work. You must sleep here like a good boy until I return from my chores, and you will be strong like a lion and we shall make much joy fucking, yes?'

'Yes, all right.'

But in a few moments he watched from the one small window as she hastened from the house carrying the child into the siesta-time sun and heat, her garment shrugged on so hurriedly that it was not completely pulled over one of her large hips.

Yonah knew that almost certainly there was no Padre Ramón in the town of Cuenca, and perhaps not even a church named for San Benito.

Dressing quickly, he went to the shady side of Margarita's house where Moise was tethered, and in a moment he was under the hot sun himself. He rode past only two men in the midday heat and neither paid him any attention. Soon he and the burro were climbing a trail into the hills of the Sierra Morena.

On a height he paused and looked down upon the

farm of Don Manuel de Zúniga. The small figures of four soldiers, the sun glinting on their weapons and mail vests, were following Margarita Vega, who was hastening toward her house.

High above and beyond them, he felt safe enough to regard Margarita with an astounded gratitude.

Thank you, my lady!

If it should be possible, he would like to know such pleasure again. To guard against betrayal by his circumcision, he decided, in the future he would tell women his conversion had taken place not in a small church but in a great cathedral. The cathedral in Barcelona, where there was an army of clerics, so many priests no one could know them all.

His nose still pained him. But riding away, he reviewed in his mind the appearance of each part of Margarita's body, the acts, the scents, the sounds.

An incredible fact: His body had entered a woman's!

He gave thanks to the remarkable Ineffable One. For allowing him to remain free and sound of limb and mind, for creating women as well as men with such wondrous skill that when they came together they fit like mated lock and key, and for permitting him to survive long enough to greet this day.

This has happened to me on the twelfth day of the month of Shebat . . .

I am not Tomás Martín, I am Yonah Toledano, son of Helkias the silversmith, of the tribe of Levi.

The other months are Adar, Nisan, Iyar, Sivan, Tammuz, Ab, Elul, Tishri, Heshvan, Kislev, and Tebet . . .

He said the names of the months over and over again, between snatches of Hebrew verse or prayer, as Moise picked a careful way upward, into the brown hills.

Part Four

THE SHEPHERD

Sierra Morena
November 11, 1495

17
The Sound of Sheep

Yonah traveled north again on Moise, slowly wandering along the border with Portugal, keeping pace with the autumn browning of the green land. Half a dozen times he stopped and performed brief labor to earn money for food, but he stayed in no one place until he reached Salamanca, where workers were being hired for the repair of the cathedral.

He told the burly foreman his name was Ramón Callicó. 'What are you able to do?' the foreman asked, no doubt hoping he was a journeyman mason or a carpenter.

'I am able to work,' Yonah said, and the man nodded.

The oxen and huge draft horses used to drag the heavy stone were kept in a nearby barn. Yonah kept Moise in the barn as well, and at night he slept next to the burro, lulled by the sounds of the animals in their stalls.

By day, he became part of a small army – laborers, masons, stone carvers, and drovers – struggling to replace blocks of the dark stone that made up the cathedral's walls, which in places were ten feet thick. The work was sweaty and terrible, noisy with the complaints of the animals, the curses and shouted orders of foremen and drovers, the tapping of hammers and banging of mauls, and the constant, grinding growl of heavy stone being moved over resistant ground. Small blocks of stone were carried by laborers. When the larger blocks had been moved as far as possible by animals, men became the beasts of power, long lines of them straining to move the stone by hauling on stout ropes, or standing side by side as they pushed, leaning against their enemy, the stone.

Yonah was somehow pleased to work on the repair of a house of worship, even one designed for the prayer of others. He wasn't the only non-Christian helping to repair the cathedral; the master artisans were Moors who worked stone and wood with wondrous skill. When Yonah's father had been approached by Padre Sebastián Alvarez to design and fashion a reliquary to hold a Christian relic, Helkias had discussed the opportunity with Rabbi Ortega, who had advised him to accept the commission. 'It is a mitzvah to help people pray,' the rabbi had said, and he had pointed out that the delicate and beautiful work on the synagogues of Toledo had been done by Moors.

The labor on the cathedral was all-consuming. Like the others, Yonah toiled dully and without laughter, speaking only in brief utterances about the work, protecting his difference from them by keeping all thought to himself. Sometimes he was teamed with a bald *peón* who was built like a block of stone, squat and wide. Yonah never learned his patronymic but the foremen called him Leon.

One morning, when Yonah had been in Salamanca for seven weeks, he was working with Leon, wrestling stone into place. He looked up from their labors to see a procession of black-cowled men walking from the cathedral after their Matins prayers, which had begun before the workers arrived.

Leon stared at the friar at the head of the procession. 'That one is Fray Tomás Torquemada. Chief inquisitor,' he whispered. 'I am from Santa Cruz, where he is prior of the monastery.'

Yonah looked and saw a tall, elderly friar with a long straight nose and a pointed chin, and brooding, contemplative eyes. Lost in thought, Torquemada was quickly past them. There were perhaps two dozen priests and friars in the straggling column, and in their midst Yonah saw another tall man, with a face he would recognize anywhere. Bonestruca came almost within Yonah's shadow, deep in conversation with a companion, so close Yonah was able to see a scratch on his neck and a sore on his upper lip.

The friar glanced up and looked Yonah squarely in the face, but the gray eyes showed no recognition or interest as they flickered away again, and even as Yonah stood frozen with apprehension, Bonestruca moved past.

'What brings Fray Torquemada to Salamanca?' Yonah asked Leon, and the *peón* shrugged.

But later in the day Yonah heard the foreman tell another worker that inquisitors from every part of Spain had gathered for a meeting in the cathedral, and he began to wonder if this was why God had saved him and brought him here, this opportunity to kill the man who had murdered both his father and his brother.

*

Next morning, he watched again as the inquisitors passed from the cathedral after Matins. He decided that the best place for him to assault Bonestruca would be to the left of the cathedral entrance, close to where he worked. He would be able to depend upon striking only once before he was overwhelmed, and he thought that to kill Bonestruca he would have to use his sharp hoe like an ax, stabbing him in the throat.

That night he lay sleepless and anxious on his bed of straw in the barn. Sometimes as a boy he had had daydreams about being a warrior, and in recent years he had told himself he would enjoy avenging the deaths of his father and his brother. But now, brought to a situation where that might be possible, he anguished, not knowing if he could kill. He asked the Lord to grant him strength when the moment arrived.

In the morning he went to the cathedral as usual.

When a friar came through the doors after Matins, Yonah picked up the hoe and went to the place near the cathedral entrance. Almost at once he began to tremble uncontrollably.

Five more friars followed the first, and then no one else came.

The foreman stared at Yonah, seeing him standing pale and idle. 'Are you sick?'

'No, señor.'

'Should you be helping to mix the mortar?' he asked, noting the hoe.

'Yes, señor.'

'Well then, go and be about it,' the man growled, and Yonah did as he was bidden.

That afternoon he heard that the meeting of the guardians of the faith had ended the afternoon before, and he knew he was stupid and foolish, unfit to be God's avenging arm. He had delayed too long and Bonestruca was gone, returned with the other inquisitors of Spain to the regions of their terrible responsibility.

The work in Salamanca lasted late into the spring. In mid-March a muscle in Leon's back tore while they moved a block of stone, and Yonah saw the *peón* roll on the ground in agony. Leon was lifted into the bed of a wagon and carried away, and Yonah never saw him again. Yonah was paired with others when there was need for two laborers, but they had nothing in common with one another. He turned away from them out of fear, and no one became his friend.

Not all the repairs had been made to the 355-year-old cathedral when the labor ended amid heated arguments about the structure's future. Many of the townfolk said their house of God wasn't large enough. Despite the fact that the Chapel of San Martín contained frescoes of the thirteenth century, the cathedral had little ornamentation and suffered in contrast to the distinguished cathedrals in other places. Already there were those who had begun to raise money to build a new cathedral in Salamanca, and further repairs on the old cathedral were postponed.

Yonah escaped into unemployment and drifted south again. On the seventh day of May, the birthday that made him eighteen years old, he was in the border town of Coria. He stopped at an inn and treated himself to a stew of goat meat and lentils, but an overheard discourse between three men at a nearby table ruined his celebration.

They were speaking of the Jews who had fled Spain for Portugal.

'In order to gain admittance to Portugal for six months,' one of the men said, 'they agreed to pay King John one-fourth of their worldly goods and one ducat for every soul allowed to cross the border. One hundred and twenty thousand ducats in all. The six months of their residency expired in February, and can you countenance what the whoseson king did then? He declared the Jews to be slaves of the state.'

'*Ai* . . . May God curse King John.'

From their tone Yonah guessed they were conversos. Most Christians would not have been so wounded about the enslavement of Jews.

He had made no sound, but one of the three glanced over and observed him sitting still and stiff, and knew he had listened. The man said something to his companions quietly, and the three rose from their chairs and left the inn.

Yonah realized once more the wisdom Abba and Uncle Aron had shown in determining that the safer course from Toledo had been east instead of west into Portugal. His appetite gone, he continued to sit at the table while his cold stew congealed.

That afternoon he rode toward the blatting of many sheep. Soon he came to a flock spreading away from its center and presently saw the reason they were allowed to wander. Their old shepherd, gaunt and white-haired, lay on the ground.

'I am stricken,' he told Yonah simply.

His face against the grass was as pale as his hair, and he made a soft sibilance each time he struggled to breathe. Yonah turned him on his back, fetched him water and tried to see after his comfort, but the old man indicated that his greatest agony was the impending loss of the flock.

'I can get your sheep,' Yonah said, and he mounted Moise and rode away. It wasn't a difficult task. Many times he had worked with Aron Toledano's flock. Uncle Aron had had fewer animals, and as many goats as sheep, but Yonah was familiar with their ways. These sheep hadn't strayed far, and after some small difficulty he herded them into a tight group.

The old man managed to gasp that his name was Geronimo Pico.

'How else can I help you?'

The shepherd was in severe pain, his arms clasping his chest. 'The sheep must be returned . . . to Don Emilio de Valladolid, near Plasencia,' he said.

'And so must you be returned,' Yonah said. He lifted the shepherd onto the burro and took up the old man's rude crook. They made slow time, for he needed to hasten over a wide area just to keep the sheep together. It was late in the afternoon when he witnessed the aged shepherd drop from Moise's back. Somehow, from the heavy fall and the nerveless sprawl of the body, he knew at once that the old man was dead.

Still, he spent time calling out to Geronimo Pico, patting the aged face and rubbing the man's wrists before acknowledging death.

'Ai, damnation . . .'

Absurdly whispering the Kaddish for the stranger, he slung the body across Moise's back, face down and arms dangling, and made certain the flock was bunched before proceeding along the trail. Plasencia was not far; presently he came to a man and a woman working in a field.

'The farm of Don Emilio de Valladolid?'

'Yes,' the man said. He gazed at the corpse and crossed himself. 'Geronimo the shepherd.'

'Yes.'

He told Yonah how to find the farmhouse. 'Past the great tree split by lightning, across the stream, and on the right you will see it.'

It was a large, well-kept finca and Yonah drove the sheep into the barnyard. Three workmen appeared who needed no explanation when they saw the corpse; they slid the shepherd from the burro, making sad little grunts of regret, and carried the body away.

The landowner was a florid-faced, sleepy-eyed man who wore fine clothes that were covered with stains. He disliked the interruption of his evening meal, and he came outside and spoke to his overseer. 'Is there reason for all this noise of the sheep?'

'The shepherd is dead. This one brought him back with the flock.'

'Get the fucking animals away from my house.'

'Yes, Don Emilio.'

The overseer was a lean man of medium height, with brown hair that was turning gray, and steady brown eyes. He and his sons helped Yonah move the flock to a field, the sons smiling and shouting insults at one another. They were Adolfo, a lanky boy who was about sixteen years of age, and Gaspar, several years younger than his brother. The man sent them to fetch two bowls of food – a thick, hot gruel of wheat – and he and Yonah sat on the ground near the sheep and ate silently.

The overseer belched and considered the stranger. 'I am Fernando Ruiz.'

'Ramón Callicó.'

'You appear to know how to care for sheep, Ramón Callicó.' Fernando Ruiz was aware that many men would have abandoned the body of Geronimo the shepherd and driven the valuable flock far away, as fast as the beasts could move. This one who sat before him hadn't done that, signifying that he was either crazy or honest, and he saw no madness in the young man's eyes.

'We need a shepherd. My boy Adolfo would do well, but he is still a year too young for such responsibility. You wish to continue to care for these sheep?'

The grazing animals were quiet save for an occasional soft bleat, a sound Yonah found comforting.

'Yes, why not?'

'But you must take them away from here.'

'Don Emilio doesn't like his sheep?'

Fernando smiled. They were alone in the field, but he leaned forward and whispered.

'Don Emilio doesn't like anything,' he said.

He was to spend thirty-four months virtually alone with the flock, becoming so familiar with it that he knew the ewes and the rams as individuals, which of them were calm and tractable and which were stubborn or mean, which were healthy and which were ailing. They were large, stupid sheep with a long, fine white wool that covered everything save their black noses and placid eyes. He thought them beautiful. Whenever the weather was kind he moved them through a mountain stream to wash away some of the dirt that clung to the greasy white wool, yellowing it.

Fernando gave him some rough provisions and a dagger that was not very good, the blade being made of poor steel. Yonah was allowed to bring the sheep any-where grass could be found, so long as he returned them to Don Emilio's farm in the spring for shearing and in the fall for castration and the slaughter of some of the young rams. He took them into the foothills of the Sierra de Gredos, riding sedately at the flock's slow pace. Uncle Aron had had a brindle dog to help with the herding, but Yonah had Moise. With each passing day the little burro became more adept at keeping the sheep in sight. At first Yonah spent hours on the burro's back, but soon Moise was acting on his own, clattering after strays like a sheep dog and braying them back to the flock.

Each time he brought the sheep back to the farm young Adolfo, Fernando's son, took him into his charge and taught him about sheep. Yonah learned to shear, although he never became fast or adept, like Fernando and his boys. He could castrate and slaughter, but when it came to skinning he was not much better with the knife than he was with the shears.

'Don't be concerned. It all comes with practice,' Adolfo said. Whenever Yonah brought the sheep back to the farm, Adolfo carried a jar of wine out to the far field where the flock was kept, and he and Yonah sat and talked of the problems encountered in sheep herding, the lack of women, the loneliness, and the threat of wolves – Adolfo recommended singing at night to keep them away.

Herding was an ideal occupation for a fugitive. Villages in the sierra were sparse and Yonah avoided them, also giving wide berth to the occasional small farm. He grazed the sheep in the grassy clearings that dotted the lower slopes of deserted mountains, and the occasional human who met him saw only an unsavory young hermit shepherd.

Even bad men avoided him, for he was large and rugged, with a wild strength in his eyes. His chestnut hair hung long and his beard had come in full and wide. During the heat of summer he went almost naked, because his clothing, bought used to replace garments he had outgrown, was worn thin. When a sheep met with a fatal accident he skinned it badly and dined with great enjoyment on lamb or mutton until the meat went high, which happened almost at once in the summer. When raw winds blew in wintertime, he tied sheepskins around his arms and legs to ward off the chill. He was comfortable in the hills. At night when he was on a crest he moved intimately under the large, bright stars.

The crook he had inherited from Geronimo Pico was a poor thing, and one morning he cut a long piece from a nut tree, a branch with a natural crook at the end. He carefully peeled it of bark and carved on it a pattern imitating a geometric design Moorish craftsmen had used in the Toledo synagogue. Then he ran his hand through the wool of the sheep until his fingers were rich with their grease and rubbed it into the wood long hours at a time, until the supple staff took on a dark patina.

At times he felt like an animal of the wild, but deep within himself he clung to his more gentle origins, saying morning and evening prayers and trying to keep track of the calendar in order to honor the holy days. Sometimes he managed to bathe before welcoming the Sabbath. It was easy during the summer heat, because anyone coming upon him immersed in a stream or a river would believe he splashed for coolness instead of religion. When the weather wasn't warm he bathed with a wet rag, shivering, but during the coldest part of winter he allowed himself to stink; after all, it was not as if he were a woman, forbidden to take her husband unto herself until she had visited the mikvah.

He wished he could immerse himself and wash clean his soul, for he was in thrall to the pleasures of the flesh. It was difficult to find a woman he trusted sufficiently. There was a tavern trull from whom he bought wine, and twice he gave her a coin to open her legs for him in her dark, odorous chamber. On occasion while the animals cropped without interest he surrendered himself to lewd pleasure and spilled his own seed, committing the sin for which the Lord took the life of Onan.

Sometimes he imagined how different his existence would have been without the catastrophes that had driven him from his father's house. By now he would have been a journeyman silversmith, married to a woman of good family, perhaps already a father himself.

Instead, although he had tried valiantly to remain a person, occasionally he felt he was becoming something low and bestial, not only the last Jew in Spain but the last human creature in the world, a concept that several times led him to take foolish chances. Sitting before a fire at night, with the animals gathered near him, he warned wolves away, bawling snatches of remembered words, sending old prayers into the black sky along with the sparks that rose from the snapping wood. Any inquisitor or denouncer drawn toward the light of his fire would have heard his reckless voice flinging forth words of Hebrew or Ladino. But no one ever came.

He tried to be reasonable about the things he prayed for. He never asked God to send the archangel Michael, the guardian of Israel, to sweep down from Paradise and slay those who murdered and did evil. But he asked God to allow him, Yonah ben Helkias Toledano, to serve the archangel. He told himself, and God, and the beasts on the silent hills, that he wanted another opportunity to become the archangel's strong right arm, killer of the killers, murderer of the murderers, slayer of those who destroyed.

The third time Yonah drove the sheep back to the farm in the autumn season, he found the family of Fernando Ruiz in mourning. The overseer, although he wasn't old, had dropped dead without warning one afternoon as he walked to inspect a picked field. The farm was in turmoil. Don Emilio de Valladolid had no idea how to run the place himself and had not been able to choose a new overseer. He was in bad humor and shouted a lot.

Yonah thought the death of Fernando Ruiz was a sign that it was time for him to move on. He drank wine in the sheep pasture with Adolfo for the last time.

'I'm sorry,' he said. He knew what it was to lose a father, and Fernando had been a very good man.

He told Adolfo he was leaving. 'Who will take over the care of the sheep?'

'I will be the shepherd,' Adolfo said.

'Shall I talk to Don Emilio?'

'I'll tell him. He won't care, so long as I keep the sheep away from his delicate nose.'

Yonah embraced Adolfo, and handed over the handsome shepherd's crook he had made, as well as the flock. Then he mounted Moise and directed the burro away from the farm and Plasencia.

That night he awoke in the dark and listened because he thought he heard something. Then he realized it was the absence of sound that had alarmed him, the fact that there were no quiet noises of sheep, and he rolled over and went back to sleep.

18
The Jester

Winter was on the way and he rode Moise toward warmth. He had a desire to glimpse the southern sea on the other side of the Sierra Nevada, but when he approached Granada the clear nights already were chill. He had no wish to challenge the snow-covered peaks of the high sierra in winter, and instead he entered the city to spend some of his earnings on comfort for himself and the burro.

He was disquieted when he arrived at Granada's walls, for over the grisly gate were suspended the rotting heads of executed criminals. Yet the display failed to discourage footpads, because as Yonah rode toward an inn where he hoped to find wine and food, he came upon two burly men intent on robbing a dwarf.

The small man was half their size, with a very large head, a strong upper torso, long arms, and tiny legs. He was watching his assailants warily as they approached him from two directions, one brandishing a wooden cudgel, the other holding a knife.

'Give over your pouch and save your little ballocks,'

the man with the knife said, feinting toward his victim.

Without thinking, Yonah seized his sharpened hoe and slid from the burro's back. Unfortunately, before he could intervene, the robber with the staff swung it and struck him on the head. In a moment he was lying on the ground, injured and dazed, while the man stood over him with the cudgel, ready to finish him off.

Semiconscious, Yonah saw the dwarf produce a wicked-looking knife from his tunic. His little legs skipped and scampered. His long arms became limber and writhing, the knife point flicking like a serpent's tongue. In a moment he had penetrated beneath the flailing defenses of the armed robber, who howled and dropped his knife when the small fighter's blade slashed his arm.

The two footpads turned and ran, and the small man picked up a stone and sent it winging hard and long to thump into one of the departing backs. Then he wiped his knife on his trousers and came to peer down into Yonah's face.

'Are you all right, then?'

'I think I shall be,' Yonah heard himself declaring hollowly. He struggled to sit up. 'Once I'm inside and have had wine.'

'Oh, you shan't get decent wine there. You must get off one of your asses and onto the other, and come with me,' the small man said, and Yonah took a proffered hand and was raised by a surprisingly strong arm.

'I am Mingo Babar.'

'I am Ramón Callicó.'

It occurred to him, as Moise was led out of the city and up an ascending trail, that this strange, small man,

144

so recently an intended victim, might himself be a robber and murderer. But though he steeled himself for signs of an attack, nothing happened. The man scuttled before the burro with a shambling, spiderlike gait, his hands at the end of the long arms brushing the trail like two extra feet.

Presently a sentry perched above them on a rock called softly, 'Mingo, is it you, then?'

'Aye, Mingo. With a friend.'

A few feet beyond, they passed a hole in the hill from which soft lamplight glowed. And then another opening, and several more. From the caves came cries.

'Ah, Mingo!'

'Mingo, a good eve to you!'

'Well come, Mingo!'

The small man returned all the greetings. He halted the burro before a similar entrance into the hill. When Yonah dismounted he followed Mingo into murkiness and was led to a sleeping mat in the strangest sort of a place.

In the morning he awakened to wonderment. He was in a cave unlike any he had ever seen. It was as though a bandit lord had set up a retreat in the den of a bear. The dim light of oil lamps merged with the gray light from the entrance, and Yonah could see richly colored carpets covering bare rock and earth. There were pieces of heavy wooden furniture, ornately carved, and a profusion of musical instruments and gleaming copper utensils.

Yonah had had a long night's sleep. Memory of the previous evening quickly returned, and he was relieved to note that his head was clear again.

A plump full-sized woman sat nearby and placidly

145

polished a copper urn. He greeted her and received a smile, a flashing of teeth.

When he ventured outside the cave Mingo was there, working a leather halter and watched by two children, a boy and a girl almost his own size. 'A good morn to you.'

'A good morn, Mingo.'

Yonah saw they were high on the hill. Below stretched the town of Granada, a mass of houses like pink and white cubes, the town surrounded by a bouquet of trees. 'It is a lovely town,' Yonah said, and Mingo nodded.

'Yes, built by Moors, so the insides of the dwellings are beautifully decorated, while the exteriors are simple.'

Overlooking the town, on the crest of a hill much smaller than the hill of the caves, was a place of rose-colored towers and battlements that made Yonah catch his breath at its sheer grace and majesty.

'What is it?' he asked, pointing.

The other man smiled. 'Why, it is the citadel and palace known as the Alhambra,' Mingo said.

Yonah perceived that he had landed among a group of singular people, and he asked many questions that Mingo answered with good humor.

The caves were in a hill named the Sacromonte. 'The Holy Mountain,' Mingo said, 'called that because Christians were martyred here in the early days of the religion.' The small man said his people, gypsies of a tribe called the Roma, had dwelt in the caves since coming to Spain when Mingo was a boy.

'From where did the Roma come?' Yonah asked.

'From there,' Mingo said, waving his hand in a circle

that indicated the entire world. 'Once – *long* ago – they came from a place far to the east, where runs a great sacred river. More recently, before coming here they wandered in France and Spain. But when they reached Granada they settled, for the caves make wondrously fine homes.'

The caves were dry and airy. Some were no larger than a room, while others were like twenty rooms strung in a row, deep within the hill. Even someone as unmilitary as Yonah could see that the site would be easily defended if attacked. Mingo said that many of the caves were connected with one another by fissures or natural passageways, offering means of concealment or escape should that ever become necessary.

The plump woman in Mingo's cave was his wife, Mana. As she brought food, the small man told Yonah proudly that he and Mana had four children, two of them grown and living away from their parents.

He could see the question Yonah dared not ask, and he smiled.

'All my children are full-sized,' he said.

Yonah met the Roma all through the day. Some straggled up from a meadow they owned below, in which they kept horses. Yonah gathered they were horse breeders and traders.

Some went to employment nearby, and still others worked at tables outside one of the caves, mending broken cooking pots, utensils, and tools they had collected from homes and businesses in Granada. Yonah watched the metalworkers with pleasure, the tapping of their hammers reminding him of Helkias Toledano's workshop.

The Roma were affable and welcoming, accepting Yonah at once because Mingo had brought him to them. Throughout the day members of the tribe came to the small man to solve their problems. By midday Yonah wasn't surprised to learn that Mingo was what they called *voivode*, chieftain of the Roma.

'And when you are not governing them, do you work with the horses or mend broken pots with the other men?'

'I was trained early to do those things, of course. But until recently, I worked down there,' he said pointing.

'In the town? What sort of work?'

'In the Alhambra. I was a fool.'

'How do you mean, a fool?'

'A jester in the sultan's court.'

'In truth?'

'In truth, of course, for I was jester to Sultan Boabdil, who ruled as Muhammad the Twelfth, last Moorish caliph of Granada.'

Once one became accustomed to the misshapen body, the *voivode* of the Roma was a man of presence. There was dignity in his face, and the men and women of the tribe plainly regarded him with respect as well as affection. It made Yonah uneasy to hear that so kind and intelligent a person had played a fool to earn his bread.

Mingo was able to discern his embarrassment. 'It was employment I relished, I assure you. I was good at it. My dwarfish and ill-made body helped my people to prosper, for while at court I was able to learn early of possible dangers the Roma should avoid, and impending opportunities for their employment.'

'What sort of man is Boabdil?' Yonah asked.

'Cruel. He was little loved when he was sultan. He

lives in the wrong century, because today Islam's military power is gone. The Muslims came from Africa to invade Iberia almost eight hundred years ago, and made all of Spain Islamic. Soon afterward, the Christian Basques fought fiercely to reestablish their independence and the Franks drove the Moors from northeastern Spain. That was the beginning. After that, through the centuries Christian armies regained most of Iberia for Catholicism.

'The Moorish sultan of Granada, Muley Hacén, refused to pay tribute to the Catholic monarchs and in 1481 launched a war against the Christians, seizing the fortified town of Zahara. Boabdil, Sultan Muley Hacén's son, had a falling out with his father. For a time, hunted by his father's forces, he sought asylum in the court of the Catholic monarchs. But in 1485 Muley Hacén died, and with the help of loyal subjects Boabdil came to occupy the throne.

'It was only a few months later,' Mingo said, 'that I came to the Alhambra to help him rule!'

'How long did you serve as his jester?' Yonah asked.

'Almost six years. By 1491, only one Islamic place remained in all of Spain. In the preceding years Ferdinand and Isabella had seized Ronda, Marbella, Loja, and Málaga. They could not tolerate that Boabdil the Muslim sat on a throne with Mingo Babar at his feet, beguiling him with witty advice. They laid siege to Granada and soon within the Alhambra we were having hungry days. Some of the population fought bravely on empty stomachs, but by the end of the year the future was plain to see.

'I recall a cold winter night when a great silver moon shimmered in the fish pond. Only Boabdil and I were in the throne room.

149

'"So you must guide my life, wise Mingo. What must I do next?" the Sultan asked.

'"You must lay down your arms and invite the Catholic monarchs to dine well, sire, and be waiting in the Court of Myrtles to greet them graciously and conduct them into the Alhambra," I said.

'Boabdil looked at me and smiled. "Spoken like a true fool," he said. "For now that my moments of ruling are almost at an end, my majesty is more precious to me than rubies. They must come and find me sitting here in the throne room like a monarch, and for those last few moments I shall behave with pride, a true caliph."

'That is what he did, signing the pact of surrender in his throne room on January second, 1492. When he fled into exile in Africa, from which his Berber ancestors came so long ago, I and others found it prudent to leave the Alhambra as well,' Mingo said.

'Have things changed a great deal for Granada, now that Christians are in power?' Yonah asked.

Mingo shrugged. 'The mosques are now churches. Men of every religion believe they alone have the ear of God.' He smiled. 'How puzzling that must be for the Lord!' he said.

That evening Yonah saw that the Roma dined communally, both men and women at their fires, cooking and roasting meat and fowl that ran with savory juices and filled the air with their aroma. They ate well, and the full skins that were passed held pleasant, musky wines. When the eating was done, instruments were brought from the caves, drums, guitars, dulcimers, viols, and lutes, and were played to produce a wild music that was new to Yonah, as was the free and sensual grace with

150

which the Roma danced. He felt a sudden rush of happiness to be in the company of men and women again.

The Roma were comely. They wore clothing of bright colors and had swarthy skins, with handsome dark eyes and curly black hair. He found himself drawn to these strange tribal folk, who seemed able to find and savor all the simple pleasures of the world.

Yonah spoke gratefully to Mingo about their friendliness and hospitality.

'They are good people, unafraid of the *gadje*, which is what we call strangers,' Mingo said. 'I myself was a *gadje*, not born into the tribe. Have you noticed that my appearance is different from theirs?'

Yonah nodded. Both knew Mingo wasn't referring to height. Some of the hair on his large head was gray, for he was not a young man, but most of his hair was almost yellow, far lighter than the hair of the other Roma, and his eyes were the color of a bright sky.

'I was given to the People while they camped near Rheims. A gentleman came to them with a new child who had been born with long arms and short legs. The stranger gave the gypsies a fat purse to take me as theirs.

'It was my good fortune,' Mingo said. 'As you know, it is common to strangle a child at birth when he comes as misshapen as I. But the Roma honored their bargain. They never kept the details of my origins from me. Indeed, they insist I am doubtless of high birth, perhaps even of French royal lineage. The man who surrendered me had fine dress and armor and weaponry, as well as an aristocratic manner of speech.'

Yonah thought the small man indeed had a noble face. 'Have you never regretted what might have been?'

'Never,' Mingo said. 'For though it is true I might

have been a baron or a duke, on the other hand it is also true that I might have been strangled at birth.' His fine blue eyes were serious. 'I did not remain a *gadje*. I drank the soul of the Roma into my body with the milk of the wet nurse who became my mother. Everyone here is my kin. I would die to protect my Romani brothers and sisters, as they would die for me.'

Yonah lingered with the People day after day, bathing in the warmth of their fellowship, sleeping off by himself in an empty cave.

To repay the tribe's hospitality, he sat with the pot repairers and joined their work. His father had patiently taught him the basics of metalwork when he was young, and the Roma were delighted to learn several of Helkias's techniques for joining metal with tight, even seams. Yonah also learned from the gypsy craftsmen, observing techniques they had passed down from father to son for hundreds of years.

One evening, after the merriment of their music and dancing, for the first time in more than three years Yonah picked up a guitar and began to play. He was tentative, but soon his fingers grew certain with old skills. He played the music of *piyyutim*, the chanted psalms of the synagogue: Yotzer, in the first blessing before the morning Shema; Zulat, sung after the Shema; the Kerovah, accompanying the first three blessings of the Amidah; and then the haunting Selihah, sung in contrition on the Day of Atonement.

When Yonah finished playing, Mana touched his arm tenderly as the people drifted off to their homes. He saw that Mingo's wise, grave eyes were studying him.

'Those are Hebrew melodies, I think. Played sadly.'

152

'Yes.' Without disclosing his own lack of conversion, Yonah told Mingo about his family, and about the terrible endings of his father Helkias and his brother Meir.

'Life is glorious, but it can be counted on to be cruel,' Mingo said finally.

Yonah nodded. 'I would greatly desire to recover my father's reliquary from its thieves.'

'There is small chance of that, my friend. From what you say, the work is unique. A piece of high art. They could not sell such an object in Castille, where people would be familiar with its theft. If it has been resold, no doubt it is gone from Spain.'

'Who would deal in such objects?'

'It is a specialized sort of theft. Over the years I have heard of two groups in Spain who buy and sell stolen relics and the like. One is in the north, and I do not have a name for anyone there . . . The other is in the southern section, led by a man named Anselmo Lavera.'

'Where would I find this Lavera?'

Mingo shook his head gravely. 'I cannot even guess. If I knew, I would be reluctant to tell you, because he is a very bad man.'

He leaned forward and looked into Yonah's eyes. 'You too must give thanks that you were not strangled at birth. You must forget the bitter past and make the future sweet.

'I wish you a restful night, my friend.'

Mingo assumed he was a converso. 'The Roma also belong to a pre-Christian religion,' he confided, 'a faith that worships apostles of light who struggle against apostles of darkness. But we find it easier to pray to the god of the country in which we find ourselves, so we

153

converted to Christianity when we came to Europe. Truth to tell, when we reached the territory of the Moors, most of us became Muslims as well.'

He was concerned that Yonah wasn't sufficiently able to protect himself when attacked. 'Your broken hoe is . . . a broken hoe. You must learn to fight with a man's weapon. I will teach you to use a knife.'

So the lessons began. Mingo scorned the poor dagger Fernando Ruiz had given Yonah when he had become a shepherd. 'Use this,' he said, and handed over a knife of Moorish steel.

He showed Yonah how to hold the knife palm up instead of knuckles up, so he was able to stab with a rising, ripping thrust. And taught him to strike quickly, before an adversary would guess whence the next blow would come.

He taught Yonah to watch his opponent's eyes and body so he could anticipate every movement before it was made, and to become like a feral cat, offering little target, allowing no escape. Yonah thought Mingo taught him with the insistence and intensity of a rabbi imparting Scripture to an *ilui*, a biblical prodigy. He learned quickly and well at the feet of a small and strangely shaped *maestro*, and presently he came to think and act like a knife fighter.

Their liking blossomed until it seemed a friendship of years instead of a few brief months.

Word had been sent to Mingo that he should come to the Alhambra and confer with its new Christian steward, a man named Don Ramón Rodriguez.

'Would it please you to see the Alhambra at close quarters?' he asked Yonah.

'It would indeed, señor!'

So next morning they rode down the Sacromonte together, the large and muscular young man, his splayed legs too long and his heft too considerable to allow comfort for his poor burro, and the tiny man perched on a splendid gray stallion like a frog on a dog.

On the way, Mingo told Yonah of the Alhambra's history. 'Muhammad the First, whom they called Al Ahmar ibn Nasir because he had red hair, built the first palace fortress here in the thirteenth century. A century later, the Court of Myrtles was built for Yusuf the First. Succeeding caliphs expanded the citadel and palace. The Court of the Lions was built by Muhammad the Fifth and the Tower of the Infantas was added by Muhammad the Seventh.'

Mingo halted their mounts when they reached the high, rose-colored wall. 'Thirteen towers rise from the wall. This is the Gate of Justice,' he said, pointing out a carving of a hand and a key on the gate's two arches. 'The five fingers represent the obligation to pray to Allah five times daily – at dawn, at noon, in the afternoon, in the evening, and at night.'

'You know a great deal about the Muslim faith,' Yonah observed, and Mingo smiled but didn't reply.

As they rode through the gate someone recognized Mingo and hailed him, but no one else paid them heed. The fortress was a hive of activity, with several thousand people busily maintaining the beauty and defenses of its fourteen hectares. They left the burro and the horse in the stables and Mingo led Yonah on foot through the vast royal compounds, down a long walk overhung with wisteria.

Yonah was awed. The Alhambra was more dazzling than when seen from afar, a seemingly endless fantasy of towers, arches and cupolas, lavishly colored and adorned with lacelike stucco, honeycomb vaulting, brilliant mosaics and delicate arabesques. In the inner courts and halls, plaster moldings painted red, blue, and gold, simulating foliage, covered the walls and ceilings. The floors were marble, and wainscots of green and yellow tile lined the lower walls. In the courtyards and inner gardens there were flowers, flowing fountains, and nightingales singing in the trees.

Mingo showed him that from several windows there were fine views of the Sacromonte and the caves of the Roma, while other windows revealed the wooded gorge rushing with water. 'The Moors understand water,' Mingo said. 'They tapped the Darro River five miles up in the hills, and directed it to this place by means of a wondrously conceived waterworks that fills the pools and fountains and brings flowing water into every bedchamber.' He translated an Arabic saying on one of the walls: 'He who comes to me tortured by thirst will find water pure and fresh, sweet and unmixed.'

Their footsteps echoed as they walked through the Hall of the Ambassadors, where Sultan Boabdil had signed the articles of surrender to Ferdinand and Isabella, and which still contained Boabdil's throne. Mingo showed Yonah a bathhouse, the Baños Árabes. 'Here is where the harem lolled unrobed and made their ablutions while the sultan watched from a balcony above, choosing his bed companion. If Boabdil still reigned we would be killed for venturing here. His father executed sixteen members of the Abencerrajes family and piled their heads on the harem fountain because their chief dallied with one of his wives.'

Yonah sat on a bench and listened to the splashing fountains while Mingo kept his appointment with the steward. It took only a short time for the small man to return. As they made their way back to the stables, Mingo said he had learned that Queen Isabella and King Ferdinand were coming to inhabit the Alhambra, along with their court. 'In the recent past they have complained about the somberness of the court. The chief steward has investigated and found that I am a practicing Christian, therefore I am summoned back to the Alhambra palace, to serve the conquering monarchs as their jester.'

'Does it please you to answer their summons?'

'It pleases me that members of the Roma will return to the Alhambra as grooms, gardeners, and *peóns*. As for being a jester . . . It is difficult to tickle the minds of monarchs. One must walk a line as narrow as the edge of a sword. A jester is expected to show cheek and daring, bandying insults that provoke laughter. But the insults must be clever and mild. Stay on one side of the line and you are cosseted and loved. Cross the line into royal fury and you are beaten, or perhaps you are dead.'

He gave an example. 'The caliph was haunted by guilty knowledge that when his father, Muley Hacén, had died, they were blood enemies. One day, Boabdil heard me speak of an ungrateful son and assumed I spoke of him. In a fury he took his sword and held its point where my legs meet, at my most precious part. When I fell to the floor, the sword followed me down and I felt the point pressing against my cods.

'"Do not prick me, sire," I cried. "My little prick does not require a prick of its own. Indeed, my small prick is petted and spoiled, cosseted and content with things as they are. The places this little prick has been, the sights it has seen!"

'"Indeed, your entire body is a mean little prick," Boabdil snarled at me. The caliph's sword stayed trained against me, but in a moment he began to tremble with laughter and then to shake, and I knew I had survived.'

Mingo saw that Yonah's face was troubled. 'Have no fear for me, friend,' he said. 'It takes work and wisdom to be a fool, but I am the very king of the jesters.' He smiled, and leaned forward toward Yonah. 'Actually, my prick is no small thing at all, and I am better endowed than Boabdil!'

Mounted again, they rode past Moorish overseers who were directing the construction of a palace wing. 'The Moors don't believe they will be driven from Spain someday, as the Jews couldn't believe it until it happened,' Mingo said. 'But the day will come when the Moors, too, will be ordered to leave. The Christians have long memories of the many Catholics who died fighting Islam. Moors made the mistake of wielding swords against Christians, as Jews made the mistake of accepting power over Christians, like birds who flew ever higher until burned by the sun.'

When Yonah was silent, Mingo looked at him. 'There are Jews in Granada.'

'Jews who have become Christians.'

'Conversos such as yourself. What else?' Mingo said, annoyed. 'If you wish to have contact with them, go to the marketplace, to the booths of the silk merchants.'

158

19
Inés Denia

Yonah had avoided conversos, seeing no profit in association with them. Still, he deeply longed for contact with Jews and felt it would do no harm to set eyes on those who once had known the Shabbat, even though they knew it no more.

On a quiet morning he rode Moise into the busyness of the town. Mingo had told him the marketplace in Granada had been reborn with the burst of building and refurbishing at the Alhambra. It was a large bazaar and he enjoyed leading the burro through it, beguiled by the market sights and smells and sounds, riding past booths offering breads and cakes; huge fishes with their heads removed and small fishes with their eyes bright and fresh; whole suckling pigs and the hams, parts and staring heads of fat hogs; lamb and mutton cooked and uncooked; bags of fleece; all manner of fowl, with great birds hung so their colorful tails burst into the vision and beckoned the buyer; apricots, plums, red pomegranates, yellow melons . . .

There were two silk merchants.

In one of the booths a sour-looking fellow showed bolts of material to two men who fingered the silk cloth dubiously.

In the other booth a man with a turban dealt with half a dozen interested buyers, but it was another face that caught Yonah and held him. The woman stood at a table cutting lengths of silk as a boy unrolled it from a bolt. Certainly he had seen faces more engaging and pleasing than hers, but he couldn't remember when or where that might have been.

The turbaned man was explaining that the difference between silks lay in the nature of the leaves eaten by the worms.

'The leaf-feed of the worms in the region that produces this pearly silk imparts a most subtle sheen to the thread. Do you see it? It gives the finished silk the faintest glints of gold.'

'But, Isaac, it is so dear,' the customer said.

'It does cost,' the merchant conceded. 'But that is because it is rare cloth, created by lowly worms and God-kissed weavers.'

Yonah wasn't listening. He tried to fade into the background of passing bodies while at the same time standing transfixed, for he greatly enjoyed watching the woman. She was young, but a grown female, her carriage erect, her slim body rounded and strong. Her thick hair was long and unfettered, the color of bronze. Her eyes were not dark; he thought they were not blue but wasn't close enough to name the exact shade. Her face, engrossed in her task, had been darkened by the sun, but when she measured the silk by using the distance between her elbow and the knuckles of her clenched fist, the sleeve of her garment rode up her arm and he saw that where her flesh had been covered from the sun it was paler than the silk.

She glanced up and caught him watching her. For the briefest of moments their eyes held one another in inadvertent contact, but at once she turned away and almost in disbelief he saw a delicious darkening of her lovely throat.

Amidst clucking and quacking and the stink of hen shit and feathers, Yonah learned from a seller of fowls that the turbaned silk merchant was Isaac Saadi.

He hovered in the vicinity of the silk booth a long time before it was free of customers. Only a few bought, but people liked to look at silk and stroke it. Finally, though, all potential buyers were gone, and he approached the man.

How to address him? Yonah decided quickly to combine elements of their double cultures. 'Peace be unto you, Señor Saadi.'

The man responded benignly to his respectful tone: 'And unto you, peace, señor.'

Beyond the man – surely her father? – the young woman busied herself with bolts of silk, not looking at them.

He knew instinctively it was not a moment for disguised identity. 'I am Yonah Toledano. I wonder if you might refer me to someone who may offer me employment?'

Señor Saadi frowned. He stared suspiciously at Yonah, noting the poor clothing, the broken nose, the shaggy hair and beard. 'I know no one in need of a worker. How do you come by my name?'

'I inquired of the seller of fowls. I have high regard for

161

silk merchants.' He smiled weakly at his own foolishness. 'In Toledo, the silk merchant Zadoq de Paternina
was a close friend of my father, Helkias Toledano, may
he rest in eternal peace. Are you acquainted with Zadoq
de Paternina?'

'No, but I know him by reputation. He is well?'

Yonah shrugged. 'He was among those who departed
from Spain.'

'Was your father a man of business?'

'My father was a great silversmith. Alas, slain during
an . . . unpleasantness.'

'Ah, ah, ah. May he rest.' Señor Saadi sighed. It was
an iron tenet of the world in which both of them had
been raised that when a Jewish stranger approached, he
must be offered hospitality. But Yonah knew this man
assumed that both of them were conversos, and these
days to invite a stranger might be to invite an Inquisition
informer.

'I wish you good fortune. Go with God,' Saadi said
uncomfortably.

'And good fortune unto you.' Yonah turned away,
but before he had taken two steps the older man had
followed him.

'You have shelter?'

'Yes, I have a place to sleep.'

Isaac Saadi nodded. 'You must come to my table to
dine.' Yonah could hear the unspoken words: Someone
who knows Zadoq de Paternina, after all. 'Friday, well
before sundown.'

The girl had raised her head from the silk now, and
Yonah could see she was smiling.

He mended his clothing and went to a stream and

162

scrubbed it, then he washed his body and his face and beard with equal vigor. Mana trimmed his hair and beard while Mingo, who had started to spend time again in the splendors of the Alhambra, regarded the preparations with great amusement.

'All this in order to dine with a rag merchant,' the little man jeered. 'I do not fuss so to dine with royalty!'

In another life Yonah would have brought an offering of kosher wine. Friday afternoon he went to the market. It was too late in the season to find grapes, but he bought some large dates, sweet with their own nectar.

Perhaps the girl wouldn't be there. Perhaps she was a servant of the shop and not the daughter of the shopkeeper, Yonah told himself as he followed Señor Saadi's directions to his home. It proved to be a small house in the Albaicin, the old Arab quarter that had been abandoned by those who had fled after the Moors had been defeated by the Catholic monarchs. Yonah was greeted carefully by Saadi, who expressed a formal gratitude as he accepted the gift of the dates.

The girl was there, she *was* a daughter; her name was Inés. Her mother was Zulaika Denia, a thin, silent woman with timid eyes. Her older sister, almost fat and with heavy breasts, was Felipa. A child, a pretty little girl of six years, was Adriana, Felipa's daughter. Saadi said that Joachim Chacon, Felipa's husband, was off buying silk in the southern ports.

The four adults eyed him nervously. Only the little girl smiled.

Zulaika served the two men the dates and then the females busied themselves preparing the meal.

'Your father, may he rest . . . You said he was a silversmith?' Isaac Saadi asked, spitting date pits into his palm.

163

'Yes, señor.'

'In Toledo, you said?'

'Yes.'

'You seek employment. You did not take over your father's shop when he died?'

'No,' Yonah said. He didn't elaborate, but Saadi was not shy about asking questions.

'Was it not a good business, perhaps?'

'My father was a wonderful silversmith, much sought after. His name is well known in that trade.'

'Ah.'

Zulaika Denia blew on live coals kept in a metal container and then ignited a sliver of wood which she used to light three oil lamps before darkness fell. Then she lit candles in the next room. Sabbath candles? Who knew? Zulaika Denia's back was turned to Yonah and he heard no praying. At first he couldn't tell whether she was renewing the covenant or supplementing illumination, but then he saw the almost imperceptible swaying.

The woman was praying over her Shabbat tapers!

Saadi had noticed him watching. The host's thin, angular face was tense. They sat together and conversed uncomfortably. As the scent of baked vegetables and potted fowl filled the little house, the rooms darkened and the lamps and candles took over. Soon Isaac Saadi led Yonah to table, while the girl Inés brought bread and wine.

When they were seated, it was apparent to Yonah that his host still was disquieted.

'Let our guest and new friend offer the invocation,' Saadi said, shrewdly turning over the responsibility to Yonah.

Yonah knew that if Saadi were a sincere Christian, he could have thanked Jesus for the food they were about to eat. The safe way, which Yonah fully intended to take, would be simply to thank God for the food. Instead, when he opened his mouth, almost without volition he took another way, responding to the woman who had imperfectly disguised her prayers. Lifting the glass of wine, Yonah began to sing in husky Hebrew, welcoming Sabbath, queen of the days, and thanking God for the fruit of the vine.

As the other three adults at the table stared silently, he took a sip of the wine and passed the loaf to Saadi. The older man hesitated, then he tore bread from the loaf and began to chant his thanks for the fruit of the earth.

The words and melodies unlocked Yonah's memory, providing pain to accompany his pleasure. It wasn't to God that he called out in the *berachot* but to his parents, to his brothers, to his uncle and his aunt, to his friends – the departed.

When the blessings were finished only Felipa looked bored, annoyed at something her child had asked in a whisper. Isaac Saadi's wary face was sad but relaxed and Zulaika's eyes were wet, while Yonah saw that Inés regarded him with interest and curiosity.

Saadi had made a decision. He set an oil lamp in front of the window and the three women served dishes Yonah had been dreaming of, the tender stewed chicken and vegetables, a rice pudding savory with raisins and saffron, pomegranate seeds steeped in wine. Before the meal was finished the first person summoned by the light in the window had arrived. He was a tall, handsome man with a red mark like a crushed berry on his neck, just below the jaw.

'This is our good neighbor, Micah Benzaquen,' Saadi told Yonah. 'And this young man is Yonah ben Helkias Toledano, a friend from Toledo.'

Benzaquen told Yonah he was well come.

Presently a man and a woman came and were introduced to Yonah as Fineas ben Sagan and his wife, Sancha Portal, and then came Abram Montelvan and his wife, Leona Patras. And two more men, Nachman Redondo and Pedro Serrano. The door opened more quickly now, until nine more men and six females had crowded into the small house. Yonah noted that everyone wore work clothes so as not to call attention to themselves by dressing formally on the Jewish Sabbath.

He was introduced to everyone by Saadi as a visiting friend.

One of the neighbor's boys was posted outside to serve as a lookout, while inside the house people already had begun to pray as Jews.

There was no Torah; Micah Benzaquen led the prayers out of memory and the others joined in, both fearful and exalted. The praying was conducted in little more than whispers, lest the sound of liturgy escape the house and undo them. They recited the eighteen benedictions and the Shema. Then in an orgy of melody they sang hymns, prayers, and the wordless traditional chanting known as niggun.

The fellowship and the experience of group prayer, once so commonplace to Yonah and now so proscribed and precious, had a profound effect on him. Too quickly, it was over. People embraced and exchanged whispered wishes for a peaceful Sabbath. They included the stranger who had been vouched for by Isaac Saadi.

'Next week in my house,' Micah Benzaquen whispered to Yonah, and he nodded gladly.

Isaac Saadi ruined the moment. He smiled at Yonah as people slipped from the house one or two at a time. 'Sunday morning,' he said, 'shall you wish to accompany us to church?'

'No, I cannot.'

'Then perhaps the following Sunday.' Saadi looked at Yonah. 'It is important. There are people who observe all of us closely, you understand,' he said.

In several days that followed, Yonah kept a close watch on the silk-seller's booth. It seemed a very long time before Isaac Saadi left his daughter to tend the shop alone.

Yonah walked to her casually. 'Good day, señorita.'

'Good day, señor. My father is not here . . .'

'Ah, so I see. No matter. I stopped merely to thank him again for the hospitality of your family. Perhaps you will extend my gratitude?'

'Yes, señor,' she said. 'We . . . You were most well come to our home.' She was blushing furiously, perhaps because he had been staring from the moment he had approached. She had large eyes, a straight nose, a mouth not as full-lipped as some, but quite revealing of her emotions, sensitive in the corners. He had been afraid to look at her overly long in her father's house, lest her family take offense. In the lamplight of her home it had seemed to him her eyes were gray. Looking at her now, in the light of day, they seemed to be blue after all, but perhaps it was the shadows in the shop.

'Thank you, señorita.'

'For nothing, Señor Toledano.'

*

The following Friday he participated again in the Shabbat services of the little group of conversos, this time in Micah Benzaquen's house. He kept stealing glances at Inés Denia, who was among the women. Even sitting, she had excellent posture. And such an interesting face.

The following week he continued to go to the marketplace and watch her from afar, but he knew his skulking would have to stop. Some of the merchants gave him hard stares, perhaps suspecting he was planning a robbery.

Then he went to the marketplace late in the afternoon instead of in the morning, and to his good fortune he arrived in time to see Felipa replacing her sister in the silk shop. Inés walked through the market with her little niece, Adriana, shopping for food, and Yonah contrived his route to meet them.

'*Hola*, señorita!'

'*Hola*, señor.' The sensitive mouth displayed a warm smile. They exchanged a few words and then he hovered while she bought lentils, rice, raisins, dates, and a pomegranate, and he went with her to another greengrocer's booth for two white cabbages.

By then her sack was heavy. 'Allow me, please.'

'No, no . . .'

'Yes, of course,' he insisted cheerfully.

He carried the laden market sack home for her. On the way they made conversation, but afterward he couldn't recall what had been said. He had a great desire to be in her company.

Now that he knew what time of day to go to the marketplace, it was easier to contrive to see her. Two days later he met her in the marketplace again, walking with the child.

Soon he was meeting Inés and the little girl regularly. 'Good afternoon,' he said gravely each time he saw her, and she would reply with similar gravity, 'Good afternoon, señor.'

After only a few of their meetings the little girl, Adriana, came to know him. She would call Yonah's name and run to meet him.

He thought Inés was interested in him. He was stunned by the intelligence in her face, moved by her shy charm, tormented by thoughts of the young body beneath her modest clothing. One afternoon they walked to the Plaza Mayor, where a piper sat against a sunny stone wall and played.

Yonah swayed to the music and began to move as he had seen the Roma dance, suddenly able to say things with his shoulders, his hips, and his feet, as the gypsies did. Things he had never expressed before. Amazed, she watched him with a half smile, but when he held out his hand to her she didn't take it. Still, he imagined that if her young niece weren't there . . . If they were somewhere private instead of being in the public square . . . If . . .

He scooped up the little girl, and Adriana squealed as he whirled with her, around and around.

Afterward they sat not far from the piper and talked while Adriana played with a small, smooth red stone. Inés said she had been born in Madrid, where her family had converted to Catholicism five years ago.

She had never been to Toledo. When he told her his loved ones either were dead or gone from Spain, her

169

eyes filled and she touched his arm. It was the only time she touched him. He sat without moving, but quickly she took her hand away.

The next afternoon Yonah went to the marketplace, as had become his custom, and strolled among the booths, waiting for Felipa to free Inés from the silk shop. But as he passed the booth of the seller of fowls, he saw that Zulaika Denia was there, conversing with the merchant. The fowl seller spied Yonah and said something to Zulaika, and Inés's mother turned and looked at Yonah sternly, as though they had never met. She asked the fowl seller a question, and after she had listened to him, she turned again and went directly to the silk shop of her husband, Isaac Saadi.

Almost at once she reappeared. This time her daughter was with her, and Yonah realized the truth he had been avoiding by concentrating on the proud way Inés held her body, or on the mystery in her large eyes, or the charm of her sensitive mouth.

She was very beautiful.

Yonah watched them walk quickly away, the mother holding the daughter's arm like an *alguacil* marching a prisoner toward her cell.

He doubted that Inés had mentioned their meetings to her family. Whenever he had walked her toward her home she had reclaimed her shopping sack before her house was in sight, and they had parted. Perhaps a trade person in the market had said something to her mother. Or maybe an innocent remark of the little girl, Adriana, had brought Zulaika's wrath down on them.

170

He had not brought dishonor to Inés. It was not so terrible a thing for her mother to learn they had walked together, he told himself.

Yet when he went back to the marketplace two days in a row, she wasn't in the silk shop. Felipa worked in her sister's place.

That night he lay sleepless and burned to imagine what it would be like to lie with a beloved woman. To have Inés as his wife, joining bodies to obey the commandment to be fruitful and multiply. How strange yet fine it would be.

He tried to gather his courage to speak to her father.

But when he went to the marketplace to do so, Micah Benzaquen, neighbor to Isaac Saadi's family, was there, waiting for him.

At the older man's suggestion, they walked to the Plaza Mayor.

'Yonah Toledano, my friend Isaac Saadi believes you have taken note of his younger daughter,' Benzaquen said delicately.

'Inés. Yes, it is so.'

'Yes, Inés. A jewel beyond price, no?'

Yonah nodded, waiting.

'Comely and accomplished in business and in the home. Her father is honored that the son of Helkias the silversmith of Toledo, may he rest, has blessed Isaac's family with friendship. But Señor Saadi has now a few questions. Is this agreeable?'

'Of course.'

'For example. Family?'

'I am descended from rabbis and scholars on both my mother's side and my father's. My maternal grandfather—'

'Of course, of course. Forebears of distinction. But *living* relatives, perhaps with a business the young man might enter?'

'I have an uncle. He left at the expulsion. I know not where . . .'

'Ah, unfortunate.'

But the young man, Benzaquen observed, had mentioned to Señor Saadi a skill taught him by his father the silversmith. 'Are you then a master silversmith?'

'When my father died I was soon to become a journeyman.'

'Oh . . . merely an *apprentice*. Unfortunate, unfortunate . . .'

'I learn easily. I could learn the silk business.'

'I'm certain that is true. Of course, Isaac Saadi already has a son-in-law in his silk business,' Benzaquen said thinly.

Yonah knew that a few years earlier it would have been a most fortunate match for the Saadi family. Everyone would have applauded, Isaac Saadi above all, but the reality was that now he was not an acceptable suitor. And they weren't aware that he was an unchristened fugitive.

Benzaquen was staring at his broken nose. 'Why do you not attend church?' he said, as if reading Yonah's mind.

'I have been . . . occupied.'

Benzaquen shrugged. With a glance at the younger man's threadbare clothes, he didn't bother to ask Yonah about his personal resources.

'In the future, when you stroll and converse with an unmarried young woman, you must allow her to carry her own market sack,' he said severely. 'Otherwise, suitors who are more . . . *eligible* . . . might believe the female too weak to fulfill the strenuous duties of a wife.'

He bade a quiet good day.

20

What Mingo Learned

Mingo had been spending more and more of his time at the Alhambra, returning to the caves on the Sacromonte only one or two nights a week, and one evening he confronted Yonah with troubling news.

'Because the monarchs soon will come to the Alhambra for an extended stay, the Inquisition is planning to examine very closely all Marranos and Moriscos in the area surrounding the fortress, lest some sign of backsliding Christians offend royal eyes.'

Yonah listened silently.

'They will search for heretics until they have them in good supply. Doubtless there will be an auto de fé to demonstrate their zeal and their efficiency, perhaps more than one, with court members, or even the Crown, in attendance.

'What I am trying to impart, my good friend Yonah,' he said gently, 'is that it would be prudent for you soon to go elsewhere, where the need for examination of each Paternoster of your life will be less urgent.'

*

Out of common decency, Yonah could not resist trying to warn those with whom recently he had prayed. Perhaps deep within him there was a wild hope that Isaac Saadi's family would react to him as a savior and look upon him more favorably.

But when he reached the small house in the Albaicin, it was empty.

So was the nearby house that had been occupied by the Benzaquen family, and the houses of the other New Christians. The converso families had heard of the approaching visit of Ferdinand and Isabella and had fully realized its danger to them. All had fled.

Alone in front of the abandoned houses, Yonah squatted in the shade of a plane tree. Idly, he marked four points in the dust: this mark represented the Old Christians of Spain; this, the Moors; here were the New Christians.

And the fourth mark represented Yonah ben Helkias Toledano.

He knew he was not the kind of Jew his father had been, or all the generations who had gone before. In his heart he yearned to be that kind of person but already he had become something else.

His true religion now was to be a Jew of simple survival. He had dedicated himself to continued existence as a group of one, standing apart and alone.

A few feet from the deserted house he found the little red stone that had been Adriana's plaything. He took it and placed it in his purse as a memento of the child's aunt, who was certain to haunt his dreams.

Mingo returned to the caves from the Alhambra to tell urgently of more overheard intelligence.

'Action against New Christians will occur at once. This day must see your departure from this place, Yonah.'

'What of your Roma?' Yonah asked him. 'Shall they be safe from harm?'

'My people are grooms and gardeners. We number among ourselves none so ambitious as Moorish architects and builders or Jewish financiers and physicians. The *gadje* don't bother to envy us. Indeed, most of them scarcely see us. When the Inquisition studies us it observes only *peóns* who are good Christians.'

He made another suggestion that sorely troubled Yonah. 'You should leave here without your burro. The creature is very close to the end of his life, and if he were ridden hard on the trail, very soon he would sicken and die.'

Yonah knew in his heart it was true.

'I give the burro to you,' he said finally, and Mingo nodded.

Yonah brought an apple down to the pasture and fed it to Moise, scratching the burro gently between the ears. It was difficult for him to turn away.

The small man did him one last service, arranging that Yonah would ride with two Romani men – the Manigo brothers, Eusabio and Macot – to deliver horses to dealers in Baena, Jaén, and Andujar. 'Macot Manigo is sending a package to Tangier, by way of a boat he is to meet in Andujar. The boat is owned by Moorish smugglers with whom we have done business for many years. Macot will try to get you on that boat, to go down the Guadalquivir River.'

There was little time for farewells. Mana gave him

bread and cheese wrapped in a cloth. Mingo gave him two handsome parting gifts, a dagger of worked Moorish steel that could keep a fine edge, and the guitar Yonah had played and admired.

'Mingo,' he said, 'you must please take care that you do not make the Catholic monarchs too angry.'

'And you must not worry about me. May you have a good life, my friend.'

Yonah dropped to his knees and embraced the *voivode* of the Roma.

The horse traders were sweet-tempered men with swarthy skins and such facility with animals that they thought nothing of driving a delivery of twenty horses. He had grown familiar with them on the Sacromonte, and now they proved pleasant travel companions. Macot was a good trail cook, and they had brought a supply of wine. Eusabio had a lute and he and Yonah played together every night, banishing their saddle soreness with music.

During the long hours of riding under the hot sun, in his mind Yonah compared two men whom nature had formed strangely. He marveled that the tall and comely friar Bonestruca had become hating and hateful, while the gypsy dwarf Mingo had gathered so much goodness into his small body.

Yonah's own large body ached from being too long in the saddle, and his soul ached with loneliness. Having tasted warm and welcoming companionship, it was wrenching for him to return to the forlorn wandering life.

He thought about Inés Saadi Denia. He was forced to accept the fact that her path through life would be far different from his own, but he allowed himself to brood more fully over another loss. A beast of burden had been his sole and constant companion for more than three years, willing and undemanding. It would be a long time before he would cease to regret bitterly the absence of the burro he called Moise.

Part Five

THE ARMORER
OF GIBRALTAR

Andalusia
April 12, 1496

21
An Ordinary Seaman

The horse dealers stayed too long in Baena, where they left five horses with a gypsy dealer who gave them a feast, and in Jaén, where they left another half dozen animals. By the time they delivered the last nine horses to a livestock broker in Andujar they were almost a full day late. Yonah and the brothers went to the riverfront in full expectation that the African boat had come and gone, but the boat was still there, tied up at the dock. Macot was greeted warmly by the captain, a burnoosed Berber with a great, bushy gray beard. He accepted Macot's package and explained that his boat was behind schedule also; he had brought a cargo of hemp from Tangier, selling it upriver, and would return to Tangier after taking on cargo at Córdova, Seville, the small ports along the Gulf of Cádiz, and Gibraltar.

Macot spoke earnestly to the mariner, turning to point at Yonah, and the captain nodded without enthusiasm after he had listened for a while.

'It is arranged,' Macot told Yonah. The brothers embraced him. 'Go with God,' Macot said.

'And you go with God,' Yonah said. As they rode away, leading the horse he had ridden, he watched wistfully, wishing he could return to Granada with them.

But at once the captain made it obvious to him that he would travel as a laborer and not as a passenger, and he was put to work with the crew, loading olive oil that would be taken to Africa.

That night, as the Arab captain allowed the strong current to carry the shallow-draft boat down the narrow channel of the upper Guadalquivir, Yonah sat with his back against a great tun of oil. While the shadowy banks glided by, he played the guitar softly and tried not to consider that he had not the slightest idea where his life was going.

On the African boat he was the lowest of the low, for he had to learn everything about life afloat, from the raising and furling of the single triangular sail to the safest way to stow cargo in the open craft, lest a crate or a tun career during a storm and damage the boat or even sink it.

The captain, name of Mahmouda, was a brute who struck with his fists when displeased. The crew – two blacks, Jesús and Cristóbal, and two Arabs who shared the cooking, Yephet and Darb – slept under the stars or the rain, wherever they were able to find a nook. All four of the crewmen were from Tangier, muscular *peóns* with whom Yonah got along because they were young and spirited. Sometimes at night, while he played the guitar those who were not on watch sang until Mahmouda shouted at them to shut their holes and go to sleep.

The work was not terribly hard until they reached a

port. In the dark early hours of the third day Yonah had been aboard, the boat docked in Córdova and took on cargo, Yonah teaming with Cristóbal, each carrying one end of large and very heavy crates. They worked by the light of pitchy torches that gave off a fearsome stink. On the other side of the dock a group of dispirited prisoners in chains was being herded onto a boat.

Cristóbal grinned at one of the armed guards. 'You have many criminals,' he said.

The guard spat. 'Conversos.'

Yonah watched them as he worked. They appeared dazed. Some already had injuries that caused them to move painfully, dragging their fetters as if they were old people who hurt when they moved.

The boat's lading was rope and cordage, knives and daggers, and oil, which was in short supply that year. In the eight days it took them to reach the long, wide mouth of the Guadalquivir River the captain had become anxious to obtain oil, which the Tangier merchants were eagerly awaiting. But at Jerez de la Frontera, where he had counted on a large consignment of excellent olive oil, there was only an apologetic trader.

'No oil? Fuck!'

'In three days. So sorry. But please wait. In three days, all you wish to buy.'

'Shit!'

Mahmouda set the crew to doing small tasks aboard the craft while they waited. In the foulest mood, he beat Cristóbal for not moving fast enough to please him.

Jerez de la Frontera was where the prisoners Yonah had glimpsed in Córdova had been taken, to join an assemblage of former Jews and former Muslims who had been convicted, in half a dozen river towns, of backsliding from their allegiance to Christ. A large detachment of soldiers was in the town. The red flag promising impending capital punishment had been displayed, and people had begun to come into Jerez de la Frontera to witness a very large auto de fé.

After the boat had been tied to the dock for two days, the ill-tempered Mahmouda exploded when Yephet, consolidating the cargo to make room for the expected oil, tipped a barrel of wine onto its side. There were no leaks, and the barrel was swiftly righted, but Mahmouda went berserk.

'Wretch!' he shouted. 'Foulness! Scum of the earth!' He beat Yephet to the floor with his fists and then picked up a section of rope and whipped him with it.

Yonah felt the sudden, bitter anger building in him. He found himself moving forward, but Cristóbal seized him and held him back until the beating was over.

That evening the captain left the boat to search for a riverfront stew that offered a bottle and a woman.

The crewmen rubbed a little of their precious cooking oil on Yephet's battered body.

'I don't think you need fear Mahmouda,' Almar told Yonah. 'He knows you are under the protection of the Roma.'

But Yonah thought that in a blind rage Mahmouda was incapable of reason, and he didn't trust his own ability to stand by and witness further beatings. Soon after night fell, he gathered his belongings and climbed soundlessly onto the dock, then he walked away from the boat into the dark.

He walked for five days, without hurrying because he

had no destination. The road followed the coast and he enjoyed looking at the sea. Sometimes the road veered inland but always Yonah could see blue water again after traveling only a little way. In several tiny villages there were fishing boats. Some of the boats were more silvered by sun and salt than others, but all of them were kept in good condition by men who depended on them for a living. Yonah saw Andalusian men intent on homely tasks, mending large nets or caulking and pitching a boat bottom. Sometimes he attempted to speak with them, but they had little to say when he asked about employment. He gathered that the fishing crews usually were related by blood or years of familial friendship. There was no employment for a stranger.

In the town of Cádiz his fortune changed. He was on the waterfront when one of the men unloading cargo from a packet ship became careless. Unable to see because of the size of a bale of cloth he carried, he took a misstep, lost his balance, and fell from the gangway. The cloth bale landed in soft sand, while the man struck his head hard on an iron mooring.

Yonah waited until the injured crewman had been carried away to a physician and the onlookers had dispersed before he approached the ship's mate, a grizzled, middle-aged sailor with a tough, scarred face and a kerchief tied around his head.

'I am Ramón Callicó. I am able to help with the cargo,' he said, and the mate saw the great, muscular body of the young man and nodded that he should go aboard, where others told him what to lift and where to set it down. He brought cargo down into the hold, where because of the heat two crewmen, Joan and César, worked almost naked. Stowing cargo, much of the time

Yonah could understand their orders, but sometimes he was forced to ask them to repeat their words, which sounded like Spanish, and yet were not.

'Are you unable to hear?' César said irritably.

'What language do you speak?' Yonah asked, and Joan grinned.

'It is Catalan. We are all Catalonians. Everyone on this ship.' But after that they spoke Castilian Spanish to Yonah, which was a relief to him.

Before the end of the loading, a physician's boy brought word that the fallen seaman was severely injured and would have to remain in Cádiz for extended care.

The *maestro* had appeared on deck. He was younger than the mate, an erect man whose hair and short beard were still untouched with gray. The mate hurried to him and Yonah, working nearby, overheard their conversation.

'Josep must remain here for mending,' the mate said.

'Hmmm.' The *maestro* was frowning. 'I do not like a short crew.'

'I understand. That one who takes his place with the loading . . . He appears to work with a will.'

Yonah saw the *maestro* studying him. 'Very well. You may talk to him.'

The mate approached Yonah. 'Are you an experienced seaman, Ramón Callicó?'

He didn't wish to lie, but he was almost out of money and needed food and shelter. 'I have experience on a riverboat,' he said, telling a form of the truth. Yet at the same time it was a lie because he didn't mention he had served the boat so briefly. But he was hired, presently joining others to heave on lines that raised three small

186

triangular sails. When the ship had been moved far enough from the shore, the deck hands raised a large mainsail that snapped loudly when it was unfurled and then bellied before the wind, taking them out to sea.

There were seven men in the crew – after a few days he sorted them out: Jaume, the ship's carpenter. Carles, who knew how to repair ropes and constantly was working on the lines. Antoni, who cooked the meals and was missing the little finger of his left hand. And María, César, Joan, and Yonah, who did whatever they were ordered. The purser was a small man who somehow managed to have a pale face when everyone around him was dark from the sun. Yonah always heard him called Señor Mezquida and never learned his last name. The captain's name was Pau Roure. He was seen little, spending much time in his cabin. When he came above deck he never said a word to the crew, sending his orders through the mate, whose name was Gaspar Gatuelles. Sometimes Gatuelles shouted his orders, but no one aboard was struck.

The ship was called *La Lleona*, the lioness. It had two masts and six sails that Yonah soon learned to identify: a large square mainsail, a slightly smaller mizzensail, two triangular topsails above each of these, and two small jib sails that stretched over the bowsprit, which was a tawny lion's body with the alabaster face of a woman. The main mast was higher than the mizzenmast, so high that from the moment the ship was under way before a brisk breeze, Yonah dreaded that he might be ordered aloft.

His first night aboard, when it became his time to sleep for four hours he did not lie down. Instead he went to the rope ladder and climbed until he was halfway up the mainmast. The deck, far beneath him, was murky save for the feeble light from the running lamps. All about the ship was the limitless sea, dark as *vino tinto*. He was unable to force himself to climb higher, and he scrambled down.

He was told the ship was small for a saltwater vessel, yet it seemed enormous when he compared it to the riverboat. There was a damp hold that contained a tiny cabin with six bunks for passengers and an even smaller cabin shared by the three officers. The crew slept on the deck wherever they could. Yonah found a place behind the rudder post. When he lay there he could hear the water hissing as it passed over the curved hull, and whenever the course was changed he felt the vibrations of the shifting rudder moving below.

The open ocean was nothing like the river. Yonah relished the fresh slap of the air and its wet salt tang, but most of the time the motion under way kept his stomach queasy. On occasion he retched and spewed, to the amusement of those who observed. Everyone on the ship was more than ten years his senior and they all spoke Catalan. When they remembered they spoke Spanish to Yonah, but they seldom remembered, and they didn't speak to him often. He knew from the very start that for him it would be a lonely ship.

His inexperience was at once apparent to officers and crew. Most of the time the mate kept him occupied at menial tasks, a nautical *peón*. On his fourth day aboard, there was a storm, and the ship was tossed. Even as Yonah staggered to the leeward side to vomit, the mate ordered him aloft, and as he climbed the rope ladder, fright caused him to forget his nausea. He went higher than he had climbed before, beyond the top of the main-sail. The lines holding taught the triangular topsail had been released from the deck, but human hands had to pull down the sail and lash it to its spar. To get in position to do so, the men had to step from the rope ladder onto a narrow strand of rope, holding on to the spar. A seaman had already started to make his way along the rope when Yonah reached the spar. When Yonah hesitated he was cursed by the two men below him on the ladder, and he stepped out onto the swaying rope, clutching the spar as he slid his feet along the tenuous support. The four of them held to the spar with one hand and pulled the heavy sail as the masts shuddered and swayed. The ship heeled one way and then the other, and each time it reached the dizzying end of a long pitch the men aloft could see the white spume of the furious sea, far below.

When finally the sail was lashed, Yonah found the rope ladder and descended, trembling, to regain the deck. He could not believe what he had done. No one took notice of him for a little while, and then the mate sent him below to check the lashings of the cargo in the groaning hold.

Sometimes sleek, dark dolphins swam alongside the ship, and once they saw a fish so large its sight filled Yonah with terror. He was a swimmer, he had been raised next to a river, yet there were limits to how far he could swim. No land was in sight, nothing but more sea in every direction. And even if he could swim to land, he thought he would be a dangling lure to the monsters. Remembering the story of his biblical name-sake, he imagined Leviathan moving up, up, up from the bottomless deep, drawn to surface feeding by the sky-lit movements of Yonah's arms and legs above, the way a trout is drawn up by the motions of living bait on a hook. The deck beneath his feet felt fragile and impermanent.

He was sent aloft four more times but never learned to like it, nor did he ever fully become a sailor, learning to live with nausea in varying degrees as the ship ventured north along the coast, making landfalls to unload and take on cargo and passengers at Malaga, Cartagena, Alicante, Denia, Valencia, and Tarragona. Sixteen days after they had left Cádiz they arrived in Barcelona, whence they sailed southeast for the island of Menorca.

Menorca, far to sea, proved to have a rugged coast and was an island of fishermen and farmers. Yonah liked the idea of living in such a cliff-bound place. It occurred to him that perhaps the island was sufficiently remote to escape watchful eyes. But in the Menorcan port of Ciutadella the ship picked up three black-cowled Dominican friars. One of the friars went directly to sit on a hogshead and read his breviary, while the others stood next to the deck rail and talked quietly for a time. Then one of them looked at Yonah and crooked a finger.

He forced himself to walk to them. 'Señor?' he said. His voice sounded to him like a croak.

'Where does this ship go when it leaves these islands?'

The friar had small brown eyes. They were not at all like the gray eyes of Bonestruca, but the black Dominican costume the man wore was enough to fill Yonah with terror.

'I do not know, señor.'

The other friar snorted, and looked at him sternly. 'This one is ignorant. He goes wherever the ship goes. You must ask an officer.'

Yonah pointed to where Gaspar Gatuelles stood in the bow, talking with the carpenter. 'He is the mate, señor,' he said, and the pair walked to the bow to talk with Gatuelles.

La Lleona carried those two friars to the larger island, Mallorca. The third friar stopped reading his breviary in time to debark on the smaller island of Ibiza, farther south.

Yonah realized that to survive he would have to continue to live in such a way as to deceive, because the Inquisition was everywhere.

22

Metalwork

When the ship returned to Cádiz, they had scarce begun to unload before the seaman whose place Yonah had taken reappeared, hale now, with only a livid scar on his forehead to show for his mishap.

He was greeted by the shouts of the mate and the crew – 'Josep! Josep!' – and it was clear Yonah's employment as a seaman on *La Lleona* was at an end. Truth to tell, that came as a welcome event. Gaspar Gatuelles thanked him and paid him off, and he walked away from the ship glad to be on firm land.

He wandered southeast along the coastal road, the weather hot by day and mild by night. Each evening before darkness fell he tried to find a haymow to sleep in, or the soft sand of a beach, but when there was neither he made do with what was at hand. Each morning he bathed in the gorgeous sea under the warm sun, never swimming out far because he feared that at any moment he might feel a monster's sharp teeth or tentacles. When he came to a brook or a horse trough he washed off some of the sea's salt that had dried on his body. Once a farmer gave him a long ride atop a load of straw in his ox-drawn wagon. Along the way he stopped his animals.

'Do you know where you are?' he asked, and Yonah shook his head, puzzled. It was just a deserted place along a deserted road.

'This is where Spain ends. It is the southernmost point of Iberia,' the man said with satisfaction, as if it were a personal accomplishment. Yonah received only one other ride along the way, in a cart full of dried cod that he helped the owner unload when they reached the village of Gibraltar, at the foot of a great rock mountain.

Handling the cod without tasting it had made him ravenous. There was a tavern in the village and he entered it and found a low-ceilinged room smelling of many years of spilled wine and wood fires and the sweat of its patrons. Half a dozen men sat drinking at two long tables, some of them also eating from a pot of fish stew that bubbled on the hearth. Yonah ordered a mug of wine that proved to be sour and a bowl of the stew that proved to be good, full of fish and onion and bits of herbs. The fishbones were sharp and plentiful, but he ate slowly and with enjoyment, and when he was finished he ordered another bowl.

While he was waiting for it an old man came into the tavern and took the empty place on the bench next to him. 'I shall have a bowl of wine, Señor Bernaldo,' he called to the proprietor, who grinned as he ladled Yonah's stew.

'Not unless you find a patron among these good men,' he called in reply, and the men at the tables laughed as if he had said something very humorous.

193

The old man was round-shouldered and soft-looking; his wispy white hair and the wounded vulnerability in his face at once reminded Yonah of Geronimo Pico, the old shepherd whose dying he had witnessed and whose flock he had inherited for several years. 'Give him a drink,' he said to the proprietor. Then, suddenly conscious of his limited funds, he added, 'A mug, not a bowl.'

'*Ai*, Vicente, you have found a spendthrift!' a man at the other table said. The words were spoken sarcastically and without humor, but they drew laughter. The speaker was short and thin, with dark hair and a small mustache. 'You're a miserable old rat, Vicente, never getting enough drink in your guts,' he said.

'Oh, Luis, close your mean mouth,' one of the other drinkers said wearily.

'Would you care to close it for me, José Gripo?'

That query seemed humorous to Yonah, because José Gripo was tall and broad, not young but obviously much younger and stronger than the other man; it seemed to Yonah that Luis would not have stood a chance in a fight.

But no one laughed. Yonah saw the man who sat next to Luis get to his feet. He looked younger than Luis, of average height, but lean and muscular. He was very fit. His face was all hard planes, even his nose made a sharp angle. He regarded José Gripo with interest and took a step toward him.

'Sit down or remove your arse from here, Angel,' Bernaldo, the proprietor, said. 'Your *maestro* has told me that if I have any more trouble from you and Luis, he's to hear at once.'

The man stopped and stared at the proprietor. Then

he shrugged and smiled. He reached for his mug and finished the rest of his wine at a gulp, and set the mug back on the table with a bang. 'Let us be off, then, Luis, for I have no desire to further enrich friend Bernaldo this night.'

The proprietor watched them leave the tavern and then served Yonah his stew. A moment later he brought the old man his wine. 'Here, Vicente. Let it be free. They are a bad sort, those two.'

'They are a strange combination,' José Gripo said. 'I've seen it before – Luis purposely provokes someone and then Angel Costa moves in and does his fighting.'

'Angel Costa fights well,' a man said at the other table.

'Yes, he is an old soldier and knows well how to fight, but he is an unpleasant bastard,' Gripo said.

'Luis is an unpleasant man, too,' Vicente said, 'but he is a marvelous worker of metal, I must say that.'

That drew Yonah's interest. 'I've done metalwork and I seek employment. What kind of metalwork goes on here?'

'There is an armory a bit down the road,' Gripo said. 'Have you experience with weapons?'

'I can use the dagger.'

Gripo shook his head. 'I refer to the manufacture of weapons.'

'No experience in that. But I have had lengthy apprenticeship in the working of silver, and much briefer experience with both iron and steel.'

Vincente finished his wine with a sigh. 'Then you must go and see our Maestro Fierro, the armorer of Gibraltar,' he said.

*

That night Yonah paid a few *sueldos* to Bernaldo and was allowed to sleep by the tavern hearth. The fee also gave him a bowl of gruel to break his fast in the morning, and he was both rested and fed when he departed from the tavern and followed the road according to Bernaldo's directions. It was a walk of only a little while. The singular stone mountain of Gibraltar loomed above the long low buildings and grounds of Manuel Fierro's armor works, and beyond that, the sea.

The armorer proved to be a short, wide-shouldered man with craggy features and a shock of rough white hair. Whether by birth or accident, his nose turned slightly to the left. It marred the symmetry of his features, but somehow the irregularity made his face homely and sympathetic. Yonah told him a story that was nearly true: He was Ramón Callicó. He had been apprentice to Helkias Toledano, master silversmith of Toledo, until the expulsion of the Jews sent Toledano away and brought an end to his service. For some months he had worked metals in the repair shop of the Roma of Córdova.

'Roma?'

'Gypsies.'

'Gypsies!'

Fierro was more amused than scornful. 'I shall give you some tests.'

The *maestro* had been working on a pair of silver spurs as they spoke, and now he set them down and took up a small piece of steel.

'Provide the chasing, as though the steel scrap were this silver spur.'

'I would rather work on the spur,' Yonah said, but

196

the *maestro* shook his head. Fierro waited without comment, and clearly without high expectation.

But he grew attentive as Yonah accomplished the chasing on the scrap without fuss, and then, the second test, completed a neat seam between two discarded sections of a steel elbow protector.

'Do you have other skills?'

'I am able to read. I write a legible hand.'

'Truly?' Fierro leaned forward and studied him with interest. 'These are not talents often found in an apprentice. How did you come by them?'

'My father taught me. He was a learned man.'

'I offer an apprenticeship. Two years.'

'I am willing.'

'It is customary in my craft that the apprentice pay for instruction. Are you able to do so?'

'Alas, no.'

'Then, at the end of two years you must work one year at a reduced income. After which, Ramón Callicó, we may discuss your entering my employment as a journeyman armorer.'

'I agree,' Yonah said.

The shop suited him. He enjoyed working with metals again, with a difference, for the making of armor and weapons employed techniques totally unfamiliar to him, allowing him to learn while also utilizing skills he had long since mastered.

He liked the place. There were always the sounds of hammers on metal, a ringing and clanging, sometimes rhythmic and sometimes not, often coming from several of the sheds at the same time, a kind of metallic music. And Fierro was a very fine teacher.

197

'Spain has much to be proud of in the development of iron,' he said, and gave a lesson. 'For thousands of years ore was placed in a deep charcoal fire that wasn't hot enough to melt the resulting iron, but sufficiently hot to soften it so it could be pounded or forged.'

Repeated heating and forging, heating and forging, forced out impurities and resulted in wrought iron, he said.

'Then our ironworkers learned to make the fire hotter by blowing air into it through a hollow tube, and later by using bellows. In the eighth century, Spanish ironworkers built a better hearth furnace, called the Catalan forge. Ore and charcoal are mixed in the furnace and air is blown into the bottom of the fire by means of waterpower. It enables us to produce better wrought iron, and much faster. Steel is made by removing impurities and most of the carbon from the iron. No matter how clever the armorer, his armor will be only as good as the steel from which it is made.'

Fierro had learned how to work steel by prenticing to a Moorish sword maker. 'The Moors make the best steel and the best swords.' He smiled at Yonah. 'I served an apprenticeship to a Moor and you served an apprenticeship to a Jew,' he said.

Yonah agreed it was amusing and busied himself cleaning the workplace to bring an end to the conversation.

On the fifteenth day of Yonah's apprenticeship Angel Costa sought him out as he sat on a bench in the cooking hut, eating his morning gruel. Costa was on his way to a hunt, carrying his longbow and a bundle of arrows. He stood before Yonah and glowered, watching him

198

without speaking. That suited Yonah, and he finished his meal leisurely.

When he was through, he set the bowl down and rose to his feet. He started to leave, but Costa blocked his path.

'What?' Yonah said softly.

'Are you good with a sword, apprentice?'

'I have never used a sword.'

Costa's smile was no more pleasant than his glare. He nodded, then he went away.

The cook, who was referred to as the other Manuel because he shared the *maestro*'s first name, looked up from scrubbing a pot with sand and followed Costa with his eyes as the master-at-arms crossed the compound. He spat. 'It is easy to dislike that one. He says he is God's representative in the Smoke House, where he keeps us on our knees in prayer morning and night.'

'Why do you allow it?'

The cook looked pained at Yonah's ignorance. 'We are afraid of him,' the other Manuel said.

The advantage of being the apprentice was that Yonah was the designated chore boy, sent to shops and warehouses all over the town of Gibraltar, which allowed him to learn something about his new haven. The community nestled at the foot of the great rock and spilled onto its lower slope. Fierro conducted business with many suppliers, and some of these merchants, proud of their environs, were happy to answer Yonah's questions.

A cooper's clerk told him the exotic town had a Moorish feel because the Moors had inhabited it for 750 years, until the Spanish recaptured it in 1462, 'on the feast day of St. Bernard.' At the chandlery the owner turned out to be José Gripo, whom Yonah had already met at the tavern. Gripo was busy, but while he measured and coiled rope he revealed that the name Gibraltar was a corruption of Jebel Tariq, Arabic for Tariq's Rock. And the chandler's ancient clerk, a slender old man with fine features, whose name was Tadeo Deza, added, 'Tariq having been the Moorish commander who built the first fort below the rock.'

Yonah learned little about Gibraltar from those with whom he worked in Fierro's armory. There were six *peóns* whose chief duty was to maintain the grounds and move the heavy metal from storerooms to workrooms and then back to storerooms again. These laborers lived with Angel Costa and the other Manuel, in a barnlike building, the Smoke House. The two top artisans, Luis Planas and Paco Parmiento, were mature men and the royalty of the workshop. Parmiento, a widower, was the master sword maker, while Planas, who had never married, was the master armorer. Yonah was assigned to live in the worker's hut with them and Vicente, the old man for whom he had bought a drink in the village bar. Vicente had trouble remembering the new apprentice's name.

'Who did you say you are, young stranger?' he asked, leaning on the broom with which he had been sweeping the dirt floor.

'I am Ramón Callicó, uncle.'

'I am Vicente Deza and I am not your uncle, for then your sire would be a whoreson.' He laughed, relishing his own feeble wit, and Yonah had to smile.

'Are you related, then, to Tadeo Deza of the chandler's shop?'

'Aye, I am cousin to Tadeo but he does not own to it,

for at times I shame him by begging for drink, as you have seen.' The old man cackled again and regarded him curiously. 'So we shall live here cheek by jowl, along with Luis and Paco. You are lucky, for this is a sound and weatherproof hut, built carefully by Jews.'

'How did it come to be built by Jews, Vicente?' Yonah asked, keeping his voice casual.

'They lived here in number once. About twenty years ago, perhaps a bit more, good Catholics rose against those who called themselves New Christians. Not real Christians. Jews is what they were. Hundreds of them from Córdova and Seville thought that Gibraltar, having been recently captured from the Moors and sparse of population, could be a safe and cozy haven for them, and they bargained with the duke of Medina Sidonia, the lord of this place.

'They gave the duke money and agreed to pay for a cavalry force to be stationed here. Hundreds of settlers came and raised structures for homes and businesses. But the cost of maintaining the military and paying for expeditions against the Portuguese soon drained them. When the duke learned that their funds were gone, he came with soldiers and soon they were gone as well.

'They had built this hut and the Smoke House as a business that smoked fish to be sent to port cities by ship. If you sniff deep on damp days, you can still smell the smoke. Our *maestro* leased the abandoned property from the duke and raised the animal barn and all the work sheds as you now see them.' The old man screwed his face into a wink of his left eye. 'You must come to me whenever you wish to know of the past, señor. For Vicente Deza knows many things.'

Later that day Yonah brought supplies to the shed

ruled by another of his hut mates, Paco Parmiento, the sword maker. Yonah had a feeling that Parmiento would be easy to get along with. He was bald and ran to fat. His clean-shaven face bore a whitened scar on his right cheek, and his eyes sometimes seemed distant, for he was constantly thinking of better ways to design and fashion swords, and apt to be absent-minded concerning the world around him. He muttered to Yonah that all were expected to keep their hut neat and clean. 'But we are fortunate, for old Vicente Deza attends to such chores.'

'Is Vicente Deza an armorer? Or a sword maker, like yourself?'

'That one? He has not worked metal at all. He lives among us only because of the *maestro*'s charity. You must not believe anything old Vicente says,' the sword maker warned, 'for he is impaired of intellect and has the mind of a slow child. Often he sees things that are not there.'

Like most of the stony places Yonah had seen in Spain, Gibraltar had caves, the largest being a commodious cavern at the very top of the rock. Fierro bought most of his steel from Moors in Córdova, but he kept a supply of a special iron ore that was mined in a small section of this great cave, whose entrance was reached by a narrow trail up the rock face.

Three times the *maestro* took Yonah with him, leading a pair of burros up the steep trail. On all three occasions Yonah wished his animal were Moise, for the trail went up, and up, and up – far higher than the crow's nest of any sailing ship – and a mishap would mean a dizzying and fatal drop. But the burros were accustomed to the trail, not even panicking when the way was blocked by a group of cinnamon-colored apes.

Fierro smiled when he saw Yonah start at the sudden appearance of the animals. There were six of them, large and tailless. One of the females was nursing a small ape child.

'They live here in the upper regions,' Fierro said. He took from a sack a quantity of stale bread and overripe fruit and threw it off the trail, up the slope, and the beasts cleared the trail quickly to get at the food.

'I never thought to see such animals in Spain.'

'Legend says they came from Africa, through a natural tunnel running beneath the strait and ending in one of the Gibraltar caverns,' Fierro said. 'Although I lean toward the probability that they escaped from a boat that had touched in at our rock.'

From the top of the trail, myth seemed possibility, for the coast of Africa appeared deceptively close in the clear air.

'How far is Africa, Señor Fierro?'

'Half a day's sail, with good wind. We are standing on one of the fabled Pillars of Hercules,' the *maestro* said. He pointed out the other Pillar of Hercules, a mountain in Morocco on the far side of the strait. The water that separated the Pillars was blue as blue, glittering under the golden sun.

Five days after their first conversation, Angel Costa approached Yonah again.

'Have you spent much time on a horse, Callicó?'

'Very little time, actually. I owned a burro.'

'A burro suits you.'

'Why do you ask these things? Are you seeking men for a military expedition?'

'Not exactly,' Costa said, and went away.

After days of being ordered to run errands, shovel ore, and carry steel, at last Yonah was assigned a task that allowed him to work metal, even though the task was lowly. He was nervous about working for Luis Planas, whose bad temper and character he had already witnessed. To his relief, although Luis spoke to him in a surly manner, he was serious about work. He bade Yonah to dress several sections of armor. 'You must search out tiny imperfections in the surface of the steel, the mere hints of the faintest scratches, and polish them interminably until they are no more,' Luis told him.

So he polished with a will. When more than a week of faithful and hard rubbing had transformed the pieces into glowing radiance, Yonah learned he had worked on parts of the cuirass – twin sections of breastplate. 'Each piece must be flawless,' Luis said severely. 'They are part of a magnificent suit of armor the Fierro armory has been creating for more than three years.'

'For whom is this armor being made?' Yonah asked.

'A nobleman in Tembleque. The Count Fernán Vasca by name.'

Yonah's heart thudded in his body, seemingly in a more pronounced rhythm than the blows of Luis Planas' hammer.

No matter how far he might flee, it seemed that Toledo followed!

He well remembered the debt that had been owed his father by the Count Vasca of Tembleque: sixty-nine *reales* and sixteen *maravedíes*, for a number of wrought objects of Helkias' silversmithing art, among them a remarkable and singular rose with a silver stem, a variety of silver mirrors and silver combs, a set of twelve drinking goblets . . .

It was a galling indebtedness that would have made life considerably easier for Yonah ben Helkias could he have but collected it.

Which he well knew he could not.

23
Saints and Gladiators

When Fierro perceived that the new prentice appeared to be dependable in every respect, Yonah was assigned the task of chasing a design into the cuirass of Count Vasca's armor. It required him to make tiny indentations in the steel with a hammer and a punch, following guide lines barely marked on the surface of the steel by Fierro or Luis Planas. Silver was much easier to chase than steel, but the harder metal was a protection against certain errors that would have been disasters in silver. In the beginning, Yonah made a light tap to ascertain that the punch was correctly placed, followed by a hard tap to complete the indentation; but as he continued to work, his sure touch returned. Soon the quick, hard blows of his hammer revealed his confidence.

'Manuel Fierro is careful to test his armor often,' Paco Parmiento told Yonah one morning. 'So from time to time we have games. The *maestro* likes his workers to pretend they are knights, in order to understand what changes he must make in his designs. He wishes you to participate.'

For the first time, Angel Costa's questions made disturbing sense. 'Of course, señor,' Yonah said.

So it happened that the following day he found himself standing in a large round pit, clad in a padded fabric undergarment and regarding with unease a disassembled and somewhat rusted and ill-used suit of metal being fitted to his body by Paco Parmiento. At the other side of the pit Angel Costa was being dressed by his friend Luis, while their fellow workers were gathered at the edges of the pit like spectators at a cockfight.

'Vicente, go to the hut and ready the boy's pallet, for he will have need of it soon!' Luis called, and there were jeers and laughter.

'Don't mind that one,' Paco said. Beads of sweat ran down Parmiento's bald pate.

The cuirass was lifted over Yonah and settled, covering his chest and his back. Mail protected his arms and legs, cuissarts covered his thighs. Steel guards were placed on his shoulders, elbows and lower arms, and knees, while leg pieces covered his shins. He pushed his feet into laminated steel shoes. When the helmet was placed over his head, Paco lowered the face guard.

'I cannot breathe, nor can I see,' Yonah said. He tried to keep his voice calm.

'The perforations allow you to breathe,' Parmiento said.

'They do not.'

Paco raised the face guard crankily. 'Leave it up,' he said. 'Everyone does so.' Yonah could see why.

He was given leather gauntlets with steel guards on the fingers, and a round shield. Everything added to the great weight carried by his body.

207

'The sword's edges and point have been blunted and rounded for your safety in the game, until it is more a club than a sword,' Parmiento said, handing it over. The weapon felt strange in Yonah's hand, which had little flexibility within the stiff gauntlet.

Angel Costa was similarly armored, and the moment came when they shambled toward one another. Yonah was still thinking of how best to strike when he saw Costa's sword already descending toward his helmeted head, and only just managed to fling up the shield on his arm.

The arm quickly became leaden as Costa struck again and again, with such swift, repeated power that Yonah was unable to react when the sword suddenly came lower. Costa dealt him such a smashing clout to the ribs as would have cleaved his body if the blade had been sharp and the armor less sound. As it was, even though he was protected by padding and well-made steel, he felt the smash of the sword to his very bones, and it was the precursor of many other assaults as Costa rained terrible blow after terrible blow.

Yonah managed to strike Costa only twice before they were stopped by the *maestro*'s reaching a pole between them, but it was clear to all who watched that if it had been real warfare, Angel would have killed him at once. At any time, Costa could have applied the *golpe de gracia*.

Yonah sat on a bench, aching and out of wind, as Paco stripped him of the heavy armor.

The *maestro* came to him and asked many questions. Had the armor inhibited him? Had any of the joints jammed? Did Yonah have any suggestions that might make the armor more protective and less imprisoning? Yonah answered truthfully that the experience had been so foreign to his experience that he had scarcely thought of any of those things.

The *maestro* had but to look at Yonah's face to be aware of his humiliation.

'You must not expect to best Angel Costa in these pursuits,' the armorer said. 'No man here is able to do so. Costa spent eighteen years tasting blood as a sergeant in constant and bitter combat with the Saracen, and now in these games of testing the steel, our master-at-arms relishes pretending that he is still fighting to the death.'

There was a large and purpled bruise on the left side of Yonah's rib cage, and he had enough achiness to wonder whether lasting damage had been done to his ribs. For several nights he had to sleep on his back only, and one midnight he suffered enough pain-filled sleeplessness to hear sounds of distress emanating from the other side of the hut.

As he arose with a stifled groan of his own, he determined that the hoarse noises came from Vicente Deza. He went and knelt by the old man's pallet in the dark.

'Vicente?'

'Peregrino . . . Santo Peregrino . . .'

Vicente was weeping raggedly. 'El Compasivo! Santo Peregrino el Compasivo!'

Saint Pilgrim the Merciful. What did that mean?

'Vicente,' Yonah said again, but the old man was off on a torrent of prayer, invoking God and the pilgrim saint. Yonah put out a hand and sighed when he touched the heat in Vicente's face.

When he stood, he knocked over Vicente's water bottle, which fell with a clatter.

'What the fuck?' Luis Planas asked, wakened on the other side of the room, and waking Paco Parmiento.

'What?' Paco said.

'It is Vicente. He has come down with the fever.'

'Keep him quiet or get him out of here to die,' Luis said.

At first Yonah didn't know what to do. But he remembered what Abba had done when he and Meir had had the fever. He left the hut and stumbled through the dark night to the forge, where a banked fire like a dragon's tongue cast a red glare over the tables and the tools. He lit a taper from the coals and used it to light an oil lamp, by which illumination he found a basin that he filled with water from a jug. Then he collected rags that had been cut and stacked against the time they would be needed for polishing metal.

When he was back inside the hut he set the lamp on the floor.

'Vicente,' he said.

The old man had gone to sleep fully clothed, and Yonah began to undress him. Perhaps he made more noise than he should have, or maybe the flickering light of the lamp drew Luis Planas from sleep again.

'Damn you!' Luis sat up. 'Did I tell you to remove him or not?'

Heartless bastard. Something within Yonah snapped.

'Listen—' Luis said.

Yonah turned and took a step toward him. 'Go to sleep.' He tried to keep from being disrespectful, but anger placed a burr in his voice.

Luis remained half sitting for a long moment, glaring across the room at the apprentice who would speak to him so. Finally he lay back and turned his face to the wall.

Paco also had been awakened. He had heard the

exchange between Luis and Yonah and was laughing quietly on his pallet.

Vicente's body seemed composed of filthy skin over bones, the dirt caked on his feet, but Yonah forced himself to bathe him painstakingly, changing the water twice, carefully wiping his body with dry rags so he would not take a chill.

In the morning Vicente's fever had broken. Yonah went to the kitchen and asked the other Manuel to thin the breakfast gruel with hot water, taking a bowl back to the hut and spooning the gruel into the old man. In the meantime he missed his own breakfast. When he hurried to report to work in Luis's shed, he was intercepted by the *maestro*.

He knew that Luis must have complained to Fierro about his impertinence and he braced for trouble, but the *maestro* spoke to him quietly. 'How is Vicente?'

'I believe he will be well again. The fever has gone.'

'That is good. I know that sometimes it is difficult to be an apprentice. I remember when I was apprentice to Abu Adal Khira in Velez Málaga. He was one of the foremost of the Muslim armorers. He is dead now, and his armory is gone.

'Luis was an apprentice with me, and when I came to Gibraltar and opened my own armory I brought him with me. Luis is a very difficult man but he is a wondrous maker of armor. I need him in my shop. Do you understand what I am saying?'

'Yes, *maestro*.'

Fierro nodded. 'I made a mistake placing Vicente in the same hut as Luis Planas. You know the small shed beyond the forge?'

211

Yonah nodded.

'It is well constructed. It has only a few tools in it. Move the tools elsewhere and you and Vicente will live in that hut. Vicente is fortunate you were willing to help him last night, Ramón Callicó. You did well. But an apprentice would be wise to remember that gross impertinence to a master craftsman will not be tolerated twice in this armory. Is it understood?'

'Yes, señor,' Yonah said.

Luis was angry that Fierro hadn't beaten the apprentice and sent him away. He was severe and cold to Yonah for a number of days, and Yonah took care to give no cause for complaint as he polished armor unendingly. The steel suit for the count of Tembleque was in its final stage of manufacture, and Yonah worked over piece after piece until they gleamed with a soft brilliance that even Luis acknowledged could not be improved.

It was a relief when he was dispatched to collect needed supplies from the merchants of the village.

Passing the time of day in the chandler's shop while Tadeo Deza filled Fierro's order, he told the elderly clerk that his cousin Vicente had been very ill with the fever.

Tadeo paused. 'Is he nearing the end?'

'No. The fever abated and then returned, abated and returned, but he appears to be recovering.'

Tadeo Deza sniffed. 'That one is too simple to die,' he said.

Yonah was leaving with his supplies when he turned back, struck by a sudden thought.

'Tadeo, do you know anything of Santo Peregrino el Compasivo?'

'Yes, a local saint.'

'Saint Pilgrim the Merciful. It is a strange name.'

'He lived in this region several hundreds of years ago. It is said he was a foreigner, perhaps from France or Germany. At any rate, he had been to Santiago de Compostela to worship at the relics of St. James. You yourself have made the pilgrimage to Santiago de Compostela, perhaps?'

'No, señor.'

'Ah, someday you must go. James was the third apostle chosen by Our Lord. He was present at the Transfiguration, so holy that the emperor Charlemagne decreed his subjects must give water, shelter, and fire to all pilgrims traveling to visit the relics of this saint.

'At any rate, the foreign pilgrim of whom we speak was himself transformed after days of praying with the relics of the apostle. Instead of returning to the life he had led before his pilgrimage, he wandered south, ending in this region. He spent the days of his life here, tending to the needs of the ill and the poor.'

'What was his given name?'

Tadeo shrugged. 'It is not known. That is why he is called Saint Pilgrim the Merciful. Nor do we know where he is buried. Some say when he was a very old man he simply wandered away from here, in much the same way he had arrived. But others say he dwelt alone and died alone, someplace nearby, and in every generation men have made a sport of seeking to find his grave hereabouts, without success.

'Where did you hear of our local saint?' Tadeo asked.

Yonah didn't want to mention Vicente and give his cousin reason for more complaint. 'I heard somebody speak of him and I grew curious.'

Tadeo smiled. 'Someone in a tavern, no doubt, for

213

drink often deepens a man's awareness of sin and provokes a desire for the saving grace of angels.'

Yonah was happy when Fierro assigned him to help in the shed of Paco Parmiento, the sword maker. Paco put Yonah to work at once, sharpening to keenness and polishing short cavalry sabers and the long, beautiful swords carried by noblemen and knights, double-edged and narrowing from hilt to point. Three times Paco turned back the first sword Yonah sharpened. 'The swordsman's arm does the work, but the sword must help. Each edge must be as finely honed as the steel will allow.'

Though Paco was a hard taskmaster, Yonah liked him. If Luis reminded Yonah of a fox, Paco brought to mind a kind and gentle bear. Away from his workbench he was forgetful and clumsy, but once he sat down to work his movements were sure and economical, and the *maestro* had told Yonah that Parmiento's blades were in great demand.

In Luis's shed Yonah had worked in virtual silence, but he found that Paco readily answered questions as they worked.

'Did you apprentice with the *maestro* and Luis?' Yonah asked him.

Paco shook his head. 'I am older than they are. When they apprenticed I was already a journeyman in Palma. The *maestro* sought me out and brought me here.'

'What does Angel do in this workshop?'

Paco shrugged. 'The *maestro* found him soon after he left off soldiering and brought him here as master-at-arms, for he is truly a warrior, an expert at every weapon. We tried to teach him to shape steel but he has no capacity for the work, so Señor Fierro placed him in charge of the *peóns*.'

They spoke less when the *maestro* was present, but still it was a relaxed place to work. At a nearby table in the sword maker's shed, Manuel Fierro often worked on a project dear to his heart. His brother, Nuño Fierro, physician of Saragossa, had sent, through traveling merchants, a set of drawings of surgical instruments. The *maestro* was using hard steel made from the special ore he and Yonah had brought down from the Gibraltar cavern, fashioning the tools with his own hands, scalpels, lancets, saws, scrapers, probes, and pincers.

In the *maestro*'s absence, Paco showed Yonah the instruments as a standard of excellence in the working of metal. 'He lavishes as much care on each small tool as he would on a full sword or a spear. It is a labor of love.'

He told Yonah proudly that he had helped Fierro fashion the *maestro*'s own sword of the special steel. 'It needed to be a unique blade, because Manuel Fierro has a better command of a sword than anyone else I have ever seen.'

Yonah stopped polishing for a moment. 'He is better than Angel Costa?'

'War has taught Angel to be an incomparable killer. In the use of all other weapons he is unchallenged. But in the use of the sword alone, the *maestro* is the better man.'

Hardly had his bruised ribs a chance to recover before Yonah once again was asked to participate in a game against Angel Costa. This time, again in full armor, he found himself astride a gray Arabian war horse, leveling a lance tipped by a padded wooden ball and galloping toward Angel, who was leveling a similar lance and galloping a glossy brown war horse toward him.

Yonah was unaccustomed to riding a spirited horse. He concentrated on not falling off. The ball at the end of his uncontrolled lance moved this way and that as he slithered and bounced on his mount's back.

The horses were protected by a low wooden wall that stretched between the contenders, but the riders were not.

There was no time to prepare, merely a short thunder of hooves and then they met. Yonah watched the ball on Costa's lance become larger and larger, assume the size of a full moon and then of the entireness of life, as it smashed into him and swept him from the horse and onto the ground, into a jarring and ignominious defeat.

Costa was not liked. There was little cheering, but Luis was enjoying every moment. As Paco and several others freed the shaken Yonah from his armor he saw Luis pointing at him and laughing until his cheeks were wet with tears of mirth.

That afternoon, Yonah tried to hide a slight limp. He walked to the Smoke House and found Angel Costa sharpening arrow points on a stone wheel.

'*Hola,*' he said, but Costa gave him no greeting, continuing with his work.

'I do not know how to fight.'

Costa gave his barking laugh. 'No,' he agreed.

'I would like to learn to use weapons. Would you be willing, perhaps, to give me instruction?'

Costa stared at him with hooded eyes. 'I do not instruct.' He tested the point of an arrowhead gingerly with his finger. 'I will tell you what you must do to learn

216

my skills. You must go for a soldier and spend twenty years fighting the Moor. You must kill and kill, using every weapon and sometimes your bare hands, and whenever possible you must cut the pizzle from the slain. When thus you have acquired more than one hundred circumcized pricks you may come back and challenge me, wagering your collection of pricks against mine. And then I will kill you quickly.'

When Yonah met the *maestro* in front of the barn, Fierro was kinder. 'A disaster, no, Ramón?' he asked Yonah cheerfully. 'Are you injured?'

'Only my pride, *maestro*.'

'I have a few words of advice. From the start of your ride you must grasp the lance more firmly, with both hands, and with the lower end of the weapon tucked tightly between your elbow and your body. You must fix your eyes on your enemy at once and keep them on him as he approaches, following him with the tip of the lance, so it will find his body as if the meeting were pre-ordained.'

'Yes, señor,' Yonah said, but so resignedly that Fierro smiled.

'It is not hopeless, but you ride without confidence. You and the horse must become as one, so you may drop the reins and give full attention to the lance. On days when you are not greatly needed for the work, take the gray horse from the stables and give him his exercise, then groom him and give him feed and water. I think both you and the animal will benefit.'

He was tired and sore when he made his way back to the hut and dropped onto his pallet.

Vicente looked over at him from his own pallet. 'At

least you have survived. Angel has a mean soul.' Vicente spoke normally and appeared rational.

'Your fever hasn't returned?'

'Apparently not.'

'Good, Vicente, I am glad.'

'I thank you for seeing after me in my illness, Ramón Callicó.' He coughed and cleared his throat. 'I had frightening dreams, under the fever. Did I speak wildly?'

Yonah smiled at him. 'Only a few times. Sometimes you prayed to the Pilgrim Saint.'

'The Pilgrim Saint. Did I?'

They were silent for a moment, and then Vicente struggled to sit up. 'There is something I would tell you, Ramón. Something I would share with you for being the only one who cared for me.'

Yonah looked at him with concern, certain from the tension and shrillness in his voice that the fevers had returned. 'What is it, Vicente?'

'I have discovered him.'

'Who?'

'Santo Peregrino el Compasivo. I have found the saint of pilgrimages,' Vicente Deza said.

'Vicente. What are you saying?' He looked over at the old man in distress. It was only three days since his night of delirium.

'You think me addled. I understand.'

Vicente was right, he did think the old man mad in a harmless way.

Vicente's hands scrabbled beneath his pallet. Then, holding something in his fist, he crawled to Yonah like a child. 'Take it,' he said, and Yonah found an object in his hand. It was small and thin. He held it up, trying to see it in the dim light.

'What is it?'

'It is a bone. From the finger of the saint.' He clutched Yonah's arm. 'You must come with me, Ramón, and see it for yourself. Let us go on Sunday morn.'

Damnation. On Sunday mornings, half a day was given to the workers to attend church services. Yonah was miserly about wasting the precious few hours he had to himself. He wanted to follow the *maestro*'s advice and take out the gray Arab horse, but he suspected he would have no peace if he continued to ignore Vicente's claims.

'We will go on Sunday if both of us are able to walk by then,' he said, and handed back the bone.

He was worried about Vicente, who continued to talk to him in feverish whispers about a discovery. In all other respects Vicente appeared to have recovered from his illness. He appeared alert and robust, and his appetite for both food and drink had returned prodigiously.

On Sunday morning, the two of them walked over the straight neck of land connecting Gibraltar to Spain. Once they were on the mainland, they walked eastward for only half an hour before Vicente lifted his hand.

'We are arrived.'

Yonah could see only a desolate place of sandy soil broken by numerous low outcroppings of granite rock. He could detect nothing unusual about the site but he followed as Vicente clambered across a number of the rock formations as if he had not been ill for a day.

Then, quite close to the trail, Vicente found the particular rocks for which he was looking, and Yonah saw that in the very center of the formation there was a wide fissure. A natural rock ramp ran down to an opening. It was quite invisible unless someone stood almost atop it.

Vicente had brought a live coal in a small metal box, and Yonah spent a moment blowing on the coal and lighting a pair of stubby candles.

Rainwater would be carried past the opening by the stone ramp that ended below in a patch of sand. Within, the cave beneath the rocks was dry and about the size of Mingo's cave on the Sacromonte. It ended in a narrow fissure that must have been connected with the surface, because Yonah could feel fresh air.

'See here,' Vicente said.

In the flickering light, Yonah saw a skeleton. The bones of the upper half of the body appeared to be intact, but the bones of both legs and feet had been moved a short distance away, and when Yonah knelt over them with the candle he could see they had been gnawed by an animal. Of the garments that had covered the body, only tufts of material remained here and there. Yonah guessed that the cloth had been consumed long ago by animals attracted to the salt of sweat.

'And here!'

It was a rough altar composed of tree branches. Before it were three shallow earthen pots. Their contents had long since been eaten, perhaps by the same creature that had gnawed the bones.

'Offerings,' Yonah said. 'Perhaps to a pagan God.'

'No,' Vicente said. He brought his candle to light the opposite wall, where there leaned a great cross.

And then he illumined the wall next to the cross, so Yonah could see that scratched into the stone was the mark of earliest Christianity, the sign of the fish.

*

'When did you find it?' Yonah asked as they walked back to the armory.

'Perhaps one month after you came. It happened one day that I found in my possession a bottle of wine—'

'You found it in your possession?'

'I stole it from the tavern when Bernaldo was occupied. But surely I must have been prompted by angels to do so, because I carried the bottle away so I would not be disturbed when I drank. My feet were directed to that place.'

'What do you intend to do with this knowledge?'

'There are those who will pay dearly for the saintly relics. I would like you to bargain with them for me. Get the best price.'

'No, Vicente.'

'I shall pay you well, of course.'

'No, Vicente.'

Vicente's eyes gleamed shrewdly. 'This is why you shall find profit in the bargaining. Very well. You shall have half of all. A full half.'

'I am not bargaining with you. The men who buy and sell relics are vipers. Were I you, I should go to the church in Gibraltar village and lead the priest – what is his name?'

'Padre Vasquez.'

'Yes. I should lead Padre Vasquez here and let him determine if the remains are those of a saint.'

'No!' Vicente appeared febrile again, his face flushed with anger. 'God has directed my feet to the saint. God has reasoned, "Save for a weakness for strong drink, Vicente is not a bad fellow. I shall bring him good fortune, that he may end his days in a bit of comfort".'

'It is your decision, Vicente. But I shall have no part in it.'

221

'Then you must keep your mouth closed concerning what you have seen this morning.'

'I shall be pleased to forget about it.'

'For if you should think of selling the relics on your own, without Vicente, I would see that you would be sorely punished.'

Yonah looked at him in amazement that so soon he should have forgotten who had nursed him through his illness. 'Deal with the relics as you may, and be damned,' he said shortly, and they continued their way onto Gibraltar in a strained silence.

24

The Chosen

The following Sunday morning, Yonah took the gray Arabian horse from the stables in the gloom of dawn, departing the compound before the other workers had stirred. In the beginning he tried only to accustom himself to the act of being on the creature's back. It took him three weeks more to work up the courage to drop the reins. The *maestro* had told him it was not enough simply to retain his seat in the saddle; he must learn to give directions to the horse without the use of reins or bit. When he wanted the horse to gallop, a kick of his heels. A single pressure of both knees to direct the animal to stop. A series of quick pressures from the knees to cause the horse to walk backward.

To his delight he found that the horse had been well trained to obey these very instructions. Yonah practiced again and again, learning to float with the rise and fall of the gallop, to anticipate the quick stop, to retreat at a walk.

He felt like a squire in training to become a knight.

*

Yonah had been an apprentice through the late summer, the fall, and the winter. This far south, spring came early. On a day of sunshine and soft air, Manuel Fierro examined each piece of the Count Vasca armor and instructed Luis Planas to assemble it.

It stood in the courtyard next to a fine sword made by Paco Parmiento, and the sun turned the burnished metal into a blaze of glory. The *maestro* said he planned to send a party of men to deliver the armor to the nobleman in Tembleque, but it could not leave until other urgently needed work had been completed.

So the armory banged and clanked with the renewed energy of the metalworkers. Both the completing of projects and the coming of spring energized Fierro, and he announced that before the departure of the delivery party there would be another game.

On the next two Sunday mornings, Yonah rode out into a deserted field and practiced riding with the lance firmly held at the ready, its balled point steadily directed as the Arab horse galloped toward a bush that served as target.

On several different evenings Vicente came very late to the hut, where he dropped to his pallet and at once snored in a drunken stupor. In the chandlery shop Tadeo Deza spoke scornfully of his cousin Vicente. 'He grows drunk quickly and unpleasantly, rewarding with the wildest stories those who ply him with the cheapest drink.'

'What manner of wild stories?' Yonah asked.

'Claims to be one of God's chosen. Says he has found the bones of a saint. Says soon he will make a generous donation to Holy Mother Church, yet never has he money even to pay for his wine.'

'Ah, well,' Yonah said uncomfortably. 'He harms no one save perhaps himself.'

'I believe in the end my cousin Vicente will kill himself with strong drink,' Tadeo said.

Manuel Fierro asked Yonah if he would participate in the new game, again to face Angel Costa on horseback. Even as Yonah agreed, he wondered if perhaps the *maestro* wished to see if he had profited from being allowed to practice with the Arab horse.

So two days later, in the coolness of morning Paco Parmiento helped him into the battered test armor once again, while at the far end of the jousting pit Luis laughed as he played squire and groom, dressing Costa.

'Ah, Luis!' Costa cried, pointing at Yonah in mock alarm. 'See his size? Alas, he is a giant. Oh, woe! What shall we do?' And shook with laughter when Luis Planas placed his palms together and raised them to the sky as if praying for mercy.

Parmiento's usually placid face glowed with anger. 'They are scum,' he said.

Each of the contestants had help in mounting. Costa had done it before and seated his horse in a few moments. Yonah was clumsier; he found it hard to raise his leg to throw it across the gray Arabian and made a mental note to describe the difficulty to the *maestro*, although perhaps that was unnecessary, for Fierro watched as he stood with the workers, and usually he noted a great deal.

When they were mounted, the two combatants turned their horses to face each other. Yonah took care to appear nervous, clutching the reins in his left hand and holding

225

the lance loosely in his right, its balled point waggling to the side.

But when the *maestro* let his kerchief fall to start the game, Yonah dropped the reins and took a firm grip on the lance as the Arab horse lunged forward. He had become accustomed to riding at a target and it was unnerving to see the target hurtling toward him, but he kept the lance pointed at the oncoming horseman. His balled tip found the very center of Angel's breastplate. Costa's lance slid harmlessly off his shoulder and for one brief moment Yonah was certain he had won, but his lance bowed and snapped, and Costa kept his seat as they moved past one another at a gallop.

Both of them turned their horses at the end of the wall. The *maestro* showed no sign of declaring the tourney over, so Yonah threw away the stub of the broken lance and rode weaponless to meet Angel.

The tip of Costa's lance grew larger as they rode at one another, but when Costa was two hoofbeats away, Yonah pressed his knees into the gray Arab's sides, and the horse stopped at once.

The lance missed Yonah only by a span, close enough to allow him to grasp it and jerk hard, even as his knees were signaling the good horse to move backward. Angel Costa was pulled almost out of the saddle, retaining his seat only because he let go of the lance as his horse continued to move past. Yonah retained a tight grip on the captured lance as he rode away. Now when they turned to face each other it was he who was armed and Angel who was defenseless.

The cheers of the workers were welcome music to him, but his exultation was quenched when the *maestro* signaled an end to the tourney.

'You did well. Wonderfully well!' Paco said as he helped Yonah out of his armor. 'I think the *maestro* stopped it to save his champion from humiliation.'

Yonah looked across the pit to where Luis was disencumbering Angel. Costa was no longer laughing. Luis was protesting to the *maestro*, who stood and regarded him coolly.

'Oh, it is a bad day for our master-at-arms,' Paco said softly.

'Why? He was not unseated. The game ended with no winner.'

'It is why he is angry, Ramón Callicó. To a savage bastard such as Angel Costa, not to win is to lose. He will bear you no love for this day's work,' the sword maker said.

No one was in Yonah's hut when he returned. He was disappointed, because he hadn't seen Vicente among those who witnessed the tourney, and he wanted the enjoyment of talking about it in detail.

The wearing of armor and the tension of combat had drained him, and weariness pulled him into sleep as soon as he lay on his pallet. He didn't wake until morning. He was still alone, and it appeared to him that Vicente hadn't been there during the night.

Paco and Manuel Fierro were already at work when he reached the sword maker's shed.

'It was done well, yesterday,' the *maestro* said, and smiled at him.

'Thank you, señor,' Yonah said with pleasure.

He was put to work sharpening dirks. 'Have you seen Vicente?' he asked.

Both men shook their heads.

'He did not come to our hut to sleep.'

'He is a drinker, no doubt deep in a drunkard's sleep behind some bush or tree,' Paco said. He broke off, doubtless remembering that the old man was a favorite of Fierro's.

'I hope his illness has not returned, and that he has not met with some other misfortune,' Fierro said.

Yonah nodded, troubled.

'I would like to be informed when next you see him,' the *maestro* said, and Yonah and Paco said they would do so.

If Fierro had not run out of ink powder while working on the armory's accounts, Yonah would not have been in the village when Vicente was found. He was approaching the chandler's shop when a hue and cry was raised from the wharf below the main street.

'A drowned man! A drowned man!'

Yonah joined those running to the wharf and arrived to see them raising Vicente from the strait, water pouring from him.

His thin hair was plastered, revealing an old man's scalp and a gash on the side of his head. His eyes stared sightlessly.

'His face is so bruised,' Yonah said.

'No doubt he has been bumping against rocks and the wharves,' José Gripo said gently.

Tadeo Deza came from the chandlery to see what the noise was about. He sank to his knees next to the body and cradled Vicente's wet head against his chest. 'My cousin . . . my cousin . . .'

'Where shall we take him?' Yonah asked.

'Maestro Fierro liked him,' Gripo said. 'Perhaps he

will allow Vicente to be buried on the property behind the armory.'

Yonah walked with Gripo and Tadeo behind the body as Vicente was borne away. Tadeo was shaken. 'We were playmates as boys. We were inseparable friends . . . As a man he had faults but his heart was good.' Vicente's cousin, who had spoken so badly of him when he was alive, burst into tears.

Gripo had guessed correctly that in Fierro's kindness toward Vicente the *maestro* would agree to a final act of charity. Vicente was buried in a small grassy place behind the sword maker's shack. Workers were released from their duties long enough to gather together in the hot sun and see the body interred and hear the funeral blessings of Padre Vasquez. Then everyone returned to work.

Death cast its pall. The hut where Yonah slept was empty and silent with Vicente gone. For several nights Yonah slept fitfully, waking to lie in the dark and listen to the scratching of mice.

Everyone in the armory worked hard, seeking to finish whatever orders could be fulfilled before the delivery party would leave to bring Count Vasca's new sword and armor to Tembleque. It was why Manuel Fierro frowned when a boy came with a message that a kinsman of Ramón Callicó had arrived in Gibraltar and desired Señor Callicó to come to the tavern in the village.

'You must go, of course,' Fierro told Yonah, who was edging swords. 'But mind that you return at once after you have seen him.'

Yonah thanked him numbly and left. He walked toward the village with extra slowness, his mind in turmoil. The man who waited was not Uncle Aron, that was clear. Ramón Callicó was an invented name Yonah had pulled from his mind when a name was needed. Could it be that there *was* a Ramón Callicó somewhere nearby, and that Yonah Toledano was about to meet the man's kinsman?

Two men waited in front of the tavern with the boy who had brought the message. Yonah saw the boy point him out to the men and then accept a coin and scamper away.

As he walked up to them he noted that one was dressed like a gentleman, in a mail vest and clothing of quality. He had a small spade beard, carefully tended. The other man had a scraggly beard and rougher clothing, but he wore a sword, too. A pair of fine horses were tied to the tavern's postern gate.

'Señor Callicó?' the man with the spade beard said.

'Yes.'

'Let us walk a bit while we converse, for we are saddle weary.'

'What are your names, señores? And which of you is my kinsman?'

The man smiled. 'All men under God are as kinsmen, is it not so?'

Yonah watched them.

'I am Anselmo Lavera.'

Yonah remembered the name. Mingo had spoken of Lavera as the man who controlled the sale of stolen relics in southern Spain.

Lavera didn't introduce the other man, who remained silent. 'We were asked by Señor Vicente Deza to see you.'

'Vicente Deza is dead.'

230

'How unfortunate. An accident?'

'He drowned and was recently buried.'

'So unfortunate. He had told us you know the whereabouts of a certain cave.'

Yonah knew with certainty that they had killed Vicente. 'You seek one of the caves in the Gibraltar rock?' he said.

'It is not in the rock. We are certain from what Deza said that it is somewhere away from Gibraltar.'

'I don't know of such a cave, señor.'

'Ah, I understand, it is sometimes difficult to remember. But we shall encourage you to remember. And we shall handsomely reward your remembering.'

'If Vicente gave you my name, why did he not give you the directions you seek?'

'As I said, his death was unfortunate. He was being encouraged to remember, and the encouragement was clumsy and too enthusiastic.'

Yonah was chilled by the fact that Lavera could make such a terrible admission so calmly.

'I was not there, you understand. I would have been better at it. By the time Vicente was willing to give the directions, he was unable. But when he was encouraged to tell who else might help us, he uttered your name at once.'

'I shall enquire to see if anyone else has knowledge of a cave Vicente knew,' Yonah said.

The man with the short beard nodded. 'Did you have opportunity to see Vicente before he was buried?'

'Yes.'

'Poor drowned fellow. Was he badly used?'

'Yes.'

'Terrible. The sea has no pity.'

231

Anselmo Lavera looked at Yonah. 'We are needed elsewhere quickly, but we will pass here again in ten days. Think about rewards, and what poor Vicente would want you to do.'

Yonah was aware he would have to be far from Gibraltar when they returned. He knew if he didn't reveal the location of the saint's cave they would kill him, and if he did, they would kill him because he could bear witness against them.

It saddened him, because for the first time since leaving Toledo, he liked where he was and what he was doing. Fierro was a good and kind man, the sort of master who was extremely rare.

'We wish you to ponder, so you will remember what we must learn. Is it agreed, my friend?'

Lavera's voice had never been less than pleasant, but Yonah was recalling the wound in Vicente's head and the terrible condition of his face and his body.

'I shall do my best to remember, señor,' he said politely.

'Did you meet with your kinsman?' Fierro asked when Yonah returned.

'Yes, *maestro*. A distant relative on my mother's side.'

'Family is important. It is good he came at this moment, for in a few days you will be gone from here.' He said he had decided to send Paco Parmiento, Luis Planas, Angel Costa, and Ramón Callicó to deliver Count Vasca's armor. 'Paco and Luis can use their skills to make any adjustment in the armor that may be needed after it is delivered. Angel will serve as commander of your little caravan.'

Fierro said he wanted Ramón Callicó to make the presentation of the armor to the count, 'because you

232

speak a purer Spanish than the others, and because you can read and write. I wish written confirmation of the receipt of the armor by the count of Tembleque. Is it understood?'

Yonah took an extra moment to answer, because he was saying a prayer of thanks.

'Yes, señor, it is understood,' he said.

Despite Yonah's relief at being far from Gibraltar when Anselmo Lavera would return, he was made apprehensive by the thought of returning to the Toledo district. Yet he told himself he had left Toledo as a boy and was returning as a large man, his features altered by growth, maturity and a broken nose, his beard full and his hair long, and his identity changed and established.

Fierro brought the four members of the party together and spoke plainly when he gave them his instructions. 'It is dangerous to travel to strange places, and I order you to work in concert and not in opposition to one another. Angel is the leader on the journey, in charge of defense and responsible to me for the safety of each of you. Luis and Paco are responsible for the condition of the armor and the sword. Ramón Callicó will turn over the armor to Count Vasca, make certain he is content with it before you depart from him, and receive and bring back a written receipt of delivery.'

One by one, he asked each of them if all of his instructions were understood, and each answered in the affirmative.

Fierro oversaw their careful preparations for the trip. For food they would take only a few sacks of dried peas and hard biscuit. 'Angel must hunt along the way to give you fresh meat,' the *maestro* said.

233

Each of the four men in the party was assigned a horse. Count Vasca's armor would be transported by four pack mules. So that Fierro would not be shamed by the appearance of his workers they were given new clothing, along with stern instructions that it should not be worn until they were approaching Tembleque. All four were issued swords, and Costa and Yonah were given vests of mail. Costa strapped large, rusty spurs to his boots and packed a longbow and several bundles of arrows.

Paco smiled. 'Angel wears the permanent scowl that marks him as a leader of men,' he whispered to Yonah, who was grateful that Paco would be on the trail with him as well as the other two.

When all was ready the four travelers led their beasts up the gangway of the first coastal ship to put into Gibraltar, which to Yonah's surprise turned out to be *La Lleona*. The ship's *maestro* greeted each passenger with a warm word.

'*Hola!* It is you,' the captain said to Yonah. Although he had never spoken to Yonah once while he was a member of the crew, the captain bowed to him now and smiled. 'You are welcome back to the *Lleona*, señor.' Paco, Angel, and Luis watched with surprise as other members of the crew greeted him.

The animals were tethered to the rails on the after-deck, and as the apprentice it was Yonah's chore to carry up hay from the hold each day and feed them.

Two days out of Gibraltar the sea turned choppy, and Luis became queasy and then vomited often. Angel and Paco were unperturbed by the ship's motion and to Yonah's surprise and pleasure, so was he. When the

234

mate called out an order to furl sail, on impulse he ran to the rope ladder at the mainmast and climbed, and soon he was helping the sailors haul in the sail and make it fast. When he reached deck again the crewman named Josep, whose injury had given Yonah opportunity to join the deck crew, grinned at him and slapped his back. Thinking about it, after the fact, Yonah realized that if he had fallen into the sea the mail vest would have helped carry him deep, and for the rest of the trip he remembered he was a passenger.

For the four passengers from Gibraltar, the days under sail were filled with tedium. Early on the morning of the third day, Angel unpacked his longbow and a bundle of arrows and prepared to shoot birds.

The others settled down to watch. 'Angel is as good with the bow as a damned Inglés,' Paco said to Yonah. 'He came from a little village in Andalusia known for its fine bowmen, and he went to his first fighting as an archer in militia.'

But Gaspar Gatuelles, the mate, hurried over to Costa. 'What are you doing, señor?'

'I shall kill a few seabirds,' Angel said easily, notching an arrow.

The mate was aghast. 'No, señor. No, you shall kill no seabirds on the *Lleona*, for to do so would bring certain disaster upon the ship and upon us.'

Costa scowled at Gatuelles, but Paco hurried over and placated him. 'Soon we shall be on land, Angel, and you will have plenty of hunting. Your skill will be needed to keep us in meat.' To the general relief, Costa unstrung the bow and put it away.

The passengers sat together and watched the sea and the sky. 'Tell us of war, Angel,' Luis said. Costa was still glowering and sulky, but Luis urged until he agreed. At first the other three men listened avidly to his memories of soldiering, for none had been to war. But soon they tired of tales of bloodshed and butchery, of villages put to the torch, of cattle slaughtered and women forced. They had had enough long before Angel finished talking.

The four passengers were aboard nine days. The sameness of their days wore on them and sometimes tempers shortened and frayed. By unspoken agreement each man began to keep to himself for long hours at a time. Yonah kept turning a problem over and over in his mind. If he should return to Gibraltar, he was certain Anselmo Lavera would kill him. Yet Costa's confrontation with Gaspar Gatuelles had caused him to begin to see his problem in a new way. Angel's authority had been overcome by the greater shipboard authority of the mate. One force had been held in check by a greater force.

Yonah told himself that he needed to find some greater force than Anselmo Lavera, a strength that could eradicate the threat of the relic thief. At first this seemed preposterous, but as he sat and watched the sea hour after hour, slowly a plan began to take shape in his mind.

Whenever the ship made port and was tied to a dock, the four men brought their animals down the gangway and exercised them, and when finally *La Lleona* nosed into the harbor at Valencia, the horses and pack mules were in good health.

Yonah had heard terrible stories of the Valencia harbor during the days of the expulsion. How the harbor had been crowded with ships, some of them in great disrepair and outfitted with sail solely to reap the bonanza of fares from the dislocated. How men, women, and children had been crammed into each hold. How, when sickness broke out, stricken passengers had been marooned on uninhabited islands and left to die. How, as soon as they were out of sight of land, some crews had killed passengers and dumped their bodies into the sea.

Yet on the day Angel led the procession from *La Lleona*, the sun was shining and the Valencia harbor was peaceful and quiet.

Yonah knew that his aunt and uncle and small brother would have come to a small seaside town nearby, seeking passage. Perhaps they had set sail and were now on foreign soil. He knew in his heart he would never see them again, yet each time he rode past a boy of the proper age, he stared, searching for Eleazar's familiar features. His brother would have thirteen years by now. If he was alive and still a Jew, he would be counted among the men of the minyan.

But Yonah saw only strange faces.

They rode westward, leaving Valencia behind. None of the horses could compare with the Arab stallion Yonah had ridden in the tourneys. His mount was a large dun mare with flat ears and a thin tail drooping between huge equine buttocks. The mare didn't make him a dashing figure but she was tireless and an easy ride, for which Yonah was grateful.

Angel rode first, followed by Paco leading two of the mules and Luis leading the other two. Yonah rode at rear guard, which suited him perfectly. Each of them developed his own trail style. Angel burst into tuneless sound from time to time, as apt to sing a sacred hymn as a bawdy tune. Paco joined in any hymns with a booming bass voice. Luis dozed in the saddle, while Yonah passed the time thinking of many things. Sometimes he dwelt on what must be done to carry out his plan against Anselmo Lavera. Somewhere near Toledo there were men who dealt in stolen relics, competing with Lavera for that illicit trade. He clung to the thought that if he could convince them to eliminate Lavera, he would be safe.

Often he passed the hours trying to remember Hebrew passages he had forgotten, the rich language that had fled his mind, the words and the melodies that had abandoned him after a few short years.

He was able to recapture some small remnant, and he repeated those fragments in imperfect silence, again and again. He could recall one short tractate of Genesis xxii in pristine perfection, since it was the passage he had chanted when he was first permitted to read from the Torah as a newly made man. 'And they came to the place which God had told him of; and Abraham built the altar there, and bound Isaac his son, and laid him on the altar, upon the wood. And Abraham stretched forth his hand, and took the knife to slay his son.' The passage had frightened him then and it frightened him now. How could Abraham have ordered his son to cut wood for a burnt offering and then prepare to kill Isaac and burn his body? Why had Abraham not questioned God, even argued with him? Abba would not have sacrificed a son; Abba had sacrificed himself in order that his son could live.

But Yonah was chilled by another thought. If God was a righteous God, why was he sacrificing the Jews of Iberia?

He knew what his father and Rabbi Ortega would say to such a question. They would say that man could not question God's motives because man could not see God's larger design. But when the design included human beings used as burnt offerings, Yonah questioned God. It was not for such a God that he forced himself to play the dangerous game of being Ramón Callicó, day after day. It was for Abba and the others, for the good things he had learned in Torah, visions of a merciful and comforting God, a God that forced people to wander into exile but delivered them finally into land that had been promised.

If he closed his eyes he was able to imagine himself part of the caravan in the wilderness, one of a host of Jews, a multitude of Jews. Seeing them pause in the desert each evening to erect the tents of the host, hearing them praying together before the sanctuary of the ark and the sacred testimony . . .

Yonah's reveries were interrupted when lengthening shadows told Angel it was time to halt. They tethered the eight animals under some trees and the four men took time to piss and fart and walk off their saddle stiffness. Then they searched for wood and built a fire, and as their evening gruel began to bubble, Angel dropped to his knees and ordered them to do likewise so they might recite the Paternoster and the Ave María.

Yonah was the last to comply. Before the fierce glare of the master-at-arms he knelt in the dust and added his mumbling to the tired, murmured words of Paco and Luis and the loud, brusque prayers of Angel Costa.

In the morning Costa was out at first light with his bow. By the time they had packed the mules he was back with

239

four doves and two partridge that they plucked as they rode slowly, leaving a trail of feathers before they stopped to gut the birds and roast them over a fire on green sticks.

Costa hunted every morning all along the route, sometimes bringing a hare or two with a variety of birdlife, so they never lacked food. They traveled constantly and when they stopped were careful to avoid rancor, as Fierro had ordered them to do.

They were eleven days in the saddle before, one evening as they made camp, they glimpsed from afar the walls of Tembleque, fading into the night. Next morning while it was still dark, Yonah left the fireside and bathed in a tiny stream before dressing in the new garments Fierro had given them, thinking grimly that no maiden ever protected her genitals from sight with more care than he. When the others awoke, they chaffed him for his eagerness to don finery.

He remembered riding to this castle with his father.

Now when they rode to the gate, Angel answered the sentry's loud challenge with equally loud and confident tones.

'We are artisans of the Gibraltar armory of Manuel Fierro, arrived with the new sword and armor of Count Fernán Vasca.'

When they were given entry, Yonah saw that the steward was not the same man who had been there years before, but the message he gave had a familiar ring.

'Count Vasca is off hunting in the forests of the north.'

'When will he be seen here again?' Angel asked.

'The count returns when he returns,' the man said sourly. When he saw what was in Angel's eyes, he glanced quickly to the reassurance of his own armed soldiers on the wall. 'I do not believe he will tarry many days,' he said grudgingly.

Costa withdrew to confer with the men from Gibraltar. 'They now know that our mules carry precious goods. If we leave here with the sword and armor we may be fallen on and killed by these or other whoresons in number, and the armor and sword stolen.' The others agreed, and Yonah went to the steward.

'We have orders that if the Count Vasca should not be here at our arrival, we must leave the sword and armor in his treasury and receive written receipt attesting to its safe delivery,' he said.

The steward frowned, not happy to take orders from strangers.

'I am certain the count has been waiting impatiently for the armor made by Maestro Fierro,' Yonah said. He did not have to add, If it should be lost on your account . . .

The steward led them into a stronghold, unlocked ponderous doors whose hinges cried out for oil, showed them where to place the armor, where to place the sword. Yonah wrote out the writ of receipt but the steward was barely literate, and it took a long time to help him read the note. Paco and Luis stared, impressed, and Angel looked away. 'Hurry on, hurry on,' he muttered, resenting Yonah's ability.

Finally the steward scrawled his mark.

The men from Gibraltar found an inn nearby, their spirits lightened by the fact that their responsibility had been turned over to the castle of Tembleque. 'God's thanks, we brought it here safely,' Paco said, and the relief in his voice spoke for all of them.

'Now I want sleep in comfort,' Luis said.

'Now I want drink!' Costa declared, slamming his hand to the table, where they fell to drinking a bitter, biting wine served by a short and heavy woman with tired eyes. While she filled their cups Angel brushed the back of his hand on the stained apron covering her full thighs and rear, and when there was no objection his hand became bolder.

'Ah, you're comely,' he said, and she made herself smile. She was accustomed to men who came to the inn after long weeks of travel without women. In a short time she and Angel removed themselves from the other men and held a consultation nearby, feverish bargaining followed by a nod.

Before Angel left with her, he returned to the other three men. 'So we must meet here at the inn in three days to determine whether the count has returned,' he said, and then hurried back to the woman.

25
The City of Toledo

Paco and Luis were content to take pallets at the inn and attempt to sleep away the tiredness of a long journey. So it happened that Yonah ben Helkias Toledano, of late called Ramón Callicó, found himself riding alone through the late morning sunlight, as though in a dream. Down the road between Tembleque and Toledo. Remembering and singing as his father had sung.

> 'Oh, the wolf shall dwell with the lamb,
> And the leopard shall lie with the kid,
> And the cow and the bear shall feed,
> While the lion eats straw like the ox . . .'

When he approached Toledo, each new glimpse was a gladness and a pain. Here was where sometimes he had walked from the city with other youths to have grave, grown-up discussions – of Talmud lessons, and of the true nature and variety of the sexual act, and of what they would be when they were men, and of the reasons for the various shapes of female breasts.

There was the rock where, only two days before he was murdered, his brother Meir, may his soul rest in peace, had sat with Yonah and taken turns playing his Moorish guitar.

There was the path to the house where once lived Bernardo Espina, former physician of Toledo, may God also grant perfect rest to his Catholic soul.

There was the path to the place where Meir was killed.

Here was where Yonah had sometimes tended the flock of his uncle Aron the cheese maker. There was the farmhouse where Aron and Juana had lived, with unfamiliar children now playing by the door.

Yonah clattered across the Rio Tagus as sunlight glinted hard on the water, hurting his eyes, the mare's hooves exploding through the bright, clear shallows, wetting his legs.

Then he was riding up the cliff trail to the height, the trail that Moise the burro had descended so surely in the dark of night, and which now the poor mare climbed clumsily and nervously in full daylight.

At the top, nothing had changed.

My God, he thought, *You have scattered and destroyed us and You have left this place exactly the same as it was.*

He rode slowly down the narrow way that ran near the cliff. The houses matched his memories of them. The old neighbor, Marcelo Troca, was still alive, there he was, grubbing in his garden while near him another burro was listlessly eating his garbage.

The Toledano house was still standing. There was a stench in the air; the closer Yonah came, the stronger was the stench. The house had been repaired. Only . . . if you knew where to look and then searched very carefully, it was still possible to see the faint signs of a past fire.

Yonah stopped the horse and dismounted.

The house was occupied. A man of middle years came through the door and was startled to see him standing there holding the horse's reins.

'*Buenos días*, señor. Is there a thing you wish of me?'

'No, señor, but I feel a dizziness, a touch of the sun. Will you permit me to go to the shade behind your house and rest for a moment?'

The man studied him uneasily, noting the horse, the mail vest, Mingo's knife, the sword hanging from his left side, the bearded stranger's hard edge. 'You may seek out our shade,' he said reluctantly. 'I have cool water. I will bring you drink.'

Behind the house, things were the same and yet vastly different. Yonah went at once to the secret place, searching for the loose stone behind which he had left the message for his brother Eleazar. There was no longer a loose stone. The place had been tightly plastered.

The odor came from behind what had been his father's workshop. There were hides and animal skins, some soaking in vats before they could be scraped, others drying in the air. He tried to identify the exact spot where his father was buried and saw that an oak tree grew from it, already almost as tall as Yonah.

The householder returned with a wooden cup and Yonah drained it of water despite the fact that it was as if he took in the heavy smell when he swallowed.

'You are a tanner, I see.'

'I bind books and make my own leathers,' the man said, watching him closely.

'May I sit for another moment?'

'As you wish, señor.' But the man remained, watchful – lest Yonah should purloin a wet and stinking skin? More likely he was fearful for valuable books in the workshop, or perhaps he had gold. Yonah closed his eyes and recited the Kaddish. Despairing, he knew he would never remove his father's body from this stinking and unmarked place.

I shall never stop being a Jew. I swear it, Abba.

When he opened his eyes, the bookbinder still stood there. Yonah saw that when he had gone inside for the water he had placed a tool in his belt, a wicked hooked knife doubtless meant to trim leather. Yonah had no quarrel with the man. Clambering to his feet, he thanked the bookbinder for his kindness. Then he returned to his horse and rode away from the house where once he had lived.

The synagogue looked much the same but now it was a church with a tall wooden cross rising from the peak of the roof.

The Jewish cemetery was gone. All the stone memorial markers had been taken away. In several areas of Spain he had seen gravestones with Hebrew inscriptions used to build walls and roadways. The cemetery had been transformed into a grazing meadow. Without markers, he knew only the approximate area of his family graves, and he went there, aware that he made a strange picture as he stood among the sheep and goats and said the prayer for the dead.

Riding toward the center of the city he came to the communal ovens, where a group of women were hectoring the baker for burning their bread. Yonah knew the ovens well. Once, they had been kosher. As a boy, each Friday he had brought the family bread there for baking. In those days the ovens were run by a Jew named Vidal, but now the baker was a hapless fat man with no means of defense.

'You are a lazy, dirty man, and a fool,' one of the women said. She was young and comely, if somewhat fleshly. As Yonah watched, she took one of the ruined breads from her basket and shook it under the baker's nose, insulting him with a vengeance. 'You think I come here to see my good bread turned into dog shit? You should be made to eat it, dumb ox!'

As she turned, Yonah saw that she was Lucía Martín, whom he had loved as a boy.

Her glance slid over him, and past, and then back to him again. But she didn't pause in her departure, trudging away with her basket of burned bread.

He rode slowly down the narrow street, not wishing to overtake her. But he had ridden scarcely beyond the houses and prying eyes when she stepped from behind a tree where she had been waiting.

'Truly, is it you?' she said.

She walked to the horse and gazed up at him.

What he must do, he knew, was deny that he knew her, smile over a mistaken identity, bid her a polite farewell, and ride away. But he dismounted.

'How has it been for you, Lucía?'

She seized his hand, her eyes widening in a kind of triumph. 'Oh, Yonah. It is beyond belief that it is *you*. Where did you vanish, and why, when you might have been my father's son? Brother to me?'

This was the first female he had seen naked. She had

been a sweet girl, he remembered, and the memory made his body stir. 'I had no wish to be your brother.'

She had been married these three years, she told him quickly, retaining a fierce grip on his hand. 'To Tomás Cabrerizo whose family owns vineyards across the river. Do you not recall Tomás Cabrerizo?'

Yonah had the vaguest memory of a sullen, rock-throwing youth who had taunted Jews.

'I have two little daughters and am with child yet again. I pray to the Blessed Mother for a son,' she said. She looked at him with wonder, noting his horse, his clothing and arms. 'Yonah. *Yonah!* Yonah, where did you go, how do you live?'

'Best you do not ask,' he said gently, and changed the subject. 'Your father is well?'

'My father is gone these two years. He was full of health, then one morning he was dead.'

'Ah. May he rest,' Yonah said with regret. Benito Martín had ever shown him kindness.

'May his soul rest with the Savior,' she said, crossing herself. Her brother Enrique had entered the order of Dominicans, she told him with evident pride.

'And your mother?'

'My mother lives on. Never go to her, Yonah. She would denounce you.'

Her piety had made him fearful. 'And you shall not denounce me?'

'Never then nor now!' Her eyes filled, but she stared at him angrily.

He succumbed to the need to flee. 'Go with the Lord, Lucía.'

'With the Lord, my childhood friend.'

He freed his hand but could not resist turning back to

a final question. 'My brother Eleazar. Have you ever seen him here again?'

'Never.'

'You have never received a word as to his whereabouts or fate?'

She shook her head. 'No word of Eleazar. No word of any of them. You are the only Jew to return here, Yonah Toledano.'

He knew what he must do now, and whom he must find, if he was to save himself from Lavera.

He rode slowly through the central part of the city. The wall about the Jewish Quarter still stood but the gates were opened wide, and Christians lived in all the houses. The cathedral of Toledo loomed over everything.

So many people.

Surely someone here in the Plaza Mayor behind the cathedral might recognize him as Lucía had done. Thinking of her, he realized that already she might have betrayed him. By now, the cruel fingers of the Inquisition might be reaching for him as a man reaches to snare a fly. There were soldiers in the plaza, and members of the guard. Yonah forced himself to ride by them slowly, but no one gave him more than a passing glance.

He promised a coin to a gap-toothed boy if he would watch the mare.

The entrance he took into the cathedral was called the Door of Joy. As a boy he had wondered whether it fulfilled the promise of its name, but now he felt no rapture. In front of him, a ragged man dipped his hand into a font and genuflected. Yonah waited until no one was in sight and then slipped into the cathedral.

The space was vast, with a high, vaulted ceiling

supported by the stone columns that divided the floor into five separate aisles. The interior looked almost empty because it was so large, but there were a lot of people scattered through the cathedral and many black-robed clerics, and the merged sound of their prayers echoed as it rose to the heights. Yonah wondered whether all the combined voices lifted to God in cathedrals and churches throughout Spain drowned out his own frightened voice when he spoke to God.

It took him a long time to make his way through the main body of the cathedral, but he didn't see the person he was seeking.

When he emerged, blinking in the bright light, he gave the boy the promised coin and asked if he knew a friar named Bonestruca.

The boy's smile disappeared. 'Yes.'

'Where might I find him?'

The boy shrugged. 'Lots of them at the Dominican house.' Grimy fingers closed upon the coin, and he ran as if pursued.

At a rude drinking place – three boards set upon casks – Yonah sat and sipped sour wine, watching the house of the Dominican order, across the way. Eventually a friar left the house and, after a long time, a pair of fiercely arguing priests.

When Fray Lorenzo de Bonestruca appeared, he was approaching the house instead of leaving it. Yonah saw the tall figure coming from far down the street yet knew him at once.

He entered the order house and remained long enough so Yonah had to ask the proprietor to add wine to his cup, which he left gladly after the friar emerged from the house and walked down the street. Yonah followed slowly on the horse, keeping Bonestruca in view but staying well behind.

Bonestruca finally turned into the doorway of a small *taberna*, a workingman's place. By the time Yonah tethered the mare and entered the dark little cellar, the friar had seated himself in the rear and already was in the midst of an argument with the proprietor.

'Perhaps you may pay a small amount toward the debt?'

'How dare you? You miserable little bastard!'

The proprietor was more than cowed, Yonah saw. He was in terror, unable to look at the inquisitor.

'I beg you, Friar, take no offense,' the man said desperately, 'your wine will be served, of course. I meant no impertinence.'

'You are a dung worm.'

Bonestruca had put on flesh, yet his features were as beautiful as Yonah remembered: an aristocratic brow, high cheekbones, a long, thin nose, a wide, full-lipped mouth over a firm and chiseled jaw. The face was betrayed by the eyes, large and gray, full of chilly dislike for the world.

The proprietor had scurried away, returning with a cup he set down in front of Bonestruca before turning to Yonah.

'A cup of wine for myself. And another cup for the good friar.'

'Yes, señor.'

Bonestruca's stony eyes made Yonah their object. 'Jesus bless you,' he muttered, paying for the drink with the benison.

'Thank you. May I have your permission to join

251

you?' he asked, and Bonestruca nodded indifferently.

Yonah went and sat at the table of the man who had caused the deaths of his father and his brother and Bernardo Espina, and doubtless many more.

'I am Ramón Callicó.'

The friar obviously had a thirst. He emptied his cup of wine quickly, and the one Yonah had bought, and nodded when Yonah ordered two more. 'Bowls, this time, señor!

'I have had the pleasure of praying in the cathedral, of which Toledo must be very proud,' Yonah ventured, and Bonestruca nodded with the reluctance of one who resents it when uninvited words interrupt his privacy.

The bowls were served.

'What is the nature of the work being done on the cathedral structure?'

Bonestruca shrugged wearily. 'I know something is being done to the doors.'

'Do you do the Lord's work on the cathedral staff, good Friar?'

'No. I do the Lord's work elsewhere,' the friar said, and drank so deeply that Yonah was forced to wonder whether the coins in his purse would be equal to this man's thirst. Yet it was money well spent, for even as he watched, the friar became more voluble, his eyes took on new life, and his body relaxed like a flower unfolding after a rain.

'And have you served God long, señor?'

'Since I was a boy.'

His tongue warmed and loosened, the friar began to talk about hereditary grace. He told Yonah matter-of-factly that he was the second son of an aristocratic family in Madrid. 'Bonestruca is a Catalan name. Many generations ago, my family came to Madrid from Barcelona. My heritage is very old, no pig's blood in us, understand, *limpieza de sangre*, purest of bloodlines.' He had been sent to the Dominicans when he was twelve. 'Fortunate for me I was not sent to the Franciscans, whom I now cannot abide. My sainted mother had a brother who was with the Franciscans in Barcelona, but my father had Dominican friars among his kin.' The penetrating gray eyes Yonah remembered were locked onto his face. Now it was Yonah who felt terror, certain that Bonestruca could see his secrets and transgressions.

'And what of you? From where do you come?'

'I come from the South. I am apprenticed to Manuel Fierro, the armorer of Gibraltar.'

'Gibraltar! By the passion, you come a distance, armor maker.' He leaned forward. 'Have you then carried here the armor so eagerly awaited these four years by a fine nobleman hereabouts? And shall I guess his name?'

Yonah didn't confirm that the friar had guessed correctly, but sent his message by not denying it, choosing to sip his wine and smile. 'I am here with a party of men,' he said politely.

Bonestruca shrugged and brought a long finger to touch his nose mockingly, amused by Yonah's reticence.

It was time, Yonah told himself, to shoot an arrow into the air and see where it would fall. 'I am seeking to find a churchly man willing to give me counsel.'

The friar appeared bored. He remained stolidly silent, evidently mistaking the overture as a prelude to another of the everyday confessions of conscience that some clerics pounce on while other clerics come to view as a plague.

'If a person were to discover . . . that is, something of

253

great sacred worth . . . Well, where should he bring such a thing? In order to . . . to see that it will receive its proper importance and place in the world?'

The gray eyes were wide awake and looking straight at him. 'A relic?'

'Well. Yes. A relic,' Yonah said cautiously.

'I suppose it is not a portion of the true Cross?' the friar said, mocking him.

'No.'

'Well, then, why should it interest anyone?' Bonestruca said – a little joke – and for the first time gave a small, chill smile.

Yonah smiled back and glanced away. 'Señor,' he called, and ordered two more bowls of wine.

'Let me suppose it is the bone of someone you believe was holy,' the friar said. 'So let me tell you that if it is the bone of a hand, almost certainly it is the hand bone of some poor murdered whoreson, a sinner who was perhaps a coachman or a pig farmer. And if it is the bone of a foot, likely it is the foot bone of some departed blackguard, a whoremaster who was in no way a Christian martyr.'

'That is possible, good Friar,' Yonah said humbly.

Bonestruca snorted. 'More than possible. Likely.'

The new bowls came and Bonestruca continued to drink. He was the sort of drinker that remained sober and dangerous, showing little effect from the wine. Yet it must dull his reactions, Yonah thought; it would be easier to kill him now, this murdering friar. But Yonah was thinking clearly, and he knew that Bonestruca must live if he himself were to return to Gibraltar without meeting his death there.

He told the proprietor to give him an accounting.

254

After they settled the debt, the man served a gift dish of bread and olives in oil, and Yonah remarked on the kindness to the friar.

Bonestruca still smoldered at the host. 'He is a backsliding Christian who shall taste justice,' he muttered. 'He is a swine of a monstrous Jew.'

Yonah carried the terrible weight of those words as he walked the mare through the sleeping streets.

26
Bombardes

Count Vasca kept the men from Gibraltar waiting four more days.

Yonah used the time searching for the widow of Bernardo Espina, hoping to find a way to deliver Espina's breviary to his son, as he had promised the physician before the auto de fé that had taken his life.

But the search ended in frustration.

'Estrella de Aranda did come back here with her children,' one of the women in the neighborhood of Espina's former home told Yonah when he inquired. 'After her husband was burned for heresy none of her kinsmen would keep her. We gave them shelter for a little time. Then she went to the Convento de la Santa Cruz to be a nun, and we heard she died there soon after. Mother Church swallowed her children, Marta and Domitila to become nuns also, and Francisco to become a monk. I don't know where they have gone,' she said.

Yonah worried that Bonestruca had had too much wine to recall what he had told the friar about his knowledge of a valuable relic. He was certain Bonestruca was part of a network that bought and stole sacred objects for lucrative sale abroad. The friar knew that Yonah was waiting to deliver armor to the count of Tembleque, and if he had taken the lure, someone should be approaching Yonah about the details.

Yet several days passed without event.

When finally the count returned from hunting he proved to be a man large enough to fill the huge suit of armor. His beard, mustache and hair were the color of ginger and there was a large bald spot in the middle of his scalp. He had the coldly imperious eyes of one born and raised to the knowledge that all the men in his world were inferior beings created to serve him.

The Gibraltar men helped dress him in the armor and then watched as he shambled about the courtyard holding the sword. When he was freed from the steel suit he was plainly delighted with the things they had brought, but he complained of a lack of room in the right shoulder. A forge was set up at once in the courtyard, and Luis and Paco went to work with a will and two hammers.

Soon after the adjustment had been made in the shoulder piece, Count Fernán Vasca sent his steward to summon Ramón Callicó to his presence.

'Has he made his mark on the receipt?' Yonah asked.

'It awaits you,' the steward said, and Yonah followed him back to the count's chambers, passing through a number of rooms. As they walked Yonah found himself trying to glimpse some of the silver objects his father had made for the count, but he saw none. The castle of Tembleque was large.

He wondered why he was summoned. He didn't

need to collect money; payment for the sword and the armor would be made through Valencia merchants who traded in Gibraltar. Yonah hoped Fierro would be more successful collecting payment from the count than his own father had been.

The steward stopped by an oaken door and knocked. 'Excellency. The man Callicó is here.'

'Send him in.'

It was a long and gloomy room. Although the day wasn't cold there was a small fire in the hearth, and three hounds lay stretched on the rush-strewn floor. Two of the animals regarded the newcomer with cold eyes and the third sprang to his feet and came at Yonah with a low growl, slinking away at the very last moment when called off by his owner.

'My lord,' Yonah said.

Vasco nodded, and passed the marked receipt to him. 'I am greatly taken with the armor. You may so inform your *maestro* Fierro.'

'My master will be happy to hear of your pleasure, lord.'

'No doubt. It is good to receive pleasant tidings. For example, I am told you have made the discovery of a holy relic.'

Ah. So this is where the arrow I shot at Fray Bonestruca has landed, Yonah thought with a chill.

'It is true,' he said cautiously.

'What is the nature of the relic?'

Yonah looked at the count.

'Come, come,' Vasca said with harsh impatience. 'Is it a bone?'

'It is many bones. It is a skeleton.'

'Whose?'

258

'A saint's. Not a saint well known. A local saint of the Gibraltar region.'

'You believe it is the skeleton of Santo Peregrino el Compasivo?'

Yonah looked at the count with new respect. 'Yes. You know the legend?'

'I know all the legends about relics,' Vasca said. 'Why do you think it is the Pilgrim Saint?'

So Yonah told him about Vicente, and how Vicente had brought him to the cave in the low rocks. He described everything he had seen in the cave, and the count listened to him carefully.

'Why did you approach Fray Bonestruca?'

'I thought he might know someone who . . . would be interested.'

'Why should you think that?'

'We were drinking together. I thought it more sensible to ask a friar who is a drinker than to approach some disapproving priest.'

'The truth is, then, that you were looking for a dealer in relics and the like, and not simply a churchman.'

'Yes.'

'Because you have a fat price for your information?'

'I have a price. It is a high price to me, but perhaps not to others.'

Count Vasca leaned forward. 'But why have you come all this way from Gibraltar to seek a dealer? Is there no dealer in relics in southern Spain?'

'There is Anselmo Lavera.' *As you well know*, Yonah thought.

He told the count of Vicente's murder, and of his own visit from Lavera. 'I know if I don't bring Lavera and his men to the cave, I shall be killed. Yet, if I do

259

bring them, I shall be killed. My instinct is to run, yet I greatly desire to return to Gibraltar and work for Maestro Fierro.'

'So, what price do you ask for your information?'

'My life.'

Vasca nodded. If he was amused it was not evident. 'That is an acceptable price,' he said.

He gave Yonah a quill and ink and paper. 'Draw a map showing how to find the saint's cave.'

Yonah composed the map as carefully and truly as he was able, placing in it whatever landmarks he could remember. 'The cave is in a barren of sand and stone, completely invisible from the trail. There is nothing there but low rocks, with a few stunted bushes and dwarfed trees.'

Vasca nodded. 'Make a copy of this map and take it back to Gibraltar with you. When Anselmo Lavera comes to you again, tell him you are unable to bring him to the cave, but give him the map. I repeat. *Do not go to the cave with him*. Do you understand?'

'Yes. I understand,' Yonah said.

He didn't see the nobleman again. The sour steward dispensed gifts of ten *maravedíes* to each of the armorers in the name of Count Vasca.

According to Fierro's instructions, Angel Costa sold the burros in Toledo, and the four men rode back to the coast unencumbered by pack animals.

In Valencia, while waiting to board a boat, the men used part of their gift money on strong drink. Yonah felt an urge to join them, but he was still taut with the menace of the past, and he entered their roistering but drank carefully and watchfully.

They had just arrived in a tavern when Luis jostled a fat man who was leaving, and then chose to become insulted. 'You clumsy cow!' Luis said. The man looked at him in astonishment. 'What is the problem, señor?' he said. He spoke with the accent of a Frank. The amusement in his eyes turned to wariness when Angel moved up, his hand on his sword.

The Frank was unarmed. 'I am sorry for my clumsiness,' he said coldly, and left the tavern.

Yonah could scarcely bear the pride in Luis's face and the satisfaction in Angel's.

'And if he returns armed, and with friends?'

'Then we will fight. Are you afraid to fight, Callicó?' Angel said.

'I will never injure or kill only because you and Luis seek a bit of amusement.'

'I think you are afraid. I think that you can stomach a game but not a man's real fight.'

But Paco came and stood between them. 'We have managed to do the *maestro*'s work without trouble,' he said. 'I do not intend to try to explain injury or death to Fierro.' He signaled the proprietor for drink to be served.

They drank late into the night and in the morning boarded a packet that sailed with the early tide. During the voyage the four men met morning and evening in prayer meetings on which Angel insisted. At other times Luis and Angel kept to themselves and when Yonah wanted conversation he sought out Paco. Most of the time he kept to himself. He was moody and sad. He felt he had made a pact with the Devil, conspiring with the men who almost certainly had brought terrible deaths to his father and his brother. Yet he was strangely happy to

261

disembark at Gibraltar. It was good to return to a place where his arrival was expected.

There was not a long rest period after the travelers reached Gibraltar. While they had been gone, several orders for both armor and swords had come in from members of the royal court. Yonah was assigned to work in Paco's shed, helping to rough out a breastplate destined for the duke of Carmona. All over the armory there was a clamor, the beat of hammers on heated steel.

Despite the new orders Fierro himself continued to work on the medical instruments he was making for his brother, Nuño Fierro, physician of Saragossa. They were sleekly beautiful, each polished like a jewel and sharpened like a sword.

When work was done at the end of the day Yonah used the glowing fire and the waning light to work on a project of his own. He had taken the steel blade of his first weapon, the broken hoe, and heated it and shaped it. Without a plan or real intent – almost without his volition – his pounding hammer had fashioned a small chalice.

He worked with steel instead of silver and gold, and the small cup wasn't finely fashioned, yet it was a replica of the reliquary his father had made for the Priory of the Annunciation. When Yonah was finished he had a strange little cup, etched crudely with only the principal figures that adorned the reliquary. But it would serve to keep him remembering, and serve also as a kiddush cup to help him celebrate the Sabbath by thanking the Creator for the fruits of the vine. He tried to comfort himself with the thought that if his belongings were searched, the cross on the cup might bolster the breviary of Bernardo Espina as evidence of his own Christianity.

Less than a fortnight after Yonah's return, a boy again came from the village with a message that one of Ramón Callicó's kinsmen waited near the tavern for a meeting with him.

This time Fierro frowned. 'We are too busy with work,' he told Yonah. 'Tell your kinsman to come here if he wishes to see you for a brief time.'

Yonah gave the message to the boy and then waited and watched while he worked. When presently he saw two men enter the compound on horseback he left the shed and hurried to meet them.

It was Anselmo Lavera and his henchman. Lavera slid from his horse and tossed the reins to his companion, who remained mounted.

'*Hola*. We returned to see you, but they said you were away.'

'Yes. Delivering armor.'

'Well, it gave you time to think. Have you remembered where the saint's bones reside, then?'

'Yes.' Yonah looked at him. 'Is there a reward for such news, señor?'

He heard the man on the horse laugh softly.

'A reward? Of course there is a reward. Bring us to the saint now and you shall be rewarded at once.'

'I am unable to go. There is much work here. I was not even allowed to go to the village.'

'Who would give a single *sueldo* about work? If you are to become rich, why must you work? Come, we'll waste no more time.'

Yonah glanced at the shed and saw that Fierro had stopped his work and was gazing out at them.

'No,' he said, 'it would be very bad for you if I were to come. The men here would pursue me. It would prevent you from getting the bones.' He took from his tunic the copy of the map he had made in Tembleque. 'Here. The cave in which the bones lie is plainly marked. It is on the mainland, just after you leave Gibraltar.'

Lavera studied the map. 'Is it east or west on the mainland road?'

'East. A very short distance.' Yonah explained how they would find it.

Lavera moved to his horse. 'We'll see. We'll return to you, after, and deliver your reward.'

The day passed slowly for him. He threw himself into his work.

They did not come.

That night he lay alone and sleepless in the hut, listening for the sound of a horse approaching in the night, or a footstep.

No one came.

A day passed, and another. And another.

Soon it was a week.

Gradually Yonah came to realize that they were not going to come, and that the count of Tembleque had paid the stipulated price.

The armory's orders were almost filled. The days became more relaxed, and Fierro asked that the games should be resumed. He put Yonah into the pit with Angel again, in full armor with the rounded swords, and

264

then once more without armor, using button-tipped dueling blades.

Costa beat him both times. The second time, as they struggled Angel whispered his contempt. 'Fight, you misery, you coward. Fight, you limp prick, you piece of shite.' His contempt was obvious to those who watched.

'Do you mind struggling against Costa?' the *maestro* asked. 'You are the only one young enough. And big enough, and sufficiently strong. Do you mind being so often in the games?'

'No, I don't mind it,' Yonah said. Yet he had to be honest with Fierro. 'I believe I might win on occasion if we could go back to the mounted tourneys,' he said, but Fierro shook his head.

'You are not a squire learning to be a knight, therefore of what use would it be for you to perfect your skills with the lance? I schedule swordplay against Angel so you can learn from it, for it is a good thing for any man to be a swordsman. Each tourney is a lesson you force Angel to give you.'

Yonah always strove, and it was true he was gaining a small skill through constant practice and imitation. He thought that with enough practice he might become able to parry and strike, able to know when to dance away and when to thrust and lunge. But the older man was faster and stronger, a true master of weaponry, and though Yonah strove he could not best Costa.

Sometimes Angel gave demonstrations with the crossbow, a weapon he didn't like. 'An unskilled man can quickly learn to send bolt after bolt into a closely formed enemy army with a crossbow,' he said, 'but it is heavy to carry, and the mechanism is easily ruined by rain. And it doesn't have the wonderful range of the longbow.'

Now and again he gave the armory workers a glimpse of war, a whiff of the bloody stink.

'When a knight is unhorsed in battle, often he must discard some of his armor lest he be left behind by the sword wielders, spearmen, pikemen, and archers, who are less protected than the horsemen but far less encumbered. The armor isn't made that can cover everything and still allow the wearer to fight well without a horse.'

They stuffed a ragged tunic with straw, marking off the places that would be unprotected by armor. Almost always, from far off Angel's longbow sent an arrow to strike the 'enemy' in one of the narrow, exposed chinks where pieces of the simulated armor failed to come together. Whenever he made a particularly difficult shot, Fierro rewarded him with a coin.

One afternoon the *maestro* gathered them at the pit and directed the positioning of a large and cumbersome instrument.

'What is it?' Luis asked.

'A French *bombarde*,' Fierro said.

'What does it do?' Paco asked.

'You shall see.'

It was a tube of hammered iron strengthened by rings. Fierro had them anchor it to the earth with great stakes and chains. They loaded into the tube a heavy stone ball bound with iron, and primed it with a powder that Fierro said combined saltpeter, charcoal, and sulfur. Fierro spent a time fussing with a hinge that elevated the *bombarde*'s angle. He stationed the workmen a safe distance away, then he placed the flaming end of a pole to the touch hole at the bottom of the *bombarde*.

When the saltpeter began to smolder, the *maestro* dropped the pole and scurried to join the others.

There was a delay as the powder burned, and then there was a terrible sound, as though God had clapped his hands.

The stone ball swam through the air with a quiet hiss. It landed well beyond the target, striking a good-sized oak and snapping its trunk with a rending of wood.

Everyone cheered, but there was laughter, too.

'Of what use is a weapon of war that doesn't come near the target?' Yonah asked.

Fierro took no offense, understanding it was a serious question. 'It doesn't seek the target because I am unskilled in its use. I am told it isn't difficult to become adept in its practice.

'Accuracy isn't so important. In battle, instead of stone balls these *bombardes* can send forth case shot, which are balls fashioned from pieces of iron and stone bound together in a cement that breaks up in the act of the discharge. Imagine what several *bombardes* will do to a line of foot soldiers or horsemen! Those who don't flee will fall like grass before a scythe.'

Paco placed his hand on the barrel and withdrew it quickly. 'It is hot.'

'Yes. I'm told if it is fired overly much, the iron sometimes parts. It's thought perhaps barrels of cast bronze would be better.'

'Truly formidable,' Costa said. 'It makes armor useless. Then, are we to manufacture these *bombardes*, *maestro*?'

Fierro stared at the broken tree and shook his head. 'I think not,' he said quietly.

27
Watching Eyes

On a bright Sunday morning several weeks after he had sent Lavera and his henchman to the cave, Yonah rode the Arab horse out to the rocky barren and tethered him to a bush.

Any tracks that had been made in the stony earth had been obliterated by the scouring winds and what little rain had fallen since then.

Inside, the cave was empty.

The bony remains of the saint were gone. As was the rude cross and the earthen vessels. In their search for sacred riches the plunderers had broken up the altar. The scattered dry branches and the drawing of the fish on the wall were the only evidence that Yonah hadn't dreamed of the cave in its former state.

On the wall under the fish was a stain of dark rust, and when he knelt with his candle he saw other rusty remainders, large pools of dried blood on the stone floor.

The ambushers who had watched and waited here had had a profitable piece of work and at the same time had wiped out those who had competed against them in southern Spain.

Yonah knew that when he had given the map to Anselmo Lavera and his companion, he had executed them as surely as if he had drawn a sharp blade over their throats. He rode back to Gibraltar feeling both light-headed relief and the heavy burden of knowledge that he was a murderer.

Since coming back from Tembleque, more then ever Angel Costa had positioned himself as Gibraltar's pious soldier of the Church.

'Why do you ride out on Sunday mornings?' he demanded of Yonah.

'Maestro Fierro has given permission.'

'God has not given permission. Sunday mornings are for the worship of the Trinity.'

'I pray a great deal of the time,' Yonah said, attempting a piety that evidently did not impress, because Costa snorted.

'Among the armorers, only you and the *maestro* do not worship respectfully. You must attend the Christian Mass. You had best repent your ways, my educated señor!'

Paco had seen and heard. When Costa was gone, he spoke to Yonah. 'Angel is a killer and a sinner for whom hellfire assuredly waits, yet he watches out for the immortal souls of the better men about him.'

Costa also had talked to Fierro.

'And I have been warned by my friend José Gripo that my absence from the Mass has brought dangerous notice to myself,' the *maestro* told Yonah. 'So you and I must change our habits. You will not ride out anymore on Sunday mornings. That time is set aside for prayer. It would be advisable for you to attend the service of worship this week.'

So the following Sunday morning Yonah went to the town and arrived at the church early, taking a place in the rear. He felt Costa's eyes on him when the master of weapons entered the church. On the other side of the church Maestro Fierro was talking comfortably with townsfolk of his acquaintance.

Yonah sat and relaxed, studying Jesus hanging on the cross above the altar.

Padre Vasquez had a high, droning voice, like the sound of bees. It wasn't difficult for Yonah to rise when people rose, to kneel when others knelt, to mouth words as though praying. He found himself enjoying the sonorous Latin of the Mass, the way he had always enjoyed hearing Hebrew.

Following the worship there were lines of people before the confessional and in front of the priest dispensing the wafers of the Eucharist. Yonah was made nervous by the sight of the wafers, for he had been raised on terrifying stories about Jews accused of stealing and desecrating the Host.

He slipped outside, hoping his departure would be unnoticed.

As he walked away from the church he saw, well ahead of him in the narrow street, the departing figure of Manuel Fierro.

Yonah went to church four Sundays in a row.

Each Sunday, Maestro Fierro also was there. Once they walked back to the armory together, chatting amiably like boys walking home from school.

'Tell me about the Jew who trained you to work silver,' Fierro said.

So Yonah told him about Abba but spoke as a former apprentice and not as a son. Still, he didn't try to keep pride and affection from his voice. 'Helkias Toledano was a wonderful man and a talented worker of metals. I was lucky to apprentice under him.'

He knew he was also lucky to apprentice now under Fierro, but shyness left the thought unspoken.

'Did he have sons?'

'Two,' Yonah said. 'One died. The other was a young boy. He took the younger one with him when he departed Spain.'

Fierro nodded and turned the subject to the netting of fish, for the boats that went out from Gibraltar were having a good season.

After that day, Manuel Fierro began to observe Yonah ever more closely. At first Yonah thought he was imagining it, for the *maestro* had always been a kind man, ready with a pleasant and encouraging word for everyone. But Fierro conversed with him more frequently than before, and at length.

Angel Costa was watching Yonah closely, too. He often felt Angel's eyes on him, and when Costa wasn't in sight, Yonah believed he was watched by others.

Once he was certain Luis followed him to the village.

More than once Yonah returned to his hut and saw that his few belongings had been moved. Nothing was stolen. He tried to inspect his own property through a hostile searcher's eyes but saw no incrimination in his few items of apparel, his guitar, the steel cup he had made, and the breviary of the late Bernardo Espina, might his soul rest.

*

271

Manuel Fierro had been a successful and influential man in Gibraltar for several decades. He had a wide circle of friends and acquaintances, and on the rare evenings when he stopped into the village tavern he almost never drank alone.

He saw nothing unusual when José Gripo sat at his table and drank a glass of wine without too many words, for he had known Gripo as long as he had been in Gibraltar, and the owner of the chandlery shop was never overly verbose.

But when Gripo whispered that Manuel must meet him at once on the wharf, and then finished his wine and said a loud good night, Fierro swallowed his own drink a few minutes later and, refusing the offer of another glass, said good night to everyone there.

As he made his way to the waterfront, he wondered why Gripo had been afraid to be seen leaving the tavern in his company.

The chandler was waiting halfway down the length of the dark wharf, behind a storage shed. He wasted no time in niceties.

'You are marked, Manuel. You would have done well to have discharged the ungrateful bastard long since, and sent him away with his sword and bow.'

'It was Costa?'

'Who else? He is a jealous man, resentful of prosperity, however well earned,' Gripo said bitterly.

Charges were made anonymously at autos de fé, but Fierro didn't ask how Gripo knew his accuser. He was aware José Gripo had half a dozen close relatives who were well-placed priests.

'On what grounds am I marked?'

'He told the inquisitors you apprenticed to a Muslim

wizard. He said he has seen you place a blood curse on each piece of armor sold to good Christians. As I have told you before, it has been noted you do not attend Mass.'

'I have attended recently.'

'Recently was too late. You are denounced as a servant of Satan and an enemy of Holy Mother Church,' Gripo said, and Fierro recognized the depth of the sadness in his voice.

'Thank you, José,' he said.

He waited there in the darkness until Gripo had left the wharf, then he made his own way back to his armory.

He told this to Yonah the next day, in the bright and lazy afternoon while together they polished the instruments he had fashioned for his brother. He spoke quietly in a flat voice devoid of emotion, as if they were discussing the progress of a piece of work. He did not identify Gripo by name, reporting only that he had learned he was denounced by Angel Costa.

'If he has warned the inquisitors of me, I am certain you are also denounced and will be taken,' Fierro said. 'Therefore, each of us must leave this place, and quickly.'

Yonah could feel his own pallor. 'Yes, señor.'

'Do you have a refuge?'

'No.'

'What of your kinsmen? The two men who visited you here.'

'They were not kinsmen. They were bad men. They have gone away.'

Fierro nodded. 'Then I ask a favor of you, Ramón

Callicó. I shall go to my brother, Nuño Fierro, physician of Saragossa. Will you come with me and be my guard until we reach his home?'

Yonah struggled to think. Finally, he spoke. 'You have shown me kindness. I will go with you, to serve you.'

Fierro nodded in appreciation. 'So we must prepare at once to leave Gibraltar,' he said.

In the middle of the night, while others slept, Yonah went to the *maestro*'s house as he had been directed, and they assembled the things they would need for the trip. Food and implements for the trail, and for each of them stout boots and spurs and a mail vest. A sword for Yonah. A sword for Fierro that took Yonah's breath away; it wasn't jeweled or scrolled like a sword made for a nobleman, but it was so finely wrought that it was beautiful, with a wonderful balance.

Fierro wrapped in soft cloths each of the surgical instruments he had made so meticulously for his brother, and placed them in a small chest.

He and Yonah went to the stable and from it led a strong mule to one of the supply sheds at the far end of the compound. It was locked, as each of the supply sheds were, and Fierro opened the door with a key. Inside, half the shed was a jumble of steel pieces, old and rusted armor and other metal dross. The other half of the space was stacked with firewood, fuel for the forge. The *maestro* set Yonah to moving billets of wood and worked with him, and when a good portion of the pile had been displaced, a small leather chest was uncovered.

It was no larger than the chest that held the surgical instruments, but when Yonah went to pick it up he grunted in surprise, because it had great weight, and he understood why the mule was necessary.

They packed the chest on the mule's back and locked the shed.

'Last thing we want is a braying that will waken the world,' Fierro said, and as Yonah led the animal back to the house the *maestro* patted the mule and gentled it in a low voice. When the chest was placed on Fierro's floor, the *maestro* told Yonah to return the mule to the stable and himself to his hut, which he did. Yonah fell onto his pallet at once, but though he was tired and tried to sleep he lay in the dark, troubled by thoughts.

Despite their precautions, next morning Costa knew something was amiss. Up to hunt at daybreak, he saw new dung in the stable yard and yet, within the barn, he noted that every creature was in its proper stall.

'Who has been using a horse or a pack animal in the night?' he asked casually, placing the question to everyone without receiving an answer.

Paco shrugged. 'No doubt a night rider lost his way and, seeing this is a dead end by the straits, rode back the way he had come,' he said, yawning.

Costa nodded reluctantly. It seemed to Yonah that each time he looked up he saw Angel's eyes.

He fretted to be off, but Fierro wouldn't leave until he took care of a final piece of business. The *maestro* left a package with an old friend who was monarchs' magistrate in the village, to be opened in a fortnight. It contained money to be divided among the men in his employ according to their length of service, and a letter granting them collective ownership of the shop and foundry, along with his wishes that they sustain themselves in the production of armor or other products of their considerable skills.

'It is time,' Fierro said to him that evening, and Yonah felt great relief. They waited until most of the night was gone, so they would have daylight by the time they were on unfamiliar ground. In the stable Fierro led from her stall his accustomed mount, a black mare said to be the best horse there.

'Take the Arab gray for yourself,' he said, and Yonah did so gladly. They saddled both horses and placed them back in their stalls, and then they led the mule to Fierro's house for the last time.

They dressed for the trail and armed themselves, and packed the mule with the things they had accumulated. When they returned to the stable they collected the horses and led the three animals through the compound of the foundry buildings in the gray birth of a new morning.

They didn't speak.

Yonah was sorry he hadn't been able to say good-bye to Paco.

He knew what it was to leave a home and thus could imagine what Fierro must be feeling. When he heard the soft grunt he mistook it for a small emission of regret, but turning to the older man Yonah saw that a feathered shaft had blossomed from the *maestro*'s throat just above the mail vest. Bright blood ran from Manuel Fierro's throat and dripped from the vest onto his horse.

Angel Costa stood perhaps forty paces away and had made such a shot in the dim light as would have earned him a gold piece from the *maestro* if it had been done in practice.

Yonah knew Angel had taken out Fierro first because he feared the *maestro*'s sword. He had no such fear of Yonah's skill, and he had already dropped the bow and drawn his sword as he ran.

Yonah's first panicked thought, which drove all else from his mind, was to leap on the horse and ride away. Yet perhaps there was something that might be done for Fierro.

He had no time left for musing, only time to draw his sword and step forward. Costa was on him and the blades clanged and clashed.

Yonah had little hope. Time after time he had been bested by Costa. The expression on Angel's face, bemused and contemptuous, was the expression he knew. Costa was determining which series of strokes would finish it quickly, choosing from a dozen maneuvers that had worked against the neophyte in the past.

With a strength born of desperation, Yonah immobilized Costa's sword, hilt to hilt, fist to fist, as they strained against one another. It was as though, then, he heard Mingo's voice in his head, bidding him precisely what he must do.

His left hand snaked down to the small scabbard at his waist, drew the dagger.

Rammed it home. Ripped it upward.

They stared at each other in the same stupefaction, both aware that it was not supposed to end like this. As Costa sagged.

Fierro was dead when Yonah returned to him. He tried to remove the arrow but it was deep and the arrowhead resisted, and he snapped the shaft close to the poor bloodied throat.

He couldn't leave Fierro to be found, knowing the corpse would be convicted and as a final indignity burned alongside the living victims of the next auto de fé.

He lifted the *maestro* and carried him well off the trail and then used his sword to scratch a shallow grave in the sandy soil, scrabbling the loosened dirt out of the grave with his hands.

The earth was full of rocks and stones, and using the sword as a shovel had ruined the blade, making it useless as a weapon. He exchanged it for Fierro's wonderfully wrought sword. He left the silver spurs on the *maestro*'s boots but took his purse and removed from about his neck the cord holding the keys to the chests.

He spent time and energy covering Fierro's body with heavy rocks to protect him from animals, and then covered the rocks with a foot of earth, spreading the surface of the grave with stones and twigs and small boulders, until from the trail the ground appeared undisturbed.

A few flies were already on Costa and before long there would be a swarm, but after checking to make certain he was dead, Yonah allowed Angel to remain slumped in the dust.

He rode away from that place finally, on the gray Arab at a brisk trot in the lambent light of early morning, leading both Fierro's black horse and the pack burro. He didn't let up on the animals after they crossed the narrow isthmus that linked Gibraltar with the mainland, riding past the looted home of the Pilgrim Saint without seeing it. By the time the sun was high in the sky he was once again in the lonely security of high mountains, and for a time he wept like a child for Fierro as he rode, feeling grief and something more. He had sent two men to their deaths, and now had taken a human life with his own hands, and what he had lost therefrom weighed heavier on him than any of the burdens carried by the burro.

When he was confident that he wasn't being pursued he eased up on the animals, walking them as he followed little-used mountain trails eastward for five days. Then he turned northeast, still keeping the protection of the hills until he neared Murcia.

He opened the leather chest only once. From its weight it could have been only one thing, so the sight of gold coins was merely confirmation that the chest contained the *maestro*'s earned capital from two decades of fashioning armor highly desired by the rich and powerful. It was a resource that wasn't real to Yonah, and he didn't touch the coins before relocking the chest and returning it to its large cloth sack. Fierro had made it his responsibility.

His hair and his beard quickly became wild and tangled once more, and his spurs and the mail vest were marred by skim rust from the dewy grasses on which he slept. He stopped twice to buy supplies in remote villages that appeared safe, but otherwise he avoided all human contact. In truth, most situations were safe, for he looked the perfect picture of a killer rogue knight, whose fine sword and warrior's horses and fearsome appearance did not encourage either attack or social intercourse.

After Murcia he turned due north, traveling through Valencia and into Aragon.

He had left Gibraltar at the end of summer. Now the days had become cool and nights were cold. From a shepherd he bought a blanket of sheepskins and slept wrapped in them. It was too cold to wash, and the poorly cured skins added to his stink.

He was numb with travel weariness by the morning he reached Saragossa.

'You know the physician of this place? A man named Fierro?' he asked a man loading cut wood into a donkey cart in the Plaza Mayor.

'Yes, of course,' the man said, watching him nervously. Yonah was directed to retrace his steps outside the town, to a small but secluded farm whose entrance trail he had passed unknowingly. There was a barn attached to the hacienda but no visible animals except a horse cropping the ragged brown grass of winter.

A woman answered his knock on the door, which emitted the odor of freshly baked bread. She opened the door only a bit; all he could see of her was half a sweet peasant face, the round of one shoulder, the swell of one breast. 'You wish the doctor?'

'Yes.'

Nuño Fierro proved to be a balding man with a big stomach and quiet, introspective eyes. Although the day was overcast he squinted his eyes as though he were looking into the sun. He was older than the *maestro*. His nose was straight, and in many other ways he didn't resemble his brother, who had been more vital, more robust. But at a second glance, when he left the house, Yonah saw the way he held his head, the walk, the expression that flickered into his face.

He stood silent and weighed down as Yonah told him his brother was dead.

'A natural death?' he said finally.

'No. He was struck down.'

'Killed, you say?'

'Yes, killed . . . and robbed,' Yonah added suddenly. There was no premeditation in the decision not to give over to this man his brother's money, only the sudden blinding knowledge that he would not. He went to the burro and untied the bundle of medical instruments.

Nuño Fierro opened the chest and stroked the scalpels, the probes, the clips.

'He made each one of them himself. He let me polish a few, but he made them all.'

The physician tenderly touched these few things his brother had made, lost in a terrible moment. Then he looked up at Yonah. No doubt seeing the marks of long travel. Probably, Yonah thought, smelling him, too.

'You must come inside.'

'No.'

'But you must—'

'No, I thank you. I wish you well,' Yonah said roughly, and went to the gray Arab and swung into the saddle.

He forced himself to keep the beasts at a walk, fleeing slowly, with Nuño Fierro standing in the dust, looking after him in puzzlement.

Yonah traveled farther north, scarcely knowing where.

The physician was an old man, he told himself, and clearly he was prosperous. He had no need for his brother's fortune.

Without being conscious of temptation, he realized he had been thinking about the money for a long time.

He had come to realize what it would mean for him to have unlimited financial resources.

Why not? Obviously, God had sent them to him. The Ineffable One had sent him a heavenly message of hope.

After a while, seated in the saddle that had come to feel like another layer of skin on his ass, he became giddy from thinking of the choices that might be available with the gold, of where he might wish to go to buy a new life.

He found himself in the foothills, glad to travel toward the comforting sanctuary of mountains, but that night he didn't sleep. There was a thin sliver of moon and the same stars that had shone on him when he was a shepherd. He built a fire in a clearing on a wooded slope and sat and gazed into the flames, seeing many things there.

The money was power.

The money would buy him a certain amount of security. A modicum of safety.

But in the chill light of early morning he got up and sighed a *peón*'s curse as he kicked dirt over what was left of his fire.

He traveled back to Saragossa slowly.

Nuño Fierro opened the door of the hacienda as Yonah was unpacking the box of coins. Yonah set the box before him, unbuckled his sword and placed it on the box.

'These were his also, and the animals.'

The intelligent Fierro eyes stared at him, comprehending everything.

'Did you kill him?'

'No, no!'

His horror was recognized as genuine.

'I loved him. He was . . . the *maestro*! He was good and just. Many loved him.'

The physician of Saragossa held wide his door.

'Come inside,' he said.

28
Books

As difficult as it was, before he rested or cleaned himself he recounted in detail for Nuño Fierro the events of the morning when Manuel Fierro had died with Angel Costa's arrow in his throat, and how he had killed Angel. Nuño Fierro listened with his eyes closed. It was a difficult narrative for him to hear, and when it was finished he nodded and went off to be alone.

The physician's housekeeper was quiet and watchful, a strong-bodied woman of perhaps forty years – older than Yonah had supposed from his first glimpse of her through the crack of the door. Her name was Reyna Fadique. She cooked well and heated his bath water without complaint, and for a day and a half he did nothing but sleep, waking to eat and use the chamber pot and then sleep again.

He found his garments laundered and fresh when he left his pallet on the afternoon of the second day. He dressed and ventured outside, and presently Nuño Fierro found him kneeling by the brook, watching small trout flying through the water.

Yonah thanked him for his hospitality. 'I am rested and ready for the trail again,' he said, then he waited awkwardly. He didn't have enough money to make an offer for the gray horse, but he thought perhaps he might buy the mule. He loathed the thought of wandering on foot.

'I have opened the leather chest,' the physician said.

Yonah detected something in the man's voice that caused him to look up sharply. 'Does something appear to be missing?'

'On the contrary. Something was there I had not expected to find.' Nuño Fierro held out a small piece of paper, torn raggedly from a larger piece. On it, in ink to which a few grains of the blotting sand still clung, was written, 'I believe the bearer to be a New Christian.'

Yonah was stunned. So there had been at least one man he had not misled with his false name and gentile ways! The *maestro* had thought him a convert, of course, but he had known Yonah for a Jew. The note showed that he had believed Yonah would deliver the wealth to his brother in the event of his own demise. A compliment of trust from the grave, which almost had not been deserved.

Yet he was disappointed because Manuel Fierro had thought it necessary to warn his brother that a Jew was in his house.

Nuño Fierro saw the confusion in his face. 'You must come with me, please.'

Inside the house in his study, Nuño removed a tapestry wall hanging, uncovering a niche in the stone wall. Within the niche were a pair of objects wrapped well in linens that had been tied carefully with strips of fabric. Unwrapped, they proved to be two books.

In Hebrew.

'I apprenticed under Gabriel ben Nissim Sporanis, one of the most revered physicians in all of Spain, and then had the honor to practice medicine with him. He was a Jew. He had lost a brother to the Inquisition. Through the mercy of God he himself died naturally, a very old man in his bed, two months prior to the edict of expulsion.

'At the time of the expulsion his two children and his sister had few funds with which to travel to safety. I bought this house and land from them, as well as these books.

'I am told that one is *A Commentary of the Medical Aphorisms of Hippocrates*, by Moses ben Maimon, whom your people call Maimonides, and that the other is the *Canon of Medicine* by Avicenna, whom the Moors know as Ibn Sina. I had written to my brother Manuel that I had these books and how I yearned to discover their secrets. And now he has sent me a New Christian.'

Yonah picked up one of the books and his vision embraced the letters he had not seen in such a long time. They appeared strange and unfamiliar, and in his nervous joy they seemed to turn into serpents that writhed.

'Have you other books by Maimonides?' he asked hoarsely. What he would give for a copy of the Mishne Torah, he thought; Abba had had that book, in which Maimonides commented on the entirety of Jewish practice, describing in detail everything Yonah had lost.

Alas, Nuño Fierro shook his head.

'No. There were several other books, but Gabriel Sporanis's sons carried them off when they departed.' He glanced at Yonah anxiously. 'Are you able to translate these?'

Yonah stared at the page. The serpents were simply beloved letters again, but . . . 'I don't know,' he said doubtfully. 'Once I had the Hebrew language effortlessly in my grasp, but I haven't read it or otherwise really used it for a long time.' Nine long years.

'Will you stay here with me, and try?'

He was stunned that he had been brought together again with the language of his father.

'I will stay for a time,' he said.

If the choice had been his he would have tried to do the Maimonides book first, because the copy was very old and the pages were dry and crumbling, but Nuño Fierro was eager to read the Avicenna, so Yonah began there.

He was uncertain he could do the translation. He worked with great deliberation, one word at a time, one thought at a time, and slowly the letters that once had been so familiar became familiar again.

'Well? What do you think?' the physician asked after the first day.

Yonah could only shrug.

The Hebrew letters unleashed memories of his father teaching him, discussing the meanings of words, how they apply to man's relationship with other men, how they apply to man's relationship with God, with the world.

He remembered the sounds of quavering old voices and strong young voices chanting raggedly together, the joy of song, the sorrow of the Kaddish. Bits of worship, fragments of verses he had thought gone forever began to spin from the depths of his memory like blossoms before a wind. The Hebrew words he translated spoke of lockjaw and pleurisy, shaking fevers, potions to ease pain; nevertheless, they brought him song and poetry and fervor that had been lost in the brutishness of his coming of age.

Some words he simply didn't know, and he could do no more than retain the Hebrew word in the Spanish sentence. But once he had known this language very well, and slowly it came back to him.

Nuño Fierro hovered anxiously in the periphery of his existence.

'How goes the work?' he asked at the end of each day.

'I begin to show progress,' Yonah finally was able to say.

Nuño Fierro was an honest man and lost little time in warning Yonah that in the past Saragossa had been a dangerous place for Jews.

'The Inquisition came here early and harshly,' he said.

Torquemada had appointed two inquisitors for Saragossa in May of 1484. So eager were these clerics to destroy recalcitrant Jews that they held their first auto de fé without bothering to issue the Edict of Grace designed to allow backsliding New Christians to confess voluntarily, thereby seeking mercy. By June 3, the first two conversos had been executed and a dead woman's body had been exhumed and burned.

'There lived in Saragossa good men, members of the Diputación de Aragon, the Council of the Estates, who were shocked and outraged. They approached the king, saying that Torquemada's appointments and executions were illegal and his confiscations of property violated the *fueros* of the kingdom of Aragon. They made no objection to trials for heresy,' Nuño Fierro said, 'but they petitioned that the Inquisition should function to bring sinners back to the bosom of Holy Mother Church by means of instruction and admonition, using milder penances. They said that aspersions should not be leveled against good and pious men, and insisted there were no notorious heretics in Aragon.'

Ferdinand had dismissed the councillors brusquely. 'He said, if there were so few heretics in Aragon, why did they bother him with this fear of the Inquisition?'

On the night of September 16, 1485, Pedro Arbués, one of the inquisitors, was murdered while at prayer in the cathedral. There were no witnesses to the crime but authorities made the immediate assumption that he had been killed by New Christians. As they had done in the cases of several other imagined insurrections of conversos elsewhere, at once they placed under arrest the leader of the New Christian population. He was a distinguished and elderly jurist, Jaime de Montesa, deputy to the chief justice of the municipality.

A number of his acquaintances were also arrested, men deeply involved in Christian life, the fathers and brothers of monks, whose ancestors had been converts. They included men in high positions of government and commerce, several of whom had been knighted for valor. One by one each was declared *judio mamas*, 'really a Jew.' Terrible tortures produced confessions of a plot. In December of 1485 two more conversos were burned at the stake, and beginning with February, 1486, monthly autos de fé were held in Saragossa.

'So you see that we must take care. Great care,' Fierro cautioned Yonah. 'Is Ramón Callicó your true name?'

'No. I am sought as a Jew under my true name.'

Nuño Fierro winced. 'Then do not reveal your true name to me,' he said quickly. 'We shall simply announce,

289

should we be asked, that you are Ramón Callicó, an Old Christian from Gibraltar, the nephew of my late brother's wife.'

It proved not to be difficult. Yonah saw no soldiers or priests. He stayed close to the hacienda, which the Jewish physician Gabriel ben Nissim Sporanis had situated cleverly, far enough from the town and sufficiently off the trail to guarantee that only those in need of medical care would bother to come.

Fierro's property covered three sides of a long, sloping hill. Whenever fatigue turned the letters to snakes again and Yonah could translate no more, he left the books and tramped over the land. It showed signs that once it had been a good farm, but it was obvious Nuño wasn't a good farmer. There was a planting of olive trees and a small fruit orchard, both healthy but desperate for pruning, and like the good *peón* he had been Yonah found a little saw in the barn and pruned several of the trees, piling the cut boughs and burning them the way he had done on the farms of earlier employment. Behind the barn was a trove of old horse manure and bedding from the stalls, and Yonah added the ashes from the fires and spread the mixture under half a dozen of the trees.

Over the crest of the hill and on its northern side was a neglected field Reyna called the Place of the Lost Ones. It was an unmarked cemetery for those unfortunates who took their own lives, because the Church said suicides were damned and barred them from interment in Christian burial grounds.

Just above the hacienda was the hill's southern slope, the best part of the property, with deep, rich topsoil and full exposure to the sun. Reyna kept a small kitchen garden, but much of it had grown to weeds and brush. Yonah saw that if someone were serious about working this land there were many possibilities.

He wasn't certain how long he would stay, but he was caught up in rediscovering the Hebrew language, and as the weeks passed it came to seem almost normal for him to be living in a house. It was a house full of the smells of cooking and baking and the warmth from the large fireplace. Yonah kept the wood box filled, for which Reyna was grateful, since that had been one of her many chores. The ground floor was one large room in which the cooking and dining was done, with two comfortable chairs by the fire. Upstairs, Yonah's pallet was in a small storeroom between the large master bedchamber and Reyna's smaller room, each of which contained a bed.

The walls were thin. He never heard her pray, but each of them was aware someone could hear when they awoke to piss into the chamber pot. Once he heard her make a small moan as she yawned and he could imagine how she looked, stretching, enjoying the luxury of a few hours spared from work. During the day he watched her surreptitiously, taking care not to be observed doing so, because from the start he knew Reyna was taken.

Several times, lying in the dark at night, he heard her door open and listened as she went into Nuño's room and closed the door behind her. Sometimes he heard the muted sounds of lovemaking.

Good for you, Physician! he thought, caught in the prison of his own unreleased loins.

He noted that in their daylight demeanor Nuño and Reyna were master and servant, pleasant to one another but devoid of intimacy.

Their sexual joining didn't happen as frequently as Yonah would have expected. Apparently Nuño Fierro's needs no longer were urgent. Yonah was a man who discerned patterns, and he noticed early that sometimes, after they had supped, Nuño told Reyna that on the morrow he would like a potted fowl, and she inclined her head. And always that night she came to Nuño's room. Soon when Yonah heard their private code, the order for a potted fowl, he was unable to sleep until he heard her going into the other man's chamber.

Yonah first realized Nuño wasn't well one afternoon when he left the small table at which he did his translating and saw that the physician was sitting quietly on the lower steps of the staircase. Fierro was pale and his eyes were closed.

'Señor, can I help you?' Yonah said, and hastened toward him, but Nuño Fierro shook his head and raised his hand.

'Allow me to be. A touch of dizziness, nothing more.'

So Yonah nodded and returned to his desk. And presently he heard Fierro get to his feet and go to his room.

Several nights later there were wild winds and a hard and persistent rain that broke a long drought. In the darkness before dawn the three of them were awakened by a hammering on the door and the loud voice of a man calling for Señor Fierro.

Reyna hurried down and shouted through the closed door. 'Yes, yes. What is it?'

'I am Ricardo Cabrera. Please, we need the señor. My father has had a terrible fall.'

292

'I am coming,' Nuño called from the top of the stairs.

Reyna opened the door only a crack, because she was in her shift. 'Where is your farm?'

'Off the Tauste road.'

'But that is across the Ebro!'

'I crossed it without difficulty,' the man said pleadingly.

Now for the first time Yonah heard the strange sound of the servant woman arguing with Nuño Fierro as if she were his wife. 'Do not place instruments and medications in your bag so calmly! It is too far, and across the river. You cannot go on such a night.'

Presently there was another knocking, this time on Yonah's door. She came in and stood over him in the dark. 'He is not strong. Go with him and help him. See that he returns safely.'

Nuño was less sanguine than he had pretended, and he seemed relieved when Yonah threw on his clothes and came downstairs.

'Why not take one of your brother's horses?' Yonah asked, but the physician shook his head. 'I have my own horse, who has crossed the Ebro many times.'

So Yonah saddled Nuño's brown horse and the gray Arab for himself, and they followed the shaggy pony of the farmer's son through the driving rain. The brook had turned into a stream and the sound of water was everywhere as they made their muddy way. Yonah carried Nuño's bag, allowing him to hold the reins with both hands.

They were thoroughly wet by the time they reached the river. There were no calm and shallow fords in this kind of a rain. The water was running hard and up over the stirrups when they crossed, but even the tough little pony made the crossing without mishap. They arrived at the farm wet through and chilled but were unable to see to their own comfort.

Pascual Cabrera lay on the barn floor while nearby his wife forked hay to their animals. He groaned when Nuño bent over him.

'I fell from the high rocks in the field,' he whispered. He appeared to have difficulty breathing, and his wife assumed the tale.

'A wolf is about and took a freshened ewe from us a fortnight ago. Ricardo has set snares and will kill the beast, but until he does so, we bring our few sheep and goats into the barn at night. My husband got all of them inside except that cursed goat,' she said, indicating a black *cabra* munching hay nearby. 'She had gone up onto a high rocky place in a corner of our field. The goats love to climb it, and she would not choose to come down.'

Her husband said something faintly, and Nuño asked him to repeat it.

'The *cabra* . . . our best milker.'

'Just so,' his wife said. 'So he went up to the top of the rocks to get her, and she got down and went directly to the barn. But the rocks are slick from the rain, and he slipped. He fell all the way to the bottom. He was out there a while before he managed to get into the barn himself. I was able to get off his clothes and cover him with a blanket, but he wouldn't let me dry him, for the pain.'

Yonah watched a different Nuño than the one he had seen at home. The physician was swift and confident. He removed the blanket and asked Yonah to hold one of the two lanterns close. The physician's hands moved over the man's body gently, assessing the damage while a pair of oxen watched from the stalls.

'You have broken several of your ribs. And perhaps you have cracked a bone in your arm,' Nuño said finally. He wrapped the moaning man's upper body tightly in cloth bindings, and soon Señor Cabrera sighed, feeling a lessening of his pain.

'Oh, that's something better,' he breathed.

'Your arm needs our help too,' Nuño said, and as he bound it for support he directed Yonah and Ricardo to tie the blanket between two long thin poles that leaned in a corner of the barn. When that was done they shifted Cabrera onto the litter and carried him to his own bed.

They were able to take their leave only after Nuño had given the señora powders for infusions that would allow her husband to sleep. It was still misting when they began their return ride but the storm was done and the river was quieter. The rain ceased before they reached home, and a sunlit dawn flooded into the sky. In the house Reyna had the fire going and hot wine waiting, and she began at once to boil water for the physician's bath.

In the gloom of his small room Yonah shivered as he rubbed his cold body dry with rough sacking. He was thoughtful as he listened to the woman's worried scolding, soft and urgent as the sound of a dove.

Yonah was willing when Nuño asked him to ride out with him again several days later. The following week they made seven visits to the sick and injured, and soon it was accepted that when the physician must ride abroad, Yonah was his company.

It was while visiting a woman stricken with sharp fevers and paroxysms of chills that Yonah received an account of further happenings in the lives of the Spanish

Jews who had fled to Portugal. While Nuño attended to the woman's ague her husband, a cloth merchant whose business took him to Lisboa, sat and passed the time of day with Yonah, speaking of Portuguese wine and food.

'As every place, Portugal has problems with its damnable Jews,' he said.

'I have heard they have been made slaves of the state.'

'They were slaves until Emanuel ascended the throne of Portugal and declared them free. But when he sought to marry young Isabella, daughter of our own Ferdinand and Isabella, our Spanish monarchs chided his overly soft heart and he made certain to be firmer. He had a problem, in that he wanted an end to Jewishness in his kingdom but could not afford to lose the Jews, who are cursedly good at trade.'

'I have heard they are,' Yonah said. 'Is it really true, then?'

'Oh, yes. I know this to be true in my own cloth trade as in many others. At any rate, at Emanuel's orders all Jewish children between the ages of four and fourteen were forcibly baptized en masse. In a failed experiment, some seven hundred of the newly baptized children were sent to live a Christian life on the isle of San Tomás, off the coast of Africa, where almost all of them quickly died of the fevers. But most of the children were allowed to remain with their families, and Jewish adults were given the choice of becoming Catholics or departing the country. As in Spain, some converted, though by our experience it is to be doubted that a man who has been *judio mamas*, really a Jew, may become a good and honest Christian, eh?'

'Where did the others go?' Yonah asked.

'I have no idea, nor do I care, so long as they never

shall return to us,' the merchant said, and a burst of groaning from his wife drew him away from Yonah and to her side.

One day a pair of gravediggers led up Nuño's lane a donkey laden with a recumbent form. When they stopped at the hacienda and begged water, Reyna asked if the physician's services were needed, and the men laughed and said it was far too late. The body on the donkey was that of an unidentified man with black skin, a wanderer who in the broad light of day had slit his own throat in the Plaza Mayor. The gravediggers gave polite thanks for the water and continued their slow way to the Place of the Lost Ones.

That night, Nuño awakened Yonah from a deep sleep. 'I need your help.'

'You have it, Señor Fierro. What can I do?'

'You should know it is a matter considered to be witchcraft and mortal sin by the Church. If you help me, and we are discovered, you will burn as well as I.'

Yonah had long since decided that Nuño Fierro was a man worthy of his trust. 'I am already wanted for burning, *maestro* Physician. They cannot burn me more than once.'

'Then fetch a spade and bridle a burro.'

The night was clear but Yonah felt its chill. Together they led the burro to the cemetery of the suicides. Nuño had gone up there before dark to find the grave, and now led the way to it in the bright light of the moon.

He set Yonah to digging at once. 'The grave is shallow, because the diggers are lazy louts and were partly drunk when Reyna spoke with them.'

It required little effort for Yonah to reclaim the shrouded corpus from the ground, and with the burro's help they took the body back over the hill to the barn, where the shroud was removed and the naked man was laid out on a table surrounded by bright oil lamps.

The form and face were those of a man of middle age, with wispy curls of black hair, thin limbs, bruised shanks, a variety of scars from old injuries, and the unpleasant neck wound that had brought him death.

'The color of the skin is not a subject for conjecture,' Nuño Fierro said. 'In climates of great heat, such as in Africa, men have developed dark skins over long centuries to protect them from the burning rays of the sun. In northern places such as the land of the Slavs, cold climate has produced skin of stark whiteness.'

He took up one of the fine scalpels his brother had fashioned for him. 'This has been done as long as there have been healing arts,' he said, and made a straight and steady incision that opened the body on the table from the breastbone to the pubis.

'Both dark and light skins and the flesh beneath them contain different kinds of glands that are the agents of the functions of the body.'

Yonah drew a sharp breath and turned his head from the stink of corruption. 'I know what you feel,' Nuño said, 'because it is what I felt the first time I saw Sporanis do this.'

His hands worked skillfully. 'I am a simple physician and not a priest or a devil. I don't know what becomes of the soul. But I know for a certainty it doesn't stay here in this house of flesh, this house that after death seeks at once to become earth.'

He mentioned what he knew about the organs he

removed, and directed Yonah to record the dimensions and weight in a book with a leather cover.

'This is the liver. The nutrition of the body depends upon it. I believe it is where the blood is born.'

'This, the spleen . . . This, the bladder of gall, regulating the temperament.'

The heart . . . When it was removed, Yonah held in his palms a man's heart!

'The heart draws blood into itself and sends it elsewhere. The nature of blood is perplexing, but it is clear the heart gives life. Without it, man would be a plant.' Nuño showed him it was like a house with four chambers. 'It is in one of these chambers, perhaps, that my own doom lies. I think God erred here when making me. Though perhaps the trouble is in the bellows of the lungs.'

'Is it bad for you, then?' Yonah could not refrain from asking.

'At times it is bad. Trouble with respiration, it comes and it goes.'

Nuño showed him how bones, membranes, and ligaments supported and protected the body. He sawed off the top of the thin man's head and showed Yonah the brain, then demonstrated that it was connected to the spinal cord and certain nerves.

It was still dark when all was put back and the incisions were sewn with the care of a seamstress. The shroud was replaced, and the two men led the burro back up the hill.

Yonah buried the thin man deeper this time, and they gave him the honor of a Christian prayer and a Jewish one. By the time the light of day drifted over the hill, each of them was in his bed.

*

In the week that followed, Yonah was enflamed by a curious unrest. He translated Avicenna's words: 'Medicine is the preservation of health and the cure of disease that arises from conscious causes which exist within the body.' When he went to see patients with Nuño he looked at them in a new way, seeing in each the skeleton and organs he had seen in the thin man.

It took him the full week to achieve the courage to approach the physician with his proposal.

'I would bind myself to you as apprentice physician.'

Nuño looked at him calmly. 'Is this a sudden desire that may drift away like a fog before a wind?'

'No, I have given it much thought. I think you do God's work.'

'God's work? Let me tell you something, Ramón. Often I believe in God. But sometimes I do not.'

Yonah was silent, not knowing what to reply.

'Do you have other reasons for your request?'

'A physician helps others throughout his life.'

'So. You would benefit humanity?'

Yonah felt Nuño toying with him and was irked. 'Yes, I would do so.'

'Do you know how long such a clerkship might be?'

'No.'

'Four years. It would be your third apprenticeship, and I could not give assurance that you would be able to finish it. I do not know if God will grant me four more years to do his work.'

Honesty forced another admission. 'I need to belong to something. To be a part of something good.'

Nuño pursed his lips and looked at him.

'I would labor hard for you.'

'You already labor hard for me,' Nuño said gently.

But in a moment he nodded. 'Well. We shall try,' he said.

Part Six

THE PHYSICIAN
OF SARAGOSSA

*Aragon
February 10, 1501*

29

The Physician's Apprentice

Now when Yonah rode out with Nuño to treat a patient he no longer waited idly for the physician to complete his task. Instead he stood at the bedside as Nuño spoke in a low voice throughout the examination and treatment. 'Do you see the dampness of the sheets? Do you detect the acidity of his breath?' Yonah listened closely as Nuño told the sick man's wife that her husband was stricken with fever and colic and prescribed a light diet free of spices, and infusions to be taken for seven days.

On the ride from house to house they kept their mounts to a businesslike canter, but on the slow ride home Yonah usually had a question or two that he had gleaned from the day's work. 'How do the symptoms of colic vary?'

'Sometimes colic is accompanied by fever and sweating, but other times, not. It may be caused by acute constipation, for which a good remedy is figs boiled in olive oil and honey until they are a thick paste. Or by diarrhea, for which rice may be parched until it is perfectly brown, and then boiled down and eaten slowly.'

Nuño always had a question or two of his own. 'How does what we have seen today match what Avicenna says regarding the detection of illness?'

'He has written that often illness may be recognized by what the body produces and expels, such as sputum, stools, sweat, and urine.'

He continued to work at his translation of the Avicenna book, which buttressed Nuño's lessons:

Symptoms are obtained through physical examination of the body. There are visible ones, such as jaundice and edema; some are perceptible to the ear, such as the gurgling of the abdomen in dropsy; the foul odor strikes at the sense of smell, for example, that of purulent ulcers; there are some accessible to taste, such as the acidity of the mouth; touch recognizes certain ones: the firmness of . . .

When he found a word he couldn't identify, he had to go to Nuño. 'It says, "the firmness of . . ." the Hebrew word is *sartán*. I'm sorry, I don't know what *sartán* means.'

Nuño read the transcribed passage and smiled. 'It almost certainly means cancer. Touch recognizes the firmness of cancer.'

In itself the process of translating such a book was educational, but Yonah found he had limited time to devote to Avicenna, because Nuño Fierro was a demanding teacher who set him straightaway to reading other books. The physician owned several classical works of medicine in the Spanish language, and Yonah became responsible for the knowledge imparted by

Teodorico Borgognoni writing on surgery, Isaac's work on fevers, and Galen on the pulse.

'Don't just read them,' Nuño warned. 'Learn them. Learn them so completely that you will not have to consult them in the future. A book may be burned or lost, but if you really have learned, the book is part of you and the knowledge will last as long as you do.'

Opportunities to perform additional dissections in the barn were rare and widely spaced, but they studied the corpse of a woman of the town who had thrown herself into the Ebro and drowned. When they cut into her womb Nuño showed him a fetus, not fully formed and the size of a fish that any angler would have thrown back.

'Life is engendered from the sperm, the issue of the penis,' Nuño told him. 'It is not understood what occurs in the woman's body to make the transformation. Some believe that seeds in the expelled male liquid are quickened into growth by the natural warmth of the female tunnel. Others suggest it might be helped by the additional heat of friction during repeated thrusting of the male member.'

They dissected a breast, Nuño pointing out that the spongelike inner tissue was sometimes the site of tumors. 'In addition to delivering mother's milk to the babe, the nipples are sensitive sexual areas. Indeed, a woman can be readied for intercourse by means of stimulation of several areas by the hands or mouth of the male, but it is a secret ignored even by many anatomists that the seat of female arousal is here,' he said, and showed Yonah the tiny organ, the size of a small pea, hidden in twin folds of skin like a wrapped jewel at the top of the vagina.

It reminded Nuño of another lesson he wished to teach. 'There are women in good number in the town, more than enough of them for any man's needs to be discreetly satisfied. But stay away from whores since many have the pox, a disease to be avoided for its terrible consequences.'

A week later, he fixed that lesson firmly in Yonah's mind by bringing him to the home of Lucía Porta, in the center of the city. 'Señora, it is the physician come to see little José and Fernando,' he called, and a woman shuffled to the door.

'*Hola*, señora,' Nuño said. She looked at them without greeting but gave them entrance. A thin, small boy stood against the wall, snuffling and regarding them dully.

'*Hola*, Fernando. Fernando has nine years,' he said, and Yonah felt a stir of pity, for the boy seemed four or five years old. His legs were underdeveloped and terribly bowed. He made no protest when they examined him. Nuño pointed out that he had a clump of dark growths on his scrotum and another on his anus, like small grapes. 'We sometimes see this, but not often,' he said. He led Fernando to the window where the light was better, and held the child's mouth open wide so Yonah could see that the palate was perforated. It was a strange mouth in other ways; the two upper front teeth were gapped like pegs, narrower at the bottom than at the top. 'The hole in the palate is very commonly seen, and so are the malformed teeth.'

A crying infant lay on a pallet, and Yonah and Nuño knelt over him.

'*Hola*, José,' Nuño murmured. The baby had sores and blebs on his mouth and about his nose.

'You have enough salve, señora?'

308

'No. All gone.'

Nuño nodded. 'Then you must go to Fray Medina's shop. I shall tell him to expect you, and to give you more.'

Yonah was glad when they were in the bright sunshine again, and walking away. 'The salve will do very little,' Nuño said. 'Nothing will do much for them. The baby's sores will go away, but his front teeth no doubt will come in like his brother's. And there may be far darker complications. I have noted that several of my patients who have gone mad – two men and a woman – had suffered from the pox while younger.' He shrugged. 'The connection between the two diseases is nothing I can prove, but it is interesting that the combination appears,' he said, and for a long time that was all he taught Yonah about pox.

Nuño said his apprentice was required to attend church regularly, although at first Yonah struggled against this rule. It had been one thing to attempt an illusion of Christian piety in Gibraltar, where he was under constant scrutiny, but he rebelled against hypocritically performing the mechanics of Catholicism while living in Nuño Fierro's household, where he sensed there was no threat to a nonbeliever.

But Nuño was unyielding. 'When your apprenticeship is completed you will go before the town officials, a candidate for licensing as a physician. I must go with you. Unless they know you as a practising Christian, you will not be licensed.' Then he delivered his decisive argument. 'If you are discovered and destroyed, Reyna and I shall be destroyed with you.'

'I have been to some services of the church only a few

times, when attendance was a necessity. I was able to mimic those who sat nearby, kneeling when they knelt, sitting when they remained seated. But church attendance is dangerous for me, because I am unskilled in the subtleties of churchly behavior.'

'It is easily taught,' Nuño replied calmly, and for a time along with the lessons in medicine there was instruction about when to rise and when to kneel, how to recite Latin prayers as though they were as familiar as the Shema, and even how to genuflect upon entering the church as if Yonah had done it all the Sundays and saint's days of his life.

Spring came to Saragossa later than it had arrived in Gibraltar, but eventually the days grew longer and warmer. The trees he had pruned and fertilized in the orchard bloomed prodigiously, and he watched as the fragrant pink petals fell and were replaced within weeks by the first small fruits, both apples and peaches, hard and green.

On a day of soft rain a widow named Loretta Cavaller came to the infirmary and complained that in the past two years her monthly flows had all but disappeared, replaced by severe cramps. Small and fair-skinned, with hair the color of a mouse's fur, she described her problems haltingly, her close-set eyes looking only at the wall and never at Yonah or Nuño. She had been to two midwifes, she said, and had been given salves and nostrums but nothing had availed.

'Are your bowels open?' Nuño asked.

'Sometimes they are not.'

For when they were not he prescribed flaxseed in cold water to be drunk seeds and all. Outside the dispensary her horse and cart waited, but Nuño told her that for a time she must leave the cart at home when she went on errands, and ride on horseback. For increasing her monthly bleeding he instructed her to boil in water cherry bark and purslane and leaves of raspberry and to sip the resulting infusion four times each day, continuing this treatment until thirty days after her flow became regulated.

'I am not certain where to find the ingredients,' she said, and Nuño told her they might be purchased at the apothecary's shop in Saragossa.

But the next afternoon Yonah collected strips of bark from a wild cherry tree and gathered purslane and new leaves from a berry bush, and that evening he carried them, along with a bottle of wine, to the woman's small house by the Ebro River. Her feet were bare when she answered his knocking at the door, but she invited him in and thanked him for the bark and the leaves. She gave him a mug of his own wine and poured a mug for herself, and they sat by the fire on two beautifully carved chairs. When Yonah complimented them she said they had been made by her late husband Jiménez Reverte, who had been a master carpenter.

'How long has it been since your husband died?' Yonah asked, and the woman said it was two years and two months since Jiménez had been stricken by the thrush and carried off, and that she prayed daily for his immortal soul.

They never knew ease with one another but conversed awkwardly, separated by silences. Yonah was aware of what he wanted to occur but unversed in the kind of conversation that might bring it about. Finally when he stood she rose too; he knew he would have to

311

leave unless he acted, and he put his arms around her and bent to touch his lips to her mouth.

Loretta Cavaller remained very still in his embrace before she disengaged and took the oil lamp and led him across the room, to where he followed her bare feet up the steep, narrow stairway. In her chamber he had only the briefest opportunity to see that Jiménez had carved her bedstead more cunningly than the chairs, all oaken grapes and figs and pomegranates, and then she carried the lamp from the chamber and left it on the floor of the hall. When she returned there was the quick rasp of material drawn against flesh as they divested themselves of clothing and dropped it onto the floor

They fell against each other then like a pair of long-parched travelers in a dry desert, as if each of them expected sweet water; yet the union brought Yonah only relief, and not the rich pleasure for which he yearned. Presently, lying in the dark room scented by what they had been doing, he explored with his hands flaccid breasts, sharp hipbones, and knobbly knees.

She put on her shift before reclaiming the lamp. Yonah was never to see her naked. Though he came back to her house to lie with her three more times their joinings lacked passion, as if he were committing an act of onanism with her borrowed body. They had almost nothing to say to one another; awkward conversation was followed by release in the fine bed, followed by spare and clumsy words as he took his leave. The fourth time he came to her house, when she answered his knocking she didn't invite him in, and he could see past her to where Roque Arellano, the Saragossa butcher, sat at her table with his shoes off, drinking wine Yonah had given her.

Several Sundays later Yonah was in church when the banns of Loretta Cavaller and Roque Arellano were read by the priest. After they were married Loretta Cavaller began to work in her husband's butcher shop, a prosperous business. Nuño kept chickens but didn't raise beef or pork and several times Reyna asked Yonah to go to the butcher's to buy meat or the fish which Arellano sometimes also carried. Loretta had become skilled; he admired the swift, sure way she cut and trimmed meat. Arellano's prices were high, but Loretta always greeted him cordially, her close-set eyes beaming, and often she gave him marrow bones that Reyna used when she made soup or potted a fowl.

Both Nuño and Reyna had come to live in the hacienda when the *maestro* of the house was Gabriel ben Nissim Sporanis, and it had been the Jewish physician's custom to bathe before sundown each Friday, preparing himself for the Sabbath. Nuño and Reyna had fallen into the habit of weekly bathing, Nuño taking to the bath on Mondays and Reyna on Wednesdays, so water would be needed to be heated for only one bath in the course of an evening. The bathing was done in a copper tub placed before the fire, where a kettle of additional water was kept heating.

It was great luxury for Yonah to bathe each Friday as Montesa had done, though he had to scrunch his large body into the confines of the tub. On Wednesday evenings sometimes he would walk outside while Reyna bathed, but more often he stayed in his room, playing his guitar or working on the Avicenna by lamplight. It was hard to concentrate on memorizing the drugs that had astringent uses on sores and those that

313

warmed and did not purge, while trying to imagine how she looked.

When the water cooled, he could hear Nuño going to her, taking the kettle off the fire and adding hot water to the tub, as she did for the *maestro* on Mondays. Nuño also provided this act of courtesy for his apprentice on Fridays, moving slowly and with exertion as he lifted the kettle, warned Yonah to swing his legs out of the way lest he be burned, and poured the hot water, his breathing labored.

'He does too much. He is no longer young,' Reyna said to Yonah one morning when Nuño was occupied in the barn.

'I try to lighten his load,' Yonah said, feeling guilty.

'I know. I asked him why he must lavish so much of his strength in teaching you,' she told him frankly. 'He said, "I do it because he is worth it."' She shrugged and sighed.

Yonah could offer her no comfort. Nuño forced himself to ride out even when the cases were so ordinary that follow-up calls could be made by the apprentice alone. It wasn't enough for Nuño that Yonah had read Rhazes, who pointed out that superfluities and poisons were eliminated from the body each time urine was voided; the *maestro* must point out to Yonah at bedside the lemony colour of the void of the patient who had a long-lasting fever, the pinkish urine occurring at the start of malarial fevers that recurred every seventy-two hours, the white spumous urine that sometimes came with pus-filled boils. He taught Yonah to detect the varied stink of disease in piss.

Nuño also demonstrated an excellent grasp in the art and science of apothecary. He knew how to dry and grind herbs to powder, and how to make unguents and perfusions, but he sacrificed the convenience of making his own medicines. Instead he patronized an aged Franciscan, Fray Luis Guerra Medina, a skilled apothecary who also had provided medications for Sporanis.

'There is much suspicion of poisonings, especially when a member of royalty dies. Sometimes the supposition is well grounded, but often it is not,' Nuño told Yonah. 'For a long time the Church forbade all Christians from taking medications prepared by Jews, lest they be poisoned. Some Jewish physicians prepared their own remedies anyway, but a number of physicians, Old Christians as well as Jews, have been accused of attempted poisonings by patients who didn't wish to pay their medical debts. Gabriel Sporanis felt safer using an apothecary who was a friar, and I use Fray Guerra also. I have found that he well knows the difference between hemp agrimony and cassia fistula.'

Yonah saw what he had risked by supplying medicinal herbs to Loretta Cavaller and understood he must never do it again. Thus he learned from the older man and listened as Nuño Fierro sought to prepare him for life as a physician, both in professional knowledge and in the homely matters that composed a successful practice.

One day, when Yonah had been an apprentice physician little more than a year, he realized that in that time, eleven of their patients had died.

He had learned enough medicine to understand that Nuño Fierro was an exceptionally good physician and to recognize his good fortune to be in the hands of such a teacher; yet it weighed on him that he was entering a profession in which the practitioner so often failed.

315

Nuño Fierro watched his pupil the way a good horse trainer studies a promising horse. He saw Yonah fight bitterly against the gathering darkness when a patient lay dying, and noted the gravity that settled into the younger man's being with every death.

He waited until one evening when teacher and student sat by the fire in weary rest, mugs of wine in hand.

'You killed the man who slew my brother. Have you taken other lives, Ramón?'

'I have.'

Nuño took a sip of wine, studying him as the apprentice told of how he had arranged for the murder of two relic dealers.

'If these incidents could be lived again, would you behave differently?' Nuño asked.

'No, because all three men would have killed me. But the thought that I have taken human life is a burden.'

'And do you wish to practice medicine as a chance to atone for the lives you have taken, by saving other lives?'

'It wasn't the reason I asked you to teach me to be a physician. Yet perhaps lately I have had similar thoughts,' he admitted.

'Then you must see the powers of the medical art more clearly. A physician is able to ease the suffering of a small number of people. We fight their disease, we bind their wounds and set their broken bones and deliver their young. Yet every living creature eventually must come to an end. So despite our learning and skill and passion, some of our patients die, and we must not overly mourn or feel guilt that we are not gods who are able to grant eternity. Instead, if they used their time well, we must be grateful they had experienced the blessing of life.'

Yonah nodded. 'I understand.'

'I hope so,' Nuño said. 'Because if you lack this understanding you will be a poor physician indeed, for you will go mad.'

30
The Testing of Ramón Callicó

By the end of the second year of Yonah's apprenticeship the way of his life seemed clear and determined, and each day continued to be an excitement to him as he absorbed what Nuño taught. Their practice extended widely into the countryside surrounding Saragossa, and they were kept busy in the dispensary and riding out to tend to patients who were unable to come to them. Most of Nuño's patients were the common people of the town and the farms. Occasionally he was summoned by a nobleman in need of a physician and he always responded, but he told Yonah that noble patients were imperious and apt to be reluctant to pay physicians for their work, and he didn't seek them out. But on the twentieth of November in the year 1504, he received a summons he could not ignore.

Late that summer both King Ferdinand and Queen Isabella had been taken with a debilitating illness. The king, a robust man whose constitution was conditioned by years of hunting and warfare, had quickly recovered, but his wife had grown steadily weaker. Now Isabella had taken a precipitous turn for the worse while visiting the town of Medina del Campo, and Ferdinand had sent a frantic summons to half a dozen physicians, including Nuño Fierro, the physician of Saragossa.

'But surely you are not able to go,' Yonah protested gently. 'It is a ride of ten days to Medina del Campo. Eight days if you kill yourself.' He meant the words literally, for he knew Nuño was not robust and shouldn't attempt such a trip.

But the physician was adamant. 'She is my queen. A monarch in need must be attended no less faithfully than a common man or woman.'

'At least allow me to travel with you,' Yonah said.

But Nuño refused. 'You must remain here to continue to provide care for our patients,' he said.

When Yonah and Reyna united to plead that he must have someone to assist him along the way, Nuño conceded the argument and hired Andrés de Ávila, a man of the town, to accompany him, and the two of them rode off early the next morning.

They returned too soon, and in foul and wet weather. Yonah had to help Nuño from his horse. While Reyna saw that the physician immediately had a hot bath, Ávila told Yonah what had occurred.

The trip had been everything Yonah had feared. Ávila said they had ridden four and a half days. By the time they had reached an inn just beyond the town of Atienza, he had been concerned that Nuño was too fatigued to go on.

'I convinced him to stop for a meal and a rest that would allow us to proceed. But within the inn we found people engaged in drinking to the memory of Isabella.'

Ávila said that Nuño had asked hoarsely if the drinkers knew for certain that she had died, and other travelers from the west assured him that even then the monarch's body was being borne south to Granada for interment in the royal tomb.

Nuño and Ávila had spent a sleepless, louse-bitten night on the inn's sleeping floor, and in the morning they began to ride east, back to Saragossa. 'This time we traveled at a slower pace,' Ávila said, 'but it has been an ill-starred journey in every way, and the entire last day of the ride has been through the cold and driving rain.'

Despite the bath Yonah was alarmed to observe Nuño's weariness and pallor. He placed the physician into his bed at once and Reyna plied him with hot drinks and nourishing food. After a week of bed rest he was somewhat recovered, but the fruitless ride toward a dying queen of Spain had sorely sapped and limited his strength.

The time came when Nuño experienced a trembling of his hands that made it impossible for him to use the surgical instruments his brother had made for him. Yonah used them instead, with the physician standing next to him, instructing, explaining, asking questions that challenged and taught the apprentice.

Before an amputation of a crushed little finger, he had Yonah feel his own finger with the fingertips of his other hand. 'Do you feel a place – the slight gap where bone meets bone? That is where the crushed finger should be severed, but you must leave the skin uncut higher up, well before the amputation. Do you know why?'

'We must construct a flap,' Yonah said, and the older man nodded in satisfaction.

While Yonah deeply regretted Nuño's misfortune, yet it was an advantage in his training, because throughout the entire last year of his apprenticeship he performed far more surgery than would otherwise have been the case.

He felt guilty because Fierro was channeling his strength toward teaching him, but when he expressed the thought to Reyna she shook her head. 'I believe the need to teach you is keeping him alive,' she said.

Indeed, when the fourth year of the apprenticeship came to an end, there was a gleam of triumph in Nuño Fierro's eyes. At once, he acted to bring Yonah before the medical examiners of the district. Each year, three days before Christmas, the municipal officers elected two physicians of the district to be examiners of candidates for medical licensing. Nuño had served as an examiner and knew the process well.

'I would have preferred that you wait for testing until the departure of one of the present examiners, Pedro de Calca,' he told Yonah. For many years Calca had envied and resented the physician of Saragossa. But Nuño's intuition told him not to delay. 'I cannot wait another year,' he told Yonah. 'And I believe you are ready.' The next day, he rode to the municipal building of Saragossa and made the appointment for Yonah's examination.

On the morning of the testing, the student and the teacher left the hacienda early and rode their horses slowly through the bright morning warmth. They spoke little in their nervousness. It was too late for priming Yonah's intellect; they had had four long years for that.

The municipal building smelled of dust and several

centuries of human traffic, though that morning only Yonah, Nuño, and the two examiners were there.

'Gentlemen, I have the honor of presenting Señor Ramón Callicó for your examination,' Nuño said calmly.

One of the examiners was Miguel de Montenegro, a small, grave man with silver hair, beard, and mustache. Nuño had known him well for many years and had assured Yonah that Montenegro would be serious and conscientious about his responsibilities as an examiner, yet fair.

The other examiner, Calca, was a smiling, hearty man with red hair and a small, sharp beard. He wore a tunic encrusted with dried and clotted blood, pus, and mucus. Nuño already had disdainfully described the tunic to Yonah as 'the man's boastful advertisement of his trade,' and had warned Yonah that Calca had read Galen and little else, so that most of his questions would come from Galen.

The four of them sat at the table. Yonah told himself that two and a half decades before, Nuño Fierro had sat in this room and taken his examination, and several decades before that, Gabriel ben Nissim Sporanis had done so too, in a time when a physician could announce that he was a Jew.

Each examiner would have two rounds of questioning, and Montenegro went first, his due as the senior physician. 'If you please, Señor Callicó. I would like you to speak to us about the advantages and the disadvantages of prescribing theriac as an antidote against fevers.'

'I shall begin with the disadvantages,' Yonah said, 'for they are few and can quickly be dealt with. The medication is complex to assemble, containing up to seventy constituent herbs, and therefore it is difficult to compound

322

and expensive to buy. Its chief advantage is that it is a proven and effective agent against fevers, intestinal ailments, and even some kinds of poisonings.' He could feel himself unwind as he moved easily from point to point, trying to make his exposition complete without being excessive. Montenegro appeared to be satisfied. 'My second question deals with the differences between quartan and tertian fevers.'

'Tertian fevers appear every third day, counting the day of occurrence as the first day. Quartan fevers appear every four days. These fevers are most likely to occur where the climate is warm and moist, and often are accompanied by chills, sweats, and great weakness.'

'Quickly and briefly answered. To cure hemorrhoids, would you remove them by knife?'

'Only if nothing else would help. Often the pain and unpleasantness can be controlled by a healthful diet that avoids sharp, salty, or very sweet foods. If there is copious bleeding, styptic medication can be applied. If they swell but do not bleed, they may be lanced or drained with leeches.'

Montenegro nodded and sat back, indicating that it was Pedro de Calca's turn.

Calca stroked his red beard. 'Speak to us, please, of the Galenic system of humoral pathology,' he said, and settled back in his chair.

Yonah was ready and he drew a breath. 'It originated as a few ideas expressed by the Hippocratic school and was modified by other early medical philosophers, especially Aristotle. Galen molded their ideas into a theory that said all things are composed of four elements – fire, earth, air, and water – producing the four qualities of hot, cold, dry, and wet. When food and drink are taken into the body, they are cooked by natural heat and transformed into four humors, blood, phlegm, yellow bile, and black bile. Air corresponds to blood, which is wet and hot, water to phlegm, which is wet and cold, fire to yellow bile, which is dry and hot, and earth to black bile, which is dry and cold.

'Galen wrote that a portion of these substances is carried by the blood to nourish the various organs of the body, while the rest is excreted as waste. He said that the proportions in which the qualities are combined in the body are very important. An ideal mixture of qualities produces a person in a state of well-being. Too much or too little of a humor upsets the balance, resulting in illness.'

Calca played with his beard again: stroke, stroke. 'Tell us about innate heat and the pneuma.'

'Hippocrates and Aristotle, and then Galen, wrote that the heat within the body is the substance of life. This internal heat is nourished by the pneuma, a spirit which is formed in the purest blood of the liver and carried by the veins. Yet it cannot be seen. It—'

'How do you know it cannot be seen?' Calca interrupted, and Yonah felt Nuño's warning knee press hard against his own.

Because thus far we have dissected the veins and the organs of three cadavers, and Nuño has shown me only tissue and blood and pointed out that we were unable to see anything that might be called the pneuma. He was a fool; Calca would realize that the only one who could know such a thing was someone who had opened a body and witnessed it. For a moment, terror seized his vocal cords.

'It is . . . something I have read.'

'Where have you read this, Señor Callicó? For it seems

324

to me I have never heard whether the pneuma can be seen or cannot be seen.'

Yonah paused. 'It was not in Avicenna or in Galen that I read it,' he said, as though trying to recall. 'I believe it was in Teodorico Borgognoni.'

Calca looked at him.

'Quite so,' said Miguel de Montenegro. 'That is it. I recall reading it in Teodorico Borgognoni myself,' and Nuño Fierro nodded in agreement.

Calca nodded as well. 'Borgognoni, of course.'

As his second round of questioning, Montenegro asked Yonah to compare the treatment of a fractured bone with the treatment of a dislocation. They listened to his answer without comment and then Montenegro asked him to list the factors necessary for health.

'Uncontaminated air, food and drink, sleep to rest the body's forces and wakefulness to make the senses active, moderate physical exercise to expel residues and impurities, elimination of wastes, and sufficient joy to make the body prosperous.'

'Tell us how disease is spread during epidemic,' Calca said.

'Poisonous miasmas are formed by decaying corpses or the fetid waters of swamps. Warm, moist air charged with corruption gives off noxious odors that, if breathed in by healthy persons, may infect and sicken their bodies. During epidemics, the healthy should be encouraged to flee, going far enough so that miasmas cannot be carried to them on the wind.'

There followed quick strokes of the red beard and a rapid series of questions about urine: 'What does urine signify when it is somewhat yellow?'

'It contains a measure of bile.'

'And when the urine is the color of fire?'

'It contains a great deal of bile.'

'Dark red piss?'

'In one who has not been eating saffron, it contains blood.'

'If the urine is seen to contain sediment?'

'It indicates internal weakness of the patient. If the sediment looks like bran and has a bad odor, it indicates that there is ulceration within the ducts. If the sediment has decomposed blood, it marks a phlegmonous tumor.'

'If one sees sand in the urine?' Calca asked.

'It reveals a calculus or stone.'

There was a silence.

'I am satisfied,' Calca said.

'I am satisfied also. A fine candidate who reflects his teacher,' Montenegro said, and proceeded to take down from a shelf the great leather-bound municipal volume. He recorded in it the names of the examiners and the nominator, as well as the intelligence that Señor Ramón Callicó of Saragossa had been examined and duly accepted and licensed as a physician on the seventeenth day of October, Anno Domini 1506.

On the way home teacher and pupil lolled in their saddles and chortled like children or drunkards.

'I believe I read it in Teodorico Borgognoni! I believe I read it in Teodorico Borgognoni!' Nuño mocked him.

'But Señor Montenegro . . . Why did he support me?'

'Miguel de Montenegro is a good and celebrated Catholic, the favorite physician of the Church and a man who is called upon to travel far and wide when a bishop or cardinal suffers illness. Yet he is a true medical scientist who makes up his own mind about what is science

326

and what is sin. He and I dissected together several times when we were younger. I am sure he perceived at once why you could attest so confidently regarding the appearance of something internal to the body.'

'I am grateful to him, and fortunate.'

'Yes, you are fortunate, but you performed in a manner that does you great credit.'

'I was most fortunate in my teacher, Maestro,' he said.

'You should refer to me as your *maestro* no longer, for now we are colleagues,' Nuño said, but Yonah shook his head.

'Two men will always have my gratitude, he said. 'Both of them are Fierro. And each will ever be *maestro* to me.'

31

A Hard Day's Work

Only a few weeks after the examination Nuño turned over a number of their patients to him. Day by day, Yonah felt more like a physician and less like an apprentice.

Late in February Nuño told him that an annual gathering of the physicians of Aragon would be held in Saragossa. 'It will be good for you to go to the gathering, and to meet your colleagues,' he told Yonah, and both of them arranged their schedules so they might attend.

When they reached the inn they found seven other physicians drinking wine and eating garlicky roasted duck. Both Pedro de Calca and Miguel de Montenegro greeted them, and Nuño derived obvious pleasure in introducing Yonah to the other five, practitioners from the outer edges of the district. When they were finished eating, Calca gave a talk on the role of the pulse in illness. Yonah thought it was ill prepared and was troubled that one of the men who had so recently examined him could present so poor a lecture. Yet when Calca finished, the other physicians stamped their feet in apparent approval, and when he asked if anyone there had a question, no man ventured to rise.

Yonah had been amazed to hear Calca state that there were three types of pulse: strong, weak and bounding. *Dare I contradict?* Yonah wondered, painfully aware how new a physician he was. Yet he could not resist, and he lifted his hand.

'Señor Callicó?' Calca said, in evident amusement.

'I would like to add . . . to point out . . . that Avicenna wrote that there are nine kinds of pulse. The first, an even, ample signal of healthy equilibrium. A steady pulse that is stronger still, signaling power in the heart. A weak pulse that is just the opposite, denoting a weak force. And varieties of weakness – a long and a short, a narrow and a full, a superficial and a deep.'

He saw with dismay that Calca was scowling at him. Next to him he could feel Nuño struggling to his feet.

'How good that we have at our meeting both a new physician fresh from book studies and an excellent and seasoned practitioner who well knows that in the daily treatment of folk, the rules of our art are made simpler by experience and hard-gained wisdom.' There were a few chuckles and a resumed stamping of feet while Calca smiled, mollified. Yonah could feel the blood risen to his face as he took his seat.

After they had arrived home, his complaint burst from him. 'How could you speak in such a manner, when you knew well that Calca was wrong and I was right?'

'Because Calca is precisely the kind of man who might go to the Inquisition and charge a rival with heresy if he is sufficiently provoked, which every physician who was there fully understood,' Nuño said. 'I pray the day may

329

come in our Spain when a physician may disagree with impunity and safely argue in public, but now is not that day, nor shall it arrive tomorrow.'

At once Yonah understood that he had been a fool, and presently he muttered his thanks and an apology. Nuño didn't make light of the incident. 'You came to me aware of the dangers that exist for you from religion. You must also be vigilant against aspects of our profession that might bring catastrophe.'

He grinned suddenly at Yonah. 'Besides, you were not completely accurate in your remarks. In the translated pages of the *Canon* you have given to me, Avicenna said there are *ten* different kinds of pulse – and then listed only nine! He also wrote that subtle differences in the pulse are useful only to skillful physicians. You will discover that this description fits only a few of the men with whom we have broken bread this day.'

Three weeks later, Nuño had a severe attack. He had been in the process of climbing the stairs to his room when a grinding pain in his chest struck him a wild and sudden blow that left him weak and gasping, so that he had to sit in order to avoid a nasty fall. Yonah had been out seeing patients and was in the barn, unsaddling the gray Arab, when a distraught Reyna opened the door. 'He is badly taken,' she said, and Yonah hurried into the house with her. Between them they managed to get Nuño into bed where, in a drenching sweat, he gasped out signs as if he were standing over a patient and lecturing to Yonah.

'Pain is . . . dull, not . . . sharp. But . . . pronounced. Very pronounced . . .'

When Yonah checked the pulse, it was so irregular it

330

frightened him. It seemed to beat in fits and starts, to no rhythm he could perceive. He gave Nuño sips of camphor in apple liquor against the pain, which persisted strongly nevertheless for almost four hours. In the evening it lifted and then was gone, leaving Nuño lying abed with no strength at all.

But he was calm, and able to speak. He bade Reyna to kill a hen and make a broth for his dinner that day, and then he fell into a deep sleep. For a time Yonah watched him, realizing too well the limitations of the physician, because he wanted to do anything that would make Nuño well but had not the slightest idea what to do.

Within three days Nuño was able to make his way slowly down the stairs with Yonah's help, to sit during the day in his chair. For ten more days Yonah held on to hope for him, but by the end of the second week it was clear he had met with serious trouble. His chest was congested and his legs had begun to swell. At first Yonah tried raising his head and chest at night, propping him up in bed against several pillows. But soon both the swelling and the breathing grew worse, and day or night, Nuño refused to be moved from his chair by the fire. At night Yonah lay on the floor a few feet away from him, listening to the bubbling respirations of the seated man.

By the third week the signs of final illness were indisputable. The liquid that gurgled in his lungs seemed to have pervaded all the tissues of his body so that he had taken on the appearance of obesity, with legs like posts and a pendulous abdomen that drooped over itself. He had tried not to speak, finding it an effort even to breathe, but at last, in breathless spurts, he gave Yonah instructions.

331

He was to be buried on his own property, on the crest of the hill. There was to be no memorial stone.

Yonah could only nod.

'My will. Write it . . . down.'

So Yonah fetched paper and ink and quill, and Nuño dictated terms in breathless spurts.

To Reyna Fadique he left the savings he had accrued in his career as a medical practitioner.

To Ramón Callicó he left his land and hacienda, his medical books and instruments, and the leather chest and contents that had belonged to Nuño's departed brother, the late Manuel Fierro.

Yonah was unable to absorb it without protest. 'It is far too much. I have no need . . .'

But Nuño closed his eyes. 'No relatives . . .' he said, and with a weak hand, gestured the subject closed. He reached out for the pen, and when he signed the will the signature was a scrawl.

'Something . . . more. You must . . . study me.'

Yonah knew what Nuño meant but didn't think he could do it. It was one thing to cut into the flesh of strangers while his *maestro* was inducting him into the secrets of anatomy. But this was *Nuño*.

Nuño's eyes blazed. 'You wish . . . to be . . . like Calca . . . or like me?'

What he wished was to be able to do this man's dying for him.

'Like you. I love you and thank you. I do promise.'

Nuño died sitting in his chair, somewhere between the rainy darkness of January 17, 1507, and the gray dawn of January 18.

Yonah sat on his pallet and looked at him for a time.

332

Then he rose and kissed his *maestro*'s forehead, which was still warm, and closed his eyes.

Despite his own size and strength he staggered under the weight as he took the body to the barn, where he carried out the dead physician's wishes as though he could hear his voice.

First he put quill to paper, making note of what he had observed before mortality. He wrote of the coughing that produced blood-tinged sputum. Of skin that was sometimes tinged purple. Of neck veins that had been enlarged and pulsating, of drenching sweats, of a heart that seemed to beat as quickly and erratically as a running mouse. Of rapid, noisy, and labored breathing, and of the softly swelling skin.

After he had finished writing he picked up one of the scalpels that Manuel Fierro had made and, for only a moment, studied Nuño's face as he lay on the table.

When he opened the chest he saw that the heart had a different appearance from the other hearts he and Nuño had examined. There was a blackened area on the outer surface, as if the tissue had been burned. When he sliced it open, the four chambers looked wrong. On the left side, a portion of one of the chambers was blackened and eaten away, part of the damaged section that went all the way to the exterior. In order to study it, he had to use cloths to soak up and wipe away the blood. He thought it had not been able to pump properly, because blood apparently had backed up and had been jammed into both of the left chambers and some neighboring veins. Yonah knew from Avicenna's *Canon* that to maintain life the blood must be pumped by the heart so that it perfused the whole body, coursing through large arteries and a network of veins that became finer and ever finer until they ended in the very fine, hairlike channels called capillaries. Nuño's ruined heart had destroyed that blood-distribution system and had cost him his life.

When he cut into the swollen tissue of the abdomen he found it was wet, and so were the lungs. Nuño had drowned in his own juices. But from where had all the wetness come?

Yonah hadn't the slightest idea.

He went through the routine he had learned well, weighing the organs and recording the statistics before he put things back into place and closed Nuño up. Then he bathed with raw soap and the bucket of water that was kept by the table, as he had been taught, and added his observations to the writing. Only when that was done did he allow himself to go into the house.

Reyna was calmly making a gruel, but she had known Nuño was dead the moment she had seen the empty chair.

'Where is he?'

'In the barn.'

'Had I best go and see him?'

'No,' Yonah said, and she breathed in sharply and crossed herself, but made no objection. Nuño had told Yonah that almost three decades of serving physicians in this hacienda had made Reyna fully aware of what went on there, and that she could be trusted absolutely. Still, Yonah hadn't known her all his life, and he worried that she might denounce him.

'I'll give you some gruel.'

'No. I have no hunger.'

'You have much to do this day,' she said quietly, and she filled two bowls. They sat together and ate without speaking, and when he was finished he asked her if there was anyone else Nuño would have wanted at his burial, but she shook her head.

'There is just us,' she said, and he went outside and began to work.

There were sawn planks in one of the animal stalls, quite old but still sound, and Yonah measured Nuño with a piece of cord and then cut the wood to size. It took him most of the morning to make the coffin. He had to ask her if there were nails anywhere about, and she found them for him.

Then he took a mattock and a spade and went up to the crest of the hill and dug the hole. The winter was upon Saragossa but the ground was unfrozen, and the grave took shape under his steady labor. It had been years since he was a *peón* and he knew his body would remind him of that the next day. He worked slowly and carefully, making the sides even and smooth, and deep enough so he had to exert himself to get out of it, heaving himself up and sending a shower of dirt and small stones back into the hole.

In the barn he rolled up the bloody rags inside a clean cloth and stuffed them into the coffin next to Nuño. It was the safest way to be rid of them, and as he hammered the top pieces onto the box he knew it was exactly what Nuño would have had him do. Even without the rags to dispose of he would have a difficult time cleaning up to leave no trace of the dissection.

The work took him the whole day. Dusk was near when he hitched Nuño's brown horse and the gray Arab to the farm wagon. Reyna had to help him carry the heavy burden from the barn.

It was devilishly hard for the two of them to get the casket into the earth. He stretched two ropes across the hole and then tied the ends into loops that he slipped over stout pegs driven into the ground. When they settled the box over the hole, the ropes held, but they had to work the loops off the pegs and hold the ropes taut on both sides of the grave, so the coffin could be lowered a little at a time. Reyna struggled with one of the loops. She was strong and work-hardened, but when finally the loop came free of the peg she lost control of the other rope long enough so a corner of the coffin dipped and dug into the side of the hole.

'Pull back hard on the rope,' he said, speaking much more calmly than he felt. But she had started to do that even before he spoke. The box still was not quite level, but there was no disaster.

'Take a step,' he said, and they both did so. That way, step by step, they advanced and lowered the coffin until it rested on the bottom.

He was able to pull up one of the rope strands but the other rope caught on something beneath the coffin. Perhaps the loop had snagged on a root; after a few hard tugs he threw his end of the rope back into the grave.

She said a Paternoster and an Ave María, crying quietly now, as if ashamed of her grief.

'Drive the wagon horses back to the barn,' he said gently. 'Then you go back into the house. I will finish things here.'

She was a country woman who knew how to handle horses, but he waited until the wagon was halfway down the hill before he picked up the spade. He took the first shovelfuls of dirt on the back side of the spade, the Jewish custom symbolizing that it was a hard duty to bury someone who would be sorely missed. Then he turned the spade right side up and drove it hard into the dirt pile, grunting. At first the rain of dirt rattled hollowly against the box but soon the sound was quieter, dirt falling on dirt.

The hole was only half filled when full night came, but there was a high white moon in the sky, and he could see well enough to work steadily and with few pauses.

He was almost finished when Reyna came back up the hill. She stopped before she reached him. 'How long shall you be?' she called.

'Only a little while now,' he said, and she didn't reply but turned around and went back to the house.

When he had mounded the grave as best he could, he placed his hand on his uncovered head and said the Kaddish for the dead, and then carried the spade and the mattock back to the barn. Inside the house, he saw that she had already gone to her room. She had carried in the copper tub and had placed it before the fire. The water it held was still hot, and there were two more kettles of water over the fire. On the table she had left him wine, bread, cheese, and olives.

He undressed near the crackling fire and left his damp and grimy clothing in a pile, then he sat scrunched in the tub with a piece of Reyna's strong brown soap in his hand, thinking of Nuño – of his wisdom and tolerance, of his love for the people he had doctored and his dedication to the practice of medicine. Of the kindness he had shown a battered young man who had drifted into his life. Of the difference Nuño Fierro had made in the life of Yonah Toledano. Long, long thoughts . . . until he realized the water was growing cold, and he began to wash himself.

32

The Solitary Practitioner

Next morning he went up the hill and neatened the grave by daylight. There was a small sapling oak nearby that reminded him of the unplanted tree growing from his father's resting place, and he dug it up carefully and transplanted it into the soft earth of Nuño's grave. This tree was quite small and bare of leaves, but in warmer weather it would grow.

'You must inform the priests,' Reyna told him, 'and give to the church so they will say a Mass for his immortal soul.'

'First I shall mourn him inside this house for seven days,' Yonah said. 'Then I'll tell the priests and we will go to the church for the Mass.'

Reyna's piety was skin-deep and brought forth only by the solemnity of death, and she shrugged and told him to do as he wished.

He was conscious that he had never observed his father's death properly. Nuño had been like a father to him, and he wished to show his respect in the ways he remembered. He rent one of his garments, went shoeless in the house, shrouded the one small mirror with a cloth, and recited the Kaddish in Nuño's memory morning and evening, as a son would do for a father.

Three times during the week someone came to the house in need of the doctor; once he took a man into the dispensary in the barn and splinted a sprained wrist, and twice he rode out to homes and doctored the sick. He also went to the homes of four patients whom he knew needed his attention, but each time he returned to the hacienda to renew his mourning.

After he had observed the week of shiva, and after the memorial Mass had been said for Nuño, Yonah was left with a life that felt strange to him, an existence for which he had to make new rules.

Reyna waited a week before asking him why he was still sleeping on the pallet in the little storeroom, when now he was the *maestro* of the house. Nuño's chamber was the best room, with two windows, one facing south and one facing east. The bed was large and commodious, made of cherrywood.

They went through the dead *maestro*'s belongings together. Nuño's clothing was of good quality but he had been smaller than Yonah, and stout. Reyna was clever with a needle and said she would alter some of the garments so they would fit Yonah. 'It will be nice for you to wear something of his now and then, and to think of him.' What Yonah couldn't use she put aside, saying she would bring the garments to her village, where each would be gratefully received.

When Yonah claimed the room, he spent the night in a bed for the first time since he had fled from Toledo. By the time he had slept there a fortnight, he felt a sense of ownership; the house and land had become part of him, and he cherished the place as if he had been born there.

When he dealt with his patients a number of them spoke sadly of Nuño's passing. 'He was ever a good and faithful physician and he had our warm affection,' Pascual Cabrera said. But Señor Cabrera and his wife – indeed, most of the patients in the practice – had grown accustomed to Ramón Callicó during his long years of training and seemed to be very satisfied with him, and it took him less time to become acclimated to being a solitary practitioner than it took for him to become conditioned to the bed. He didn't truly feel alone as a physician. When he attended a difficult patient he heard a number of voices in his mind, Avicenna's, and Galen's and Borgognoni's. But always there was Nuño's overriding voice that seemed to say, 'Remember what the great ones wrote, and the things that I taught you. And then look at the patient with your eyes, and smell the patient with your nose, and feel the patient with your hands, and use your own good sense to decide what must be done.'

He and Reyna settled into a quiet and somewhat awkward routine. When he was home he read from the small medical library or worked at his translation, while she took care not to disturb him as she went about her chores.

One evening several months after Nuño's death, as Yonah settled into his chair by the fire she refilled his glass with wine. 'Is there anything special you will want for your dinner tomorrow?' she asked.

Yonah felt the heat of the wine and the heat of the fire. He looked at her standing there, a good servant, as if she had not seen him homeless and desperate, as if he had always been lord of the finca.

'I would appreciate it if you will make a potted fowl.'

They regarded one another. It was impossible for him to guess what she was thinking. But she inclined her head, and that night she came to his room for the first time.

She was older than he, perhaps by even as much as two decades. There was white hair among the black, but her body was firm from a life of the kind of hard work that had not made an old woman of her early, and she was more than willing to share his bed. From time to time she made a remark that gave Yonah reason to believe that when she was a young woman she had also shared the bed of Nuño's Jewish *maestro*, Gabriel Sporanis. It was not that she came with the property. He understood that having a man's body made her feel alive, and she had happened to work alone with three men of whom, over time, she had grown fond.

Yet in the morning she was as proper and respectful a housekeeper for Yonah as she always had been to Nuño.

He quickly grew to be very contented, what with the work he loved astonishingly, and her good food and the ease they brought to one another regularly in his own wooden bed.

When he walked the property it bothered him that the land wasn't properly utilized, but he didn't plan to work it, for the same reason that its earlier physician-owners hadn't done so: it would not do to have *peóns* on the place to observe that the barn attached to the house contained not only a dispensary and a surgical table but was occasionally used for anatomical study that many might term witchcraft.

So when spring came that year he husbanded only so much of the farm as he could manage with his own hands and available time. He established three hives of bees for honey, and pruned a few of the olive and fruit trees, manuring them with the waste of the horses. Later in the year the orchard brought them their first good harvest of fruit for cooking and the table. It was a life that allowed Yonah to enjoy the rotation of the seasons.

He did not allow himself the dangerous outward manifestations of a Jew, but on the eves of Sabbath he always burned two tapers in his chamber and whispered the prayer: 'Blessed art Thou, Lord our God, King of the Universe, who has sanctified us with His commandments, and commanded us to light the Sabbath candles.'

Medicine filled his life richly, almost as if it were a religion he could practice in public, but he struggled to keep alive an inner existence as a Jew. Translating had brought back much of his skill with the Hebrew language, but he had lost the ability to pray in his father's tradition. He recalled only snatches of prayers. Even the framework of the Sabbath service had slipped from his grasp. For example, he could remember that the part of the service that called for prayer while standing – the Amidah – was made up of Eighteen Benedictions. Try as he might, with anguish and frustration, he remembered only seventeen. Furthermore, of the prayers he could recall, one of them troubled him terribly. The twelfth benediction was a prayer for the destruction of heretics.

When he had memorized the prayers as a boy in his father's house he hadn't pondered too deeply concerning their meaning. But now, living in the dark shadow of an Inquisition that sought to destroy heretics, this prayer arrowed its way into his heart.

Did it mean that if Jews were in power instead of the Church, they would also use God to destroy nonbelievers? Was it an axiom that absolute religious power must bring with it absolute cruelty?

Ha-Rakhaman, Our Father in Heaven, one God of all, why do You allow slaughter to be done so carelessly in Your name?

Yonah was certain that the ancients who composed the Eighteen Benedictions were godly men and scholars. But the author of the twelfth benediction would not have written it if he had been the last Jew in Spain.

One day, in a pile of worthless junk behind which a one-eyed beggar-pedlar sat in the Plaza Mayor, Yonah saw an object that made him catch his breath. It was a small cup. The kind of kiddush cup, used for the blessing of the wine, that his father had made for so many Jewish patrons. He forced himself to pick up other things first, a steel bit so bent it wouldn't fit in a horse's mouth, a filthy cloth bag, a wasp's nest still attached to a bit of branch.

When he turned the cup over he saw with disappointment that it hadn't been made by his father, for it lacked the HT mark that Helkias Toledano had placed in the bottom of every cup he had made. Probably it had been made by a silversmith who had lived somewhere in the region of Saragossa. Doubtless the cup had been abandoned or bartered away at the time of the expulsion, and apparently it had not been polished since then, for it was black with the dirt and tarnish of years, and also was badly scratched.

Still it was a kiddush cup and he wanted it badly. Yet he was held back from buying it by a terrible fear. It was an object which only Jews were likely to react to. Perhaps it had been placed amidst the beggar's trash as bait, so that

343

when it was glimpsed and bought by a Jew, condemning eyes would note the identity of the purchaser.

He nodded to the beggar and walked away, circumnavigating the plaza slowly, and examining each doorway, roof, and window for a sign that someone watched.

Yet he saw no one who appeared to mark his presence, and when he returned to the beggar he went back to rummaging among the things. He chose half a dozen objects for which he had no use or desire and included the cup, taking care to engage in the usual bargaining over price.

When he reached home he polished the kiddush cup tenderly. Its surface was marred by several deep scratches that no amount of polishing would remove, but it quickly became one of his most cherished possessions.

The autumn of 1507 was wet and cold. The sound of coughing was heard in all the public places, and Yonah worked long hours, some of the time afflicted with the same racking cough that bedeviled his patients.

In October he was summoned to the home of Doña Sancha Berga, an elderly Old Christian woman who lived in a large and well-appointed house in a fine section of Saragossa. Her son, Don Berenguer Bartolomé, and her daughter, Monica, wife of a nobleman of Alagón, were in attendance when Yonah examined their mother. She had another son, Geraldo, a merchant of Saragossa.

Doña Sancha was the widow of a famous cartographer, Martín Bartolomé. She was a slim and intelligent woman of seventy-four years. She didn't appear to be terribly ill, but because of her age he prescribed wine in hot water, to be taken four times a day, and sips of honey.

'Do you have any other complaints, señora?'

'Only my eyes. My vision has grown increasingly dim,' Doña Sancha said.

Yonah pushed the draperies on her window, allowing light to flood into her chamber, and then put his face very close to hers. When he lifted her eyelids one at a time he was able to see the faint opacity in the lens.

'It is a disease called catarata,' he said.

'Blindness in old age is a family inheritance. My mother was blind when she died,' Doña Sancha said resignedly.

'Can nothing be done for this catarata?' her son inquired.

'Yes, there is a surgical treatment called "couching," in which the clouded lens is removed. In many cases, sight is somewhat improved.'

'Do you believe this couching might be done to me?' Doña Sancha asked.

He leaned over her again and studied her eyes. He had done the operation three times, once on a cadaver and twice with Nuño standing at his elbow, talking him through the procedure. In addition, he had seen Nuño do it twice.

'Do you have any vision at present?'

'I do,' she said. 'But it grows gradually worse, and I fear the coming blindness.'

'I believe it can be done for you, but I must warn you against expecting too much improvement. While vision remains to you, however imperfect, we shall wait. The catarata is easier to remove when it is ripe. So we must be patient. I will watch, and tell you when the procedure should be done.'

Doña Sancha thanked him, and Don Berenguer invited him into his library for a glass of wine. Yonah hesitated. Usually he avoided dangerous social contact with Old Christians whenever possible, wishing to guard against situations in which they might ask of his family and inquire into possible churchly connections and mutual friends. But the invitation was friendly and gracious, and it would have been difficult to refuse, so presently he found himself seated before the fire in a wonderful room furnished with a drafting desk and four large tables covered with charts and maps.

Don Berenguer was excited and hopeful about the prospects of improved vision for his mother. 'Can you recommend a suitable surgeon to do the procedure when the catarata ripens?' he asked.

'I can do it,' Yonah said cautiously. 'Or if you prefer, I believe Señor Miguel de Montenegro would be an excellent choice.'

'You are a surgeon as well as a physician?' Don Berenguer asked in surprise, pouring wine from a heavy glass decanter.

Yonah smiled. 'As is Señor Montenegro. It is true that most practitioners concentrate either on surgery or on medicine. But a few men, some of them excellent at both professions, combine the practices. My late *maestro* and uncle, Señor Nuño Fierro, believed that too often surgeons mistakenly believe the only real cure is with a knife, while many physicians are capable of total dependence of physick when surgery should be called for.'

Don Berenguer nodded thoughtfully as he handed Yonah a glass. The wine was mellow and very good, the kind of vintage Yonah would expect to be offered by an aristocratic family. He soon relaxed and began to enjoy himself, for his host offered no inquiry into subjects that would cause him discomfort.

Don Berenguer disclosed that he was a cartographer, as his father and his grandfather had been before him. 'My grandfather, Blas Bartolomé, created the first scientific charts of the Spanish coastal waters,' he said. 'My father concentrated on river charts, while I have contented myself with forays into our mountain regions to map altitudes, trails and passes.'

Don Berenguer showed him chart after chart, and Yonah forgot his fears as they pored over them together. He revealed to the cartographer that in his youth for a brief time he had been an ordinary seaman, and he traced his river and sea voyages on the charts, warmed by the good wine and the company of an interesting man who, his intuition told him, might become his friend.

33
The Witness

In the first week of April, a man from the office of the *alguacil* of Saragossa came and informed Yonah that he was required to appear as a witness before the municipal court, 'in a judgment to take place on Thursday a fortnight hence.'

The evening before the hearing, Yonah came downstairs while Reyna was in her cooling bath in front of the fire. He took the kettle from its hook over the flames, and as he poured fresh heat into the bath water they talked of his summons to the court. 'It is about the two boys,' he told her.

The case was already celebrated in the district. On a midwinter's morning two boys, both fourteen years of age and fast friends since they were small, had had a falling-out over a little wooden horse. The boys, Oliverio Pita and Guillermo de Roda, had played with the horse for years. It was crudely carved, little more than a trinket, but one day they quarreled about its ownership.

Each claimed the horse as property he had gladly shared with his friend.

As often happens with boys, the quarrel became physical. Had they been a few years older an altercation might have resulted in a challenge and a duel, but they resorted to fists and hard feelings. Things were made worse when a parent of each of the boys reported a memory that *their* family owned the horse.

The next time the boys met, they threw stones at one another. Oliverio was by far the better marksman; he was untouched, but several of the missiles he launched found Guillermo, one of the stones raking his right temple. When he appeared at home with his face covered with blood, his frightened mother had sent for the physician at once, and Yonah had gone to the Roda home and treated the boy. The incident might have had a chance to fade away in time, had not Guillermo subsequently contracted a fever and died.

Yonah had explained to the grief-stricken parents that Guillermo had died of a contagious disease and not from the slight injury he had suffered weeks before. But in his grief Ramiro de Roda had gone to the *alguacil* and sworn out a charge against Oliverio Pita, stating that the illness had followed the head injury, and that therefore Oliverio had been the cause of Guillermo's demise. The *alguacil* had scheduled the hearing to determine whether the boy would be charged with homicide.

'It is a tragedy,' Reyna said, 'and now the physician of Saragossa has been drawn into it.' She was able to sense the extent to which Yonah was troubled. 'But what have you to fear in this tale of two boys.'

'I have heard that a new inquisitor has been assigned to Saragossa, and he will be looking for trouble. In testifying, I shall alienate a powerful Saragossa family. As we both know, physicians can be denounced anonymously to the Inquisition. I am not eager to make enemies of the Rodas.'

Reyna nodded. 'Yet you do not dare ignore an order from the *alguacil*.'

'No. And there is a question of justice that must be settled. It leaves me with one alternative.'

'What is that?' Reyna asked, soaping an arm.

'To make my appearance and tell the truth,' Yonah said.

The hearing was held in the small meeting hall on the upper story of the municipal building, which was already crowded when Yonah arrived.

José Pita and his wife, Rosa Menendez, looked straight at Yonah when he entered the room. They had come to him soon after their son had been charged, and he had told them the truth as he saw it.

The boy Oliverio Pita sat alone, his eyes large, facing the unsmiling and businesslike magistrate who began the proceedings without delay by rapping his great ring of office against the tabletop.

Alberto Porreño, the monarch's prosecutor, with whom Yonah had a greeting acquaintance, was a short man with a head enlarged by a great mane of black hair. For his first witness he called Ramiro de Roda.

'Señor Roda, your son, Guillermo de Roda, age fourteen years, expired on the fourteenth day of February, the year of Our Lord 1502?'

'Yes, señor.'

'Of what did he die, Señor Roda?'

'He was struck on the head by a rock hurled at him in anger, the murderous injury leading to a terrible illness that carried him off.' He looked over to where Yonah was sitting. 'The physician could not save Guillermo, my only son.'

'Who threw the rock?'

'He.' He extended his arm and pointed a finger. 'Oliverio Pita.' The Pita boy, very pale, stared at the table in front of him.

'How do you know this?'

'It was seen by a mutual neighbor, Señor Rodrigo Zurita.'

'Is Señor Zurita present?' the prosecutor asked, and when a skinny, white-bearded man raised his hand, the prosecutor moved to him.

'How did you come to see the boys throwing stones at one another?'

'I was sitting by my house, warming my bones in the sun. I saw the whole thing.'

'What did you see?'

'I saw José Pita's son, the boy over there, throw the stone that struck poor Guillermo, that good lad.'

'You saw where it hit him?'

'Yes. It struck him on the head,' he said, pointing to his forehead, between his eyes. 'I saw it clearly. He was struck so cruelly, I saw blood and pus come from the wound.'

'Thank you, señor.'

Señor Porreño now approached Yonah. 'Señor Callicó, you treated the boy following the incident?'

'I did, señor.'

'And what did you find?'

'He could not have been struck squarely by the stone,' Yonah said uncomfortably. 'Rather, it had grazed him in the region of the right temple, just above and in front of the right ear.'

351

'Not . . . here?' The prosecutor touched his finger to the centre of Yonah's forehead.

'No, señor. Here,' Yonah said, and touched his temple.

'Could you tell anything else from the wound.'

'It was a minor wound. More of a scratch. I washed the dried blood from his face and from the scratch. Such scrapes and scratches usually do well when they are bathed in wine, so I soaked a cloth with wine and wiped the wound, but otherwise I left it alone.

'At the time,' Yonah said, 'I could not help but feel that Guillermo was a fortunate youth, because if the stone had struck him just a bit to the left his injury would have been far more serious.'

'Is it not a serious injury when blood and pus appear from a wound?'

Within himself, Yonah sighed; but there was no escape from the truth.

'There was no pus.' He saw Señor Zurita's furious eyes. 'Pus is not something that exists within the skin of humans, to ooze free when the skin is punctured. Pus often appears *after* the injury, engendered when a breakage of the skin allows an open wound to come under the influence of putrid scents in the air, the stink of such things as ordure or rotting flesh. There was no pus in the wound when first I saw it, and there was no discharge of any sort when I saw Guillermo three weeks later. By then the scratch had developed a scab. It was cool to the touch, it was not angry looking. I considered him almost healed.'

'Yet two weeks later he was dead,' the prosecutor said.

'Yes. But not of the slight injury to his head.'

'Of what then, señor?'

352

'Of a ragged coughing and mucus in the lungs that brought on his final fever.'

'And what caused the malady?'

'I do not know, señor. Would that I knew. A physician sees such illness with discouraging regularity, and some of the afflicted die.'

'You are certain that the stone thrown by Oliverio Pita did not cause the death of Guillermo de Roda?'

'I am certain.'

'Will you take your oath on it, Señor Physician?'

'I shall.'

When the town-owned bible was brought, Yonah placed his hand on it and swore that his testimony had been true.

The prosecutor nodded and instructed the accused to rise. The magistrate warned the youth that he would face swift and severe punishment if any of his actions should bring him back to stand before the bar of justice. Rapping the table a final time with his heavy ring, he declared Oliverio Pita to be free.

'Señor,' José Pita said. He was still embracing his weeping son. 'We are in your debt for all time.'

'I merely testified to what is true,' Yonah said.

He made his escape at once and soon rode from the center of town, trying to forget the cold dislike he had seen in Ramiro de Roda's eyes. He knew the Roda family and their friends would die still believing that young Guillermo had been slain by a thrown stone, but he had testified truly and was glad to be done with it.

From the other end of the street, three horsemen were riding towards him. As they drew nearer, Yonah could see two men-at-arms and a cleric in black habit.

A friar. Tall, even as he rode.

Dear God, no.

But as the distance between them closed, Yonah knew who it was. When they drew abreast he saw that in middle age the friar had put on flesh. There were dark veins in his nose and his unruly hair was cut in a tonsure that showed gray.

'A good day to you,' Yonah said politely to the group as they passed and the friar gave a small nod of his head.

But before Yonah's horse had taken half a dozen steps, he heard the voice.

'Señor!'

He turned the gray Arab and went back.

'I seem to know you, señor.'

'Yes, Fray Bonestruca. We met some years ago in Toledo.'

Bonestruca waved his hand. 'Yes, in Toledo. But . . . your name . . . ?'

'Ramón Callicó. I had come to Toledo in order to deliver a suit of armor to the count of Tembleque.'

'Yes, by my faith, the armorer's apprentice from Gibraltar! I have admired Count Vasca's fine armor, of which he is rightfully proud. Are you in Saragossa on a similar errand?'

'No, I reside here. My *maestro* and uncle, the armorer Manuel Fierro, passed on, and I came to Saragossa to apprentice with his brother, Nuño, a physician.'

Bonestruca nodded with interest. 'I would say you have been rich in uncles.'

'And I would agree with you. Sadly, Nuño has gone to his rest as well, and now I am the physician of this place.'

'The physician . . . Well, then we shall see one another from time to time, for I am come here to stay.'

354

'Then I trust Saragossa will please you, for it is a town of good people.'

'Indeed? Truly good people are treasures beyond price. But I have long since discovered that often beneath an appearance of rectitude there is something darker and far less benign than goodness.'

'I am certain that is true.'

'It is good to discover an acquaintance when one is uprooted and transferred to a new location. We must meet again, Señor Callicó.'

'We must indeed.'

'For now, Christ be with you.'

'Christ be with *you*, Fray Bonestruca.'

Yonah was numb as he rode away, lost in thought. Halfway home the reins dropped from his hands and the Arab horse moved to the side of the track and began to graze in the shade of a tree while his rider sat in the saddle, unheeding. Yonah had failed to kill Bonestruca once before, in his youth, when opportunity had presented itself. And then he had used the friar to rid himself of enemies who would have killed him.

And now the inquisitor was going to be in close proximity to him. Every day.

He realized, almost with surprise, that he would never again attempt to kill Bonestruca. He had become a healer, ruined for work as an assassin. If he committed murder, even if no one else knew about it, it would change him, spoil him as a doctor. Somewhere during his apprenticeship to Nuño Fierro he had crossed an important line. Being a physician – fighting death – was the most important part of him, the tether that anchored him to the earth. It was a priesthood that had taken the place of religion, culture, and family, and it far outweighed any dry and bitter satisfaction to be found in a revenge that could not bring back his loved ones.

Yet he hated Bonestruca and Count Vasca and had no forgiveness in his heart for the men who had been involved in the deaths of his father and his brother. He told himself that if Bonestruca was to be in close proximity, he would keep a watch on him, in the hope that circumstances might yet permit him to bring this rogue friar to justice.

Comforted and resolute, he picked up the reins again and directed the Arabian back onto the road that took them home.

34

The Friar's House

Fray Lorenzo de Bonestruca had not been transferred to Saragossa as a reward or a promotion, but rather as a rebuke and a punishment. The sources of his troubles had been the late queen, Isabella of Spain, and Archbishop Francisco Jiménez de Cisneros. When Cisneros had become archbishop of Toledo in 1495, he recruited the queen to join him in a campaign to reform the Spanish clergy, which had fallen into a period of vice and corruption. Clerics had grown accustomed to an opulent style of living; they had vast land holdings under their private ownership, as well as servants, mistresses, and the trappings of wealth.

Cisneros and Isabella divided the units of the Church between them. She traveled to convents, where she used her position and persuasive powers, cajoling and threatening the nuns until they agreed to return to the simple living style that had characterized the early Church. The archbishop, dressed in a simple brown habit and leading a mule, visited each priory and monastery, cataloguing its wealth and urging its friars and monks to donate to the poor anything not essential to their daily existence. Archbishop Cisneros reinstituted the requirement for tonsure. He had emended Bonestruca's head with his own hands, shaving off all hair but a close-cropped ring to form St. Peter's tonsure, representing the crown of thorns worn by Jesus.

Fray Bonestruca had been caught in the web of reform.

He had spent only four years as a celibate friar. Once his body experienced the sweetness of fusing with female flesh, he had succumbed to sexual passion easily and often. For the past ten years he had kept as mistress a woman named María Juana Salazar, on whom he had sired five children. One died at birth, another after six weeks of life. Maria was his wife in every way save name, and he had not tried to keep her presence in his life a great secret; there had been no need, for he was doing only what so many others did. But a number of people knew about Fray Bonestruca and María Juana Salazar. First the elderly priest who had been his confessor for years was recruited to warn him that the days of laxness were over, and that contrition and genuine change were the keys to survival. When Bonestruca had ignored the warning, he was summoned to the chancery for an interview with the archbishop. Cisneros had wasted no time on idle talk.

'You must rid yourself of her. You must do it at once. If you do not, you shall feel my wrath.'

Now Bonestruca decided to try secrecy and subterfuge. He moved María Juana and the children to another village, midway between Toledo and Tembleque, and told no one. He behaved discreetly when he visited, and sometimes he stayed away from them for weeks. In this way he had gained six additional years in which he had enjoyed his little family.

Still, one day he received word that the chancery had called for him again. But this time when he went there he was met by a Dominican priest who told him that because of his disobedience he had been transferred to the office of the Inquisition in the town of Saragossa. He was ordered to depart for Saragossa at once.

'And alone,' the priest had said sardonically.

He had obeyed, but by the time he had finished the long journey, he understood that what others had considered a punishment for him was in fact an opportunity to achieve the privacy he required.

More than a double fortnight after he had met the inquisitor in the street, Yonah was summoned by a brown-robed novice who said that Fray Bonestruca wished the physician to come at once to the Plaza Mayor.

When he responded, he found Fray Bonestruca sitting in the shade of the plaza's only tree.

The friar nodded to him as he rose from the bench. 'I will take you to a place. No word of what you will see or do should be repeated to any person, lest you receive my anger. I promise you that my anger can be terrible. Do you understand?'

Yonah fought for equanimity. 'I do understand,' he said evenly.

'You will come with me.'

He strode ahead, Yonah following on the horse. Several times Bonestruca looked back, his gaze going beyond Yonah to determine that they were not followed. But at the edge of the river Bonestruca didn't hesitate, lifting the skirt of his black robe above the shallow, rushing water. On the far bank he led Yonah to a finca, small but in sound condition, the new wood in a windowpane showing evidence of recent repairs. Bonestruca opened the door and swept inside without knocking. Yonah saw several bags of cloth and leather, and a wooden crate that had not been opened and unpacked. A woman stood holding a baby, two other children standing behind her, clutching her garment.

'This is María Juana,' Bonestruca said.

Yonah removed his hat. 'Señora.'

She was a plump woman, brown skinned, with a heart-shaped face, wide dark eyes, and very full, red lips. Her milk stained the material over her rounded breasts. 'He is Callicó, a physician,' Bonestruca told her. 'He will see to Filomena.'

The object of his concern was a baby, feverish and troubled by sores about the mouth. The oldest child, Hortensia, was seven, a pretty girl who appeared to be in good health, and there was a five-year-old boy, named Dionisio. Yonah's heart sank when he saw the boy. He appeared feeble and slow of mind. One of his legs was markedly bowed, and when Yonah examined him he found that the boy had the perforated palate and distinctive, pegged upper front teeth that Nuño had taught Yonah to recognize. The child squinted because of poor vision, and Yonah could see areas of opacity in both of his eyes.

Bonestruca said that his three children were exhausted and out of sorts, having arrived from Toledo with their mother only two days before. 'As for Filomena's sores, I trust that eventually they will go away. I remember when the other children had them as well.'

360

'Even Hortensia?'

'Yes, Hortensia also.'

'You are the children's father, Fray Bonestruca?'

'Of course.'

'When you were a younger man . . . did you have the pox, malum venereum, ever?'

'Do not many young men get a taste of the pox, sooner or later? I was covered with sores like scales. But after a time I was cured, and no symptoms have returned.'

Yonah nodded discreetly. 'Well . . . you gave the pox to your . . . to María Juana.'

'That is true.'

'And she has given it to each of your children at birth. It is the pox that has twisted your son's limb and dimmed his eyes.'

'Then why are my Hortensia's limbs straight and her eyes bright?'

'The disease affects people differently.'

'After all, Filomena's sores will go away,' the friar said again.

'Yes,' Yonah said. But the boy's crooked leg and pegged teeth will not, he thought. And who knew what other tragedies the pox might bring into their lives.

He finished examining the children and prescribed a salve for the baby's sores. 'I shall return to see her in a week,' Yonah said. When Bonestruca asked him what was owed, Yonah quoted his usual fee for a home visit, taking care to maintain a businesslike tone. He had no wish to encourage a growing friendship with Fray Bonestruca.

Next day, a man named Evaristo Montalvo led his

elderly wife, Blasa de Gualda, into the dispensary to see the physician.

'She is blind, señor.'

'Allow me to look,' Yonah said, and he led the woman into the bright light near the window.

He could see clouding in both her eyes. It was more advanced than similar clouding he had seen recently in the eyes of Doña Sancha Berga, Don Berenguer Bartolomé's mother, so ripe it made this woman's lenses appear to be a yellowish white.

'Is it possible for you to help me, señor?'

'I cannot promise to help you, señor. But it is possible for me to try, if that is what you wish. It would require surgery.'

'Cutting on my eyes?'

'Yes, cutting. You have what are called cataratas in each eye. The lenses have become cloudy, and they block your sight the way a shade blocks the light from entering a window.'

'I wish to see again, señor.'

'You will never see the way you did when you were young,' he said gently. 'Even if we are successful, you will not be able to fix your eyes on distant objects. You will be able to see only what is close at hand.'

'But that would allow me to cook. Perhaps even to sew, eh?'

'Perhaps . . . but if we fail, doubtless you will be permanently blind.'

'But I am blind now, señor. So I beg you to try this . . . surgery.'

Yonah bade them to come back early the next day. That afternoon he readied the operating table and the things he would need, and throughout the evening he sat next to the oil lamp and read, several times, what Teodorico Borgognoni had written about couching the eyes.

'I am going to need your help,' he told Reyna. He showed her, by lifting her own eyelids, how he wanted her to hold the patient's eyes open and prevent her from blinking.

'I may not be able to watch a cutting of the eyes,' she said.

'You may turn your head away, but you must keep her eyelids raised firmly. Can you do it?'

Reyna nodded doubtfully but said she would try.

Next morning when Evaristo Montalvo came with Blasa de Gualda, Yonah directed the old man to take a long walk before returning, then he gave Blasa two cupfuls of strong spirits in which soporific powders had been infused.

He and Reyna helped the elderly woman to lie on the table and then bound her to it with strips of strong fabric that were wide enough not to cut into her flesh, tying down her wrists and ankles and forehead so she could not move.

He took the smallest of the scalpels in the Fierro collection and nodded to Reyna. 'Let us begin.'

When the lids were raised he made tiny incisions around the lens of the left eye.

Blasa drew a shuddering breath.

'It won't take long,' Yonah said. He used the small, keen blade as a fulcrum to tip the clouded lens until it fell back, into the eye's interior regions and out of the way. Then he repeated the process on the right eye.

When he was done he thanked Reyna and told her to

363

allow the lids to close, and they unbound Blasa and covered her eyes with cool, wet compresses.

After a time he removed the compresses and bent over her. Her closed eyes were tearing or she was weeping, and he wiped her cheeks gently.

'Señora Gualda. Open your eyes.'

Her lids unlocked. Blinking against the light, she peered up.

'You have a very good face, señor,' she said.

How strange, to find that a man he scorned and hated as a murderer and a thief was so loving and concerned as a father!

He had hoped Bonestruca would be absent when he paid his next visit to the finca by the river, but he hid his chagrin when the friar greeted him at the door. The three children, rested from the rigors of travel, appeared to be stronger and in better spirits, and Yonah discussed their diet with their mother, who mentioned with offhand pride that her children were accustomed to meat and eggs in abundance.

'And I am accustomed to excellent wine,' Bonestruca said lightly, 'which I shall now insist on sharing with you.'

It was evident that he brooked no refusal, and Yonah allowed himself to be led into a study where he had to fight to remain composed, because it contained relics of the friar's war against the Jews: a set of phylacteries, a skullcap, and – an unbelievable sight to Yonah – a Torah scroll.

The wine *was* good. As Yonah sipped and attempted not to stare at the Torah, he regarded the host who was his foe, and wondered how soon he could flee this man's house.

'Do you know how to play Turkish draughts?' Bonestruca asked.

'No. I have never heard of Turkish draughts.'

'It is a most excellent game that uses the mind. I shall teach it to you,' he said, and to Yonah's annoyance he rose and took from the shelf a square board that he placed on the small table between them, and two cloth bags.

The board was marked with alternating light and dark squares, sixty-four of them according to Bonestruca. Each of the bags contained twelve small, smooth stones; the stones in one bag were black while those in the other bag were a light gray. Bonestruca handed over the black stones and told Yonah to place them on the dark squares found in the first two rows of the board, while the friar similarly placed the lighter stones on his side. 'Thus we have made four rows of soldiers, and we are at war, señor!'

The friar showed him that play consisted of moving a stone forward diagonally, to an adjoining vacant square. 'Black moves first. If my soldier is in an adjoining vacant square, with a space beyond, he must be captured and removed. Movement of the soldiers is always forward, but when a hero achieves the opponent's back row he is crowned a monarch by placing on him another piece of the same color. Such a doubled piece may go forward or back, for no one can tell a king where he may not go.

'An army is conquered when an opponent's soldiers are all captured or blocked so they cannot move.' Bonestruca placed all the pieces back into position. 'And now, Physician, have at me!'

They played five games of war. The first two battles were over quickly for Yonah but they taught him that moves could not be made randomly. Several times Bonestruca lured him into making a foolish move, sacrificing one of his soldiers in order to win several of Yonah's. Finally, Yonah was able to recognize a trap and move away from it.

'Ah, you learn quickly,' the friar said. 'You will be a worthy opponent in the shortest of time, I can see it.'

What Yonah soon could see was that the game required a constant inspection of the board to review the purpose of the opponent's moves and gauge the possibilities that might arise. He noted the ways in which Bonestruca worked constantly to lure him into traps. By the end of the fifth game he had learned some of the defenses that were possible.

'Ah, señor, you are clever as a fox or a general,' Bonestruca said, but the friar's supple mind had defeated Yonah easily.

'I must go,' Yonah said reluctantly.

'Then you must return to play again. Tomorrow afternoon, or the day after?'

'My afternoons, I am afraid, are spent with patients.'

'I understand, a busy physician. Suppose we meet here on Wednesday evening? Come as early as you can, I shall be here.'

Why not? Yonah asked himself. 'Yes, I shall come,' he said. It would be interesting to try to understand the way Bonestruca's mind worked, as revealed from his play of draughts.

On Wednesday evening he returned to the finca by the river, and he and Bonestruca sat in the study and drank the good wine and cracked almond shells and ate the meats as they perused the board and made their moves.

Yonah watched the board and his opponent's face, seeking to discern the way the friar thought, but he could learn nothing from Bonestruca's features.

With every game they played, he learned a little about the game of draughts and a tiny bit about Bonestruca. That evening they played five games, as they had at their first meeting.

'The games last longer now,' Bonestruca observed. When he suggested that they meet Wednesday eve on the following week, Yonah assented so readily that the friar smiled.

'Ah, I see that the game has captured your soul.'

'Only my mind, surely, Fray Bonestruca.'

'Then I shall work on your soul as we play, señor,' Bonestruca said.

It took Yonah two more evenings of playing draughts before he won his first game, and then he didn't win again for several weeks. But after that he began to win sometimes, and the games became harder fought and longer lasting as he came to know Bonestruca's strategies.

He thought that Bonestruca played at draughts the way he played at life, feinting, taking, toying with his opponent. The friar usually greeted him with a disarming, sunny friendliness, but Yonah never relaxed in his presence, aware of the darkness that lurked only seconds away.

'You do not have a first-rate mind after all, Physician,' Bonestruca said contemptuously after winning an easy game. Yet each time they played he was insistent that Yonah play with him again, and soon.

Yonah concentrated on learning to best him. He

suspected that Bonestruca was a bully, made more powerful by fear, yet perhaps vulnerable to one who would stand up to him.

'I have been in Saragossa but a brief time, yet I have unmasked a Jew,' the friar told him one Wednesday evening, jumping one of his soldiers.

'Ah?' Yonah said casually. He moved one of his own pieces into place to repel the attack.

'Yes, a backsliding Jew, yet who pretends to be an Old Christian.'

Would the friar now bring about his ruin?

Yonah kept his eyes on the board. He moved a soldier into a square where he was jumped, and then jumped two of Bonestruca's pieces. 'Your soul rejoices to catch a Jew. I hear it in your voice,' he said, and wondered at the coolness of his own voice.

'Think on it. Is it not written that they who have sown the wind, they shall reap the whirlwind?'

To hell with him, Yonah thought, and lifted his eyes from the board to meet the friar's glance. 'Is it not also written that blessed are the merciful, for they shall obtain mercy?'

Bonestruca smiled. He was enjoying himself. 'It is so written, by Matthew. But . . . consider. "I am the resurrection and the life. He that believeth in me, though he were dead, yet shall he live. And whosoever liveth and believeth in me shall never die." Is it not then an act of mercy to save an everlasting soul from hell? For that is what we do when we reconcile Jewish souls with Christ before the flames. We end sorry lives of error and grant them peace and glory for eternity.'

'And what of one who refuses such a reconciliation?'

'We are admonished by Matthew, "If thy right eye offend thee, pluck it out and cast it from thee. For it is profitable for thee that one of thy members should perish, and not that thy whole body shall be cast into hell."'

He smiled as he told Yonah that the Jew who pretended to be an Old Christian was about to be placed under arrest.

Through a sleepless night and the next day, Yonah was caught up in an agony of apprehension. He was prepared to flee for his life, yet he had learned enough about Bonestruca's thinking to believe that perhaps this mention of a counterfeit Old Christian might be nothing more than a trap. Suppose Bonestruca was watching to see if the physician had taken the bait and would run? If all the inquisitor had was a suspicion, Yonah would do well to spend each day in his normal living.

That morning he attended the daily clinic in his dispensary. In the afternoon he called on patients. He had just returned home and was removing the saddle from the horse when a pair of soldiers of the *alguacil* rode down the lane to the house.

He had been expecting this moment and was armed. There was no point in surrendering to those who would wish to bring him in for the Inquisition. If they tried to take him, perhaps his sword would be lucky against the soldiers or, if he were killed, it would be a better death than the flames.

But one of the riders leaned forward respectfully.

'Señor Callicó, the *alguacil* asks that you accompany us at once to the Saragossa prison, where there is need for the skills of your profession.'

'What kind of need?' Yonah asked, not at all convinced.

'A Jew has tried to cut off his prick,' the soldier said baldly, and his companion snickered.

'What is the Jew's name?'

'Bartolomé.'

It struck him an almost physical blow. He remembered the beautiful house, the aristocratic man who had talked with such intelligence in the gracious study that was crowded with maps and charts. 'Don Berenguer Bartolomé? The cartographer?'

The soldier shrugged, but his companion nodded, and spat.

'The same,' he said.

Within the prison a young black-robed priest sat behind a table, probably assigned the task of noting the names of anyone who applied to see the prisoners.

'We have brought the physician,' the soldier said.

The priest nodded. 'Don Berenguer Bartolomé broke his water mug and used a shard to circumcize himself,' he told Yonah, and motioned for the guard to unlock the outer door. The guard led Yonah down a corridor, to a cell where Berenguer lay on the floor. He unlocked the cell door to allow Yonah to enter, and then locked him inside.

'When you are ready to leave, shout for me and I will let you out,' he said, and went away.

Berenguer's trousers were stiff with blood. A don and the descendant of dons, Yonah thought, a distinguished man whose grandfather had charted the coast of Spain. He lay on the prison floor, stinking of blood and urine.

'I am sorry, Don Berenguer.'

Berenguer nodded. He grunted as Yonah opened the trousers and pulled them down.

Yonah kept a flask of strong spirits in the medical bag. Berenguer received it eagerly and needed no urging to drink, in great swallows.

The penis was a horror. Yonah saw that Berenguer had cut away most of the foreskin but some remained, and the incisions had been done raggedly. He marveled that Berenguer had been able to carry it out at all, using a sharp shard on himself. He knew the pain was very bad and he was sorry to add to it, but he took a scalpel and trimmed the ragged tissue, completing the circumcision. The man on the floor groaned, sucking in the last of the strong drink like a thirsty child.

When it was over, he lay gasping as Yonah applied a soothing salve and a loose dressing.

'It will be a fortnight before it heals. Until then, you will have pain. Leave the trousers off. If you are cold, cover yourself, but keep the blanket away from yourself with your hands.' They looked at one another.

'Why have you done this? What does it gain?'

'You would not understand,' Berenguer said.

Yonah sighed and nodded. 'I'll come tomorrow if I am allowed. Is there anything you wish?'

'If you could bring my mother some fruit . . .'

He was shocked. 'Doña Sancha Berga is here?'

Berenguer nodded. 'All of us. My mother. My sister, Monica, and her husband, Andrés, and my brother, Geraldo.'

'I will do what I can,' Yonah said numbly, and called for the guard to unlock the cell.

In the entryway, before he could inquire about the condition of the other members of the Bartolomé family, the priest asked him if he would examine Doña Sancha Berga. 'She sorely has need of a physician,' the priest said. He seemed a decent young man, and troubled.

When they took Yonah to Doña Sancha, the beautiful old woman lay like a broken flower. She gazed at him sightlessly and he saw that her cataratas had ripened; they were almost sufficiently developed to allow surgery, but he knew he would never touch these eyes.

'It is Callicó the physician, señora,' he said gently.

'I am . . . injured, señor.'

'How did the injuries occur, señora?'

'They placed me on the rack.'

He could see that the torture had dislocated her right shoulder. He had to summon the guard to help him pull the shoulder back into place while she shrieked. Afterward, she could not stop weeping.

'Señora. Is the shoulder not better?'

'I have condemned my beautiful children,' she whispered.

'How is she?' the priest asked.

'She is old, her bones are soft and brittle. I'm certain she has multiple fractures. I think she is dying,' he said.

Yonah was in despair as he rode home from the prison.

When he returned there next day bearing a quantity of raisins and dates and the figs, he found Don Berenguer still in great pain.

'How is my mother?'

'I am doing what I can for her.'

Berenguer nodded. 'I thank you.'

'How did all this come to be?'

'We are Old Christians and have always stated so. My father's Catholic family goes back in time. My mother's parents were converted Jews and she was raised with certain harmless rituals that became our family habit as well. She told us stories of her girlhood and always lighted tapers as dusk fell on Fridays. I am not certain why, perhaps in memory of her departed. And gathered her children each week on that evening for a bountiful dinner, with blessings and thanks for the food and the wine.'

Yonah nodded.

'Someone denounced her. She had no enemies, but . . . she had recently discharged a servant for repeated drunkenness. It is possible that this kitchen maid is the source of our troubles.

'I had to listen to my own mother's screams while they tortured her. Can you imagine such horror? I was told afterwards by my interrogators that in the end our mother implicated all of us, my brothers and sisters – even the memory of our father – in a Judaizing plot.

'So I knew that we are lost, each and every one. My family, which has always known we are Old Christians. Yet a part of us *is* Jewish, so that we have been neither fully Catholic nor Jewish, adrift between two shores. In my despair I felt that if I am to burn at the stake as a Jew I should come before my Maker as a Jew, and I broke my drinking cup and cut myself with the shard.

'I am aware you will not be able to understand,' he said to Yonah, as he had said the previous evening.

'You are wrong, Don Berenguer,' Yonah told him. 'I understand you very well.'

As he was leaving the prison he overheard a guard

speaking to the young priest. 'Yes, Padre Espina,' the man said.

Yonah turned and came back.

'Padre,' he said. 'Did he call you Espina?'

'That is my name.'

'May I ask your full name?'

'I am Francisco Rivera de la Espina.'

'Is your mother, by chance, Estrella de Aranda?'

'Estrella de Aranda was my mother. She is gone. I pray for her soul.' He stared. 'Do I know you, Señor Physician?'

'You were born in Toledo?'

'Yes,' the priest said reluctantly.

'I have something that belongs to you,' Yonah told him.

35

A Fulfilled Responsibility

When Yonah brought the breviary to the prison the young priest led him down a dank stone corridor to a cubby where they could sit unobserved. He accepted the breviary as if it were an item bewitched. Yonah watched as he opened it and read what was written behind the cover.

'"To my son, Francisco Rivera de la Espina, these words of daily prayer to Jesus Christ, our heavenly Savior, with the undying love of his father on earth. Bernardo de la Espina."'

'What a strange sentiment, from one who was a convicted heretic!'

'Your father was not a heretic.'

'My father *was* a heretic, señor, and burned at the stake for it. In Ciudad Real. It happened when I was a boy, but I have been informed. I am acquainted with his history.'

'Then you are falsely, and certainly not fully, acquainted, Padre Espina. I was there, in Ciudad Real. I saw your father daily in the days before his death. When

I knew him I was a youth and he was a man, a most skilled and tender physician. About to die, and lacking the presence of even one other friend, he asked me to try to find his young son, and to deliver his breviary to you. Everywhere I have traveled, these many years, I have searched for you.'

'You are certain about what you tell me, señor?'

'Absolutely. Your father was innocent of the charges for which he was killed.'

'You know this for fact?' the priest asked in a low voice.

'For firm fact, Padre Espina. He made his daily devotions from this book, almost up to the moment when he was put to death. When he marked it for you, he was leaving you his faith.'

Padre Espina appeared to be a man accustomed to controlling his emotions, yet he was betrayed by paleness. 'I have been raised by the Church. My father has been the shame of my life. My face has been rubbed into his supposed apostacy like a puppy's into piss, so it would not happen again.'

His appearance did not favor his father greatly, Yonah thought, except that he had Bernardo de la Espina's eyes. 'Your father was steadfastly the most believing Christian ever I have known, and one of the finest men of my memory,' Yonah told him.

They sat and talked for a long time, their voices low and steady. Padre Espina said that after his father's burning, his mother, Estrella de Aranda, had entered the Convento de la Santa Cruz to be a nun, leaving her three children to the charity of several families of cousins in Escalona. Within a year she had died of a malignant

376

fever, and by the time her son had reached the age of ten years his relatives had handed him to the Dominicans, and his sisters, Marta and Domitila, had taken the veil. All three had disappeared into the vast world of the Church.

'I have not seen my sisters since we stayed with our cousins in Escalona. I don't know of Domitila's whereabouts, or if she still lives. I learned two years ago that Marta is in a convent in Madrid. I dream of visiting her someday.'

Yonah told him a few things about himself. He spoke of the fact that after he had been a jail boy in Ciudad Real he had apprenticed, first with the armorer Manuel Fierro and then with the physician Nuño Fierro, leading to his becoming the physician of Saragossa.

If there were things he held back from the young priest, he could sense that there were also matters about which Padre Espina could not allow himself to speak freely. But Yonah gathered that he had been assigned only temporarily to the Office of the Inquisition, and that he had little stomach for its activities.

He had been ordained eight months before. 'I shall be leaving here in a few days. One of my teachers, Padre Enrique Sagasta, has been made auxiliary bishop of Toledo. He has arranged for me to be assigned as his aide. He is a noted Catholic scholar and historian, and he encourages my wish to follow his path. So I am about to begin an apprenticeship, as you had done.'

'Your father would be proud of you, Padre Espina.'

'I cannot thank you enough, señor. You have given my father back to me,' the priest said.

'May I return tomorrow to see my patients?'

Padre Espina was visibly uncomfortable. Yonah knew

377

he didn't wish to appear ungrateful yet was unable to grant too much lest he bring trouble to himself. 'You may come in the morning. But I warn you, it may well be the last visit that will be allowed.'

When he appeared next day, he learned that Doña Sancha Berga had died during the night.

Don Berenguer received the news of his mother's death stoically. 'I am glad she is free,' he said.

Each surviving member of the family had been notified that morning that they were formally condemned for heresy and would be executed at an auto de fé in the near future. Yonah knew there was no delicate way to broach what was burdening his soul.

'Don Berenguer, burning is the worst way to die.'

Between them there flashed shared knowledge of horrible, drawn-out pain, of flesh as charring meat, of blood boiling.

'Why do you tell me so cruel a thing? You think I am unaware?'

'There is a way to escape it. You must reconcile yourself with the Church.'

Berenguer looked at him and saw a disapproving Catholic he had never noted before. 'Indeed, must I, Señor Physician?' he said coldly. 'It is too late. The sentence is cast in steel.'

'Too late to save your life, but not too late to buy a quick end from the garrote.'

'You think I cut my flesh on an idle whim, and bound myself to my mother's faith only to renounce it? Have I not told you of my determination to die a Jew?'

'You *can* die a Jew in your heart. Merely tell them you repent, and buy release. You are forever a Jew, because by Jewish law consecration to the faith is passed from mother to child. Since your mother was born of a Jewish mother, so were you. No declaration can change that. By the ancient law of Moses you are a Jew, and by stating that which they are eager to hear, you will gain a quick strangling and avoid the torture of a slow and terrible death.'

Berenguer closed his eyes. 'Yet it is a coward's way, robbing me of the one noble moment, the single satisfaction I am able to find in my dying.'

'It is not cowardly. Most rabbis are agreed that it is not a sin to accept conversion at the point of a sword.'

'What do you know of rabbis and the law of Moses?' Berenguer stared at him. Yonah could see realization manifest itself in the other man's eyes.

'My God,' Berenguer said.

'Are you able to have contact with the others of your family?'

'Sometimes they lead us to the courtyard for exercise at the same time. It is possible to exchange a few words.'

'You must tell them to seek Jesus and gain the mercy of a quicker end.'

'My sister, Monica, and her husband, Andrés, are devout Christians. I shall advise my brother, Geraldo, to do as you suggest.'

'I am not to be allowed to see you again.' He walked to Berenguer and embraced him, and kissed him on both cheeks.

'May we meet in a happier place,' Don Berenguer said. 'Go in peace.'

'Peace be with you,' Yonah said, and called for the guard.

*

That Wednesday evening, in the middle of a game of draughts that Yonah was winning, Friar Bonestruca left the game board and began to caper in front of his children. For a little while it was charming. Bonestruca made wry faces and soft merry sounds as he leaped this way and that. His children laughed and pointed. Squinting, Dionisio ran towards his playful father to see him better and threw a small wooden ball at him.

On and on the friar frolicked. His smile vanished, the sounds grew less merry and more guttural, and still he capered and leaped. His face grew rosy with effort and then dark and bitter, yet still the tall figure caroused and whirled, his black habit billowing, his bobbing face become ugly with rage.

The children grew silent and frightened. They huddled away from him, watching wide-eyed, the girl Hortensia open-mouthed as if soundlessly screaming. María Juana, their mother, spoke to them quietly and herded them from the room. Yonah wished he could go too, but he could not. He sat at the table watching the terrible dance as it slowed and slowed. Finally it ceased, Bonestruca dropping in exhaustion to his knees.

Presently María Juana came back. She wiped her friar's face with a moistened cloth and left again, this time to return with wine. Bonestruca drank two glasses and then allowed her to help him back to his seat.

It was a while before he looked up. 'I am taken sometimes by spells.'

'I see,' Yonah said.

'Do you, indeed? And what is it that you see?'

'Nothing, señor. It is a manner of speech.'

'It has happened in the company of the priests and

friars with whom I carry on my duties. They are watching me.'

Was it the sick man's imagination? Yonah wondered.

'They have followed me here. They know of María Juana and the children.'

It was probably true, Yonah decided. 'What will they do?'

Bonestruca shrugged. 'I think they are waiting to see if the spells are a passing thing.' He frowned at Yonah. 'What do you think is the cause?'

It was a form of madness. Yonah thought this but couldn't say it. Nuño had told him once, when talking of insanity, that he had noted a commonality in the history of some of the persons whom he had treated. The shared fact was that the afflicted person had had malum venereum when young and had become mad only after years had passed. Nuño had not drawn a theory from this observation, but he had found it interesting enough to pass on to his apprentice, and now it came to Yonah's mind.

'I can't be certain, but . . . perhaps it has to do with the pox.'

'The pox, is it! You are wrong, Physician, for I have not had the pox for ever so long. I think it is Satan, come to wrestle for my soul. It is grievous labor fighting the Devil, but I have managed to drive off the archfiend each time.'

Yonah was speechless but he was saved by Bonestruca's attention being reclaimed by the draughts board. 'Was it your turn to land a blow with your soldiers or my own?'

'It was yours, señor,' Yonah said.

He was disturbed and played poorly the rest of the

evening, while Bonestruca appeared to be refreshed and clear-minded. The friar ended the game in short order and was cheerful and content with his victory.

Despite what Padre Espina had said, on the following day Yonah went to the prison and attempted to see Don Berenguer, but in Espina's place there was an older priest who looked at him and merely shook his head, sending him away.

The auto de fé was held six days later. The morning before the executions, the physician Callicó left Saragossa and rode far away, going to visit patients at the far edge of the district, a trip that forced him to spend several days away from home.

He had fears that this time he had overstepped, and that under torture Berenguer might reveal the presence and identity of another Judaizer, but it did not happen. When Yonah returned to Saragossa there were those among his patients who were happy to fill him in on the details of the act of faith, which had been well attended as always. Each member of the Jew Bartolomé family had died in a state of grace, kissing the cross held to their lips and then strangled before the burning by quick rotations of the screw that tightened the steel garrote.

36
Draught Games

When next Yonah appeared at the finca by the river for an evening of draughts, he saw that María Juana had a large, fresh darkening under her swollen left eye and covering most of her cheek, and he also noted bruises on the arms of the little girl named Hortensia.

Bonestruca greeted him with a nod and spoke little, concentrating so that he won the first game after a close battle. During the second game the friar was sullen and played badly, and soon it was apparent that the game was lost to him.

When the baby, Filomena, began to wail, Bonestruca leaped to his feet. 'I want *silence!*'

María Juana picked up the baby and ushered her children hastily into the other room. The two men played in a quietness broken only by the clacking of the stone pieces against the wooden board.

Presently, during the third game, María Juana appeared to serve a plate of dates and fill the wine-glasses.

Bonestruca regarded her moodily until she left the

room. Then he looked at Yonah. 'Where is it that you live?'

When Yonah told him, he nodded. 'That is where we shall play draughts next week. Is it agreeable to you?'

'Yes, of course,' Yonah said.

It was less than agreeable to Reyna. She knew the visitor when he appeared at the front door. Everyone in Saragossa was aware of this friar and knew what he was.

She ushered him into the house and seated him comfortably, then announced his presence to Yonah. When she served them with wine and refreshment she kept her gaze down, and she withdrew as soon as possible.

It was obvious that it frightened her to see Yonah consorting with Bonestruca. The next day, he saw puzzlement in her face, but she didn't ask him any questions. She was never the least bit unclear about their roles; she knew that it was his house and she was a servant every place but in bed. But a week later, she went to her village for three days, and when she returned she informed him she had bought a house of her own and would be leaving his employ.

'When?' he said, dismayed.

'I don't know. Before too long.'

'And why?'

'To return home. The money Nuño left has made me a very rich woman by my village's standards.'

'I shall miss you,' he said truthfully.

'But not terribly. I am a convenience for you.' When he started to protest she held up her hand. 'Yonah. I am old enough to be your mother. It is nice to feel tenderness when we share a bed, but more often I think of you as a son or a nephew of whom I am fond.'

She told him not to fret. 'I will send a strong girl to take my place, a young girl who is a good worker.'

Within ten days a boy from her village drove a donkey cart to Yonah's house and helped her load it. The belongings she had accumulated while working for three *maestros* made up a sparse collection that easily fit into the small cart.

'Reyna. Are you certain you want to do this?' Yonah asked her, and she made the only gesture that broke the servant-and-master convention under which they had lived. She reached out and placed her warm palm against his face, and the look she gave him contained tenderness and respect, and also an unmistakable farewell.

When she was gone there was a stillness in the rooms, and it seemed to Yonah as though the house had been emptied.

He had forgotten the bitter taste of loneliness. He threw himself into work, riding out ever farther to care for those in need, lingering in the homes of patients for a few more minutes of human contact, chatting at length with shopkeepers about business, and with farmers about crops. On his own property he pruned a dozen more of the old olive trees. He spent more time translating the Avicenna; he had already translated a major part of *The Canon of Medicine*, and that fact excited him and spurred him on.

True to her word, Reyna sent him a young woman, named Carla Santella, to serve him as housekeeper. She was a stocky girl who worked willingly and kept the house clean, but she never spoke and he disliked her cooking. After several weeks, he sent her away. Reyna sent as a replacement Petronila Salva, a widow with facial warts; she cooked well but distracted him by talking too much, and he kept her only four days.

After that, Reyna sent no one else.

He was fast coming to dread his weekly mock wars with Bonestruca over the draughts board, not knowing whether the friar would appear as a brilliant competitor or as the dark-tempered man in whom reason and stability were fast slipping away.

On a Wednesday evening when they were to play at the friar's finca again, María Juana let him in and motioned him toward the inner room, where he found Bonestruca seated before the table, which held an open book instead of the draughts board. The friar was studying his own face in a hand mirror.

For a moment he didn't acknowledge Yonah's greeting. Then, still gazing into the mirror, he said, 'Do you see evil when you look at me, physician?'

Yonah chose each word carefully. 'I see a most comely face.'

'Gracious features, would you say?'

'Most handsome, señor.'

'The face of a just man?'

'A face that has stayed remarkably innocent and unchanged by time's passing.'

'Do you know the long poem called *The Divine Comedy*, by the Florentine, Dante Alighieri?'

'No, señor.'

'Pity.'

He turned his eyes on Yonah. 'The first section of the poem, called *Inferno*, is a portrait of the lower reaches of Hell.'

Yonah had no reply. 'The Florentine poet has long been dead, no?'

'Yes . . . he is dead.' Bonestruca continued to peer into the mirror.

'Shall I get the board and lay out the pieces?' Yonah suggested. He stood and walked to the table. Seeing the back of the mirror for the first time, he realized it was made of silver, greatly tarnished. He could see the silversmith's mark, near the top of the handle: HT. And knew it for one of the mirrors his father had made for the count of Tembleque.

'Fray Bonestruca,' he said. He recognized the betraying tension in his own voice, but Bonestruca didn't appear to have heard. His eyes were on the mirrored image but unfocused, like a blind man's, the gaze of someone sleeping with open eyes.

Yonah was unable to resist rashness in an attempt to examine an object made by his father, but when he tried to take it from Bonestruca he found that the friar's hands were immovable. For a moment he struggled to free the mirror until the thought came to him that Bonestruca was pretending to madness and aware of everything. Yonah abandoned him in terror and made his way through the door.

'Señor?' María Juana said as he entered the outer room, but in his perturbation he walked past her and fled the finca.

The following afternoon when he rode back to his own house after visiting patients, he found María Juana waiting for him near the barn, nursing her baby in the shade produced by her tethered donkey.

He offered her the hospitality of his house but she

387

refused, saying she must return to her other children. 'What is to be done with him?' she asked.

He could only shake his head. He felt great pity for María Juana. He could guess how she had been, a foolish girl, younger and prettier. Had Bonestruca calmed her terror and seduced her? The first time, had she been debauched? Or had she been a reckless young woman who perhaps had thought it wonderfully amusing to lie down with so strange a cleric, never knowing the kind of existence that lay ahead of her.

'When I first met him he beat me. But he did not beat me for years, after that. Until now. He becomes more and more unbalanced.'

'When did it start?'

'Several years ago. It grows steadily worse. What is the cause?'

'I don't know. Perhaps it has something to do with the pox, which he has had for a long time.'

'He has not suffered from the pox for many years.'

'I know, but that is the nature of the disease. Perhaps now he has begun to suffer from it once more.'

'Can nothing be done?'

'In truth, señora, I know precious little of the cause of an unbalanced mind, nor can I refer you to a colleague more skilled than I in its treatment. Madness is mystery and magic to us. Last night, how long did he sit motionless with the mirror?'

'For a long time, until just before midnight. I gave him warmed wine then, and he drank and fell on the bed and into sleep.'

Yonah had slept poorly himself after sitting up late, reading by candlelight about insanity. The year before he had added to the medical library Nuño had left him, spending two months' income on a tract entitled *De Parte Operativa*. In it, Arnau de Vilanova had written that mania occurred when an overabundance of choler dried, heating the brain and resulting in restlessness, clamor, and aggression. 'When the friar becomes . . . excited, you must give him an infusion of tamarind and borage in cool water.' For periods such as the previous evening's, when Bonestruca had become stuporous – Vilanova said the French called such episodes *folie paralitica* – Avicenna had written that the patient must be warmed, and Yonah prescribed a powder of ground peppers, to be mixed with heated wine.

María Juana was in despair. 'He has been acting so oddly. He is capable of . . . imprudent actions. I am so fearful of our future.'

It was a hard existence for a woman and children to be tied so closely to Lorenzo de Bonestruca. Yonah wrote out the prescriptions and bade her to take them to Fray Medina's apothecary shop. Then, as he removed the saddle from his horse, he watched her donkey carrying her away.

He would have liked to have waited several days to return to the finca by the river, but instead he went there the next morning, impelled by fears that harm could come to the woman or her children.

But he found Bonestruca sitting passively in the back room of the house. María Juana whispered that he had been weeping. The friar nodded at him in return for his greeting.

'How do you feel this day, Fray Bonestruca?'

'Poorly. When I shit, it burns like fire.'

'That is the tonic I prescribed. The burning will go away.'

'Who are you?'

'I am Callicó the physician. You don't remember me?'

'No.'

'Do you recall your father?'

Bonestruca looked at him.

'Your mother? . . . Well, no matter, you will remember them some other time. Are you sad, señor?'

'Of course I am sad. I have been sad all of my life.'

'For what reason?'

'Because He was slain.'

'It is a good reason to be sad. Do you perhaps grieve as well for others who have died?'

The friar looked at him but didn't answer.

'Do you remember Toledo?'

'Toledo, yes . . .'

'Do you remember the Plaza Mayor? The cathedral? The cliffs over the river?'

Bonestruca was watching him silently.

'Do you recall riding out at night?'

There was silence.

'Do you remember riding out at night?' Yonah said again. 'With whom did you ride?'

Bonestruca watched him.

'Who was your companion when you rode at night?'

The room was quiet. The time passed.

'The count,' Bonestruca said.

Yonah heard it clearly. 'Vasca,' he said, but Bonestruca sank into silence once again.

'Do you recall the boy who carried the ciborium to the priory? The boy who was taken and killed in the olive grove?'

Bonestruca looked away. He was speaking to himself, so softly that Yonah had to lean forward to catch the words.

'They are everywhere, the fucking Jews. May they be cursed,' he whispered.

The next day, María Juana came to Yonah alone and almost incoherent, riding the donkey that showed signs of having been whipped.

'They have taken him to the smaller prison, the place for madmen and paupers.'

She said she had left her children with a neighbor's girl, and he told her to return to them. 'I'll go to the prison and see if there is anything I can do,' he said, and straightaway went to the table to saddle his horse.

The prison for paupers and madmen had a reputation for exceedingly bad food and very little of it, and so he stopped on the way and bought two loaves of bread and two small rounds of goat's cheese. When he reached the prison his heart sank, for the place assailed all the senses. Even before he walked under the raised portcullis at the entrance the prodigious stink – an essence of defecation and filth – caused his insides to churn, while the cacophony of screams and shouts, curses and imprecations, laughter and wailing, oration and babble, fed into the great united noise like streams contributing to the roar of a great river. The sound of the madhouse.

The Inquisition had no interest in this place, and once Yonah had made the gift of a coin to the guard there was no difficulty in gaining permission to attempt to see a prisoner.

'I wish to visit with Fray Bonestruca.'

'Well, you must see if you can glimpse him amongst

the humanity,' the guard said. He was a middle-aged
man with expressionless eyes and a pasty, pocked face.
'If you give me the food, I'll see he gets it. Give it to him,
and it's wasted. They'll all pounce on him and take it
away.'

He glared when Yonah shook his head.

There were no cells, only a wall composed of the same
heavy grating that had been used to fashion the
portcullis. On one side were the guard and Yonah. On
the other side was a large open space, a world inhabited
by the lost.

Yonah stood by the grate and stared into the huge
cage of bodies on the other side. He could not distin-
guish the debtors, because everyone he studied appeared to be mad.

He saw the friar finally, slumped on the dirt floor
with his back to the far wall.

'Fray Bonestruca!'

He shouted it repeatedly but his voice was lost within
the greater bedlam. The friar did not raise his bowed
head, but Yonah's cries drew the attention of a ragged
man who looked hungrily at the bread. Yonah broke a
piece from one of the loaves and held it through the
grate, where it was snatched up and quickly eaten.

'Bring me the friar,' Yonah said, pointing, 'and you
shall have half the loaf.'

The man went at once, dragging the sitting
Bonestruca to his feet and leading him to where Yonah
waited on the other side of the grating. Yonah delivered
the half loaf that had been promised, but the ragged man
did not move very far, his eyes on the other provisions
Yonah held.

A sizable crowd of prisoners had gathered.

392

Fray Bonestruca looked at Yonah. It was not a blank stare. There was a certain intelligence within the gaze, an awareness and a sense of horror, but he showed no recognition. 'I am Callicó,' Yonah said. 'Do you not recall, Ramón Callicó, the physician? . . .

'I have brought you a few things,' he said. He handed the pair of small cheeses through a square in the grate, and Bonestruca accepted them wordlessly.

But when Yonah tried to carry on conversation with him, the friar looked away mutely, and Yonah knew it would be hopeless to question him.

'I can do nothing to secure your release unless your sanity should return,' he felt impelled to report. Witnessing, hearing, smelling the place, it was a hard thing for him to say despite the part of him that would always hate Bonestruca for his terrible crimes against the Toledano family and so many others.

He handed the half loaf of bread through the grate, and then the full loaf; in order to accept them, Bonestruca transferred the two cheeses from his right hand to his left and lost control of one of them. The fallen cheese was grabbed up by the ragged man, while a naked boy snatched the breads from Bonestruca's grasp. Many hands turned against the boy; there was a heaving and thrashing among the bodies that brought to Yonah's mind the feeding frenzies of fish in the sea.

A bald old woman threw herself at the grate, reaching through to grasp Yonah's arm in a wiry claw, seeking food he didn't have. Even as he leaped backward to free himself, to escape the stink and curse of the terrible place, Yonah was conscious of Bonestruca's great fist striking out at the others about him until the friar stood alone with his mouth agape, while from him issued a scream of wolfish despair, part wail and part roar, that seemed to follow after Yonah as he fled.

He rode to the finca by the river and forced himself to tell María Juana of his instinctual feeling that Bonestruca's madness would become worse and not better. She listened without tears, having expected the news even while she had dreaded it.

'Three men of the Church have been here. They will come for me and the children this afternoon. They promise to bring us to a convent and not to the workhouse.'

'I am sorry, señora.'

'Do you perhaps know of a home nearby where a housekeeper is needed? I am not afraid of hard work. The children eat very little.'

He knew only of his own home. He thought of how it would be to live with them, of time passing while he watched its effect, devoting his life to this poor doomed woman and her poor doomed children. But he knew he was not good enough, not strong enough, not saintly enough to make such a gesture.

He put the idea from his head and thought instead of Bonestruca's collection of Jewish objects. The phylacteries. The Torah! 'Perhaps you will be willing to sell me some of the friar's belongings?'

'When they came this morning they took everything.' She led him into the next room. 'You see?'

The only things left were the crude draughts board and the small stones that were the playing pieces. They had even taken the book of Dante's poem, but too hurriedly, for several loose pages lay under the draughts board. He picked them up and read the top page, which he soon saw was a description of hell:

*Here we heard people whine in the chasm, and knock
and thump themselves with open palms, and blubber
through their snouts as if in a spasm. Streaming from
that pit, a vapor rose over the banks, crusting them
with a slime that sickened my eyes and hammered at
my nose. That chasm sinks so deep we could not sight
its bottom anywhere until we climbed along the rock
arch to its greatest height. Once there, I peered down;
and I saw long lines of people in a river of excrement
that seemed the overflow of the world's latrines. I saw
among the felons of that pit one wraith who might or
might not have been tonsured – one could not tell, he
was so smeared with shit.*

Yonah understood suddenly that no punishment God
or man might think of could possibly be worse than the
existence faced by Lorenzo de Bonestruca. Filled with
terror, he accepted the draughts game she pushed into
his hands. He emptied his purse of gold and silver and
left it on the table; then he wished the Lord's protection
on the woman and her children, and he rode away.

37

A Trip to Huesca

Fevers were always a problem, but at the end of winter an abundance of coughing fevers kept him especially busy. The home visits were much the same.

'Señor Callicó, there is a pain in my very bones (coughing) ... The thrush is severe, I cannot swallow ... The pain (coughing) ...

'Sometimes I am on fire, other times I shiver with cold (coughing).'

An old man, a youth, two old women and a child died. He hated not saving them, but he could hear Nuño telling him to think of those who lived. He went from house to house, prescribing hot drinks, honey with heated wine. And theriac against the fever.

It was by no means a pandemic or even a notable epidemic, but there were so many house calls to be made. He told himself that so long as everybody's fever cycle didn't begin and end on the same day, he would be able to manage. He promised each patient that if they followed directions for ten days, magically the illness would be gone. For most, it was so.

Often when he got home he was too tired to do house-work or cook a hot meal. Sometimes he would set the pieces on the draughts board and try to play, making the moves for both sides, but it was not at all enjoyable to play that way. He felt a general dissatisfaction and unrest, and when finally the fevers had abated and the coughing had eased, he decided to take a day off and ride out to see Reyna.

The place in which she lived was merely a collection of tiny farms and the houses of woodcutters, half an hour's ride from the outer limits of Saragossa. It had no name or government, but the people who had lived there for generations shared a sense of community, and they were accustomed to referring to the place as El Pueblecito, the Village.

When he came to the little settlement he stopped his horse by an old woman sitting in the sun; he asked for Reyna and was directed to a house next to a sawyer's. Close to the walls of the house, two men in breech-clouts – a man with long white hair and a younger, more muscular fellow – stood in a pit and thrust a long saw back and forth across a pine log, sawdust clinging to their sweaty skin.

Inside, he found Reyna shoeless and on her hands and knees, scrubbing the stones of the flagged floor. She looked as healthy as always but somehow older than he had remembered. When she saw who had entered she stopped working and smiled, wiping her hands on her dress as she got to her feet.

'I brought you some wine. The kind you like,' he said, and she thanked him as she accepted the jar.

'Sit at the table, if you please,' she said, and then took

out two cups and a jar of her own. It proved to hold *coñac*.

'*Salud*.'

'*Salud*.' It was good. Its strength made him blink.

'Have you found yourself a housekeeper by now?'

'Not yet.'

'Two good women I sent you. Carla and Petronila. They said you told them to go away.'

'Perhaps I was accustomed to the way you kept the house.'

'You must accept change. All of life is change,' she said. 'Do you wish me to send somebody else? In the spring it will be time for a thorough cleaning of the house.'

'I shall clean my house.'

'You? You should be the physician. You must not spend your time so,' she said severely.

'You have found yourself a very good house,' he observed, to change the subject.

'Yes, it will make a hostelry. There is no other shelter for hire nearby, and we are on the road to Monzon and Catalonia, with many travelers.' She said she had not begun to take in paying guests, as the house required additional carpentry before it could serve as an inn.

They sat and sipped the *coñac* and he brought her up to date with the news and gossip of Saragossa while she described the life of the Village. From outside came the soft rasping sound of the saw.

'When have you last eaten?'

'Not since early morning.'

'Then I shall make you a meal,' she said, standing.

'Will you make me a potted fowl?'

'I don't make that dish anymore.'

398

She sat again and looked at him. 'Did you see the two men cutting wood out there?'

'Yes.'

'Soon I will be married to one of them.'

'Ah. The younger one?'

'No, the other. His name is Álvaro.' She smiled. 'His hair is white but he is very strong,' she said drily. 'And he is a wonderful worker.'

'I wish you the good fortune you deserve, Reyna.'

'Thank you.'

He knew she was aware that he had traveled to the Village to persuade her to come back to his house, but they smiled at one another, and in a little while she got up again and set food on the table: a loaf of fresh bread, eggs cooked hard, garlic paste, half a yellow cheese, onion, tiny olives with wonderful flavor.

They each had several cups of the wine he had brought, and he left after a little while. Outside, the two men were fitting a fresh log over the pit.

'Good afternoon,' Yonah said. The younger man didn't reply, but the one called Álvaro nodded as he picked up the saw.

Yonah knew Passover was approaching, although he wasn't certain of the date, and he threw himself into the task of spring cleaning – dusting and scrubbing everything, opening the windows to the fresh, cold air, beating and airing carpets, cutting fresh rushes and spreading them on the stone floor. He took advantage of his privacy by making a credible version of unleavened bread, baking irregular portions on a metal sheet suspended over the fire. The resultant product was a bit burned and somewhat softer than he remembered, but it was definitely matzos, and he ate it triumphantly at a one-man seder, for which he cooked a leg of paschal lamb and prepared bitter herbs to remind him of the trials of Israel's children, fleeing Egypt.

'Why is this night different from all other nights?' he asked the quiet house, but there was no answer, only a silence more bitter than the herbs. Because he wasn't certain of the dates, he held the seder every night for a week, relishing the lamb meat for three nights before it went high and then burying the rest in the orchard on the hill.

For a few days winter seemed to have left, but it came back, chill and rainy, turning the roads into rivers of deep, cold muck. He sat in front of his table for hours at a time, thinking long thoughts. He was a wealthy man, a respected physician, living in a stout stone hacienda surrounded by good land that he owned. Yet sometimes in the sleepless night he seemed to hear, louder than the strident howl of rainy wind, his father's gentle voice telling him he was only partially alive.

He was weary of being a minyan of one, tired of being caught in a cage, even though the cage was as large as all of Spain. He thought of fleeing to France or Portugal. But he had neither the French nor the Portuguese language. Even though he might slip across one of the borders, if someone demanded proof of his baptism, in France he might burn and in Portugal he would surely be enslaved. At least in Saragossa he was known and accepted as an Old Christian. His work as a physician made up for a great deal that was missing from his life.

Yet he had a yearning for something nameless, something he couldn't identify. When he slept he dreamed of the dead or of women who drew the seed from his sleeping body. Sometimes he was certain he was going to go as mad as the friar, and when the warm and sunny days finally came he regarded the season with suspicion, unable to believe the bad weather had departed.

It was fortunate the fevers didn't return, because talking with Fray Luis Guerra Medina, the apothecary, he learned that there was no theriac to be bought anywhere in the district.

'How do we obtain more?' he asked Fray Medina.

'I don't know,' the old Franciscan said worriedly. 'It is available in good quality only from the Aurelio family of Huesca. Each year I have traveled to Huesca myself to buy theriac from the Aurelios. But it is a ride of five days, and I have grown too old. I cannot go.'

Yonah shrugged. 'Let us send a rider.'

'No, if I send someone who is not familiar with theriac they will give him a compound that is worthless as medicine because it is years old. It must be bought by someone they will respect, someone who knows the appearance and qualities of sound theriac. It must be freshly compounded, and purchased in a quantity that will last no more than a year.'

Yonah's home had become a prison, and here was a reprieve.

'All right. I will ride to Huesca,' he said.

Six months before, Miguel de Montenegro had been summoned to Montalvan, where the bishop of Teruel had been stricken by a trembling fever, and Yonah had cared for his patients in his absence. Now Montenegro and another physician named Pedro Palma, for whom Montenegro vouched, agreed to care for Señor

401

Callicó's practice, content that they and their own patients would benefit from the theriac he was to bring back. He took the gray Arab and a single pack burro. As usual, his spirits lightened as he began to wander over the land. The weather was fine and he could have made better time, but the Arabian horse was growing old and he spared the animal, seeing no need for haste. The trail wasn't difficult. In the foothills there were valleys with fields in which livestock grazed, and small farms where pigs snuffled on land that would be planted soon with grain or vegetables. He always chose a place of beauty in which to camp for the night. The hills quickly turned into small mountains, and then larger ones.

When he reached Huesca he sought out the Aurelio family and found them doing business in a converted stable that was fragrant with the odors of herbs. Three men and a woman worked at powdering and compounding the dried plants. The *maestro* herbalist, Reinaldo Aurelio, was a pleasant, sharp-eyed man wearing a rough leather apron covered with chaff.

'And what can I do for the señor?'

'I need theriac. I am Ramón Callicó, physician of Saragossa. Ordering for Fray Luis Guerra Medina of Saragossa.'

'Ah, it is for Fray Luis! But why does he not come for it himself? How is his health?'

'His health is good, but he is growing older, so he has sent me.'

'Oh, yes, we can supply you with theriac, Señor Callicó.' He went to a shelf and opened a wooden bin.

'May I see it?' Yonah said. He crumbled a bit between his fingers, sniffed it, and shook his head. 'No,' he said

402

softly. 'If I brought this back to Fray Luis he would geld me, and deservedly.'

The herbalist smiled. 'Fray Luis is most particular.'

'For which we physicians are grateful. I need fresh theriac in quantity, a sufficient amount of the compound so Fray Luis may supply a number of physicians in the districts around Saragossa.'

Señor Aurelio nodded. 'That is not a problem, but it will of course take us time to compound that much fresh theriac.'

'How much time?'

'At least ten days. Perhaps a bit more.'

Yonah had no choice except to agree. Indeed, the situation didn't displease him because it left him free to continue to wander into the Pyrenees. They calculated what the charge for the herbs would come to and he paid in advance. Fray Luis had said their word was sacred, and he didn't wish to be burdened by carrying the gold. He arranged to leave the pack burro with the Aurelios while he was gone, and promised that he would stay away from the herbalists for at least a fortnight so they would have time to do their work.

He rode due north, through foothills. He had heard that between Huesca and the border with France the mountains rose so sharply that they appeared to reach the heavens. Indeed, he saw mountains before he had traveled far, some with snowy peaks. In a meadow rich with early flowers he found a brook filled with tiny, brightly clad trout. In a moment he had taken a hooked line from his bag, as well as a little tin box that held worms from his manure pile back in Saragossa. The fish were eager to bite; too soon, he had his meal. Each trout provided no more than a mouthful but they were gutted in an instant, and he spitted them on a green wand and broiled them over a small fire, relishing the melting bones along with the tender flesh.

He let the horse crop the grass and flowers for a time, and then he followed the trail up into the mountains. The lower regions were thickly forested with beech, chestnut, and oak, rising to stands of fir and pine that he knew would thin and then disappear at the higher levels where even small plants would be sparse. The warm sun sent snow melt tinkling and rushing toward lower ground, filling the banks of a roaring stream with muscular rapids.

As the afternoon came he saw his first snow in a fir grove. It contained the perfect tracks of a bear, so discrete he knew they were freshly made. The air was sharper there, and night would be colder; he decided he wanted to sleep in lower, milder air, and he turned the horse around and descended again until he came to a likely spot under the protection of a great pine that offered dead branches for fuel. Remembering the bear tracks, he tethered the horse close to him and kept a fire burning all through the night, waking now and then to break the dry wood from the living tree with loud snapping sounds that warned of his presence, then sleeping again as the fire burned high.

On the afternoon of the third day out of Huesca he was turned back by deep snow in a high pass. It would have been safe to ride through it but hard on the horse, and to do so would have made no sense. Ascending, he looked for a side trail that would take him around that mountain, but he saw none. It was only when the gray Arab sought to turn in that he saw what the horse had perceived, a path almost indiscernible in the wall of trees. When he investigated, it became a wide and stony trail along a tumbling stream that over long centuries had cut its way through a sheer rock face descending the mountain.

He rode down and down.

After a long descent, he smelled the smoke of a wood fire, and presently he emerged from the trees and found himself in a small valley, gazing at a village. He could see perhaps a dozen small stone houses with steep slate roofs, and the cross-topped roof of a church poking up over the low horizon. Cows and horses grazed in a pasture, and he saw several cultivated fields, the soil black.

He rode past two houses without seeing anyone, but a woman had gone from the third house to the stream for water and now was carrying back the laden bucket. When she noticed him she began to hurry towards the shelter of the house, the water slopping over the rim of the bucket, but he reached her before she was halfway there.

'A good day to you. What village is this, if you please?'

She stopped in her tracks as if frozen. 'It is Pradogrande, señor,' she said in a clear and guarded voice, and as the horse brought him closer the sight of her face struck him sharply, so he could hear his own breathing.

'Inés. Is it you?'

He dismounted clumsily and she fell back in fear. 'No, señor.'

'You are not Inés Saadi Denia, daughter of Isaac Saadi?' he said stupidly. The girl was staring at him.

'No, señor. I am Adriana. I am Adriana Chacon.'

Of course, he was a fool, he told himself. This was a young woman. When last he saw Inés she was little younger than this girl, and since then all the hard years had passed.

'Inés was my aunt, may her soul rest in eternal peace.'

Ah, Inés was dead. It gave him a pang to hear that she was gone: another door was closed. 'May she rest,' he muttered.

'I remember you,' he said suddenly. He realized this woman had been the child Inés had cared for, the small daughter of her older sister, Felipa. He remembered walking with Inés in Granada with that little girl between them, he and Inés each holding one of her hands.

The woman was looking at him uncertainly.

Yonah turned at a shout that said his presence was discovered by others. Men were running toward them desperately, three men from one direction, two men from another, holding work tools like weapons they would use to kill an invader.

38

The High Meadow

Before the running field workers could reach them, a spare, robust man came from one of the nearby houses. He had aged, but not so much that Yonah did not at once know Micah Benzaquen, who had been the Saadis' friend and neighbor in Granada. Benzaquen had been middle-aged when Yonah had met him; now he was still vigorous, but an old man. He peered at Yonah for a long moment, and when he smiled, Yonah saw that Benzaquen also recognized him.

'You have matured well, señor,' Benzaquen said. 'When I knew you last you were an enormous and ragged young shepherd, all hair and beard, as if you had a bush about your head. But what is your name? It is like the name of a beautiful city . . .'

Yonah saw that during the brief time he would remain in this remote place it would be impossible to insist he was Ramón Callicó. 'Toledano.'

'Yes, Toledano, by my soul!'

'Yonah Toledano. Well met, Señor Benzaquen.'

'Where do you live now, Señor Toledano?'

'Guadalajara,' Yonah said, aware that he did not dare associate the name of Toledano with Saragossa. To his regret, the woman had lifted her bucket of water and made her escape as he and Benzaquen exchanged greetings. The running men had slowed to a walk, having noted that the stranger's sword and knife remained sheathed. By the time they arrived, still carrying farm implements with which he could have been skewered and hacked, he and Benzaquen were standing at ease and talking amicably.

Benzaquen introduced Pedro Abulafin, David Vidal, and Durante Chazan Halevi; and then a second group, Joachim Chacon, Asher de Segarra, José Diaz, and Fineas ben Portal.

Several men tended to Yonah's horse while he was led to the hospitality of Benzaquen's finca. Leah Chazan, Benzaquen's wife, was warm and gray-haired, with all the virtues of a Spanish mother. She gave him a bowl of hot water and a cloth and brought him to the privacy of the barn. By the time he was washed and refreshed, the small house was beginning to fill with the scent of baking spring lamb. His host awaited him with a jar of drink and two cups. 'Visitors to our little valley are extremely rare, so this is an occasion,' Benzaquen said, pouring *coñac*, and they drank to one another's health.

Benzaquen had noted Yonah's Arabian horse and the excellent quality of his clothing and weaponry. 'You are no longer a ragged shepherd,' he said, and smiled.

'I am a physician.'

'A physician? How fine!' Benzaquen said. Over the excellent meal soon served by his wife, he told Yonah what had befallen the converts after they and Yonah had taken separate paths.

'We left Granada in a caravan, thirty-eight wagons all

408

bound for Pamplona, the principal city of Navarre, which we reached after agonizingly slow and difficult travel.'

They had stayed in Pamplona two years. 'Several of our people married there. Including Inés Denia. She became the wife of Isadoro Sabino, a carpenter,' Benzaquen said delicately, for both men had unpleasant memories of their discussion concerning Inés Denia the last time they had met.

'Alas,' Benzaquen said, 'for those of us from Granada, our joyous times in Pamplona were vastly overshadowed by tragedy.' One out of every five of the Granada New Christians had died in Pamplona of burning fever and bloody flux. Four members of the Saadi family were among those taken cruelly and swiftly in the terrible month of Nisan. 'Isaac Saadi and his wife Zulaika Denia died within hours of one another. Then their daughter Felipa sickened and died, and finally both Inés and her new husband, Isadoro Sabino, who had been married less than three months.

'The people of Pamplona blamed any newcomers for bringing death to their city, and when the pestilence had run its course those of us who had survived knew we must flee again.

'After much discussion we determined to cross the border into France and attempt to settle in Toulouse, although the decision was controversial. I, for one, was unhappy with both the route and the destination,' Benzaquen said. 'I pointed out that for centuries Toulouse had had a tradition of permitting violent acts against the Jews, and that we were separated from France by the high Pyrenees, through which we had to take our wagons, a prospect that seemed impossible.'

But some of Benzaquen's fellow conversos had

scoffed at his fears, pointing out that they would come to France as Catholics and not as Jews. As for getting through the mountains, they knew that in the village of Jaca, which lay ahead, there were professional mountain guides, conversos like themselves, who could be hired to bring them through the passes. If the wagons could not get through the mountains, they said, they would take their most valuable possessions into France on the backs of pack animals. And so the chain of wagons had set out along the trail to Jaca.

'How did you locate this valley?' Yonah asked.

Benzaquen smiled. 'By accident.'

On the long, wooded mountain slopes, good camping sites for so large a party were hard to find. Often the travelers slept in their wagons, the vehicles strung out along the side of the trail. On such a night, between their sleeping and rising, one of Benzaquen's draft horses – a valuable animal, and needed – pulled its tether and wandered away. 'As soon as its absence was discovered in the first gray light, with four other men I set out to search, cursing the beast.'

Following flattened brush and broken branches, an occasional hoofprint, and droppings, they found themselves on a kind of natural stony trail that dropped downhill alongside a rushing stream. Finally they emerged from the woods and saw the horse grazing on the rich fodder of a small, hidden valley.

'We were immediately impressed by the good water and grass. We returned to the caravan and led the others to the valley because it offered a safe and sheltered resting place. We had only to widen the natural trail a bit in two places, and move several large rocks, and then we were able to bring the wagons down.

'At first we thought to stay only four or five days, to allow humans and animals to rest and restore their energy.' But everyone was struck by the beauty of the valley, and by the obvious fertility of the soil, he said. It wasn't lost to them that the place was wonderfully remote. To the east, it was two days of difficult travel to the closest village, Jaca, itself an isolated community that drew few travelers. And to the southeast it was three equally difficult days' travel to the nearest city, Huesca. Some of the New Christians noted that people might live here in peace, without ever seeing an inquisitor or a soldier. It occurred to them that perhaps they should go no farther, but stay in the valley and make it their home.

'Not everyone concurred,' Benzaquen said. After a great deal of argument and discussion, of the twenty-six families that had left Pamplona, seventeen decided to stay in the valley. 'Everyone pitched in to help the nine families who were going to Toulouse. It took the morning and the better part of the afternoon to get their wagons back up to the trail. After the embraces and a few tears they disappeared over the mountain, and those of us who had refused to go with them went down into the valley again.'

Among the settlers were four families whose members had earned their living from farming. In arranging the transfers from Granada to Pamplona and then to Toulouse, these farmers had been abashed, leaving the planning and decisions to the merchants whose travel experience and sophistication had stood the group in good stead.

But now the farmers became the leaders of the settlement, exploring and plotting the sections of the valley, determining which crops would be planted, and where.

411

All over the valley grew rich, healthy fodder, and from the start they called the place Pradogrande, the High Meadow.

The men of each family worked together to divide the valley into seventeen equitable holdings, giving each plot a number, and drawing the numbers from a hat to establish ownership. Each man agreed to work cooperatively in planting and harvesting, the order of work to be rotated each year so no owner would have a permanent advantage over any other. The four farmers suggested where houses should be situated to take advantage of the sun and the shade and exist well with the elements. They built the fincas one at a time, everyone working together. There was plenty of stone on the slopes and the structures were solid farmhouses with stables and barns either in the lower level or attached to the living quarters.

The first summer in the valley they built three fincas, and the women and children huddled in them communally during the winter, the men camping out in the wagons. Over the next five summers they built the other houses and the church.

The four experienced farmers became the community's purchasing committee. 'They traveled to Jaca first,' Benzaquen said, 'where they bought a few sheep and some seeds, but Jaca was too small to satisfy their needs and in their next trip they went the extra distance to Huesca, where they found a greater variety of livestock for sale. They brought back to us sacks of good seeds, a variety of implements, fruit tree seedlings, more sheep and goats, hogs, chickens and geese.'

One of the men had been a leather worker and another man had been a carpenter, both skills that were blessings in the new community. 'But most of us had been merchants. When we decided to stay in Pradogrande we knew we would have to change our livelihoods and our lives. At first it was discouraging, and difficult to accustom tradesmen's bodies to the ruder demands of labor, but we were excited about the possibilities of the future and eager to learn. Gradually, we toughened.

'We have been here eleven years, and we have broken the ground for fields and established crops and orchards,' Benzaquen said.

'You have done well,' Yonah said, truly impressed.

'Darkness is about to fall, but tomorrow I shall take you through the valley so you may see it for yourself.'

Yonah nodded absently. 'The woman Adriana . . . Is her husband a farmer?'

'Everyone in Pradogrande is a farmer. But Adriana Chacon's husband is gone. She is a widow,' Benzaquen said, cutting another slice of lamb and urging his guest to take advantage of the opportunity to eat good meat.

'He says he remembers me when I was a child,' Adriana Chacon told her father that evening. 'How curious, for I don't remember him at all. Do you recall him?'

Joachim Chacon shook his head. 'I do not. But perhaps I met him. Your grandfather Isaac knew a great many people.'

It seemed strange to her that this newcomer in the valley could lay claim to memories about her that she couldn't share. When she thought back to her childhood it was like trying to peer across a vast landscape from a mountaintop, the closer objects sharp and clear, the earlier ones fading into the remote distance until they

413

couldn't be seen. She had no memory of Granada and only a few memories of Pamplona. She remembered riding for a long time in the back of a wagon. The wagons were covered against the sun but became so hot that the caravan did most of its traveling in the early mornings and late afternoons, the drivers stopping their horses in the midday heat when they came to shade. She remembered the hard and constant jostling of the wagon over difficult trails, the creaking of leather harness, the sound of plodding hooves. The eternal gray dust that sometimes gritted between her teeth. The grassy smells of the round droppings that spilled out behind the horses and the burros, to be compacted by the wagons that came after theirs.

Adriana was eight years old then, desperately bereft as she rode alone and yearned for her loved ones who had recently died. Her father, Joachim Chacon, treated her tenderly when he thought of it; but most of the time he sat up front and drove his horses in silence, almost sightless with his own grief. Her recollections of what happened after they entered the mountains were muddled; she remembered only that one day they had come to the valley, and that she had been content to stop traveling.

Her father, who in another life had bought and sold silk cloth, did his share of the farming now, but in their first Pradogrande years he had worked at building their houses. He had become a creditable mason, learning to fit stones so they embraced one another and made sturdy walls. The houses, built of river stone and timber, were allotted in turn to the largest families. Thus, Adriana and her father had to live in the homes of others for five years, their house being the last one built by the community. It was also the smallest of the houses, yet it was as well built as any of the rest and seemed grandly private to her when at last they moved into it. That year – the year she turned thirteen years old – was her happiest time in Pradogrande. She was mistress of her father's house and as besotted by the valley as they all were. She cooked and cleaned, singing much of the time, content with her lot. It was the year her breasts began to appear; that was a little frightening yet it seemed natural, because all around her things were growing and blossoming. She had gotten her first bleeding when she was eleven, and Leona Patras, an old woman who was the wife of Abram Montelvan, had been very kind to her, showing her how to care for herself in the monthly times.

The following year the community suffered its first death when Carlos ben Sagan died of a lung disease. Three months after Sagan's burial, Adriana's father told her that he would marry Carlos's widow, Sancha Portal. Joachim explained to his daughter that the hardworking men of Pradogrande, afraid to seek immigration from the outside, were aware that in years to come they would need every pair of hands they could get. They were agreed that large families were the key to the future, and single adults were encouraged to marry as soon as it was possible. Sancha Portal had agreed to marry Joachim; she was still a handsome and robust woman, and he was decidedly cheerful about doing his duty. He told Adriana he would go to Sancha's finca to live, but she had five children and her house was already crowded. So Adriana would continue to live in her father's small house, joining her new family for meals on Sundays and holy days.

After a small church and a pastor's house had been raised in the center of the valley, Joachim had been among the delegates who traveled to Huesca and requested that a priest should be assigned to their new community. Padre Pedro Serafino, a quiet, diffident man in black, had accompanied them back to Pradogrande, staying long enough to marry Joachim and Sancha. When he returned to Huesca he had told his superiors about the new little church and the snug but empty rectory, and several months later the priest rode out of the forest and announced to the settlers his permanent appointment as their pastor.

The villagers were delighted to attend his Mass, feeling as Catholic as any bishop. 'Now, if unfriendly eyes shall ever scrutinize our community,' Joachim had told his daughter, 'even the Inquisition will have to note the prominence of our church and rectory. And observing our priest constantly riding his little burro about the valley, they will be forced to conclude that Pradogrande is a community of real Christians.'

In those days Adriana was glad to live alone. It was easy to keep the house neat and clean when there was only one person in it. She was busy, baking bread and raising food in her garden to help feed her father's large family, and spinning wool from his sheep. In the beginning everyone smiled to see her, the women as well as the men. Her body underwent the last of the changes from girlhood; her breasts didn't grow large but they were beautifully shaped, and her young frame was long and lithe yet very womanly. Soon the wives of the village noticed the way men stared, and some of the women began to sound cold and angry when they spoke to her.

416

She was innocent of experience but not knowledge; once she had seen horses mating, the neighing stallion with a pizzle like a club climbing onto the mare's back. She had watched rams with ewes. She knew human mating was done differently and wondered about the details of the act when women were with men.

She was distressed when Leona Patras took ill that spring. She visited her and tried to repay her kindness, cooking meals for Leona's elderly husband, Abram Montelvan, setting pots of water to boil on the fire so steam might ease the sick woman's breathing, and spreading goose fat and camphor on her chest. But Leona's coughing increased, and just before summer, she died. Adriana wept at the funeral; it seemed to her that death took any woman who showed her tenderness.

She helped bathe Leona's body before it was placed in the earth, and she cleaned the dead woman's house and brought several meals to the widower, leaving them on Abram Montelvan's table.

That summer the valley was almost overblown in its beauty, the heavy trees and tall grass full of darting songbirds in bright coats, the air drenched with the scent of blossoms. Sometimes it made her almost drunk with its loveliness, so that her mind wandered even in the midst of conversation. So at first she thought she had misheard when her father told her she was to be married to Abram Montelvan.

Before she and her father had received the last finca that had been built in Pradogrande they had sheltered in the houses of several other families, among them the home of Abram Montelvan and Leona Patras. Her father knew that Abram Montelvan was difficult, a sour-smelling old man with bulbous eyes and a temper; but Joachim spoke bluntly to her. 'Abram is willing to take you, and there is no one else for you. We are only seventeen families. Subtracting me and the late Carlos ben Sagan, whose family is now my family, there are only fifteen families from whose males you may seek a husband. But those men already are husbands and fathers. You would have to wait for some other man's wife to die.'

'I will wait,' she said wildly, but Joachim shook his head.

'You must do your duty to the community,' he said. He was firm. He said if she did not obey she would shame him; and in the end she had agreed.

Abram Montelvan seemed absentminded at the wedding. During the nuptial Mass in the church he didn't speak to her or look at her. After the marrying, the celebration was held in three homes, and it was a boisterous affair with three kinds of meat – lamb, kid, and chicken – and dancing until the early hours of the morning. Adriana and her bridegroom spent part of the evening in all three of the fincas, ending the wedding festivities in Sancha Portal's house, where Padre Serafino sat with them and drank a glass of wine and told them repeatedly about the sanctity of marriage.

Abram was tipsy when they left Sancha Portal's house to general cheers and laughter. He stumbled several times getting to the wagon, then they drove under cold moonlight to his house. Unclothed in his bedchamber, on the bed in which her friend Leona Patras had died, she was frightened but resigned. He had an ugly body, with a drooping stomach and skinny arms. He bade her spread her legs as she lay, and moved the oil lamp the better to see her nakedness. But evidently

418

human mating was more difficult than for the horses and sheep she had watched; when he mounted her he could not enter her body with his limp pizzle though he bucked and cursed her, spraying her with his breath. Finally he had rolled from her and gone to sleep, leaving her to get up to extinguish the lamp. When she reentered the bed she lay sleepless on the edge, as far from him as possible.

Next morning he tried again, grunting with effort, but succeeded only to produce a spurtle of matter that clung to the fine hair of her loins until he departed the house and she could scrub away all traces of him.

He turned out to be a surly husband whom she feared. He struck her on the first day of their marriage, shouting 'Do you call that an egg pudding?' That afternoon he bade her cook a fine meal for nine places next day. She killed two hens and plucked and cooked them, baked bread, and carried fresh water for cool drinking. Her father and her stepmother came to dinner, as did Abram's son Anselmo and his wife Azucena Aluza, and their three children to whom Adriana was now a fourteen-year-old grandmother – two daughters, Clara and Leonor, and a little boy named Joseph. No one spoke to her as she served, not even her father, who was laughing as Anselmo described the antics of his goats.

To her distress her husband kept at her in bed, and the time came, some three weeks after they were wed, when he had enough stiffness to push his way into her. She cried out faintly with the pain of the tearing, and listened with resentment to his crow of triumph as almost immediately he made a sticky withdrawal and hastened to capture on a rag the small spot of blood, evidence of his prowess.

After that for a time he largely left her alone, as if having climbed the mountain he saw no need to make repeated attempts. Except that many a morning she would be wakened by his hateful hand beneath the undergarment in which she slept, probing between her legs in a manner that could never be described as a caress. Much of the time he ignored her, but he fell into the habit of striking her freely and often.

His mottled hands made hard fists. Once, when she burned the bread, he whipped her legs with a switch.

'Please, Abram! No, please! No! No!' she had cried, weeping, but her husband made no reply, breathing deeply each time he struck.

He told her father he was forced to beat her for her shortcomings, and her father came to the house to talk with her.

'You must stop being a willful child and learn to be a good wife, as your mother was,' he said, and she could not meet his eyes, but told him she would do better.

As she learned to do things in the manner Abram wished, the beatings were less frequent, but they continued, and with each passing month he was crankier. It hurt him to lie down. He walked stiffly and gasped with the pain of it. Where before he had had little patience, now he had none.

Her life changed one evening, when they had been married more than a year. She cooked dinner but didn't serve it, for she spilled water on the table while filling his cup and he stood and punched her in the breast. Although it had never before entered her mind to do so, she turned on him now and attacked his face, slapping him twice, so hard that he might have fallen had he not been able to sprawl back into his chair.

She stood over him. 'You are not to touch me, señor. Ever again.'

Abram stared up at her with amazement and began to weep in baffled anger and humiliation.

'Do you understand?' she asked, but he didn't answer.

When she looked at him through her own tears she saw he was a contemptible old man but also foolish and weak, not a creature to fear. She left him there in the chair and went upstairs. After a time he climbed the stairs himself, slowly removed his clothing, and entered the bed. This time it was he who lay at the edge, as far from her as possible.

She was certain he would go to the priest or to her father, and she awaited with resignation the punishment they might decree, whether it was whipping or worse. But she heard no condemning word, and gradually she realized that he would not complain of her because he feared the ridicule that might ensue, preferring to be viewed by the other men as a potent old lion who knew how to keep so young a wife in hand.

After that, every night she placed a blanket in the common room downstairs and slept on the floor. Every day she worked in his garden and cooked for him, and washed his clothes and kept his house. When they had been married a few days short of two years he began to cough and took to his bed, which he never left. For nine weeks she tended him, heating wine and goat's milk for him, feeding him his food, bringing the chamber pot, wiping his bottom, washing his body.

When he died, there had swept over her an abiding thankfulness and her first adult feeling of peace.

*

For a time after that she was decently left alone, for which she was grateful.

But less than half a year after Abram's death, her father raised the subject of her status as a Pradogrande widow.

'The men have decided that a property may be held only in the name of a man who will join in the work on the farms.'

She considered him. 'I will join in the work.'

He smiled at her. 'You will not be able to contribute enough labor.'

'I can learn to labor as well as a silk merchant. I am able to garden very well. I would work harder in a field than Abram Montelvan was able to do.'

Her father continued to smile. 'Nevertheless, it is not allowed. To keep the holding you would have to be engaged to marry. Barring that, ownership of your land will be shared by each of the other farmers.'

'I do not wish to marry, ever again.'

'Abram's son Anselmo desires to keep your holding intact and within his family.'

'How does he propose to do that? Does he wish to take me as a second wife?'

Her father frowned at her tone but exhibited patience. 'He proposes that you accept a betrothal with his eldest son, Joseph.'

'Eldest son! Joseph is a little boy of only seven years!'

'Nevertheless, the betrothal will serve to keep the land intact. There is no one else for you,' her father said, just as he had spoken to her when telling her to marry Abram. He shrugged. 'You say you do not wish to marry. Perhaps Joseph will die while still a child. Or if not, it will take years for him to grow. It may be that he will turn out well. When he has become a man, it is possible you will welcome him.'

Adriana had never realized how much she disliked her father. She watched him go through her basket of vegetables and remove the green onions she had picked for herself earlier in the day. 'I will bring these home with me, for Sancha, who prefers your onions to all others,' he told her, beaming as he delivered the compliment.

The second betrothal had given her a period of time without harassment. Three planting seasons and three harvests had come and gone since Abram Montelvan's death. The rich fields had been seeded each spring, the hay cut and stacked each summer, the bearded wheat harvested each fall, with only a few grumblings to be heard from the men. Some of the wives in the valley looked at Adriana with hostility again. A few of their husbands had gone beyond staring, indicating their interest in her with soft words, but the marriage bed still was unpleasantly fresh in her mind and she wanted nothing of men; she learned to turn them away with a quip or a little smile at their foolishness.

On occasion when she left her finca and walked, she saw the male to whom she was promised. Joseph Montelvan was small for his age, with a dark mop of curly hair. He seemed a likely little boy as he played in the fields. By now he was ten. How old would be old enough? A boy should have at least fourteen or fifteen years, she supposed, before being put out to stud.

Once she passed close by him and saw his nostrils flowing. Taking a rag from her pocket she stopped and wiped the nose of the astonished child. 'You must never come abed bearing snot, señor. You must promise me that,' she had said, and was able to laugh at life as he ran like a startled rabbit.

Within her a small lump of coldness was growing like an unwanted child. She had no means of escape but began to contemplate simply going away, walking higher and higher up the mountain until she could walk no more. She didn't fear death but hated the knowledge that she would be eaten by beasts.

She had learned it was folly to expect good things of the world. On the afternoon when the stranger had ridden out of the woods, like some cursed knight in his rusted mail vest and on his beautiful gray horse, she would have fled him had it been possible. And so she was less than pleased when Benzaquen knocked on her door the following morning to ask humbly if she could take his place in showing the visitor their valley. 'My sheep have begun to drop lambs prodigiously and some will need my tending today,' he said, leaving her no choice.

He told her what he knew of the man, who he said was a physician from Guadalajara.

39

The Visiting Physician

Yonah had slept snugly in Benzaquen's hayloft. Not wishing to be a bother to Benzaquen's wife, he stole into the house while still they slept and took a live coal from the cooking fire, then he made a small fire close to the stream that ran nearby and cooked himself a pease gruel from his own dwindling supplies. He was rested and fed when Adriana Chacon came and told him she would guide him about the village instead of Benzaquen.

She told him not to saddle the horse. 'Today I shall show you the eastern portion of the valley. We will do better to walk. Perhaps tomorrow someone will show you the other part and you will ride,' she said, and he nodded.

He still marveled that she was greatly like Inés in appearance, yet on reflection he recognized that she was different from Inés in a number of respects, being taller, broader in the shoulder, more delicate in the bosom. Her long body was as comely as her interesting face; when she had walked toward him, her round thighs had moved against the gray spun cloth of her garment. Yet she gave the sense of not realizing she was beautiful; there was no coy foolishness in her.

He took the small basket she had brought, covered by a napkin, and carried it as they walked. They passed a field in which men were working and she raised a hand to them but didn't interrupt their work in order to introduce him. 'That man doling out the seed is my father, Joachim Chacon,' she said.

'Ah, I met him yesterday. He was one of those who ran to protect you.'

'He didn't remember you from Granada either,' she told him.

'He had nothing to remember. While I was in Granada I was told he was traveling in the south, buying silk.'

'Micah Benzaquen told me you tried to marry my aunt.'

Micah Benzaquen was a damned gossip, he thought wryly; but truth was truth, after all. 'Yes, I tried to marry Inés Saadi Denia. Benzaquen was your grandfather's close friend. He served as a go-between, interviewing me for Isaac Saadi to determine my financial prospects. I was young and very poor, with little to hope for the future. I was wishing Isaac Saadi would teach me his silk business, but Benzaquen told me that Isaac Saadi already had a son-in-law working with him – your father – and that Inés must marry a man with a business or a trade. He made it clear that your grandfather had no need for a son-in-law who required financial assistance, and he sent me on my way.'

'And were you sorely wounded?' she said, speaking lightly to indicate that after all the years that had passed, his youthful rejection was not so horrible a matter.

'Indeed I was, and by the loss of you as well as the loss of Inés. I wished to marry her but I had become enchanted by her small niece. After you left I found a smooth red pebble that you had used as a plaything. I took it for a keepsake and had it with me for more than a year before it was lost.'

She gave him a glance. 'Truly?'

'God's truth. It is too bad Isaac did not take me into the family. I might have been your uncle and helped to raise you.'

'Or you might have died with Inés in Pamplona, in Isadoro Sabino's stead,' she said.

'What a practical woman you are. Indeed, that might have happened.'

They came to the stink of a piggery in which many hogs lolled in their mud wallows. Beyond the heavy smell loomed a smokehouse and a gaunt pig farmer named Rudolfo García, to whom Adriana introduced Yonah.

'I heard we had a visitor from outside,' García said.

'I am here to show him the valley's pride,' she told him. They took Yonah into the smokehouse where great, deep-colored haunches hung from the eaves. Adriana told him that the pigs were raised on acorns from the mountainside. 'The hams are rubbed with spices and herbs and slowly smoked, and the result is a lean, dark meat with its own rich flavor.'

García had fields where green shoots already thrust through the earth. 'His crops are always first to bear in the springtime,' she told Yonah, and the farmer explained it was because of the pigs. 'I move their pens once a year. Wherever I put them, their sharp hooves and rooting snouts churn the sod into the earth along with their accumulated shit, making a rich field begging for seed.'

They bade him good-bye and walked again, following a stream through field and forest until they came to a log workshop, fragrant with wood shavings, in which a man named Jacob Orabuena made sturdy furniture, wooden implements, and sawn lumber. 'There is enough wood on the mountainside to keep me busy forever,' he told Yonah, 'but we are a small group and our needs for the things I fashion are quickly met. The remoteness of this valley, which we prize for our safety, makes it impossible to sell what we produce. The marketplaces are too far away. And though we might fill a wagon or two and make the difficult journey to bring them to Jaca or Huesca, we must not encourage people to come here looking for more of Rudolfo's fine hams or my furniture. We do not wish to call attention to ourselves. So when I have no work in my shop I help in the fields.'

He said he had a favor to ask of Yonah. 'Señora Chacon says you are a physician.'

'Yes?'

'My mother often gets the headache. When it occurs, terrible pain.'

'I will be happy to look at her,' Yonah said. He was struck by a thought.

'Tell her . . . or anyone who wishes to see a physician . . . that I may be found tomorrow morning in Micah Benzaquen's barn.'

Orabuena smiled and nodded. 'I will bring my mother,' he said.

They followed the stream and found a shaded pool to rest by. The little cloth-covered basket he carried for her proved to contain bread, goat's cheese, green onions and raisins, which they washed down with cold water from the stream, cupped in their hands. The act of their drinking startled trout of good size that darted into the shelter among the roots of the undercut bank.

'It is a wonderful place to live, this valley of yours,' he said.

She didn't answer but shook the sack, spilling bread crumbs into the pool for the fish. 'Time for a siesta, I think,' she said. She settled her back against the bole of a tree and closed her eyes, and he followed her wise example. The world intruded only with birdsong and water sounds, a lulling, and he dozed for a little while, a resting without dreams. When he opened his eyes she was still asleep and he stared at her with interest, at his leisure. She had the Saadi face, the long straight nose, the wide, thin-lipped mouth with its sensitive corners that revealed her emotions. He was somehow certain she was a woman capable of strong passions; yet she seemed to have little concern for enticing a man, flying none of the signal flags that indicate, however politely, a woman's availability. Perhaps it was simply that he didn't arouse her interest. Or it might be she still mourned the dead husband, he told himself, for a silly moment envying her vanished lover. Her body was slim but strong. She had very good bones, he thought; and in that moment her eyes opened and she was looking at Yonah raptly studying how she was fashioned.

'Shall we go on now?' she said, and he nodded and got up, giving her a hand to help her up too; her fingers in his were cool and dry.

In the afternoon they visited herds of goats and sheep, and he met a man who spent his days walking the

429

streams, collecting and hauling likely building stones, which were piled like cairns or monuments near his finca, against the day when somebody wanted to build something.

They were both tired when Adriana brought him back to Benzaquen's finca late in the afternoon. They had said good day and parted, when she turned back. 'Whenever you are through being a physician, I will be happy to show you the rest of the valley,' she said, and he thanked her again for her kindness and told her he would like that.

Early the next morning, the first person to seek out the visiting physician was a woman named Viola Valenci. 'The devil is in my eyetooth,' she told him.

When he peered into her open mouth the problem was apparent at once, because a canine tooth was discolored and the gums around it were pale. 'I wish I had seen this earlier, señora,' he muttered, but he had forceps in his medical pack and the tooth clearly had to come out. Just as he feared, it was already rotten, and it splintered during the extraction. Though he had to struggle to make certain that the offending roots were plucked, in the end the pieces lay in the dirt at Señora Valenci's feet. Spitting blood, she sang his praises as she went away.

By that time, several people had gathered, and he worked steadily through the morning, dealing with one patient at a time, asking the others to wait a distance away so there could be privacy. He trimmed back the ingrown toenail in Durand Chazan Halevi's foot and then listened to Asher de Sogarra describe the choloric flux that periodically bothered his stomach.

'I have no medicines with me and you are distant

from an apothecary shop,' he told Señor Sogarra. 'But soon roses will be in bloom. If you will boil a cupful of petals in water with honey, cool it well and beat into it a hen's egg, it will supply a drink that will ease your stomach.'

At midday Leah Chazan brought him bread in a bowl of broth, and he consumed it gratefully and then returned to lancing carbuncles, discussing digestion and diet, sending people behind the barn to void into a cup so he could examine their urine.

At one point Adriana Chacon appeared. She stood and talked with the others who waited. Several times she looked over to where he was treating somebody.

But the next time he looked up and wanted to see her, she was gone.

The next morning Adriana appeared on a mare the color of brown moss, named Doña. They rode first to the church, where she introduced him to Padre Serafino. The priest asked him where he was from, and Yonah told him Guadalajara. Padre Serafino pursed his lips. 'You have traveled far.'

The trouble with lying, Yonah had discovered long ago, was that a single lie engendered many other lies. He hastened to change the subject by remarking on the pleasant aspect of the small stone-and-timber church. 'Does it have a name?'

'I am thinking of suggesting several names to the congregants, who must guide me in that decision. I first considered the Church of Saint Dominic, but so many other churches have that name. What is your opinion of calling it the Church of Cosmas and Damian?'

'Were they saints, Padre?' Adriana asked.

431

'No, my child, they were early martyrs, twin brothers born in Arabia. They both became physicians and treated the poor without payment, healing many. When the Roman emperor Diocletian began to persecute Christians he ordered the brothers to recant their faith, and when they refused he had them beheaded by the sword.

'I have heard this morning of another physician who treated suffering people and refused all payment,' he said.

Yonah felt unjustly praised and had no wish to be spoken of in the company of martyrs. 'I customarily accept payment for my services, and gladly,' he said. 'But in this instance, I am a guest in the valley. It would be a poor guest who accepted payment from his hosts.'

'You have cast your bread upon the waters,' Padre Serafino said, not to be denied. He blessed them when they took their leave.

There were several fincas in the far end of the valley, the homes of herdsmen who had built up large flocks of sheep and goats. Yonah and Adriana didn't stop to knock on doors, however, but skirted the houses, letting their horses amble along in quiet harmony.

He had asked her to bring no food, certain he could catch a few trout to make a meal for them; but she had brought some bread and cheese and it satisfied them both, so he skipped the simple exertion with the fish-line. They tethered the horses in shaded grasses nearby and spent the midday as they had the day before, asleep under a tree near the stream.

The day grew hotter and he slept on pleasantly for a long while. When he awoke he thought she still slept, but when he went to the stream and splashed the very cold water on his face, she came up and knelt nearby to do the same. They cupped water in their hands. As they drank, each looked over their dripping hands, directly at the other, but at once she averted her gaze. Riding back, he allowed her horse to lead slightly so he could glimpse her sitting sidesaddle with a perfectly straight spine, maintaining her balance easily even during a canter. Sometimes her loose brown hair blew in the breeze.

At her house he unsaddled her horse. 'Thank you for showing me about again,' he said, and she smiled and nodded. He didn't want to leave, but there was no invitation to stay.

He rode the gray Arabian to Benzaquen's and let him graze near the barn. The men of the valley had started digging a ditch to carry irrigation water from the stream to parts of the meadow that suffered from dryness. For an hour he helped them, carrying away buckets of the earth they dug and spreading it in a low place, but even the hard work didn't dispel the curious restlessness and irritability that gripped him.

The next day was Saturday. The first thing he thought of when he opened his eyes was that he wanted to go at once to see Adriana Chacon, but almost at once Micah Benzaquen came into the barn and asked if he would go into the woods with several men, to point out medicinal herbs that might help them fight sickness when Señor Toledano was gone and they were without a physician once more.

'Unless, of course, you plan to stay here indefinitely?' Micah said. Yonah sensed that the question was half-serious, but he smiled and shook his head.

Presently he set off, accompanied by Benzaquen,

Asher de Segarra, and Pedro Abulafin. He was certain he would overlook a number of valuable plants out of ignorance, but Nuño had trained him well, and he knew these men lived in the midst of an apothecary's treasure trove. To begin with, he didn't allow them to leave the meadow before he had pointed out bitter vetch that would mollify ulcers or, mixed with wine for a poultice, ease snakebite. And lupine, to be taken with wine to ease sciatic pain and with vinegar to expel worms from the bowel. In their gardens, he told them, were other valuable herbs. 'Lentils, eaten with their husks, will bind bowels afflicted with flux. So will medlars, cut into small pieces and mixed with wine or vinegar. Rhubarb will open bowels that are overly bound. Sesame seeds in wine will help an aching head and turnip will calm the gout.'

In the forest he showed them the wild pea, good for scabs and jaundice when mixed with barley and honey. And fenugreek, which needed to be mixed with nitre and vinegar to ease the monthly cramps of women. And hyacinth, to be burnt with a fishhead and merged with olive oil to make an ointment for painful joints.

At one point Pedro Abulafin, being closest to his finca, slipped away and soon returned with two loaves of bread and a jar of drink, and they sat on rocks by the stream and tore and ate the bread, and passed the jar, which contained a sour wine that had been allowed to grow stronger so it was almost like *coñac*.

The four of them were mellow and full of good fellowship when they came out of the woods. Yonah was wondering whether there yet might be time for the visit to Adriana he had contemplated earlier, but when he returned to Benzaquen's barn, Rudolfo García was waiting there for him.

'I wonder if you might help me, señor. It is one of my best sows. She has been trying to deliver, but despite a day of labor, she is stuck. I know that you doctor people, but . . .'

So in García's company he had departed at once for the piggery, where the sow lay panting weakly on her side, clearly in difficulty, and Yonah had removed his shirt and greased his hand and arm with lard. After a bit of manipulation he had extracted a plump dead piglet from the sow, and it was like uncorking a bottle. Within a brief time eight living pigs emerged and soon were sucking mother's milk into their bodies.

Yonah's fee was a bath. García's tub was brought to the barn and the pig farmer heated and carried in two large pots of water, while Yonah scrubbed himself in contentment. When he returned to Benzaquen's he found a covered dish left by Leah Chazan, containing bread and a small round of cheese, and a cup of a sweet, light wine. Yonah ate and then went out and pissed against a tree in the moonlight. He climbed into the hayloft and moved his blanket next to the unglazed window so he could see the stars, and went to sleep at once.

On Sunday morning he accompanied Micah and Leah to the church, where he saw that Adriana sat next to her father, with his wife on the other side of him. There were empty benches available but Yonah went directly to Adriana's side and sat next to her, Leah and Micah following him to take their places on his left.

'Good morning,' he said to Adriana.

'Good morning.'

He wanted to speak with her but was prevented from

doing so by the start of the service. Padre Serafino led them in a businesslike Mass. Sometimes as they knelt and rose, their bodies brushed. Yonah was aware of people watching.

Padre Serafino announced that in the morning he would appear on the western meadow to bless the drainage ditch that was being dug. After the final hymn, people lined up. As the priest went into the confessional, Leah said that unless Señor Toledano wished to confess they had best leave at once, since she had to prepare refreshment for the residents of Pradogrande who would visit her house that day in order to meet their guest and pay respects. Groaning within, Yonah had to follow them out the door.

The visitors came bearing gifts for him, honey cakes, olive oil, wine, a small ham. Jacob Orabuena gave him a remarkable woodcarving of a thrush in flight, lifelike with colors Orabuena had gained from woodland herbs.

Adriana and her father and stepmother were among those who came to call, but there was no opportunity for him to speak with her alone. Eventually she left, and inwardly he fretted and fumed.

40
Adriana Chacon

Adriana's interest in him had grown when she had observed him treating the people at Micah's barn. She was impressed by how absorbed he had been, and by the fact that he treated each person with respect. She saw that he was a tender man.

'Anselmo Montelvan is angry,' her father told her on Sunday. 'He says you are seen too much with this physician. He says it dishonors his son, your betrothed.'

'Anselmo Montelvan cares little for his small son Joseph and certainly he cares nothing for me,' she said. 'All he is concerned about is gaining control of the land that was his father's.'

'It would be best not to be seen with Señor Toledano. Unless, of course, you believe his intentions are serious. It would be a very good thing to have a physician living here.'

'I have no reason to believe he has any intentions at all,' she said peevishly.

Still, her heart leaped when Yonah Toledano appeared at her door on Monday morning.

'Will you walk with me, Adriana?'

'I have already shown you both sides of the valley, señor.'

'Please, show them to me again.'

They retraced the path along the stream, talking lazily. At midday he took his hooked line from his pocket, and a tiny can containing wriggling worms he said he had gathered at the ditch being dug in the meadow. She went to her house for a live coal from her cooking fire, and when she carried it back in a little tin pail, he had already caught and gutted four small trout for each of them. He snapped dry wood from the trees for a fire, and soon they ate the sweet blackened flesh of the trout from their hands, licking their fingers.

This time when they napped he lay down not far from her. While she was falling asleep she was aware of his quiet breathing, the rising and falling of his chest. When she awoke he was seated nearby, a tall, quiet man watching over her.

They walked together each day. The villagers grew accustomed to seeing them strolling, utterly absorbed, deep in conversation, or merely proceeding in companionable silence. On Thursday morning, as though crossing a visible line, she told him they would go to her house, where she would prepare food for a midday meal. As they walked there, she began speaking of the past. Without offering details, she said that her marriage to Abram Montelvan had been difficult and unhappy. She told him what she remembered about her mother, her grandparents, and her aunt Inés. 'Inés was more a mother to me than Felipa. To lose one of them would have been a catastrophe, but both died, and then also my grandfather and my beloved grandmother, Zulaika.'

He took her hand and held it tightly. 'Tell me about your family,' she said.

He told her frightening stories. Of his mother who had died of illness. Of a murdered older brother, and of a father who had been slain by a Jew-hating mob. Of a younger brother taken from him.

'Long ago I reconciled myself to the loss of those who are dead. I find it harder not to continually mourn my brother Eleazar, because something within me feels he is alive. If so, by now he is a grown man, but living *where* in the great world? He is gone from me as completely as the others. I know that he exists yet I will never see him again, and that is terrible to bear.'

The men digging the irrigation ditch had reached a place quite close to her house, and the diggers watched the man and the woman pass them by talking and listening, walking closely together.

When the door of her house closed behind them, Adriana began to tell him to be seated in the common room, but the words died in her mouth because they had turned to one another without thought, and he was kissing her face. In a moment she was kissing him also, and their mouths and bodies met.

She was soon dazed by their mutual ardor, but when he raised her skirt and then lifted the inner garment, she grew faint. She wanted to flee when she felt his hand. It must be something all men did, not only Abram Montelvan, she thought in terror and disgust. But as his mouth paid her homage with small kisses his hand spoke to her and it was different. Loving. And a warmth rose within her, spreading most pleasantly to weaken her limbs until she sank down on nerveless knees. He sank to his knees too and continued to kiss and caress her.

439

From outside came the voice of one of the diggers shouting to others far away: 'No, no. You must place some of the cursed stones back on the dam, Durand. Yes, back on the dam, else it won't hold the water.'

Inside the house, she and he were lying together half-dressed, the rushes on the floor beneath them rustling and crackling.

When she arched to meet him, it was easily done. He had none of Abram's difficulty, no difficulty at all; well, a physician, she told herself wildly . . . She knew it was dark sin to think it the most pleasurable moment of her life, but that thought, all thoughts, fled as gradually she began to feel fright again. Because something alien was happening to her. She became certain of impending death. *Please, God*, she begged, wonderfully alive till the end as her entire world began to convulse and shudder, and she gripped Yonah Toledano with both hands so she would not fall off.

For the next two evenings Yonah played a new kind of game when the light faded, bidding good night early to Micah and Leah, waiting impatiently for the full, plum-colored darkness that would allow him to slip from Benzaquen's barn. He avoided the moonshine, moving in deep shadows when he could find them, making his way to her house with as much stealth as some savage determined to slit throats. Both nights her door was unlatched for him and she was just behind it, waiting to fall upon him with a wanting that matched his own. Each time she sent him out of her house well before light, since all the village folk were farmers who rose early to care for animals.

They thought they were discreet and careful. Perhaps

they were, yet on Friday morning Benzaquen asked for Yonah's company. 'So we may have a discussion.'

The two of them traveled afoot to a place not far beyond the village church. Micah showed him a broad piece of verdant land stretching from the edge of the river to the rocky rise of the mountain.

'It is in the very center of the valley,' Micah pointed out. 'A good site, easily reached by any villager who might need a physician.'

Yonah was thinking of an earlier time when he had been a suitor and Benzaquen had dismissed him out of hand. He guessed that now Micah was courting him for the village.

'This land was part of the property of the late Carlos ben Sagan, may his soul rest, but has been owned by Joachim Chacon since his marriage. He has seen your interest in his daughter and has asked me to offer it to the pair of you.'

They were using Adriana as their bait, Yonah realized. It was such a nice piece of wooded land, where a house could stand on high ground yet be close enough to the stream so its sounds would be heard. A family living here might splash in the pools during the warm days of summer. There was a small field in front, the wooded mountainside beyond.

'It is centrally located in the valley. Everyone could walk to your dispensary. The men of Pradogrande would build you a fine house.

'Our population is small,' Benzaquen said carefully, fighting to be honest. 'You would have to treat animals as well as humans, and perhaps do a bit of farming if you liked.'

It was a fine offer and deserved an answer. A gentle

441

refusal was on his lips; he had seen the valley as Eden's garden, but he had never considered that it was for him. Yet he was afraid to refuse until he was able to determine the effect his decision would have on Adriana Chacon's life.

'Let me think on it,' he said, and Benzaquen nodded, satisfied that there had not been a refusal.

On the walk back, he asked Benzaquen to do something for him. 'Do you recall when we met each other in Isaac Saadi's house in Granada, at a Sabbath service of the old religion? Would you invite your friends to a similar service tonight?'

Benzaquen frowned. He looked at Yonah, perhaps seeing problems in him he hadn't seen before, then gave a worried smile. 'If it is something you strongly desire me to do . . .'

'It is, Micah.'

'Then I will spread the word.'

But that evening, only Asher de Segarra and Pedro Abulafin came to Benzaquen's house, and from their abashed manner Yonah suspected they were there not out of piety but because they had grown to like him as a man.

Along with Micah and Leah, they sat and waited well after the third star became visible in the evening sky and signified the beginning of the Sabbath.

'I don't remember very much of the praying,' Asher said.

'Nor do I,' Yonah said. He might have led them in the Shema. But the previous Sunday Padre Serafino had spoken in the church about the Trinity, telling his flock, 'There are three. The Father creates. The Son

442

saves souls. The Ghost makes the sinners of the world holy.'

It was what the New Christians of Pradogrande had come to believe, Yonah realized. They appeared to be happy as Catholics so long as the Inquisition left them alone. Who was Yonah Toledano to ask them to chant, 'Hear, O Israel, the Lord our God, the Lord is One?'

Asher de Segarra put his hand on Yonah's shoulder. 'It does not pay to be sentimental about what is past.'

'You are right,' Yonah said.

Soon he thanked them and said good night. They were good men; but if he couldn't have a minyan of Jews, he didn't want the reluctant participation of these apostates, praying as a favor to him. He knew he would gain more comfort from praying by himself, as he had done for a very long time.

That night at Adriana's house, he touched a sliver of wood to her cooking fire until it flamed, and then he lit her lamp. 'Sit down, Adriana,' he said. 'There are things I must tell you.'

For a moment she didn't speak. '. . . Is it that you already have a wife?'

'I already have a God.'

In spare language he disclosed that he was a Jew who since boyhood had managed to avoid both conversion and the Inquisition. She listened, sitting straight and still in her chair, her eyes never leaving his face.

'I have been asked to stay here in Pradogrande, by your father and others. But I would not survive here, where every man knows the daily life of every other man. I know myself. I would not change, and sooner or later someone would betray me out of fear.'

443

'Do you live in a safer place?'

He told her of the hacienda in which he lived on a secluded piece of land, close to the city yet away from prying eyes. 'The Inquisition is strong there, but I am believed to be an Old Christian. I attend Mass. I make certain to tithe to the Church from an excellent income. I have never been bothered.'

'Take me away from here, Yonah.'

'I want so much to take you home as my wife, but I'm filled with fear. If I am someday discovered, I will burn. My wife would face a terrible death.'

'A terrible death may come to anyone, at any time,' she said calmly: he saw that she was always practical. She got up now and came to him and held him in a fierce embrace. 'I am honored that you trust me with your life by confiding in me. You have survived. We will survive together.' Her face was wet on his, yet he could feel her mouth turn up when she smiled. 'I think you will die in my arms when we are very old.'

'We have to leave here without delay. People in this valley are so fearful. If they know you are a Jew and sought by the Inquisition, they would kill you themselves.

'Strange,' she said. 'Your people were my own people. When I was a babe my grandfather Isaac decided we were no longer to be Jews. Yet for the rest of her life my grandmother Zulaika prepared a fine meal for the family each Friday eve, and lighted the Sabbath tapers. I have her copper candlesticks.'

'You will bring them with us,' Yonah said.

They rode away next morning just as the blackness turned to gray light on the stony trail leading up from the valley. Yonah was nervous, reminded of a similar dawn ride he had made with Manuel Fierro, on a morning when an arrow had seemed to come from nowhere to end the life of the man he still thought of as the *maestro*.

No one tried to kill them now. He maintained an uneasy vigilance and didn't slow their horses' canter until they were off the mountain trail and had turned onto the road to Huesca, without a sign of pursuit.

Whenever he looked at her, he wanted to shout.

In Huesca he found that the Aurelio family had readied a large bundle of theriac of excellent quality, and in a short time he had reclaimed the packhorse and they were on their way again. From that moment on he didn't hurry, looking out for her comfort, careful not to ride overlong on a single day.

As they traveled he revealed to her the things about him that were false – that they were not going to Guadalajara, and that she must become accustomed to being the wife of Ramón Callicó, the physician of Saragossa. Adriana understood at once the reason for the falsehoods. 'I like the name Ramón Callicó,' she said, and it was what she called him from then on, in order to accustom herself to it.

When finally they reached Saragossa she looked at everything as they rode through the town, and when they turned into his own lane she was excited and eager. What Yonah yearned for was a bath, a bowl of gruel, a glass of wine, and Adriana in his own bed, followed by a long sleep; but she begged until, yawning, he led her forth to see what there was to see, walking with her over the land, showing her the olive trees, Nuño's grave, the brook and its tiny trout, the fruit orchard, the neglected

445

garden that had fallen into ruinous condition, and the hacienda.

When finally, then, he was able to have the things he wanted, they slept through half the day and all of the night.

The following day, they married themselves. Yonah lashed four straight sticks to chairs in the common room and hung a blanket over them, a wedding canopy. He lighted candles and they stood together, as under a tent.

'Blessed art Thou, O Lord our God, who has hallowed us with Thy commandments and has brought me this woman in marriage.'

She looked at him. 'Blessed art Thou, O Lord our God, who has hallowed us with Thy commandments and has brought me this man in marriage,' she said, her eyes full and shining. He placed on her finger the silver ring his father had made for him when he had turned thirteen, and it was very large. 'Never mind,' he told her. 'You will wear it about your neck on a little chain.'

He broke a glass under his heel to mourn the destruction of the Temple in Jerusalem, but in truth there was little mourning in their hearts that day.

'*Mazel tov*, Adriana.'

'*Mazel tov*, Yonah.'

For her wedding trip she went to the garden and pulled weeds and thinned the onions. Yonah went to the farm of his patient Pascual Cabrera and reclaimed the black horse, which he had boarded out to Cabrera's care. Soon the black horse was running in the field with the Arab gray and Adriana's horse, Doña. 'Why do you call your horses the Black and the Gray?' she asked. 'Why do they not have names?'

How could he explain that once long ago a youth had had and lost a burro with two names, and that since then he hadn't been able to give a name to an animal. He shrugged and smiled.

'May I name them?' she asked, and he told her that would be fine. His gray Arab became Sultán. She said the black mare that had been Manuel Fierro's looked like a nun, and she named that horse Hermana, Sister.

That afternoon she began to work on the hacienda. The house had grown a bit musty in his absence and she threw open the door and let in the air. She scrubbed and dusted and polished. She gathered fresh rushes to spread on the floor, moved the comfortable chairs a bit closer to the fire. Her grandmother's candlesticks and the carved bird from Pradogrande went on the mantle.

Within two days, it was as though she had lived there always, and the hacienda was Adriana's.

Part Seven

THE SILENT MAN

Aragon
April 3, 1509

41
A Letter from Toledo

Next to Nuño Fierro, Miguel de Montenegro was the best physician Yonah had ever met. Known as 'the physician to bishops' because of his frequent consultation by the prelates of the Church, he was a valuable friend to someone in Yonah's position. His practice overlapped Yonah's, but the two physicians had been able to support each other without any feeling of competition. Montenegro had overseen the apprenticeship of Pedro Palma and recently had made Palma his partner.

'But Pedro has gaps in his knowledge and experience,' Montenegro told Yonah one day as they relaxed over a glass of wine in a Saragossa *taberna*. 'I especially feel he requires more experience in the science of anatomy. He would learn a lot by working with you, if the occasion arose.'

Each of them knew that Montenegro was asking Yonah to allow Palma to dissect with him.

It was difficult for Yonah to refuse him anything, but since he had married he had become very conscious of his responsibilities to Adriana, and he didn't want to

451

risk her safety. 'I think you are an excellent surgeon and therefore should teach him yourself, as your friend Nuño taught me,' he said.

Montenegro nodded, understanding his decision and accepting it without rancor. 'How is your wife faring, Ramón?'

'She is the same, Miguel.'

'Ah. Well, as you know, sometimes these things take their own time. She is such a charming woman. You will please extend my greetings?' he said, and Yonah nodded and finished his wine.

He was unable to guess whether Adriana was barren or whether the fault lay within him, because to his knowledge he had never impregnated a woman. Their inability to conceive was the only unhappiness in their marriage. Yonah knew how much his wife wanted a family and it hurt him to see sadness creep into her eyes when she looked at other women's children.

When he had consulted Montenegro the two of them had studied the available medical literature together and had decided to give her an infusion of pulse, camphor, sugar, barley water, and ground mandrake root in wine, reported to be the prescription of the Islamic physician Ali ibn Ridwa. For two years Adriana had been faithfully taking the dosage and a number of other medications, but with no results.

They led a quiet and orderly existence. To keep up appearances Adriana accompanied him to church several Sundays a month but otherwise seldom went to town, where she was treated with respect as the physician's wife. She kept an enlarged kitchen garden, and she and Yonah slowly but steadily had brought to fruition more of the orchard and the olive grove. She greatly enjoyed working on their own land like a *peón*.

It was a satisfying time for Yonah. In addition to the wife he loved, he had work that he cherished, and even the pleasures of scholarship. Only a few months after their arrival from Pradogrande he had reached the final page of *The Canon of Medicine*. Almost reluctantly he had translated the last folio of Hebrew characters – a warning to physicians that patients who were in a feeble state, as well as those who had diarrhea or nausea, should not be bled.

And then at last he was able to write on his own sheet of paper the final words:

> *The Seal of the Work, and an Act of Thanks.*
> *May this our compendious discourse upon the*
> *general principles pertaining to the science of medicine*
> *be found sufficient.*
> *Our next task will be to compile the work*
> *on Simples, with the permission of*
> *Allah. May He be our*
> *aid, and Him do we*
> *thank for all His*
> *innumerable*
> *mercies.*
>
> *The end of the first book of*
> *the Canon of Medicin*
> *Avicenna the Chief*
> *of Physicians.*

Yonah used fine sand to blot the ink and carefully shook it off, then he added the page to the pile of manuscript that rose an impressive distance from the surface of his table. He was filled with a special joy that he thought must come only to writers and scholars who have labored at great length and in perfect loneliness to complete a work, and regretted that Nuño Fierro could not see the end product of the task he had set for his apprentice.

Yonah put the Spanish Avicenna away on a shelf and the Hebrew Avicenna back into its hiding niche in the wall, exchanging it for the second half of Nuño's assignment, the Maimonides book on medical aphorisms. And with the time left before Adriana summoned him to their dinner, he sat again at his writing table and began to translate the first page.

They saw few people socially. When Adriana had first arrived in Saragossa they had had Montenegro to dinner. The small, energetic physician was a widower, and he had reciprocated by bringing them to a good dinner at an inn in the city, beginning a pattern they had enjoyed with him ever since.

Adriana was fascinated with the history of their house. 'Tell me about the people who have lived here, Ramón,' she said. She was interested to learn that Reyna Fadique had served as housekeeper to all three of the physicians who had made the hacienda their home. 'How unusual a woman she must be, to be able to satisfy three different *maestros* of her house,' she said. 'I would like very much to meet her.'

Yonah hoped she would forget that request, but she didn't, until finally he rode to deliver an invitation to Reyna. Each of them accepted congratulations, for both had been married since their last meeting. Work was proceeding splendidly on the house that was on its way to becoming an inn, and Reyna said she was pleased to hear that his bride had invited her, and Álvaro – whose last name turned out to be Saravía – to dinner in the house where she had been a servant for so long.

When they came, bearing gifts of a honeycomb and wine, the two women seemed overly polite to one another for a time. Yonah and the white-haired Álvaro went to walk the land, leaving the women to become acquainted. Álvaro had grown up on a small farm and he praised the efforts Yonah and Adriana had made to bring back some of the trees. 'If you continue to save trees, it would be most useful to build a small barn near the orchard and the olive grove on the upper slope of the hill, where farm implements and picked fruit could be stored.'

It seemed a good suggestion, and they were discussing the cost of the labor and the quantity of stones that would be needed for the walls, when they returned to find the women beaming at one another and talking volubly. The meal was pleasant, and Adriana and Reyna, clearly already friends, embraced when the guests took their leave.

Adriana discussed them warmly as she emptied the table of the remains of the dinner. 'She feels like a mother to you, and I think she is eager to be a grandmother. She asked me if there was perhaps a bun in the oven.'

Yonah was aghast, knowing his wife's sadness and sensitivity about the subject of pregnancy. 'What did you say?'

Adriana smiled. 'I told her not yet, because until now we have only been practicing,' she said.

*

On the first day of February Yonah rode head down against the wind to attend the annual meeting of the physicians of Aragon. Despite the bitter weather eight other physicians attended to hear Yonah deliver a talk about the circulation of the blood according to Avicenna. It was well received and drew questions and good discussion, after which Miguel de Montenegro read a letter that had been delivered to him out of the mail packet of the Saragossa diocese.

To Miguel de Montenegro, physician, I send the greetings of the Toledo diocese, and the hope that you are in good health.

I am assistant to the Most Reverend Enrique Sagasta, auxiliary bishop of Toledo. Bishop Sagasta is head of the Office of Religious Faith in the Toledo See, in which capacity there has come to his attention a nobleman of Tembleque who has been grievously afflicted.

Count Fernán Vasca is his name. A knight of Calatrava who has been an exceedingly generous friend of Holy Mother Church, he has a malady that has left him mute and frozen as any stone, yet painfully in life.

Several physicians have been consulted in his behalf without avail. Recalling the high esteem in which you are held, Bishop Sagasta prays that you may be able to come to Castille. The Church and His Reverence, would consider it a most gracious favor if you will come or, if you are unable, if you will recommend this patient to another skilled physician of your acquaintance, the local physicians having failed in their attempts to help Count Vasca.

The bishop is assured that you or another of your choosing will be well compensated, with double payment if the physician is able to bring about a cure.

Thank you for your attention.

Yours in Christ,

Padre Francisco Rivera de la Espina, Order of Preachers

'I cannot go,' Montenegro said. 'I am growing old. It is bad enough I must travel to sick bishops. Once I start answering the summonses for sick laymen in their districts, I am truly lost. Nor can Pedro Palma go, for he is too new a physician.

'Is anyone else interested in this matter?' he asked, but there were only grins and a shuffling of feet by those in attendance.

'It is a long way to ride. And noblemen are notoriously small payers,' offered a physician from Ocaña, to general laughter.

'Well, the bishop guarantees payment,' Montenegro pointed out. 'Although I do not know either this Bishop Sagasta or the priest who wrote the letter.'

'I know the priest,' Yonah heard himself saying. 'Padre Espina served for a time in Saragossa. He seemed to me to be a most worthy priest.'

Still, nobody showed further interest in the matter, and Miguel de Montenegro shrugged and placed the letter back in his pocket.

Of course Yonah would not even consider going to Toledo, he told himself at first.

He didn't wish to leave Adriana. Tembleque was too far away, and the time needed for such a trip would be great.

457

If he owed anything to the count of Tembleque, it was revenge.

Yet he seemed to hear Nuño's voice asking if a physician had the right to treat only those members of humanity of whom he approved, or for whom he held respect or affection.

That day and the next, slowly he came to admit to himself that he had unfinished pieces of his life in Tembleque.

Only by responding to Padre Espina's summons to Montenegro, which seemed fated, could he attempt to answer the questions that had always weighed on him, about the murders that had destroyed his family.

At first Adriana asked him not to go. Then she asked that she be allowed to go with him.

The journey itself could be difficult and dangerous, and he had no idea what he might find when he got there. 'It is not possible,' he said gently.

It would have been easier if he had seen anger in her eyes, but what he saw was fright. Several times he had been called to travel a distance for a consultation, and she had been alone for two or three days. But this would be an extended absence.

'I am coming back to you,' he told her.

When he said he would leave her enough money for any emergency, she was angered. 'What if I take it and just go away?' she said.

He brought her behind the house and showed her where he had buried the leather bag containing Manuel Fierro's money, and then had built a manure pile above it. 'You may take it all if ever you truly wish to leave me.'

458

'It would be too much digging,' she said, and he took her into his arms and kissed her and comforted her.

He went to Álvaro Saravía, who promised to visit Adriana once a week, to make certain that firewood would always be stacked where she could get it easily, and that there would always be a pile of hay where she could fork it into the horses' stalls.

Miguel de Montenegro and Pedro Palma were not enthusiastic about caring for Yonah's patients for an extended time, but they didn't refuse him. 'You must ever watch out for noblemen. Once cured they will screw the physician,' Montenegro said.

Yonah decided not to take the gray Arabian, because age had begun to slow the horse. Manuel Fierro's black mare was still strong and he took her instead. Adriana packed a saddlebag with two loaves, fried meat, dried peas, a sack of raisins. He kissed her and left quickly in a morning mist.

He rode the horse southwest at an easy trot. For the first time, being free to travel didn't lift his gypsy spirits. His wife's face stayed in his mind and he had a terrible urge to turn the horse about and ride home, but he did not.

He made good progress. That night he camped behind a windbreak of trees in a brown field that was distant from Saragossa. 'You did well,' he told the mare as he unburdened her of the saddle. 'You are a wonderful animal, Hermana,' he said, stroking and patting the black horse.

42
In the Castle

Nine days later he rode across the red clay of the Sagra plain, approaching the walls of Toledo. He saw the city from far off, sharp and clear on its high rock in the afternoon sun. He was a lifetime away from the terror-stricken youth who had escaped from Toledo on a burro, yet as he passed through the Bisagra Gate he was assailed by troublesome memories. He rode past the headquarters of the Inquisition, marked by its stone escutcheon displaying the cross, the olive branch, and the sword. Once when he was a boy in his father's house he had heard David Mendoza explain the meaning of the symbols to Helkias Toledano: 'If you accept the cross they give you the olive branch. If you refuse it, they give you the sword.'

In front of the diocesan offices he tethered the black horse. Stiff from his long days in the saddle he walked inside, where a friar seated behind a table asked his errand and then motioned him to a stone bench.

Padre Espina appeared after the briefest of waits, beaming. 'How good it is to see you again, Señor

Callicó!' He was older and more mature, of course, and more relaxed than Yonah had remembered, a more polished priest.

They sat and talked. To Yonah's relief, Padre Espina showed no disappointment that his letter had produced the physician Callicó instead of the physician Montenegro. 'When you get to the castle, you must announce that you are there at the request of Bishop Sagasta and Padre Espina. The count was without a steward when he took ill, and the Church supplied a steward to aid his wife, the Countess María del Mar Cano. She is the daughter of Gonzalo Cano, a rich and influential marquis in Madrid. The steward is Padre Alberto Guzmán.' He looked at Yonah. 'As I wrote in my letter, several other physicians have tried to help the count.'

'I understand. I can only try as well.'

Padre Espina asked questions about Saragossa and spoke briefly about the joy he was taking in his work. 'My bishop is a Catholic historian, engaged in composing a book of the lives of saints, a blessed project which has the support of our Most Holy Father in Rome, and in which it is my honor and pleasure to assist.' He smiled at Yonah. 'I read daily from my father's breviary and you are often blessed for bringing it to me. I appreciate that you would ride so far in answer to my letter to Señor Montenegro. You have been the kindest of benefactors, giving me back the memory of my father. If ever there is any way I may help you, please tell me of it.

'Would you care to stay and rest here, and go to Tembleque in the morning?' the priest said. 'I can offer you a monastery supper, and a monk's cell in which to rest your head.'

461

But Yonah had no desire for a monk's cell. 'No, I shall go on, in order to examine the count as soon as possible.'

Padre Espina gave him directions to Tembleque and he repeated them aloud, but he remembered the way.

'I prescribe medication but don't compound it,' Yonah said. 'Do you know of an excellent apothecary who is nearby?'

Espina nodded. 'Santiago López, in the shadow of the cathedral's northern wall. Go with God, señor.'

The shop was tiny and untended, but it had a reassuringly strong scent of herbs. Yonah had to shout the apothecary down from his apartment upstairs. He was middle-aged and balding, with squinting eyes that didn't hide the intelligence lurking there.

'Do you have myrtle? Balsam, acacia nilotica?' Yonah asked him. 'Do you have acid beet? Colocynth? Seeds of pharbitis?'

López took no offence at Yonah's questioning. 'I have most things, señor. As you know, one cannot have all. Should you call for something I do not have, with your permission I will make it known to you and suggest one or more substitute drugs.'

He nodded gravely when Yonah told him he would be ordering medications from the castle of Tembleque. 'I hope you have not come this long way on an impossible errand, señor.'

Yonah nodded. 'We shall see,' he said, and took his leave.

By the time he reached the castle it had been dark for an hour and the barred gate was down.

'Halloo the wall!'

'Who is it that calls?'

'Ramón Callicó, physician of Saragossa.'

'Hold.'

The sentry hurried off but soon returned, this time accompanied by someone with a torch. The two figures peering down at Yonah were captured in a yellow cone of light that moved away with them.

'Enter, Señor Physician!' the sentry called.

The gate was lifted with a fearsome clanking, causing the black horse to shy before she went forward, her shod hooves clattering and striking sparks on the great stone squares of the courtyard.

Padre Alberto Guzmán, round-shouldered and unsmiling, offered him food and drink.

'Yes, thank you, I would like both, but later, after I have met with the count,' Yonah said.

'Best not to disturb him tonight, but to wait until tomorrow to examine him,' the priest said brusquely. Behind him hovered a stocky, red-faced old man in the rough clothing of a *peón*, with a cloud of white hair and a full beard of the same colour.

'The count cannot move or speak, or understand when he is addressed. There is no reason for you to be in a hurry to see him,' Padre Guzmán said.

Yonah met his gaze. 'Nevertheless, I shall need candles and lamps about the bed. Many, to provide a bright light.'

Padre Guzmán's lips thinned in annoyance. 'As you wish. Padre Sebbo will see to the light.' The old man behind him nodded, and Yonah realized that he was a priest and not a workman.

Padre Guzmán took up a lamp and Yonah followed

him on a march down corridors and up stone stairways. They passed through a room Yonah remembered, the chamber in which he had had an audience with the count after delivering his armor, and they proceeded into the bedchamber beyond, a black space, the priest's lamp causing the shadows of the giant bedstead to leap crazily on the stone walls. The air was heavily foul.

Yonah took the lamp and held it close to the face on the bed. Vasca, the count of Tembleque, had lost a great deal of weight. His eyes appeared to stare past Yonah. The left side of Vasca's mouth was pulled down in a permanent sneer.

'I need the illumination.'

Padre Guzmán went to the door and shouted harshly, but Padre Sebbo already was arriving, leading two men and a woman carrying candles and lamps, and after a period of arrangement and setting flames to wicks, the count was bathed in light.

Yonah leaned over the face. 'Count Vasca,' he said. 'I am Ramón Callicó, the physician of Saragossa.' The eyes stared up at him, the pupils of unequal size.

'As I said, he cannot speak,' Guzmán said.

Vasca was covered by a blanket, not clean. When Yonah threw it back, the stench was multiplied.

'His back is eaten by malignancy,' Padre Guzmán said.

Vasca lay stiffly, his arms held rigidly above his abdomen. His pulse was hard to compress, resisting Yonah's fingertips, signifying that the blood in the count's body was under great pressure.

The body on the bed was long, but Yonah turned it easily and grunted at the revealed sight, a panoply of ugly carbuncles, some suppurating.

464

'They are bedsores,' he said. He indicated the servants, who had been hovering outside the door. 'They must heat water over the fire and bring it here without delay, along with clean rags.'

Padre Guzmán cleared his throat. 'The last physician, Carlos Sifrina of Fonseca, made it clear there should be no bathing for Count Vasca, lest he absorb the humors of the water.'

'The last physician, Carlos Sifrina of Fonseca, doubtless has never been left to lie in his own shit.' It was time to establish himself, and Yonah did it quietly. 'Hot water in good supply, and soap and soft rags. I have a salve, but get me quill and ink and paper, that without delay I may write out what other unguents and medicines I will need, and send a rider to Santiago López, the apothecary of Toledo. The rider must wake the apothecary from sleep if necessary.'

Padre Guzmán looked pained but resigned. As he turned away, Yonah stopped him. 'Get soft, thick fleeces to spread beneath him. Clean ones. Bring me fresh nightshirts and an unsoiled blanket,' he said.

It was late before he was finished, the thin body washed, the sores dressed with salve, the sheepskins spread, the bed and the nightshirt changed.

When at last he turned to food to fill his growling belly it was bread and a piece of strong and fatty mutton, and sour wine. He was led to a small chamber containing a bed redolent with the bitter body scent of its last occupant, perhaps Carlos Sifrina, the physician of Fonseca, he thought as he fell into a weary sleep.

In the morning he broke his fast with bread and ham and a better wine, careful to eat the meat bountifully.

The morning light mostly evaded the patient's chamber, there being only one tiny window high in the wall. Yonah had the servants prepare a couch in the large outer sitting chamber next to a lower, sunny window, and moved Count Vasca out there.

By daylight Vasca's condition was even more daunting. Atrophied muscles had pulled both of his hands into a fully opened, exaggerated position with the inside of the knuckle bones at the apex of the arch. Yonah asked a servant to cut two small sections from a round tree branch; he curled Vasca's hands around the wood and tied them into place with cloths.

All four of the man's limbs appeared lifeless. When he scraped the blunt end of a scalpel over Vasca's hands, the backs of his legs, and his feet, there appeared to be a slight response in the right limb, but by any practical measure the entire physical being was stricken. The only things in the count's body that moved were his eyes and eyelids. Vasca could open and close his eyes, and he could look at something or look away.

Yonah addressed the eyes with his own, talking to him all the while. 'Do you feel this, Count Vasca? Or this?

'Is there any sensation when I touch you, Count Vasca?

'Are you in pain, Count Vasca?'

Occasionally a grunt of a moan issued from the supine figure, but never in answer to a question.

Padre Guzmán came at times to watch some of Yonah's efforts with undisguised scorn. Finally he said, 'He understands nothing. He feels nothing and understands nothing.'

'Are you certain?'

The priest nodded. 'You have come on a fruitless errand. He is nearing the divine journey that beckons to each of us.'

Presently a woman came into the sickroom, carrying a bowl and a spoon. She was perhaps Adriana's age, with yellow hair and very white skin. She had a pretty, feline face, a small mouth, high cheekbones, puffy little cheeks, large eyes that she gave the shape of almonds by extending their corners with dark paint. Her gown was very fine but stained, and she smelled of wine. For a moment he believed she had a strawberry birthmark on her long throat but then he concluded it was the kind of mark made by a sucking mouth.

'The new physician,' she said, regarding him.

'Yes. And you are the countess?'

'The same. Shall you be able to do anything for him?'

'It is too early to tell, Countess . . . I am told he has been ill for more than a year?'

'Closer to fourteen months.'

'I see. How long have you been his wife?'

'Four years next spring.'

'You were with him when the illness struck?'

'Mmm.'

'It would help me to learn in detail what occurred to him that day.'

She shrugged. 'He rode and hunted early in the day.'

'What did he do when he returned from hunting?'

'It was fourteen months ago, señor. But . . . near as I can remember . . . Well, for one thing. He took me into his bed.'

'That was late in the morning?'

'Midday.' She smiled at the sick man. 'When it came

467

to bedding he never cared about time. Daytime or the middle of the night.'

'Countess, if you will forgive the question . . . Was he strenuous in his sexual activity that day?'

She looked at him appraisingly. 'I don't recall. But he was always strenuous at every activity.'

She said he had seemed normal enough most of the day. 'Late in the afternoon he told me his head ached, but he was well enough to go to table for the evening meal. As the fowl was being served I noticed his mouth pulling down . . . the way it is. He appeared to have trouble drawing a breath. And he seemed to slip in his chair.

'His hounds had to be killed. They would allow no one near enough to help him.'

'Has he had a similar attack since that day?'

'Once more. He was not as you see him now, after the first attack. He was able to move his right limbs and he could speak. Though his words were clumsy and indistinct, he was able to give me instruction about his funeral. But another spell struck him two weeks after the first, and from then on he has been frozen and mute.'

'I thank you for telling me these things, Countess.'

She nodded, and turned to study the figure in the bed. 'He could be rough, as many strong men are. I have seen him act cruelly. Yet always he was a kind lord and husband to me . . .'

Yonah propped up the patient with pillows and then watched with interest as she spooned thin gruel into his mouth.

'He has always been able to swallow?'

'He chokes on wine or broth. Nor can he chew meat. But when we sit him up and feed him gruel, he swallows it, as you see, enabling him to receive the nourishment that keeps him in life.'

She fed her husband in silence until the bowl was empty.

As she was leaving, she turned back to Yonah.

'You have not said what you are called?'

'Callicó.'

Her eyes held him for just a moment, then she nodded again and went away.

43

The Countess

His room was at the far end of a corridor, with the countess's apartment at the other end, and another bed-chamber in between. It was the next night before Yonah saw the other guest in the castle. In the middle of the night, leaving his room to empty the piss from his night jug, Yonah saw a man come from the countess's apart-ment with something in his arms. There were two pitch torches burning in the hallway sconces and Yonah saw him clearly, a wide, naked man with a fleshy face, car-rying his clothes.

Yonah would have been silent, but the man noticed him and stared for a frozen moment.

'Good evening,' Yonah said.

The other said nothing but went into the chamber next door to Yonah's.

The following morning, Yonah was moving the count to the sunny room again, aided by Padre Sebbo. He had found that the grizzled old priest was the only person in the castle with whom he could talk easily.

While they were settling the count on the couch, a man came into the room. Yonah recognized him as the man he had seen nude in the corridor a few hours before.

'Where the fucking hell has she gone?'

A brawler, Yonah thought. He had small, annoyed eyes in a round, fleshy face, a short black beard and a fringe of black hair around a mostly bald scalp. His body was powerfully muscular, but turning to fat. He had thick fingers; his hands were like a gladiator's, each adorned with a flamboyant and heavy ring.

'Where is she?' he demanded.

'I don't know, señor.' Yonah hadn't known Padre Sebbo long, but he could tell from the cool dryness of his voice that the old priest disliked this man, who ignored Yonah completely, turning and leaving them without another word.

Together Yonah and Padre Sebbo covered Vasca with a light blanket.

'Who is the rude gentleman who gave us the pleasure of his company?'

'That is Daniel Fidel Tapia, an associate of Count Vasca. Lately he has described himself as the count's partner,' Padre Sebbo said.

'Has she no name, the woman he was looking for?'

'He knew I understood he was looking for the countess. She and Tapia are special friends,' Padre Sebbo said.

Sometimes Vasca's pulse was full and rapid, while at other times it was like the skittering of a small, frightened animal. Padre Guzmán appeared once a day for a few moments, usually to look at the count's face and remark that his condition seemed more grave than the day before. 'God tells me he is dying.'

Why would God tell you? Yonah thought.

He doubted there was anything he could do to save Vasca's life, but he had to keep trying. The malady that was killing the count was not especially rare. In the time Yonah had been a physician he had seen other persons thus afflicted, some of them with deformed mouths and stiff and useless arms and legs. Often only one side of the body was affected; more rarely, both sides. He had no idea what caused the condition or if there was anything that might cure it.

Somewhere in the complicated human body there must be a center that governed man's strength and movement, he thought. Perhaps in Vasca that center resembled the blackened, damaged area Yonah had seen in Nuño's heart.

He wished that he could dissect Count Vasca's body when he died.

'How I would like to take you into my barn in Saragossa!' he murmured aloud.

The eyes, which had been closed, drifted open now and gazed up at him. Yonah would swear the count's eyes were puzzled, and a shocking suspicion came to him. He thought it was possible that at least some of the time Fernán Vasca understood what was happening in the world around him.

Yet, perhaps not . . .

He spent a lot of time alone with his patient, seated by the bed or leaning over it, talking to Vasca, but the moment in which their eyes had made connection wasn't repeated. Much of the time Vasca appeared to sleep, his breathing slow and snoring, his cheeks puffing out with each exhalation. Twice a day Padre Sebbo came

472

and read aloud from his book of devotions in a voice that sounded worn and hoarse, pausing often to clear his throat because of a chronic catarrh. Yonah ordered a spirit of camphor for him, for which the old priest expressed his gratitude.

'You must rest while I am here. Go and take a nap, señor,' Padre Sebbo urged, and sometimes Yonah escaped during the long sessions of prayer. He wandered through the silent chambers of the castle with little restriction, because it was vast and largely deserted, a chill and gloomy home, full of hearths that were devoid of fire. He was looking for the items his father had fashioned for the count, and for which Vasca had never deigned to pay. He would especially have liked to find the golden flower with the silver stem, to see if it could be as beautiful as his boyhood memory of it.

Count Vasca had made preparation for his own death. In a storeroom there was a great limestone casket, an enormous sarcophagus carved with a Latin inscription – CVM MATRE MATRIS SALVVS. It had a stone cover heavy enough to keep out worms or dragons. But Yonah saw neither the golden rose nor anything else that was familiar to him, until he entered an armor room and was startled by a glorious knight girded for battle.

It was the suit of armor he had delivered with Angel and Paco and Luis, and with a sense of wonder he touched some of the chasing and hammering that he himself had put into the steel under the tutelage of Manuel Fierro, the armorer of Gibraltar.

Padre Sebbo came to the sickroom each day and didn't hurry away, to Yonah's pleasure, for he had come to like

473

the old priest. He noted with interest that the old man's hand were as work-hardened as those of any field *peón*.

'Padre Sebbo, tell me about yourself.'

'There is nothing of interest, señor.'

'I think you are a very interesting man. Tell me, Padre, why do you not dress like other priests?'

'Once I wore ill-fitting vanity and ambition, along with black habits beautifully tailored to my body. But I failed in my responsibility and angered my superiors, and as punishment they sent me out to become a mendicant, to preach the word of God and beg for my daily bread.

'I felt they had doomed me, and I went forth in horror to take my punishment. I didn't know where to go, I simply moved my feet and allowed them to take me where they would. At first I was too proud and arrogant to beg. I ate berries in the woods. Though I was a man of God, I stole from gardens. But people can be kind, and some of the poorest gave of their meager fare and kept me alive.

'In time my black habit rotted and fell away, and I wandered ragged and unshorn. I lived and worked with the poor, who prayed with me and shared their bread and water, and I inherited their garments, sometimes from men who had died. For the first time I began to understand Saint Francis, though I didn't go into the world naked as he did, nor go blind, nor did stigmatas appear on my body. I am just a simple and baffled man, but I have been smiled upon, and for many years now I have been God's vagabond.'

'But if you work with the poor, why are you here, in a castle?'

'I have been drawn here from time to time. I stay long

enough to hear the confessions of the servants and the soldiers of the guard, and to give Communion, and then I move on. This time Padre Guzmán has asked me to stay until the count has died.'

'Padre Sebbo, I have never heard your given name,' Yonah said, and the priest smiled.

'Sebbo is not my patronymic. It is what the people began to call me in affection, a shortening of my given name, which is Sebastián. I am Sebastián Alvarez.'

Yonah sat still but didn't jump to conclusions; there were men who shared the same name, after all. He studied the face, trying to see into the past. 'Padre, what was your churchly duty before you became a wandering priest?'

'I seldom think on it, for it seems to me that it was another man, in another existence. I was the head of the Priory of the Assumption, in Toledo,' the old man said.

That night as Yonah sat alone by the count's bedside he thought back to the time before his brother Meir was killed, the days before his father had started fashioning the ciborium for the Priory of the Assumption, but was making preliminary drawings. Yonah had seen the prior only twice, each time when he had accompanied his father to meet with Padre Alvarez at the priory. He remembered an autocratic, impatient cleric, and marveled now at the transformation that had taken place.

He was certain Padre Sebbo was drawn back to the castle because he knew, as Yonah knew, that Fernán Vasca had been behind the thefts of the ciborium and the relic of Santa Ana.

He continued talking to the count in the hope that he

might engage him into consciousness. He grew tired of his own voice speaking to an apparently somnolent Fernán Vasca. If Vasca could hear him, doubtless he, too, was bored by the droning voice; Yonah had talked of the weather, about the outlook for crops in the next harvest, about seeing a hawk floating high in the sky, a speck against the clouds.

He tried a different tack.

'Count Vasca, it is time for us to consider my fee,' he said. 'In fairness, it should be balanced by what we have owed each other in the past. Ten years ago I visited this place to deliver a wonderful suit of armor to you, and you gave me ten *maravedíes* for my trouble. But we have had other dealings, for I told you of a saint's relics in a cave on the southern coast, and in return you ended the lives of two men who would have taken mine.'

He saw a movement behind the closed eyelids.

'I sent two men to their deaths in a hermit's cave. And you rid yourself of rivals and gained relics. Do you recall?'

The eyes opened slowly, and Yonah saw something in them he had not seen before.

Interest.

'The world is strange, for now I am not an armor maker but your physician who wishes to help you. You must work with me.'

He had given thought to how he would proceed if able to engage the count's conscious mind.

'It is difficult having no speech. But there is a way in which we may talk with each other. I will ask you a question. You will blink your eyes once for yes and twice for no. Keep your eyes closed for a moment with each blink, so I will know it for an answer.

'Once for yes, twice for no. Do you comprehend?'

476

But Vasca only looked at him.

'Blink once for yes, and twice for no. Do you understand, Count Vasca?'

A single blink!

'Good. That is very good, Count Vasca, you are doing well. Do you have feelings in your legs or feet?'

Two blinks.

'In your head?'

A single blink.

'Do you have pain or discomfort somewhere in the region of your head?'

Yes.

'In your mouth or jaw?'

No.

'Your nose?'

No

'Eyes?'

Vasca blinked once.

'So. The eyes. Is it a sharp pain?'

No.

'An itching?'

One blink, the eyes held closed for a moment, as if for emphasis.

Yonah was exhilarated. He bathed the eyes gently with warmed water and sent a rider to the apothecary's for an eye ointment.

The countess came to the sickroom late in the morning, and when Yonah took her into the corridor outside the chamber and told her what had happened, she grew pale with excitement. 'Does it mean he is getting well?'

Yonah didn't think so. 'It may be a temporary time of consciousness, or perhaps his mind has always been aware in that frozen body.'

'But we may hope and pray,' she said.

'We must always hope and pray, my lady. But . . .' He left unspoken his belief that at any time Vasca might have another attack that would bring the end.

She went to the bedside and held one of the large hands that was still wrapped onto the piece of wood that guarded Vasca from deformity. His eyes were closed.

'Perhaps he sleeps,' Yonah said, but she was not to be denied.

'My lord husband,' she said.

And again, and yet again.

'My husband . . .'

'Ah, God, Fernán, open your eyes, look at me for Christ's own sweet sake!'

He did awake.

She bent close and fixed her eyes with his. 'My lord,' she said. 'Are you my love?'

Vasca blinked once, and Yonah left them to their privacy.

That night in the prison of Yonah's own sleeplessness it occurred to him that perhaps the shock of more aggressive questioning might bring greater stimulation to Vasca's consciousness than had been achieved by gentle nursing. The following morning he spent a time questioning Vasca about his condition, the blinking revealing that the pain from Vasca's bedsores was eased, his eyes were more comfortable, but there was a deep ache in the ball of his left foot, which Yonah was able to massage away.

Yonah leaned over his face again. 'Count Vasca, do you recall Helkias Toledano, who was a silversmith in Toledo?'

478

Vasca gazed up at him.

'You owned a number of objects he had made. For example, a remarkable rose made of gold and silver. I would dearly like to see some of the things Toledano fashioned. Do you know where they are kept?'

He received no answers. Vasca continued to look at him. There were a few random blinks, natural reflexes and not answers to his questions, and presently Vasca closed his eyes.

'Damnation. Count Vasca? *Hola?*'

The eyes stayed closed.

'Helkias was a Jew. He was my father. I am still a Jew. The physician who tends you and tries to bring you back to life is a Jew, my lord.'

The lids flew open. The eyes had turned so hard! Vasca searched his face, and Yonah felt the emotions of a lifetime as they spilled out of him.

'The work of my father's hand, your fucking lordship,' he said savagely. 'Three large bowls. Four small silver mirrors and two large. A gold flower with a silver stem. Eight short combs and a long comb. And a dozen goblets of silver and electrum, not to mention his ciborium. Where are my father's works?'

Vasca continued to look at him. The ruined mouth seemed to turn up; it was difficult to tell, but Yonah sensed amusement in Fernán Vasca's eyes, just before they closed.

The following morning the count responded to his wife's questioning for a time, but then his eyes closed against her, also.

As she sat bleakly in her seat next to the bed, Yonah saw two fresh bruises on her left cheek.

'Countess . . . Is there something with which you need help?'

It was clumsily put, and she became cold and distant. 'No, thank you, señor.'

But early the following morning, a servant woke him and told him the physician was required in the countess's apartment. He found her lying across her bed with a bloodied rag to her face. There was an ugly two-inch gash in her left cheek, where the bruises had been.

'Was this made by his ring?'

She didn't reply. Tapia must have hit her with his open hand, Yonah reasoned, because if his fist had been closed there would be more tearing from the ring. He took waxed thread and a fine needle from his bag. Before he closed the cut he had her drink a dram of *coñac*. Still, she winced and grunted, but he took his time and sewed with small stitches. He poured a splash of wine on a cloth and held it against the wound.

When he was finished she started to thank him but then fell back, sobbing soundlessly.

'Countess . . .' She wore a silk sleeping gown that revealed whatever there was to be seen of her, and he forced his eyes away as she sat and dried her eyes with the back of her hands, like a child.

He remembered what Padre Espina had told him about her father's wealth and power in Madrid.

'Señora, I believe your husband will soon die,' he said gently. 'If that should happen, have you considered going to the protection of your family?'

'Tapia says if I run he will come after me. And kill me.'

Yonah sighed. Tapia could not be that stupid. He told himself that perhaps he could talk reason into the man, or maybe Padre Sebbo or Padre Espina could do it.

'Let me see what can be done,' he said uncomfortably. But to his further discomfort he began to hear more about Tapia and the countess than he wanted to know.

'It is my fault,' she said. 'He had been looking at me for a long time. I didn't discourage him, but rather enjoyed keeping the hunger in his eyes, to be true about it. I felt completely safe, because Tapia was afraid of my lord and never would have tried to take his wife.

'Daniel Tapia has worked for my husband for many years, as a buyer of sacred relics. Fernán knows people in the religious communities and was able to arrange the sale of many of the things Tapia bought.'

Yonah waited in silence.

'After my husband became ill, I was fearful. I am a woman who needs the comfort of someone's arms, and I went to Tapia one night,' she said, and Yonah was silent, admiring her honesty.

'But it did not turn out as I hoped. He is a beastly man, and he means to marry me when that is possible. There are no heirs to the count's title, and when I die the property will revert to the monarchy. But Daniel Tapia will see that I live a long life,' she said bitterly. 'He wants the money.

'There is something else,' she said. 'He is convinced that Fernán has hidden something here, something of very great value. I think he finally believes I don't know anything that will help him, but he searches for it constantly.'

For a moment Yonah didn't dare to speak. 'Is it a relic?' he asked.

'I don't know. I hope you will not add your own questioning to my torment, señor,' she said.

She stood shakily, and reached up and touched her face. 'Will there be a scar?'

'Yes. A small one. It will be red at first, but it will fade. I hope it will be as white as your skin,' he said, and he took his bag and went to tend her husband.

44
Springtime

That very day, when he went searching again after Padre Sebbo relieved him in the sickroom, he had evidence that his memory of his father's work had not been faulty.

In a cellar closet filled with dusty picture frames and broken chairs, on a shelf he found a double row of heavy dark cups.

When he took one out of the closet and to a window, he saw it was a goblet made by his father. There was no doubt. The color was almost black because the silver had tarnished thickly over years of neglect, but when he turned it over, the HT mark was legible in the bottom. Placed there by his father's hands.

He brought each of the cups out to the window, one at a time. They were simple, heavy goblets made beautifully out of massy silver, with bases of electrum. Two of the cups were badly dented and scratched, as if someone had hurled them in a rage. He remembered that the count had owed his father for a full set of twelve drinking vessels, but though he searched the closet diligently, removing chairs and frames and feeling in all the dark corners, there were only ten cups.

For the next two days he made his way to the closet and held the cups again simply to enjoy their solidity and weight in his hands. But the third time he went there he found Daniel Tapia, who had obviously been searching. Objects from the closet were strewn on the floor.

Tapia stared at Yonah. 'What is it you want?'

'I want nothing, señor,' Yonah said easily. 'I am simply admiring the castle's beauty so that someday I may describe it to my children.'

'Is the count going to die?'

'I believe so, señor.'

'When?'

Yonah shrugged and looked at him calmly.

Since their marriage, Adriana had unburdened herself to Yonah about the mistreatment she had suffered from her first husband. Over time, he had seen the pain leave his wife's eyes, but he couldn't abide the thought of men who beat women. 'Recently I have had to treat Count Vasca's wife . . . I trust the countess will suffer no additional injury,' he said deliberately.

Tapia's glance held disbelief that the physician should feel free to talk to him in that way. 'Injuries often occur, and none of us is immune,' he said. 'For example, if I were you I should not walk about this castle without escort, lest someone mistake you for a thief, señor, and kill you.'

'It would be a pity if someone were to try, for it is a long time since I was unable to take care of myself against cutthroats,' Yonah said, and wandered away, making certain he moved slowly.

*

Indeed, the threat acted only to spur him on in his search of the castle, for obviously Tapia thought something so precious was hidden there that he wanted no one else to stumble on it. Yonah hunted diligently, even reaching into every wall niche on the chance that it had been used the way the niche in his own home hid his Hebrew manuscripts, but he pulled nothing from the dark places save a nest of mice and a variety of spidered webs, and soon he found he was back in rooms where he had searched before.

In the storeroom he stood in front of the great stone casket, a coffin worthy of a prince, and again studied the inscription carved in the stone.

CVM MATRE MATRIS SALVVS.

His Latin was almost nonexistent, but on his way back to the sickroom he passed the steward overseeing workmen making a repair to a balustrade on the stairway.

'Padre Guzmán,' he said. 'Do you have a knowledge of Latin?'

'Of course I do,' Padre Guzmán said importantly.

'The inscription on the stone casket that awaits the count, "Cum Matre Matris Salvus." What does it mean?'

'It declares that after death, for eternity he will be with the Virgin Mary,' Padre Guzmán said.

So why could Yonah not sleep that night?

Early the following morning, as a spring cloudburst drummed against the thin alabaster windowpane, he arose and took a torch from the sconce, carrying it to the storeroom, where he held it high as he studied the casket by its flickering light.

By midmorning, when Padre Sebbo appeared in the

485

sickroom, Yonah was awaiting him anxiously. 'Padre, how is your grasp of Latin?'

Padre Sebbo grinned. 'It has been a lifelong temptation for sinful pride.'

'"Cum Matre Matris Salvus."'

The priest's smile disappeared. 'Here, now,' he said roughly.

'What does it mean?'

'Where did you get those . . . particular words?'

'Padre, we have not known each other long, you and I. But you must ask yourself if you can trust me.'

Sebbo looked at him and sighed. 'I can. I must. It means, "Safe with the Mother's Mother."'

Yonah saw that the ruddiness was gone from the old priest's face. 'I know what you have been missing for so many years, Padre Sebastián, and I believe we have found it,' he said.

The two of them went over the casket carefully. The great stone lid, which leaned against the wall at the top of the coffin, was a solid, single piece of stone. So were the sections that made up the bottom of the stone box, and three of its sides.

'But see here,' Yonah said. The fourth side of the casket was different, wider than the wall at the casket's other end. The panel with the Latin inscription was set into the top of that side.

Yonah tapped it so Padre Sebbo could hear that it was hollow. 'We must remove the panel.'

The priest agreed but counseled caution. 'The storeroom is too close to the sleeping chambers. And not far from the dining room. People pass at odd times of day, and the soldiers of the guard are quickly summoned.

We must wait for a time when the attention of others in the castle has been diverted,' he said.

Yet events robbed them of the luxury of waiting, for early the next morning Yonah was summoned out of sleep by a woman servant who had been sitting by Vasca's bed during the night. The count was wracked by a fresh attack. His face drooped more alarmingly and his eyes no longer were on an even plane, the left eye lower than the right. His pulse was full and rapid, his respirations slow and snoring. Yonah heard a new rattling sigh and recognized the finality of the sound.

'Hurry and fetch the countess and then the priests,' Yonah told the woman.

The countess and the priests arrived together, the dying man's wife disheveled and saying her beads silently, Padre Guzmán wearing his death robes – purple cassock and surplice – and come so hastily that Padre Sebbo was still trying to adjust the purple stole about the younger priest's neck as they entered the door.

The count, eyes bulging, was gasping his last; his appearance reminded Yonah of a description of impending death by Hippocrates: 'The nose sharp, the temples fallen in, the ears cold and drawn and their lobes distorted, the skin of the face hard, stretched and dry, the color of the face dusky.'

Padre Sebbo opened the small gold bottle containing the Oil of the Sick. He wetted Father Guzmán's splayed right thumb with chrism, and the priest anointed Vasca's eyes, ears, hands and feet. The air was filled with the scent of the heavy balm and the spice of the scented oil, as the fourteenth and last count of Tembleque exhaled for the last time, a long and strangled sighing.

487

'He is shriven,' Padre Guzmán said, 'and even now he is meeting our Lord.'

Padre Sebbo and Yonah exchanged a long look, for each was aware that now it would not be long before the stone casket was placed deep in the earth.

'We must tell the staff and soldiers of the passing of their lord and *maestro* and conduct a memorial Mass with them, in the courtyard,' Padre Sebbo said to Padre Guzmán.

Guzmán frowned. 'Do you believe so? There is so much that now needs to be done.'

'This should be done first,' the older priest said firmly. 'I will assist, but you must give the message following the Mass, for you speak so much better than I.'

'Ah, it is not true,' Padre Guzmán said modestly, but he was obviously pleased by the compliment and agreed to give the message.

'In the meantime,' Padre Sebastián said, 'the physician must wash the deceased and prepare him for interment,' and Yonah nodded.

He made certain he was not finished with the task until he could hear that the Mass had begun in the courtyard below. When he was able to make out the low droning of Padre Sebastián's voice and the higher chanting of Padre Guzmán, and the sonorous response of the worshipers, he hurried to the storeroom.

Using a surgical probe, he began to scrape the mortar from around the engraved panel in the casket. It was a usage that Manuel Fierro had never imagined for the instrument when he had fashioned it, yet it worked very well. Yonah had finished removing the mortar from two sides of the panel before he heard the voice behind him.

'What is it you are doing, healer?'

Daniel Tapia's eyes were on the panel in the casket as he stepped into the room.

'I am making certain everything is all right.'

'Of course you are.' Tapia said. 'So you believe something is in there? I hope you are correct.'

He pulled his knife from its sheath and moved towards Yonah.

Yonah saw at once that Tapia was not interested in raising an alarm and summoning soldiers, meaning to complete the pilfering himself. He was as tall as Yonah and far heavier; obviously he thought he was competent to take care of an unarmed physician with his knife. Yonah feinted with the tiny probe and leaped to one side as the knife made a wide sweep meant to lay him open.

It was a close thing; the blade missed his body by the thickness of cloth. The point caught on the fabric of his tunic, slicing it open but snagging for a brief moment that allowed Yonah to grasp the arm behind the knife.

He yanked, more by reflex than design, and Tapia lost his balance and sprawled forward over the open casket. He was fast for a big man and still held the knife, but instinctively Yonah grasped the casket lid that rested against the wall. It was so heavy that moving it required all his strength, but the top of the stone casket cover came away from the wall and its great weight carried it forward. Tapia had started to raise himself, but the ponderous lid came down on him like a trap claiming an animal. His body muffled much of the noise; instead of the clatter of stone on stone there was a thud.

Still, the ugly sound was loud enough, and Yonah

489

froze, listening. But the responsive voices raised in prayer continued without pause.

Tapia's hand still was clenched on the knife, which Yonah had to pry from his fingers. He raised the stone lid gingerly, but there was no need for caution.

'Tapia?'

There was no breathing. 'No, ah, damnation.' He saw that the man's spine was broken, and that he was dead.

Yonah had no time for regrets. He carried Tapia to the chamber next to his own and placed him on the bed. Then he removed Tapia's outer clothing and closed his eyes. He shut the door as he left.

Now when he returned to the storeroom he was desperate to hurry, for he could hear that the Mass was over and the nasal voice of Padre Guzmán was extolling the life of Fernán Vasca.

When he finished removing the thin layer of grout, he lifted the stone panel free and discovered a space.

He reached inside with trepidation and felt a nest of rags. Cushioned in the nest, like a large and precious egg, was an object wrapped in linen, and beneath the linen was a bag of embroidered silk. Yonah trembled as he removed the bag, for within it he found what had brought death and destruction to his family.

That afternoon Countess María del Mar Cano went to Tapia's room and found him dead. The physician and the priests were summoned at once.

Twice before, Yonah had caused death; he had long since wrestled with the demons of conscience and decided it was justifiable to protect himself when someone tried to kill him. But now the physician had the unsettling experience of having to declare someone dead

490

whom he had killed, and it troubled him to use his profession shabbily and in a manner he would not have wished to disclose to Nuño Fierro.

'He died at once,' he said, which was true. Adding, 'In his sleep,' which was not.

'Is it a pestilence that could affect us all?' Padre Guzmán asked fearfully. Yonah told him it wasn't, and that it was coincidence that the count and Tapia had died on the same day. He was conscious of the countess's white face turned toward him.

'Daniel Tapia had no living relatives,' she said. She had quickly composed herself after the shock of discovery. 'His rites must not interfere with the count's,' she said firmly.

So Tapia was wrapped in the blanket on which he lay, and carried out onto the plain, where a grave was dug and he was buried quickly with prayers from Padre Sebastián. Yonah attended and uttered amens, and two troopers of the guard dug the grave and filled it in.

Meanwhile, work had continued in the castle. By dusk the count's funeral had been readied to his widow's satisfaction and all night he lay in the castle's great room, surrounded by a profusion of candles and waked by a group of women of the staff, who sat and conversed in hushed tones until daylight brought the castle to life once more.

Midmorning the casket was lifted by twelve strong men-at-arms and carried outside, to the centre of the courtyard. Soon a slow parade of servants and soldiers filed past it. If investigating hands had probed the thin cracks surrounding the stone panel inscribed with the Latin benison, they would have found that the panel's edges were held in place by a thin coat of luteous eye salve mixed with grains of pulverized stone grout, the mixture forced back into place and hurriedly smoothed.

But no gaze noted such details, for all eyes were on the figure laid out within the sarcophagus. Fernán Vasca, count of Tembleque, lay in knightly splendor, his soldier's hands folded in peace. He was dressed in the full glory of his armor. The beautiful sword made by Paco Parmiento was at one side, his helmet at the other. The midday sun emblazoned the burnished steel until the count appeared to be a sleeping saint engulfed in fire.

The sun of early springtime was very strong, and the armor absorbed heat like a cooking pot. Aromatic herbs had been strewn on the flagstones and were crushed by passing feet, but the odor of death was soon pervading. María del Mar Cano had planned to have the body rest in state in the courtyard for several days, to allow the 'little people' in the surrounding country to come and offer farewells, but she soon saw that it could not be.

A grave had been dug in a corner of the courtyard, next to the graves of three earlier counts of the district. A small army of men moved the great casket to the edge of the grave, but as the coffin was about to be closed Countess María del Mar Cano quietly instructed the funeral detail to desist.

She hurried back into the castle, to reappear in a few moments with a single long-stemmed rose that she placed in her dead husband's hands.

Yonah was standing eight paces away. It was not until the coffin lid was lifted again by the soldiers and had begun to be lowered that he was struck by a thought that made him stare at the flower.

It appeared to be only a rose. Yet perhaps the loveliest rose he had ever seen.

Yonah could not restrain himself from taking a step toward the casket, but in a moment, far too soon, the heavy stone lid settled over the Latin inscription, the dead knight, and the golden rose with the silver stem.

45
Departures

In the morning María del Mar Cano came to him while he was packing his saddlebags. She wore mourning, a black gown heavy enough for travel. The veil of her black cap hid the small scar on her cheek, from which he had removed the stitches only a few days before.

'I am going home. My father will send a factor to deal with the matters of property and inheritance. Will you come to Madrid with me, Physician?'

'It is not possible, Countess. My wife waits for me in Saragossa.'

'Ah,' she said in regret. But she smiled. 'Then you must come and visit someday when you may need a change. My father will want to reward you handsomely. Daniel Tapia might have done me great injury.'

It took him a moment to realize that she thought he had killed a man for striking her.

'You are confused about what has happened here.'

She lifted her veil, leaned forward. 'I am not confused. You must come to Madrid, for I would reward you handsomely, as well,' she said, and kissed him on the

494

mouth and departed, leaving him depressed and angry. No doubt her father – or anyone else who heard her – would assume that the physician of Saragossa had used poisons to kill. He did not want that kind of intelligence to be whispered about.

María del Mar Cano was young and would be a temptation to men even when she was old, but her presence in Madrid would ensure that he would never go there.

By the time he finished packing he was in better humor. When he looked from the window he saw the Countess of Tembleque riding through the front gate, and despite himself he was amused to note that she would be well protected on the ride to Madrid, for she had found herself a strong young member of the guard to accompany her.

He made his farewells to the two priests in the courtyard. Padre Sebbo had his pack on his back and a very long staff in hand.

'In the matter of my fee,' Yonah said to Padre Guzmán.

'Ah, the fee. It cannot be paid, of course, until the details of the estate are settled. It will be forwarded to you.'

'I have noticed ten silver goblets among the count's possessions. I am willing that they should be my fee.'

The priest steward appeared interested, yet shocked. 'Ten goblets of silver are worth far more than a fee for failure,' he said drily. You did not keep him alive, his eyes told Yonah. 'Take four if you are interested.'

'Fray Francisco Rivera de la Espina said I would be well compensated.'

Padre Guzmán knew from experience that one must

495

keep any matter out of the hands of meddling diocesan officials. 'Six, then,' he said, a hard steward.

'I will take them if I may buy the other four. Two are damaged.'

The steward named a price that was unfair, yet the goblets were worth more to Yonah than money and he agreed at once, although with some small show of reluctance.

Padre Sebbo had listened to the exchange with a small smile. Now he said his farewells, and with a lifted hand and a last blessing for the guards strode through the gate like a man with the world as his destination.

An hour later, when Yonah sought to ride through the same gate, he was halted.

'I am sorry, señor. We have been instructed to inspect your belongings,' the sergeant of the guards told him.

They took out everything he had so carefully packed but he kept a check on his temper, though his stomach began to knot.

'I have a receipt for the goblets,' he said.

Finally the sergeant nodded to him, and he led Hermana to the side while he repacked his belongings. Then he remounted and gladly left the castle of Tembleque behind.

They met in Toledo, in front of the diocesan building.

'No trouble?'

'No,' Padre Sebbo said. 'A driver who knew me stopped his empty coach. I rode here like the pope.'

They went into the building and announced themselves and sat together on a bench without speaking, until the friar came and told them that Padre Espina was now able to see them in private.

Yonah knew Padre Espina was puzzled to see them together.

'I would tell you a story,' Padre Sebastián Alvarez said, when they were settled into chairs.

'I shall listen.'

The grizzled old man told of a young priest, beset with ambition and blessed with family connections, who had begged for a relic that would make him the abbot of a great monastery. He told of intrigue and theft and murder. And of a physician of Toledo who had lost his life at the stake because he had not refused a request from a priest of his chosen faith. 'That was your father, Padre Espina.'

Padre Sebbo said that down through the long years wherever he had wandered he had asked about stolen relics. 'Most people shrugged. It was difficult to gather information, but I garnered a word here and a word there, and the words pointed me to Count Fernán Vasca. So I began to go to the castle of Tembleque every so often, but not until this year did God see fit to bring me together with this physician at that castle, for which I thank Him.'

Padre Espina listened with rapt attention that turned to amazement as Padre Sebbo took an object from his bag and unwrapped it with great care.

The three men fell silent as they sat and studied the reliquary.

The silver was black with tarnish but the color of the gold was pure, and even beneath the tarnish the sacred figures and the decorations of fruits and plants called out to the viewer.

'God moved the hands of the maker,' Padre Espina said.

'Yes,' Padre Sebbo said. He removed the cover of the ciborium and they gazed at the relic within. The two priests made the sign of the cross.

'Fill your eyes,' Padre Sebbo said, 'for Santa Ana's relic and the reliquary must be sent to Rome as soon as possible, and our friends of the papal curia are notoriously slow in reaffirming authenticity when a stolen relic is recovered. It may not happen in our lifetime.'

'But it will happen,' Padre Espina said, 'and because of the two of you. The legend of Toledo's stolen relic of Santa Ana is known everywhere, and both of you will be lauded as the heroes of its recovery.'

'Recently you told me that if I needed your help I had but to ask,' Yonah said. 'I am asking for it now. My name must not be mentioned in connection with this matter.'

Padre Espina was disturbed by the unexpected turn, and he regarded Yonah silently.

'What do you think of Señor Callicó's request, Padre Sebastián?'

'I support it wholly,' the old priest said. 'I have come to know his goodness. In times that are strange and difficult, sometimes anonymity can be a benison, even to a good man.'

Padre Espina nodded finally. 'I am aware there was a time when my own father might have made such a request. Whatever your reasons, I shall not cause you pain. But is there any additional way in which I may help you?'

'No, Padre. I thank you.'

Padre Espina turned to Padre Sebbo. 'You, at least, as a priest must be available to testify about what happened at the castle of Tembleque, Padre Sebastián. Can I not seek to find you easier work than wandering among the poor, begging for your supper?'

But Padre Sebbo wished to remain a begging priest. 'Santa Ana changed my life and vocation, leading me to a priesthood I had not imagined. I ask your help in seeing that I am mentioned only as is necessary, so my priesthood may continue.'

Padre Espina nodded. 'You must write a report of how these objects were recovered. Bishop Enrique Sagasta knows and trusts me, as a man and as a priest. I am confident I can convince him to send the precious objects on to Rome, stating that they were recovered by the Toledo See's Office of Religious Faith, from the castle of Tembleque after the death of Count Fernán Vasca, known to be a dealer in relics.

'The ancient Basilica of Constantine in Rome has been razed and a great church is to be erected over the tomb of Saint Peter. Bishop Sagasta yearns to be transferred to the Vatican, and I yearn to be taken there with him.'

He smiled. 'It will not hurt the bishop's reputation as a Church historian to receive credit for the recovery of Santa Ana's relic and such a reliquary.'

The two men stood in the street outside the diocesan building and regarded each other.

'Do you know who I am?'

Padre Sebbo placed a callused hand on Yonah's mouth. 'I do not wish to hear a name.'

But he looked into Yonah's eyes. 'I have noted that your features resemble the good face of a man once known to me, a fine man of wonderful skill and art.'

Yonah smiled. 'Good-bye, Padre.'

They embraced.

'Go with God, my son.'

He stood and watched Sebastián Alvarez walk away, the mane of white hair and the mendicant's tall staff bobbing down the crowded street of the city.

He rode to the outskirts of Toledo, to the field that had been the Jewish cemetery. No sheep or goats had been there in a while; the grass was greening nicely above all the Jewish bones, and he let the horse crop while he stood and said the Kaddish for his mother and Meir and all who lay there, then he got up into the saddle again and walked the horse back into Toledo, through the streets where the happiest and most innocent days of his life had been spent, up onto the cliff road overlooking the river.

The synagogue had been taken over by woodcutters, at least for the time being. Billets of firewood were stacked and piled on the front steps and along the face of the building.

He reined the horse to a halt when he came to the former house and atelier of the family Toledano.

Still a Jew, Abba, he called silently.

The tree over his father's grave had grown high, and behind the house the leafy branches hung over the low roof, giving shade, swaying in the breeze.

He felt the strong presence of his father.

Whether it was real or imagined, he reveled in it. Without words he told his father what had happened. There was no regaining the dead; what had been lost was lost, but it felt to him that the affair of the reliquary had come full circle and was done.

He patted Hermana, studying the house where his mother had died.

Sebastián Alvarez had said he looked like his father. Did Eleazar Toledano look like their father as well? If Yonah passed him in the street, in a crowd of people, would there be anything to make him realize that Eleazar Toledano was his brother?

Everywhere he looked he seemed to see a skinny boy with a large head.

Yonah, shall we go to the river?

Yonah, am I not to come along with you?

He was brought back to the present by the sudden sharp awareness of the stink; the leather tannery was still in operation.

I love you, Abba.

When he rode past the adjoining property of the neighbor, Marcelo Troca, he saw that the old man was still alive and in his field, placing a halter over a burro's head.

'*Hola!*' Yonah called.

'A good day to you, Señor Troca!' he shouted, and touched his heels to the horse's flanks.

Marcelo Troca stood with his hand on the burro's neck, peering in puzzlement after the black horse until the rider was out of sight.

46
The Barn

The place and he were a good match. The rectangular piece of property, really just a long, low hill with a meager brook running through it, was not Eden, nor could the hacienda be compared with a castle, yet the land and the house suited Yonah exactly.

That year spring had come to Saragossa early. The fruit trees he and Adriana had pruned and fertilized were heavy with buds by the time he arrived home. Adriana welcomed him with tears and laughter, as if he had returned from the dead.

She was in awe of the plain silver goblets his father had made. The black tarnish proved stubborn and mean, but Yonah collected the winter's accumulation from the henhouse floor and soaked each cup in the acidic embrace of wet chickenshit; then he rubbed and rubbed with more of the terrible mixture on a soft cloth, and after a soapy scrubbing and more rubbing with dry cloths, each cup gleamed like Count Vasca's armor. Adriana placed the goblets on a small table situated so they richly caught the leaping reflections of the fire, and she turned toward the wall the damaged portions of the two dented and scratched cups.

In the grove near the hilltop, the trees soon were heavy with small, hard green olives, and Adriana gloated over them and planned to press oil at the moment of perfect ripeness. In Yonah's absence she had bought a few goats for a small herd. Though the seller had claimed that three of the she-goats had been freshened, only a single goat showed any sign of being with kid. But Adriana was untroubled by such annoyances, because in the last week of summer it became clear that she was pregnant herself. Yonah was very pleased, and Adriana dwelt in calm ecstasy.

But the coming child made the difference.

In early autumn Reyna and Álvaro came to visit, and while the women sat and drank a glass of wine, the two men went to the hilltop and paced off the dimensions of a new barn.

Álvaro scratched his head when he saw what Yonah wanted. 'Shall you need a barn quite that deep, Ramón?'

But Yonah shook his head and smiled. 'So long as we are building, let us build,' he said.

Álvaro had constructed several houses, and Yonah contracted with him to raise the outer walls of a barn with a tile roof to match the roof of the hacienda. All through the autumn and winter Álvaro and Lope, the young man who was his assistant, collected stone and hauled it to the hilltop in a wagon pulled by oxen.

Adriana gave birth in March, laboring through a long, windy night and bearing her infant in the chill light of morning. Yonah extracted the man-child from her and as

503

the baby opened his mouth and yowled he felt the last aloneness melt within him.

'He is Helkias Callicó,' Adriana said, and when he placed the swaddled infant into her arms she said words that were never uttered, even in their most private moments. 'Son of Yonah Toledano,' she whispered

The following spring, Álvaro and Lope dug a shallow trench to Yonah's specifications and laid the foundation. As the walls began to rise under their labor, Yonah took to working with the two builders, using every moment he could spare from his patients. He learned to choose and mate the stones carefully, and how to balance stone on stone so their stresses became the wall's strength. He even insisted on learning how to mix the mortar, blending pulverized shale with clay, sand, limestone, and water to make a rough cement. Álvaro was amused by his questions and his energy. 'You wish to cease being a physician and work at my trade,' he said, but they enjoyed the experience of laboring together.

The barn was finished during the first week of June. When Álvaro and Lope had been paid and had departed, Yonah began to labor alone in the cooler parts of the day, collecting additional materials in early morning and before dusk. Through the late summer and into the fall, on his own land he lifted rocks and stones into his barrow and unloaded them within the barn.

It was November before he could put the stones to use. He ran a line that cut a narrow slice of the barn's space from the rear of the structure and began to build an interior stone wall, to duplicate the outer rear wall.

In the darkest corner of the barn he built a low, narrow doorway through the new wall, and around the doorway he constructed a bin of pine logs. The bin was divided. In the front portion he stacked cut firewood, while over the section closest to the wall he installed a trapdoor at a shallow depth. The trapdoor allowed him access to the secret room, while whenever it was not in use it was hidden completely when more firewood was stacked on it.

In the long, narrow space between the walls he assembled a table and brought in two chairs and every outward manifestation of his Jewishness – his kiddush cup, Sabbath candles, the two medical books in Hebrew, and a few scrawled pages of remembered blessings, idioms, and legends.

On the first Friday evening after the barn was completed, he stood on the hilltop near Nuño's grave with Adriana, who held their son. Together they studied the darkening sky until they could identify the white glitter of the first three stars.

Earlier he had lighted a lamp in the barn to preclude having to do so after the Sabbath had begun, and now in its light he cleared away the firewood and opened the trapdoor. He went in first and took the baby from Adriana, stooping to carry the child through the small door and into the dark space beyond. In a moment Adriana had joined them with the lamp.

It was a simple service. Adriana lighted the candles and they said the blessing together, welcoming the Sabbath Queen. Then Yonah chanted the Shema: Hear, O Israel, the Lord our God, the Lord is One.

It was all they had of liturgy.

'A peaceful Sabbath,' he said, and kissed her.

'A peaceful Sabbath, Ramón.'

They sat in the quiet place.

'See the light,' Yonah said to the child.

He was not Abraham and the little boy was not Isaac, to be made a martyr on an Inquisition stake, a burnt offering to God.

This was the only time Helkias would see the secret room until he could think as a man.

Yonah's Jewishness would live on in his own soul, where it could not be molested, and he would come here and visit his artifacts whenever it was safe. If he was preserved in life long enough to see his children reach the age of reason, he would bring each son or daughter into this secret place.

He would light the tapers and sing unfamiliar prayers, and attempt to help the next generation of the Callicó family to understand what had gone before. He would tell the tales – stories of grandparents and uncles the child would never know, of a man whose hands and mind made beauty out of metal, of glorious sacred objects, of a golden rose with a silver stem. Stories of a better time, and of a departed family, and of a vanished world. After that, he and Adriana were agreed, it was up to God.